THE APOSTATE THEORY

BY

MR. PAT

authorHOUSE®

AuthorHouse™
1663 Liberty Drive, Suite 200
Bloomington, IN 47403
www.authorhouse.com
Phone: 1-800-839-8640

First published by AuthorHouse   4/7/2009

ISBN: 978-1-4389-6109-5 (sc)
ISBN: 978-1-4389-6110-1 (hc)

Printed in the United States of America
Bloomington, Indiana

This book is printed on acid-free paper.

Although Muslim ancestry is the focal point, the story line is fiction. All the characters appearing in the work are fictitious. Any resemblance to real persons, living or dead is purely coincidental.

DEDICATION

For

Mary Ellen

One of those too few special people,
We meet in this world,
Who make our lives worthwhile.

ACKNOWLEDGMENT

Thank you, Maureen, not only for the hundreds of hours you spent editing through this process, but also for your patience and your friendship all these past years.

Thank you too, Fred, for looking after things and giving me the time to write.

And

Of course, there is still Brandy, the puppy under my desk, who patiently shares these long hours.

AUTHOR'S NOTE

This is a fiction novel, but it deals with real issues. As the author, I want to make it clear; *it does not matter what you or I believe*. What does matter is what the world of Islam believes. **Islamic / Muslim law** does not allow a person the freedom to choose a religion.

A man has no control over his ancestry, but if someone's father was a Muslim and they do not practice the religion of Islam they are an apostate in the eyes of the Islamic / Muslim world. In Islam, **apostasy is ridda**, which means turning back, and it is a profound insult to Allah. A person born of a **Muslim male parent**, who rejects Islam, is a **murtad fitri**, or **natural apostate**. In the Islamic societies of Saudi Arabia, Yemen, Iran, Sudan, Mauritania, Qatar, the Comoros, and the tribal regions of Pakistan and Afghanistan the law is explicit. **Apostasy is punishable by death.**

The Qur'an and *hadith*, which is a collection of sayings attributed to Muhammad, are quoted on the cover of the hard copy of this book; both support the death penalty for *apostasy in Islam.*

Let there be no compulsion in religion:
Clearly the Right Path of Islam,
Is distinct from the crooked path.
Quran

Those who believe and then reject Faith, then
believe again, and again reject Faith, and go
on increasing in Unbelief – Allah will not
forgive them or guide them on their way.
Quran - Surah 4-137

Kill whoever changes his religion.
Hadith Sahih Bukhari 9 – 84 – 57

The blood of a Muslim cannot be shed
Except in three cases:
1 - for Murder,
2 -for a person who commits adultery
3 - for one who leaves the religion of Islam.
Hadith – Sahih Bukhari – 9 – 83 – 17

Islam online, a website, contained a fatwa dated 21 March 2004, which is an Islamic legal declaration, stating that it is an obligation for the caliph to ask the *apostate* to repent and return to Islam. If he refuses, he is to be killed immediately.

I have asked myself why, during the two years prior to the November 2008 election night, most of the American media subverted reports of Muslim atrocities occurring on an increasing scale worldwide. However, within days after the election, stories of Somalia Muslim pirates hijacking dozens of ships, and suicide bombs going off in the streets of Afghanistan, Pakistan, Iraq and Indonesia flooded the pages of the newspapers and filled our television screens.

One month before the 2008 American presidential election, the democratic vice-presidential candidate stated publicly that the world would test his running mate within six months of his inauguration.

Shortly after the 2008 presidential election Muslim militants from Pakistan bombed the tourist section of Mumbai, India. Close to two hundred civilians died, scores more were wounded. The intent of the Muslim crusaders was to target British and American tourists, but also to kill thousands of Hindus and then die in Allah's War of Jihad.

In November 2008, Iran supplied the weapons and Hamas accelerated rocket attacks on the civilian populations of Israel believing the world would condemn Israel when Israel retaliated. *Most of the world did!*

On December 2, 2008, major news networks in the U.S. began predicting a biological or a nuclear attack on America by Muslim extremists would occur within ten years. Based on the events transpiring in Pakistan, the proliferation of nuclear weapons in North Korea and Iran's stated agenda of the pursuit of nuclear research, *I'm inclined to believe they are right.*

On March 20, 2009, after the new American President reached out to Iran, Iran's supreme religious leader, Ayatollah Ali Khamenei stated that : *"He insulted the Islamic Republic of Iran from the first day. What is the sign of that change"*

PROLOGUE

The Quran references an afterlife basking in rivers of wine, milk and honey for those crusaders who join, and die in the war of Jihad against the infidels.

Mohammad, Allah's messenger, promised Muslim martyrs seventy virgin companions who would fulfill all their desires for eternity, but he also told his followers that Allah reserves these rewards only for those men who die in his service.

Militant Muslims have ties to fishing fleets in Iran, Sudan, Syria, Lebanon, Egypt, Saudi Arabia, Ethiopia, Pakistan, Yemen and India. The trawlers following migrating schools of tuna and sardines in the Mediterranean, Red Sea, Gulf of Aden, Arabian Sea and the Indian Ocean, also smuggle military cargo, passengers, slaves and heroin between the ports on the connecting waterways.

America's pending withdrawal of its military from the Middle East in the wake of the *Apostate's* promises and congressional demands, has made the fishing ports at Marka, Somalia on the shores of the Indian Ocean, and the Port of Sudan on the Red Sea, the locations of choice for the new Muslim terrorist camps and the Muslim pirates pillaging the passing ships.

In 2006, Israel invaded Lebanon and Palestine, destroying infrastructure and setting progress back ten years after Hezbollah rocket attacks on Israel. Hamas followed suit lobbing hundreds of rockets into Israel and shortly after the November 2008 presidential election, Israel struck back at Hamas. America's support of the Israeli military response to Hezbollah and Hamas met with widespread rioting and condemnation in the Islamic world.

Ghalib was a seasoned soldier in Hezbollah. As the election progressed and the *Apostate* drew the world's attention, Ghalib asked for new volunteers. He handpicked those for the mission who had shown the most courage in the recent conflicts.

The migration started a month earlier when Ghalib arrived in Somalia. Dr. Hakeem, the new head of Pakistan's Nuclear Regulatory Commission, provided the trawler from the port of Gwadar, Pakistan that would be joining with the Blue Coral, a research ship moving south following a large school of tuna.

Ghalib and his men spent months training in the tribal regions of Pakistan before boarding the trawler in Gwadar. They posed as fishermen, and then left the trawler by rafts as they passed Marka, Somalia.

Ghalib approached the camp on the outskirts of Marka with a convoy carrying men, guns and posters the Lion Sheik promised the day the *Apostate* officially became the democratic presidential candidate.

Volunteers from Mogtada al-Sadar's army in Iraq, led by Mash'al, followed in the second truck. They would join Ghalib on his journey of martyrdom toward paradise, by way of the cities of the Great Satan, *America*.

Jawdah led the group recruited from the Islamic Center of North America in Dearborn, Michigan, USA. They arrived in Jeddah with a group of American Muslims on a pilgrimage to Mecca. The American volunteers would assure that the migrating crusaders would have men among them fluent in English and familiar with American laws and customs.

Ghalib assembled the men on the firing range. The instructors had replaced the old targets with posters of the new American president. Mannequins with the *Apostate's* features were scattered across the hillside. Ghalib raised his rifle to his shoulder, and then put a bullet between the eyes of the nearest mannequin.

This mission called for fifty men. Thousands were volunteering. The final selection process started as two hundred men raised their rifles in the air to a chant of *Kill the Apostate! Kill the Americans! Allah Akabar! Allah Akabar! Allah Akabar! God is great! God is great! God is great!*

Yaq'ab stood on the canyon rim near Chaman, Pakistan with the satellite phone to his ear. The roar of the men in the desert of Somalia meant the martyrs had arrived; the training had begun.

The Lion Sheik would be pleased. The Americans had spit in Allah's face when they chose the *Apostate* over the woman. Men were flocking to the camps to avenge Allah and his messenger. The Twin Towers would soon no longer be America's worst nightmare.

CHAPTER 1

Pictures taken by satellite camera over the camp in the desert of Somalia lay scattered on the desk. Eric Ludlow, the CIA's Chief of Operations for Middle East Affairs, and Ron Edwards, the CIA European liaison to the Pentagon, were meeting with Admiral Michaels, the senior military Chief of Staff at the Pentagon.

In preparation for the meeting, Eric and his staff developed reports on the crime of *apostasy* in Islam, and the 21st century process of Islamization taking place in Europe and the U.S. He took two copies of the reports out of his briefcase and handed one to Ron Edwards and the other to Admiral Michaels.

"What does this mean, Eric?"

"It means the Islamic world believes he is Muslim, Ron."

"That's ridiculous. His voting record in the senate says he would lead the gay parade and assist the doctor scrambling the brains of a premature baby born alive during an abortion, or for that matter any baby still partially in the birth canal. Nothing about the President is Muslim."

"Does anyone really know who he is, Ron? He shifts his position whichever way the tide of public approval is running. I do not think anyone besides the President himself knows what he believes, but that's not the point. The Islamic world knows his father was Muslim. To the religion of Islam his denial makes him an *apostate*. To devout Muslims he is still a Muslim and Muslims are not allowed to leave the religion."

"Enlighten me, Eric. Although it has not always been true, rational people in the secular world believe religion should be a personal choice. We aren't ready to accept that someone is committed to a point of view simply because a parent was a member of a certain religion or a cult."

"The Muslim family and the religion of Islam are widely misunderstood, Admiral. To believe in God, or not to believe, or to choose one religion over another is a fundamental right of a free society. The world of Islam has a different point of view.

Islam teaches that if the male parent is a Muslim the child is a Muslim. There is no requirement for baptism, and it does not require a conscious effort to join. Muslim men may marry non-Muslim women, but Muslim women cannot marry non-Muslim men. In the eyes of the Muslim world, anyone whose father is a Muslim is a Muslim."

As the CIA's Chief of Operations for Middle East Affairs, Eric had been following the reaction of the Islamic world to the 2008 American presidential race.

After graduating with a PhD in religious studies at Harvard, Eric earned an associate degree in Arabic and Islamic studies at Cairo University before joining the CIA. After three decades in the Middle East, he had an acute understanding of the religion of Islam and the Muslim family. When the question of the *Apostate's* ancestry became an issue in the presidential race, he expected an outcry from the Islamic world, but that had not happened.

Eric felt something was amiss in the Muslim world. By definition, the American President is an *apostate* and devout Muslims believe he has committed the gravest of all sins in Islam. What was happening did not follow the pattern.

Eric believed it to be a warning and *The Apostate Theory* formed in his mind when Iran followed Sudan's lead and formally reinstated the death penalty for *apostasy* during his campaign for the presidency. The *Apostate* ignored the Islamic Fatwa, and he offered to meet unconditionally with the renegades leading Iran and Syria. He also made overtures to both militant organizations, Hamas and Hezbollah.

It appeared, except for Al-Queda and the warlords in Pakistan, the public world of Islam was ignoring Islamic law and had embraced the *Apostate* as the future leader of the free world.

After America's second invasion of Iraq, Eric had been meeting weekly with Admiral Michaels about Muslim threats to America's military bases in Iraq and Afghanistan.

After President Musharraf's abdication, Pakistan had become the focal point of Eric's attention. Eric was familiar with the corruption in the secular governments of the Middle and Near East, and he was concerned that Pakistan's undocumented nuclear arsenal was now at risk. However, led by the Speaker of the House and the Senate Majority leader, there was a majority in Congress openly condemning America's past support of Musharraf. They had rallied congress behind the new governing body.

When General Musharraf stepped down in August of 2008, hundreds of nuclear weapons suddenly came within reach of the militant Muslims seeking changes to what remained of Pakistan's secular law.

Eric flashed a warning to the CIA and the Pentagon, but the warning was shelved when the special interest lobbies petitioned

Congress for additional aid funds for Pakistan. Believing more money would keep the lid on Pakistan's weapons facilities and out of the hands of Al-Queda, the doves in the Pentagon and Congress agreed.

Eric's opinions of the worldwide Muslim conflict with the secular world differed from that of the majority members of Congress and Jim Symington. The *Apostate,* as the President is referenced to in Eric's theory, liked his attitude and kept Symington as head of the Anti Terrorist Task Force (ATTF) that was established during the Bush administration after 9-11.

The honeymoon had just started, but more troops were promised for Afghanistan and more money for Pakistan. It became apparent to the press and the public that he would ignore his campaign promises that could not be kept. Rather than criticize the *Apostate,* Iraq, and Afghanistan became old news, and although Israel and Palestine were in the news daily, the congressional committees and the press were ignoring what was happening in Pakistan.

For a time the *Apostate* would leave the status quo alone. Although it was obvious to the military the wars would drag on, the American public looked the other way. The economic meltdown took precedent and complacency was setting in as the euphoric *Apostate* and the Democratic Congress looked to a wave of new social programs.

Jim Symington's influence with the congressional committee had convinced the *Apostate* and Congress that Muslim threats within the borders of the U.S. had been contained after 9-11. He believed it was time to set some of the methods aside that infringe on the personal liberties of suspects.

Eric disagreed; he was of the opinion that there was a worldwide effort by militant Muslim leaders to conquer the secular world and replace it with Islamic rule. The military men in charge of operations in the Persian Gulf and Afghanistan shared his views.

"Eric, we need a definition from the world of Islam itself, and some backup for the Task Force. Jim Symington recruited most of his people from the liberal colleges that define a militant Muslim as someone perverting the peaceful side of Islam.

To them any Muslim, except those under Al-Queda's direct influence and control, are moderates. They do not believe Muslims living in America pose a risk to this country. Nothing short of another 9-11 will convince them, and even then, they will side with the terrorists and place the blame on America's past nation building policies and our support of Israel."

"It's a difficult exercise, Admiral. Any on-line dictionary, or a Google of *apostasy* will tell the true story, but Islam has its own definition. You must go beyond the secular definition and deal with the Qur'an, and the hadith which references the life of Muhammad. However, anyone who does the research will realize there is no question in the Islamic world as to what constitutes *apostasy* or the punishment prescribed."

"If that's true, why has the most famous *apostate* of all time, been ignored by the Islamic world?"

"It's a theory I'm still working on, Admiral."

Eric's sources were convinced the word coming out of the tribal regions of Pakistan indicated Al-Queda was gearing up for a major offensive on American soil.

Admiral Michaels felt military intervention may be required to help the local law enforcement agencies in the U.S. deal with the threat. However, although a governor of a state may call in the National Guard, the American military does not have in-country authority without presidential approval. Admiral Michaels would need to sell the report to Jim Symington; a report he was having difficulty digesting himself.

"Jim Symington has agreed to meet with us in the morning, Eric. However, we need to connect the dots between Saudi Arabia and the Muslim cells in London and Miami. Symington will not be an easy sell."

"Dr. Abraham is the most qualified man we have on staff, Admiral. After the revolution, Iran's religious council condemned him as an *apostate*."

"I know him, Ron. Bring him to the meeting. With his background maybe he can convince them."

After the attack on the World Trade Center, Congress established the *ATTF*. Although they would work with Homeland Security and the individual states, the *ATTF* had jurisdiction and absolute authority over all terrorist activities within the U.S. borders.

Jim Symington was a weasel of a man the lame duck administration appointed to pacify an antagonistic press and a democratically controlled Congress.

Symington and his connections in Congress favored a reduction in funds to Homeland Security and the state agencies. As state budgets were reduced, a corresponding increased budget for the *ATTF* was granted.

Symington was power hungry and saw his position with the ATTF leading to a senate seat. He had followed the *Apostate's* lead. He had purged the ranks of the *ATTF* of anyone who disagreed with him. He then rehired a bunch of neophytes fresh out of college who do not believe in profiling.

The *ATTF* treats terrorists as misguided concerned citizens, disillusioned because of America's nation building policies and *meddling* in the Middle East. Neither Ron Edwards nor Admiral Michaels are fond of the man and his sympathies based on ignorance of an enemy that has no rules to live by.

During the primaries, the *Apostate* had professed that terrorists should be processed through the in-place legal system and rehabilitated. After the election, the democratic majority in Congress went along with him.

At the request of Symington and his staff, the Congressional Committee on Terrorism instructed what was left of Homeland Security and the state security agencies to discontinue profiling, search warrants and wiretaps, except in cases where there was absolute proof of guilt. They also issued a directive to Homeland Security to simply collect information and then turn it over to the local law enforcement authorities.

It is a self-defeating approach. Without profiling, wiretaps and warrants it is impossible to build a case. In the few isolated cases where terrorists have been caught red-handed, the loopholes in the court system and sympathetic judges were turning them loose.

Admiral Michaels was waiting for Ron's report which identified a Saudi Arabia / Miami connection. Hoping to tie the two together, Ron and his Paris staff had been dealing with a British operative in Nassau.

Ron had enlisted Eric, whose contacts in the tribal regions of Afghanistan and Pakistan were the key, but the Afghan moles were difficult to reach and it sometimes took days to set a safe meeting.

"You have kept this pretty close to your vest, Ron. How extensive is it?"

"It appears to lead from the tribal regions of Pakistan through Saudi Arabia and then to London, Admiral. Our moles in London tell us Muslims carrying British passports have been using Saudi money to buy up waterfront estates on Andros Island and along the Miami waterfront. We also have information the properties are being used to assimilate militant refugees into our general populations."

Ron received notice from British MI5 Foreign Intelligence that British Immigration in Nassau cleared a group of political refugees who would be arriving from Somalia. The sympathetic report said the men lost their families when Christian soldiers from Ethiopia invaded Somalia and destroyed their village. British Immigration accepted their applications after the new owners of an estate on Andros Island guaranteed their employment.

Ron contacted British Immigration and questioned the actions, but he was put off. He was told it was a done deal and that it was a courtesy notice about a group of political refugees who would use a pilgrimage to Mecca as an excuse to separate themselves from the warlords in Somalia.

It was rumored that a member of the Saudi royal family was taking delivery of a new mega yacht the first of the year. The men would be given temporary asylum in Saudi Arabia and then board at Jeddah for the trip to Andros Island after they completed their pilgrimage to Mecca.

After receiving the report, Ron had his staff dial in the CIA satellite cameras on the Bahamas.

"Our satellites are picking up men on yachts around Andros Island who have connections to known terrorist organizations. How about Miami, Admiral, what have you heard?"

"The FBI reports say the Saudis kept their funding to the cells under wraps in the past. They laundered money through the mosques using offshore banks. Times have changed since the election. There is an open flow of money coming into the country. What isn't used for investment pays for the lobby in Washington."

When the price of oil dropped below eighty-five dollars a barrel the social programs in the oil rich countries that keep the poverty stricken populations at bay had to be cut. The cuts threaten stability.

The regimes in Saudi Arabia and other Middle East money finances a segment of the green movement in the states and is trying to keep America from developing its own resources to prop up the price of OPEC oil.

People have forgotten, but it worked in the seventies with the Carter administration after the OPEC embargo, and leaving our resources in the ground is a popular choice with the new President and the Democratic Congress today. There is lots of backroom chatter about the Saudi influence, but no formal objection is being raised.

"What's happened to oversight, Admiral? The President won on a promise of change."

"There is change, but it's going the wrong direction. With an eight hundred billion dollar bailout and another trillion of so called stimulus, there are too many new programs and administrative employees to oversee. It's a feeding frenzy and Congress has put the animals in charge of the zoo. The lobbies are throwing lots of lavish parties and passing out perks to the new recruits who are gobbling them up."

"There has to be a way to get Symington to look into the Miami purchases, Ron."

"We tried, Admiral, but the President has made it clear he is working toward pulling our military out of the Middle East. He wants to mend fences and develop closer ties to the Islamic world. Now, with the democrats in control of both houses and the President pushing the changes in our anti-terrorism policies, the Saudis have become brazen.

We have confirmation they are buying along the Miami seaboard through their connections in Washington. They do not seem to care if we know it is Saudi money, but we do not know who the principals in the consortium are. The speculation in our circles is that it is the Saudi royal family and their friends who are hedging their bets for the future."

Eric had followed the politics in the Middle East for almost thirty years. The rulers live in luxury while the masses live in squalor and poverty. The smart Arab money knows it will end and the religious leaders will take over when the Americans leave. They also know that time is rapidly approaching.

The Saudi and Syrian royal families are corrupt, but there will be no safe bank account in the Middle East when religious rule replaces what is left of secular law. In Islam all things belong to Allah, and Allah's wishes are administered by the corrupt clerics.

Investment by Middle East oil interests and Arab power brokers in U.S. properties through American intermediaries has been a safe haven for years. The sons of many rich Arabs who have been educated in the U.S. have stayed in the U.S. gaining citizenship and with it private access to the banking industry and real estate markets.

Symington and the Task Force ignored the obvious. The Middle East has been a tinderbox since it was partitioned after World War 1. Rising birthrates and the expanding Muslim populations fuel the fire. Israel is holding on through the grace of the U.S. naval fleet in the Persian Gulf and the American support that continues to supply them with replacement arms.

Iran and Syria are funding Hezbollah and Hamas, and were funding some factions of Al-Queda, but their economies are based on eighty-five dollar a barrel oil. They need to pay attention to their own social services first.

None-the-less, Israel's existence is threatened by the growing populations of Israeli Muslims. The Muslim birth rate is three times that of the Israelis. If it continues at the present rate, they will outnumber the Jews in another forty years.

Apartheid was unacceptable to the Americans and the rest of the civilized world in South Africa. When they have the vote the Muslims will rule Israel and the last of the Jews in the Middle East will be forced to migrate to their last safe haven on the planet, the U.S.

When the Jews leave, the Americans will leave. The Muslims believe Europe is won. The Sunni / Shiite conflict continues but the Sunni side of the Muslim war of Jihad being directed from the mosques in Mecca and Medina has refocused on America.

For now, the Saudi Arabia royal family encourages the terrorists, but is staying on the sidelines. They live lavish life-styles and want to continue to do so. They have their sights set on being free to continue their way of life in America.

Jim Symington had little reason to be concerned and he rebuked Ron's prodding. Symington's response when Ron confronted him with the proof of purchases was, *with the turmoil in the Middle East, it makes sense for them to invest in high-end real estate. Since there is no law against it, we are not concerned. My orders are to leave them alone.*

How many properties and how much money is involved, Ron?"

"We know of a dozen or more, Admiral. Some of them in the fifty to hundred million range. Anyone with the money can find a way to buy property on U.S. soil, but an influx of large deposits into local banks for the transactions would raise eyebrows. The Saudi's know it attracts less attention to use a Washington law firm with its own escrow department."

"Can you put a trace on the properties and the money?"

"We tried, Admiral, but Symington blocked the warrants and the Miami branch of the law firm handling their transactions is screaming, *client's privilege*. Without solid probable cause, no warrants, so it will take time to filter the paper trail."

"What about the Andros Island properties, Ron?"

"Andros Island properties can be bought and sold in Nassau or in London, Eric. There are many Muslims with dual citizenships. By the time the deeds are recorded in Nassau there is an umbrella of legitimate companies involved."

"But it's British territory. I would think they would be in the loop."

"The British have a history of making concessions to Muslims in London, but the Muslims are outpacing the social services. The

Muslim community in the suburbs of London is expanding and the violence is escalating along with the demands for religious concessions. British politicians are content with the more radical Muslims and the vocal imams relocating. As far as they are concerned, they can turn the entire island into a Muslim enclave so long as they leave the British subways alone."

"Andros Island puts them within a stone's throw of Miami with no oversight, Ron. If Bin Laden's friends in Saudi are building a base a hundred fifty miles from Miami and buying property along Florida's coast, there is a connection. It seems everyone is aware of the surge in purchases in both areas. I understand the British attitude, but Miami is accessible to us; why no action on our part?"

"Admiral, I told Symington our satellites have picked up a lot of recent movement between the mainland and the island. I asked the question again when the satellite pictures started picking up men in military dress carrying guns on the yachts and on the beaches. However, the walled-in compounds, fifty million dollar mansions and mega-yachts justify the security to the boys upstairs."

"Congress has turned adamantly anti-gun and is trying to pass new legislation. Why not use that approach?"

"Yes, gun control is on their minds, Admiral, but the dollar is soft and Miami is a bargain for foreign investment. Washington interests control a lot of depressed Miami property. With prices in the toilet and American buyers scarce, it is politically correct politics as usual. There is a hands-off policy all the way to the top."

"Admiral, we know heroin is funding the Al-Queda leaders in Pakistan, and there has been a recent flood of heroin into the market. Can we approach it from offshore? We could make it a drug problem instead of a Muslim / terrorist issue, and get it out of Symington's ball park."

"We tried to make it an Afghanistan / Pakistan connection, Eric, but Al-Queda's financial roots are in Saudi. The Saudis wine and dine the politicians and so long as the money keeps flowing from the Saudi lobby to their pet projects, congressional committees will continue to look the other way."

"Admiral, the Al-Queda Pakistan connections are dealing in heroin. We can make that the issue in the Bahamas."

"The Saudi connections in Washington have prevented our Coast Guard from interfering at sea, and after they dock we need a search warrant to board the yachts and enter the private properties. Give me a reason besides drugs and a few real estate purchases, Eric. We need proof to open the door. Push for answers tonight and bring what you have tomorrow."

Ron picked up the report, studying the title. "I hope it is just a bunch of rich Arabs throwing their money around, and this is a dead end, Admiral."

"We all do, but the pilots on 9-11 trained in Orlando and had deep connections in Miami. Tell your people our hands are tied until we get proof they are mounting some sort of attack."

Ron settled in his suite at the Marriot and then poured himself a scotch before picking up the resume.

Dr. Abraham was born in Iran in 1943 during the reign of Shaw Mohammad Reza Pahlavi. His life as a religious student at the Islamic seminary in Qom started in his fifteenth year. He remained in Iran through his doctorate in religious studies and took up teaching at the University Mosque in Tehran, Iran.

He was at odds with the Shaw who had suppressed religion in the region and led the movement inside Iran to depose the Shaw and bring Ayatollah Khomeini to power.

After the revolution, Dr. Abraham was second to Ayatollah Khomeini in Iran's ruling Religious Council. Khomeini had been Dr. Abraham's teacher and mentor at the Qom seminary. Khomeini entrusted Dr. Abraham with the task of drafting the new constitution.

He fell out of favor with Khomeini when he questioned the direction to steer from the democratic process promised pre-revolution, to the autocratic rule of Khomeini.

A few years after the constitution passed, Dr. Abraham gave a speech to students drowning in the repression of the new ruler. His comment, *for a few years we all lost our minds, but as a system that promised us Heaven, it has created a hell on earth*, infuriated Khomeini, and Abraham was forced to flee Iran.

Dr. Abraham fled to the Muslim ghettos in France, but his view of Islam changed. He relocated to the United States where he met and married a Christian, eventually joining her church. For a time he became an outspoken critic of Khomeini's rule and the religion of Islam.

Prior to Khomeini's death, Khomeini declared Dr. Abraham an *apostate* and imposed a death sentence. Dr. Abraham was on a lecture circuit at the time and the mood of the Muslims became ugly at a seminar in Detroit, Michigan.

The ensuing riot caused him to seek protection for himself and his family. His knowledge of Islam and his connections in Iran were highly valued. The CIA moved him and his family to Washington and provided for their protection. He now works for the CIA as an advisor on Islamic affairs. There is no one better qualified to define *apostasy* within the framework of the religion of Islam than Dr. Abraham.

Dr. Abraham had attached a comment to his resume pointing out modern day Islamic author Abdul Ala Mawdudi (1903-1979) was the most influential Muslim thinker of the 20th century. As the founder of *Jamat-I Islami*, he brought a fundamental Islamic revival to modern times. His message was a return to the teachings of the Qur'an and the criminal penalties prescribed in Shari'a law. Mawdudi argued in his book, *Apostasy in Islam*, that the Qur'an *prescribes death* as the penalty for all *apostates*.

In his summary, Dr. Abraham stated there is no question. The American President is an *apostate* in the eyes and mind of the Islamic world. Dr. Abraham referenced a number of his contacts in Pakistan, Afghanistan, Syria and Iran.

They agreed; the consensus was that at the direction of the leaders in Mecca and Medina, the imams in the mosques around the world are controlling the response while the militants use it as a recruiting tool. The question is not when, but how the *Apostate* will become an issue for America.

CHAPTER 2

S audi Arabia was the home of the prophet Muhammad.
The cities of Mecca and Medina are the birthplace of Islam.
Jerusalem is the city Muhammad is said to have visited
Heaven from, and it is the third holiest place in the Islamic world.

For the past few years the world has focused on Iran's pursuit of
a nuclear arsenal. What the world has not focused on is the Shiite
/ Sunni conflict which rages over the holy sites of Islam that are
dominated by the Sunnis in Saudi Arabia, and the Jews in Israel.
A study of the Sunni / Shiite conflict would lead one to believe
that the Middle East countries of Saudi Arabia and Israel are Iran's
future targets, not the United States.

Iran's population is predominantly of the Persian race. They are
not Arabs. They are Shiite Muslims who have been at war with
their Arab Sunni enemies since the seventh century when the
Sunni's threw Muhammad's family out of their homes to roam the
barren desert.

Saudi Arabia sits on the largest known oil deposits in the world. In the Shiite leaders' minds the Sunnis are usurpers. The oil belongs to Allah and the Muslim family, but is being used to provide a decadent lifestyle for the rich Arab rulers.

The majority Shiite population of Iraq had been subjected by their Sunni enemies from the time the country was established after World War 1. Most of the remaining Shiite shrines were destroyed by the Sunnis during Saddam Hussein's regime. That tide has turned with the Shiite clerics with ties to Iran gaining control of Iraq after Saddam Hussein was replaced.

Under America's leadership, while the world has focused on Iran, Iraq, Afghanistan and Israel, the real home base of the War of Terror and the major threat to America has been ignored.

Osama Bin-Laden chose to base his operations in Pakistan for a reason. After losing East Pakistan in a war to India in 1971, Prime Minister Zulfiqar Ali Bhutto initiated Pakistan's rush to develop nuclear weapons. India followed suit and during the subsequent years, India and Pakistan acquired full nuclear capabilities.

There has been little oversight of their nuclear program and weapons manufacturing of either country. Accurate counts of warheads by nuclear watchdogs have been impossible to maintain.

In 2002, America's War on Terror moved into the tribal regions of Afghanistan ruled by the Taliban. As a result, Islamic militants took refuge in Kashmir and joined Al-Queda in the tribal region of Pakistan.

As the militants gained power in the villages, and the refugee camps along the borders began to swell, Pakistan's claim on Kashmir encouraged the Muslim refugees' attacks on the minority Hindu population. India has been moving in troops, and as the rhetoric escalates, Pakistan and India have begun stockpiling weapons along their borders.

With a predominantly Hindu population of over one billion, to Pakistan at 175 million, India is a mortal enemy of the colonizing Islamic ideology of Pakistan's Taliban warlords. Conflicts with the Muslim refugees and hostilities in the local villages continue to flare with militant Muslim bombings plaguing areas around Mumbai and Jaipur, India.

What little is left of moderate secular Pakistan is facing a war on two fronts. India is on one side and tribal leaders siding with the Afghanistan Taliban in their surge to move Pakistan toward their brand of an Islamic state are on the other.

Militant sympathizers were encouraging Taliban encroachment and escalating violence in the cities when General Pervez Musharraf seized power in 1999 in a military coup. He subsequently suspended the constitution of Pakistan and imposed martial law.

More dictator than democratic, Musharraf clamped a lid on the militant Muslims. India and the rest of the world breathed a sigh of relief as Musharraf tightened security and locked down Pakistan's nuclear arsenal.

The United States was one of the first to recognize Musharraf as the new leader of Pakistan, but Musharraf walked a tightrope for nine years.

After 9-11, in exchange for additional U.S. aid, Musharraf reluctantly assisted the U.S. in the War on Terror. However, Islamic radicals throughout Pakistan have strong roots to the Taliban and are sympathetic to Al-Queda's cause.

The *Great Satan*, as they refer to America in the Islamic world, is Islam's mortal enemy, and its focal point in Islam's war of Jihad on the secular world. When Musharraf broke ties with the Afghanistan Taliban government and sided with the Americans against Al-Queda, violent anti American demonstrations flared in the tribal regions along the Pakistan / Afghanistan border.

Musharraf ignored the religious leaders and for a time helped the American forces locate leaders of Al-Queda. After the riots resulting from the arrest of Khalid Shaikh Mohammad, who masterminded the 9-11 attack, Musharraf moved 25,000 troops to the tribal regions to maintain control.

American aid and heroin funded the country, but without secular oversight, graft and corruption plagued his government. On August 18, 2008, after the recent elections, Musharraf resigned under impeachment pressure from the new coalition government.

Eric believed that if a strong military commander could not contain corruption and the terrorist organizations, it is unlikely white collared, corrupt politicians will challenge them.

He was right. In a few short months with Musharraf gone, the Taliban began killing Pakistan police and military personnel on sight, and reestablished the punishments outlined in Islamic law.

The police have left and the local military has discarded their uniforms and rejoined the Taliban. The tribal regions on the Pakistan / Afghanistan border have become a safe haven for the leaders of the Islamic extremists.

America's military influence diminished after the 2008 Pakistan elections. Pakistan's new government has insisted American forces in Afghanistan leave the Taliban warlords and Al-Queda to them.

Al-Queda's Osama Bin Laden and al-Jawahiri are living freely in the rugged mountain canyons inside the Pakistan border with the displaced Taliban who were driven from Afghanistan.

The Taliban are being funded by Saudi Arabia oil and Al-Queda's heroin operations in Pakistan. They are now waiting for the Americans to leave Afghanistan so they can regain their ancestral poppy fields.

The gap in America's relations in the region widened when the *Apostate* was elected in America. Within days, volunteers from Kashmir, Pakistan, Afghanistan and the Middle East swarmed to the mountains in Pakistan.

Overwhelmed by the number of volunteers, Al-Queda is filtering the volunteers from Syria, Iraq and Lebanon toward re-building the ranks of the crusaders in the offshore camps of Somalia and Sudan.

Ron and Eric arrived at Admiral Michaels' office shortly before nine. Part of the puzzle was still missing. Ron and Admiral Michaels were familiar with the Muslim reaction to insults hurled at the religion of Islam in the past.

"I don't understand, Eric. They rioted in the streets of Khartoum over a *Teddy Bear* named Muhammad and across the entire Middle East over a few cartoons. If Dr. Abraham's report is correct and the Islamic world believes he is an *apostate*, why no outcry from Islam?"

"The imams in the mosques control the radicals, Admiral. Everything is organized and then orchestrated. The majority Sunni Muslims are under complete control of the imams in Saudi Arabia. They only riot when told to do so. I think the Muslim leaders were looking forward to an *apostate* being elected as leader of their archenemy, the *Great Satin,* and have kept a lid on their followers.

"You've lost me, Eric; they riot over cartoons about Muhammad and someone using a page of the Qur'an to wipe their ass. If the report is accurate, Islam demands an *apostate* pay with his life; again, why no outcry?"

"The report is accurate, Admiral. The information has been verified."

"That does not tell us how an *apostate* in the Oval Office helps their cause."

"Think of him as a tool, Admiral. If you listen to Bin Laden's messages, 9-11 was a boost for Muslim conversions and recruiting to the terrorists' camps. Since then our military has taken a toll on Al-Queda leaders in Afghanistan and along the Pakistan border. The American forces have also killed thousands of their crusaders in Iraq; they were having trouble getting new volunteers."

"What's your take, Ron? Violence has escalated across the Middle East and Europe since 9-11. It seems to me Al-Queda is as strong as ever."

"Actually, Admiral, it's stronger in Europe than before 9-11. The overall Muslim population in France is now ten percent, but twenty-five percent of the French population under twenty-five are Muslim. At their current birth rate, the Muslims will be the majority in France within 25 years. The borders of Europe are wide open and the population in the rest of the Muslim ghettos of Europe has reached a point where the terrorists can recruit from their own ranks. As the rioting and violence escalates, the European politicians are caving into their demands; the more concessions, the more riots, it's the Muslim strategy."

"Maybe, Ron, but it's been quiet in America since 9-11, and the Muslim communities have been portraying Islam as a religion of peace. Even the Sunni and Shiites in America appear to be getting along. It seems it is working for them. They are making inroads and the politicians are pushing for concessions. Why would they do something stupid that would set their advances back again? It's a tough sell."

Eric had spent his adult life following the Muslim march across North Africa, and the colonization of the European slums. During that time, the Muslims purged the Jews from Arab lands now ruled by Islamic law, and the few Christians that remain in the Middle East and North Africa de-Christianized their communities and assimilated into the Islamic culture.

"Admiral, one of our researchers coined the term *Islamization*. The Muslims do not care how long the process takes, but in the meantime they want to live by their own laws, not follow those of secular societies. They will colonize an area and begin petitioning for concessions within the framework of the local law while they build their communities.

As their communities grow, they will vote for changes in local laws. When they have the majority, they will install Islamic law. It started the same in Europe, slowly at first, but now Europe is in their palm. If blood starts flowing in our streets, as it has in London, Spain and France, the meek will cave in. They have the money and the weapons are available in Pakistan. Now all Al-Queda needs are sufficient recruits willing to die to stage a series of bloody events."

The terrorist organizations move their camps frequently. The American naval forces in the connecting waterways of the Middle and Near East maintain a network of satellites that are on a never-ending search of the land, seas and skies. The films are patched daily to the CIA office in Washington, DC.

"What's going on in the camps, Ron?"

"It's been a flurry of activity since the election. Now that a large segment of America has created a messiah out of an *apostate*, the training camps in Pakistan, Somalia and Sudan are overrun with new recruits, Admiral.

The main camp to watch is near Marka, Somalia. Law in Somalia has disintegrated and the rest of the world has stood by while the pirates pillage the shipping lanes. Al-Queda is funding the camps with the ransom money and using the entire country as a training ground.

"Ron, give us a rundown on Europe today. What is the real picture?"

"Eric is the expert on the world of Islam, Admiral."

"Eric?"

"Muslims view time differently than we do, Admiral. The attitude in the Muslim world is that although it may take another hundred years, Europe is won unless there is a major shift in policies. Based on what is happening in France and the Netherlands, I am inclined to agree with them. It is only a matter of time before Muslim rule replaces the secular societies. The fact is, even if the

Sunni and Shiites never settle their differences, the U.S. is all that stands in the way of Muslim domination of the free world."

Eric paused to reach for his briefcase and removed his report. "I believe this paints a clear picture of what has taken place in the past and the direction we are heading."

Picking up the report Admiral Michaels made an observation. "It's been quiet since 9-11 on U.S. soil. Nobody is going to believe this until it's too late."

The summary would have been enough to get the Admiral's attention.

> Muslims make up 91 % of the population of the Middle and Near East, 46 % of Africa, 22 % of Asia, 6 % of Europe and 1 % of the Americas.

> Every Muslim country or community is growing at a rate of over three percent annually, an alarming figure, doubling every twenty years.

> Iran had a population of less than ten million at the end of World War 1. Today the population is over sixty million.

> Secular populations barely replace themselves. Muslim leaders are concerned only with the quantity of Muslims, not with the quality of life. If they maintain their present growth rate, and if there is enough food to maintain the populations, by the year 2100 there will be six billion Muslims on the planet.

Admiral Michaels spent the day reviewing the part of Eric's theory on *Apostasy* and *Modern Islamization*. He added to the pile when the new package arrived from the Paris office. After reading the *Islam Tomorrow* report, the puzzle began to take shape in his mind. Islam's subtle sweep into the schools and courts in America followed the pattern. If they could recruit the volunteers and lay their hands on the weapons, violence on a wide scale would follow.

Eric believed that the Muslims were convinced that an ultimate strike with a nuclear weapon that would kill hundreds of thousands, or even millions, in one of the major cities and the fear of a repeat performance, would assure American congressional capitulation.

"Good afternoon, Admiral."

"Hello, Ron, sit down. I read the reports. This is not going to go over well with the President or his friends in Congress. They have been playing down his Muslim heritage from the beginning. If we release this without absolute proof of a pending attack, you and I will be out of a job."

"None of us will have a job if a nuke ignites in Washington. Eric delivered a third report to me a few hours ago, I see you have a copy on your desk. Have you had time to read it?

"Yes, but it deals with a subject America has ignored for decades; what makes you think it will matter now?"

"Times have changed, Admiral. Oil money has made the difference in a very short time, and we have rumblings from reliable sources that Al-Queda has infiltrated Pakistan's nuclear facilities. The Pakistan government is corrupt and the Saudis and Iranians have the money to buy what they want. All they need now is the conduit. I think Andros and Miami are their link. The Muslims have very deep pockets. They have cracked some of the most conservative offices in Washington. For the time being, they can get away with it because the people on the Hill are buying into it."

"Then what's the point, Ron? We have a sympathetic administration and a complacent public. Unless the militants do something stupid, we can't get Washington's attention."

"I'm going on record and suggest we leak the reports to the friendly press, including the information we have on the property transactions. This report on *Islam Tomorrow* may convince them it is time we took a stand before we have to start dismantling our way of life. We need to convince them to move some Navy backup into the area of the Bahamas for the Coast Guard."

"You will need London's blessing. Our treaty allows the Coast Guard access, but under British watch. Our Navy is restricted to international waters."

"Pakistan is in chaos and has a warehouse of nuclear warheads. We know Bin Laden and his crazies have safe refuge in Pakistan. The dots connect. A nuclear threat to Nassau will get British attention, Admiral. We need to convince the British to tighten security in Nassau. We can use drugs as an excuse to step up drug enforcement to board the yachts as they approach Miami."

Eric arrived in a somber mood. Two of his Middle East operatives died the day before on the border of Pakistan, which has become headquarters for the Pakistan militants. They had been visiting a contact in one of the Taliban strongholds and were carrying proof Al-Queda had their hands on nuclear material.

Two others who survived were on their way to the U.S. Embassy in Cyprus for a debriefing. They had made contact with Eric on the way.

When General Musharraf resigned, Pakistan's new parliament replaced the head of their nuclear program. The subject of Dr. Hakeem's past ties to the Taliban tribal regions along the Pakistan / Afghanistan border did not come up.

Dr. Hakeem made a deal with Al-Queda, but would need to shift the blame if the shortage was discovered. He began hiring new personnel and moving old employees to different facilities.

Wahid had been educated in the U.S. and wanted to return. After Dr. Hakeem replaced the personnel, giving Al-Queda access to the weapons storage facility in Mardan, Wahid took a half kilogram of enriched plutonium from the processing area at the laboratory in Rawalpindi to give to the CIA. He would tell them about the new

Al-Queda infiltration. The plutonium was proof Wahid worked in the assembly area. Wahid believed the information would buy him and his family a new life.

Wahid delivered the package to his brother in his village in the mountains. Isma'il gave it to the Americans who came to his village, which is outside the city of Thal, near the Afghanistan border.

Before the new Pakistan government closed the tribal regions to the Americans it would have been a routine crossing into Afghanistan. The Pakistan army had driven the Taliban out of the village in 2003. Since that time and until Musharraf resigned, the army served as escorts to the Americans who maintained a camp near Thal.

The Americans were now unwelcome in the region, but some villages were trying to break the yoke the Taliban warlords were resettling on their lives.

The American team made it to the village avoiding both the Taliban militia and the Pakistan Army. However, the Taliban would kill on sight, and the new government had issued orders to the military to engage the Americans if they continued to ignore Pakistan's sovereignty.

One of the village men, sympathetic to the Taliban, sent word to the Pakistan military and the Taliban warlord in the neighboring village that the Americans had arrived. The Pakistan military blocked the canyon on the border of Afghanistan before the Americans returned. The Taliban caught them at the border.

The American covert operation came under fire from the Taliban and they called for a helicopter pick up. General Sampson, the American commanding officer in Kabul, Afghanistan, was unaware of the CIA mission and sent word he would need clearance from the Secretary of State before sending Special Forces officers, Colonel Rogers and Captain Pitt on a mission that violated current U.S. policy.

One of the men hid the package in a shallow cave near their camp while they waited for a decision. By the time the helicopters crossed the canyon rim, two of the men died.

Colonel Rogers flew cover, disbursing the Taliban while Captain Pitt picked up the remaining men. The man who had hidden the package died with the secret of where he had put it.

"Why are you so glum, Eric?"

"I lost two men in Pakistan, Admiral. Two others survived, but the news is disturbing and we lost the proof. We think Al-Queda has acquired a nuke and has picked a target."

The admiral assumed it was tied to the report on his desk. "The *Apostate*, Washington?"

"Maybe not, Admiral, one of the survivors met with a Taliban connection near Kabul. He says the *Apostate* is a tool they do not want to lose. So long as he is in office and on the political scene, he will attract money and new crusaders to their cause."

"What then, Eric?"

"We don't have a target, Admiral, but our mole at the laboratory in Rawalpindi, Pakistan claimed the material was plutonium. The man carrying it out died and the sample was lost. I sent a message that we need another. That will take time, but for now all we have is a crude map with circles around Andros Island and Miami, and some hearsay."

"Admiral, I think this is enough to get the Navy involved. Would you ask Jim Symington to move up the meeting and then join us there?"

"I will, Ron, but we need to convince him the threat is real. The Task Force will also need to come up to speed on this view of the Muslim issue. The quickest way to do that is to read these reports. I will have copies sent over before the meeting."

"I doubt Symington will agree, but it's worth a try, Admiral."

Too much was unresolved. Eric and Ron met Admiral Michaels for a late lunch. "If there is a target we need proof they have the weapons and what the target is, Admiral."

"If we send another team in by helicopter Pakistan's new government will scream and then order their military to fire on them. It will get messy in Washington. We need to send someone who can pass for a local and cross into the tribal regions. We also need someone the locals will confide in. That's a difficult combination."

"We have someone in Kabul with connections in the tribal regions. She might get through."

It was Eric's territory and although Ron's European connections had trained her, she would be in Eric's jurisdiction.

"It would be Ayeza's first field trip, Ron. We do not send a rookie without a seasoned partner. I would prefer someone with more experience."

Ron and Eric had taken a joint approach to the young woman's training. Ayeza was a displaced Pakistan refugee who had converted from Islam to Christianity. She was raised in the tribal region of Pakistan, but had been living with an American military family in Germany. Recruits of her caliber were highly sought, but seldom found.

The CIA aggressively pursued Ayeza after learning of her connection to the CIA mole in Pakistan's nuclear laboratory. Eric did not want to lose her on her first mission.

Ayeza was born and raised in a Pakistan village, but had spent the past seven years in Germany. She had just recently returned to Kabul and was still in training.

Ayeza had excelled in school in Germany. She also scored in the top five percent on the tests for all CIA applicants for the current year. She was in superb physical condition; sky diving was her hobby, and she had earned a fifth degree belt in her martial arts classes.

On the surface, she was the perfect candidate, but her supervisor in Germany was concerned that she had not yet dealt with her history.

Germany had a large community of refugee families from the Afghan / Russian conflict who had left Afghanistan with young children. Many of those children had returned to work in the refugee camps. Ayeza had returned to Kabul with a German passport posing as a nurse to work with the children orphaned in the current U.S. / Taliban conflict.

Unlike others who had little memory of their lives in Afghanistan, Ayeza would need time to adjust to her new identity and deal with her past. It had only been a few months. She had not been re-evaluated and approved for a field trip.

Ron knew Ayeza was alienated from her village and her family. If the village had slipped back under Taliban control, Ayeza would be at some risk. However, she left the village as a child. It was unlikely that she would be recognized.

"She is the cream of the crop of the new recruits, and she was raised in the Regions, Eric."

"She doesn't have the experience, Ron, and a woman cannot travel in the Regions alone."

Admiral Michaels was out of the loop. "We don't have time to be choosy, Eric. If she doesn't travel by land, I need to go upstairs for a Special Forces mission."

"The girl is young and the mission is critical. She is not ready and should have an experienced partner on her first mission. She needs a qualified escort or I would prefer someone with more experience."

"All right, if that's our only option. If we can bring Symington on board by tomorrow, we'll send her in by helicopter with the Special Forces."

Admiral Michaels returned to his office. On his desk was the study of Islam from the Paris office. He had breezed through it earlier. Sitting at his desk, he reached into the bottom drawer pulling out a bottle of scotch. A re-read before the meeting would take some fortification.

Ron and Eric sat as Jim Symington admonished them for their anti-Islamic presentation. "These reports are biased and Dr. Abraham has an ax to grind with the Muslims. You have no proof of a connection between Andros Island and Miami. Even if you did, there is nothing to insinuate there is a threat to the United States mainland."

"The British won't let us in without a word from the Task Force, Jim."

"The British can take care of their own, Mr. Edwards. We have prevented further attacks since 9-11 in this country, and that is my primary concern. My orders are to mend fences with the Islamic leaders in this country and with their help, concentrate on the radicals in their midst, not to butt into politics in London or Pakistan."

"We had the proof, but we lost the two men who were carrying it out of the tribal region in Pakistan."

"I should have been notified if it involved a threat to U.S. soil, Mr. Ludlow. Your men had no business in Pakistan. Congress has established a new Military Foreign Relations Committee to deal with Pakistan and Afghanistan. We have agreed to honor Pakistan's sovereignty and to stay clear of their borders. Your office was part of that agreement."

"Jim, you know damn well the agreement is a sham. The Pakistan government is aware of our activities. So long as we keep pouring money into their bank accounts they will look the other way."

"That does not appear to be the case, Mr. Ludlow. You lost two men because the Pakistan Army was blocking the way."

"They were killed by the Taliban. The Pakistan Army did not get involved."

"Obviously they did not help. The new Pakistan government is holding on by threads. Your job is to keep us informed about what is going on, not set foreign policy. If I had my way, I would bring your spies home. I can't do that, but I will notify the Committee and they will see to it our military stays off Pakistan soil and out of their air space."

As a member of the Joint Chiefs, Admiral Michaels was the ranking member in the room. "Enough, Jim, we are all working toward the same end and we think there is reason for concern. Your job starts at the borders of this country. Eric's people reach into the heart of the Islamic world. We have different perspectives, and quite honestly, I wish your view of the world was correct, but the proof is in the reality of a world that is correctly outlined in these reports."

"We know there are a few radicals in our midst, Admiral, but we believe we have identified them and we are tracking them. If they actually had a nuke, which I doubt, and if there was a pending strike, we would know about it!"

"Our borders are wide open, Jim. You can't possibly know what is going on behind the closed doors of the mosques."

"I resent that, Admiral. We have moles in every Muslim community. We do know what's going on! The Muslims in this country are mostly law-abiding refugees, concerned with their families and their religion. The American Muslims are not our enemy!"

Admiral Michaels picked up his copies of the reports. It was a useless exercise. "Jim, Bin Laden and his Saudi connections work independently of the American community. Something is coming down, and this side of our borders is your territory. We think there is a connection between Pakistan, Andros Island and Miami."

"You *think*, doesn't work, Admiral. I need proof before I go upstairs or to a judge. The governor, not the military is in charge of the National Guard. I have my orders and I am passing them on. Keep your hands off Miami and leave the area to us. Come back if you get proof."

The meeting was abruptly over; Symington left the room. "What now, Admiral?"

"Symington will go upstairs with this to cover his own ass. The Special Forces are out, but he does not know about the girl, Ron. There is no other choice. Get the proof. If nuclear material is involved, everyone is expendable. Send her in."

"Can we pick her up if she gets into trouble?"

"General Sampson leans our way. I'll bring the military in Kabul on board, but she is on her own unless she gets proof there is nuclear material involved. Symington does not trust the military. He knows General Sampson and I are close. They will tell him to stand down."

"Can they retrieve her if she gets the proof? It's a long trip back across the mountains and we would risk losing it again."

"I'll commit to that, but it's going to get messy. The doves in Congress and on the Hill want General Sampson replaced. They are looking for an excuse. I am sure Symington headed for the White House as soon as he left the meeting. After our discussion, I would expect the Pakistani military will be looking for helicopters crossing from Kabul. General Sampson cannot risk a failed mission without a justifiable reason for going in."

"How do we get her out if she gets it?"

"General Sampson is with us, so is the Special Forces team assigned to the base in Kabul. They will put their careers on the line to prevent a disaster at home. I will suggest the Forces stand by and then make the pickup, but only if the girl has the proof."

"The journey from Kabul across the mountain to her village will take three days, Admiral."

"It can't be helped, Eric. I will contact General Sampson; he will be waiting for her call. Oh and Ron, we need to know what is going on with the Brits. There is a friendly charter service in Ft. Lauderdale; send someone to Nassau who likes to fish.

CHAPTER 3

A yeza was born in a Pakistan village on the border with Afghanistan. Her green eyes, exceptional beauty and blossoming body at the early age of twelve meant a substantial dowry and security for her parents.

Ayeza had numerous suitors. Her parents chose Faisal, a wealthy arms merchant from a village near Kabul, Afghanistan when she was thirteen years old.

Faisal, forty-four years old at the time, was trading arms to the Afghan Mujahedeen for heroin, which he was selling to the Russians. After the Mujahedeen drove the Russians out of Afghanistan, civil war erupted between the Taliban tribes with ties to Saudi Arabia and the less militant Afghan Islamic society. Faisal's tribe sided with the Taliban.

Female circumcision is widely practiced in the Taliban society of Afghanistan and Pakistan. However, Ayeza's village shied from the practice, which was performed in the outer villages without the aid of anesthetics or the use of sterile knives or scissors. The barbarian surgery requires a painful healing process and often causes infection resulting in the death of the child.

Faisal was outraged on their wedding night when he found Ayeza still had her female genitals and that her birth canal had not been sown shut.

Islam teaches that women are here to please men and bear children. No one knows when the practice started, but for centuries female genital mutilation has been Islam's method to control the desires of women and to keep them pure.

Faisal was still dealing heroin to the Russian drug lords from his base in Kabul when American forces landed in Afghanistan after 9-11. Shortly after the wedding, the couple returned to Kabul. Faisal ridiculed her in front of his other wives and told them they would circumcise Ayeza after he returned from his trip back into Pakistan. He assigned her the duties of servant to his eldest wife, and then exiled Ayeza to a hut of her own to wait until he returned.

Faisal was returning from the tribal region of Pakistan when his eldest wife beat the child bride with a stick for failing to complete her chores. The beating had become a daily ritual, but this time the second wife joined in and Ayeza fled from the village seeking shelter elsewhere.

Faisal's brother was with Taliban forces fleeing Kabul and came across Ayeza that evening. She was on the road talking to a young Mujahedeen soldier from a neighboring village. The Taliban killed the boy and gang raped Ayeza.

Rape is not a crime for a man in Islam. Islam assumes the woman enticed the man, or in this case men, and treats it as adultery committed by the woman. The punishment is death by stoning. Encouraged by Faisal's other wives, a village Taliban imam condemned Ayeza for being alone with the boy, enticing the rape.

Ayeza was isolated from the village and imprisoned in a stone hut when Faisal returned. Faisal, who shared the belief that a woman is mere chattel, born to serve the needs of men and to raise children, sided with the religious leaders when they sentenced her to death by stoning.

Faisal would cast the first stone. He dragged Ayeza to the village square followed by the angry mob that would join him and carry out the sentence.

A troop of American military were patrolling the road to Kabul, passing through the village. The Americans intervened, stopping the mob of religious zealots who were pelting her with stones.

Her pelvis broken and bleeding profusely from a wound to her head caused by a stone thrown by Faisal, Ayeza lay conscious, but dying in the street. The Americans approached the crowd, firing their weapons in the air.

The men and women of the village backed off, except for Sajid, Faisal's brother who had been part of the Taliban party that raped the girl.

Carrying his rifle in one hand and a rock the size of a baseball in the other, Sajid turned, scowling at the sergeant leading the Americans, now just a few feet away. When he raised his arm to cast the stone at the sobbing child, the soldier put a bullet in his brain.

In the ensuing melee, seven Taliban died before the troops withdrew, carrying the unconscious girl.

Ayeza was pregnant with her first child. She lost the baby and the ability to carry another to a stone the size of a football dropped on her unborn child by one Faisal's brothers.

Ayeza's recovery in a U.S. military hospital on the outskirts of Kabul was a slow process. Her wounds healed, but the memories of the frenzied actions of her husband's friends and family imbedded in her a chronic fear of male attachment.

Religion had been a way of life in her village. Although she could neither read nor write at the time, she had memorized many passages of the Qur'an the men and women chanted five times a day. She grew up believing Islam was a religion of peace and the only way to true happiness was to follow in the footsteps of the Prophet. However, the fanatical zeal of the mob led by her husband that had killed her child and broken her body turned her against Islam.

Knowing she was innocent of any wrongdoing, Ayeza was bitter at first. As the months passed, her heart was softened by the American army Chaplain who came daily to administer to her, bringing a message of a loving, forgiving God, rather than one of revenge and hate.

Ayeza's body healed, but she had no place to go. She left the hospital for a bunk in one of the women's tents on the base. Banished from her own kind, with a sentence of death hanging over her, she lapsed into depression and seldom left the tent. A few weeks later the Chaplain visited her and offered her a job in the American camp hospital.

Faisal still traveled the tribal region dealing in arms and heroin and would occasionally pass her village. Alone for the first time and unable to return to her family in Pakistan, Ayeza was drawn to the wards, caring for American soldiers who had been wounded defending strangers in a hostile land.

Water was scarce in the arid region of her village. Ayeza had spent her life living on dirt floors and sleeping on beds made of straw, covered with unwashed rags. She had been a servant to her family as a child and then bound to her husband's whims and demands. Daily baths, a soft bed with clean sheets, and the welcoming smiles of the friendly soldiers were a refreshing change.

Ayeza had never seen a book, a fork or a bed with a mattress, but she had a gift for learning. English came easy and in the friendly atmosphere, she dedicated herself to American methods in the hospital, as well as their way of life.

An outcast among her own people, the Americans became the source of her only comfort. The young nurse's aide changed clothes daily when she left the common areas. After shedding the traditional Muslim clothes she said she hated, she dressed in smart blouses and skirts made of military khaki. The soldiers enjoyed the company of the unveiled beauty with smoldering green eyes and satin hair, in a land where women hid behind black cotton cloth that covered all but their eyes.

Ayeza reminded Colonel Hudson of his daughter, who had recently left Germany to live with his brother's family and attend graduate school in the States. Friendly conversations and the sympathetic ear of a wounded American colonel resulted in an offer to go to school and train at a U.S. military hospital in Germany.

Germany had been home for twelve years. Colonel Hudson worked long hours as a surgeon at the hospital and often left for weeks at a time visiting field hospitals in Afghanistan and Iraq. His wife missed her own family and with their only child grown and gone, she was becoming lonely and depressed.

Ayeza and Cathy Hudson's moods changed when they met. Having grown up in a society of brutal male dominance over women, Colonel Hudson and his wife's relationship was beyond Ayeza's understanding. Ayeza, lonely and frightened when she arrived, blossomed at the opportunity to share her life with the caring couple.

Colonel Hudson and Cathy had a run-in with a group of Neo-Nazi Skinheads on a back street of Frankfurt the first year they were in Germany. It was their first holiday in Europe. Colonel Hudson was in uniform and they were sightseeing with others from the American base when they came face to face with the band of youths bent on mischief.

Standing on the street a few feet from the Americans, the gang gestured to the women yelling obscenities in German. The boys passed to the other side of the street without incident when the soldiers stepped forward, ready for the fight.

Cathy and the other women understood the language and knew that if they been there on their own, they could not have defended themselves.

When they returned to the base, Cathy asked the base commander to allow her to organize martial arts self-defense classes for the wives of the soldiers.

As time passed and some of the women's skills improved, they began regular exercise three times a week in the gym where the Special Forces worked out.

Cathy wanted the women to be able to defend themselves against the larger and stronger men, and as time passed the women merged with the classes for the men. A few months after Ayeza arrived, Cathy invited her to attend a session.

Ayeza was shy at first and in fear of the men who treated the women as their equals. Although discipline was the order of the day and they were supposed to pull their punches, one or the other would slip at times and a woman would go down in a grimace of pain.

Cathy worked with Ayeza at home until the girl gained strength and trust. A few months later Ayeza asked to join the class. As her skills improved so did her confidence. She approached an instructor she knew worked out daily and asked permission to join his class.

Ayeza threw herself into the program, earning her first black belt on her sixteenth birthday. By her eighteenth, she had moved up to fourth degree and could hold her own with the instructors.

Colonel Hudson advanced to the rank of Brigadier General and accepted the position of chief of staff at the base hospital. His new position allowed the base commander to overlook the civilian women in army fatigues competing with the men.

At nineteen, Ayeza was teaching the new women enlistees on the base when Colonel Miller arrived to start a high altitude paratrooper class.

Ayeza's strength and confidence had grown to that of the men in her weight class. One day in an exhibition match, behind in points, one recent male recruit became angry and neglected to pull a punch that sent her to the floor dazed, but coherent.

Waving off the referee, Ayeza, spitting out the blood, regained her feet and went on the attack. The referee stepped back allowing her the latitude. A few minutes later the soldier, winded and sprouting numerous bruises and a bleeding, nasty cut to his left cheek from a kick he never saw coming, backed off in submission.

Ayeza would be nursing a few bruises of her own, but as she walked off the floor to a rousing cheer from the mostly male audience. Ayeza knew she would never again cower in fear of a man.

Colonel Miller witnessed the match and inquired about the beautiful young civilian woman with special privileges. A martial arts expert himself, he worked out with the class and a few days later, he invited her to ride with the flight crew to watch the first scheduled jump.

Ayeza ignored the obvious pass. "I would rather make the jump than watch it from the cabin of the plane, Colonel."

"Sorry, miss, but the class is for military personnel only."

"I'm a martial arts instructor on the base, Colonel. They would make an exception if you were to approve."

"I won't ask, but if you get permission I won't object."

It was a foregone conclusion. "Thank you, Colonel, I'll be there. When is the pre-flight instruction scheduled?"

Colonel Miller took the rebuff to his personal advances in stride and developed a friendship with Ayeza. Ayeza made her first jump from five thousand feet, her chute cord attached to the wire insuring it would open safely. A few months later, although she was still teaching martial arts at the base, she was skydiving from heights to twenty thousand feet on weekends.

The military jump class ended with a competition. Ayeza could not compete as a civilian, but Colonel Miller invited her to join him and two other guests in a demonstration jump from thirty-five thousand feet.

"It's cold up there and the air is pretty thin, Colonel."

"Yes, it can be forty below zero or colder and you need to pack oxygen, but it's the next step and it will be your only opportunity to experience it; there are no non-military high altitude jumpers in Europe. One of my team died in Afghanistan and has not been replaced. His moon suit is available. We have time to have it resized if you are interested."

The exhilarating experience was as close to free flight as a human can attain. Two months later Ayeza set a women's altitude record with a jump from a hot air balloon at seventy thousand feet. It was well below the men's record of over one hundred thousand feet set in 1960 and still unbroken, but an accomplishment just the same.

Ayeza volunteered her free time to the physical therapy unit at the hospital on the American airbase. Injured men continued to arrive for rehabilitation as the wars in Afghanistan and Iraq dragged on.

Ayeza was drawn into their stories of military and civilian blood and gore resulting from the brutality inflicted on the innocents by the suicide missions of the misguided crusaders.

Some of the men lost multiple limbs as well as their friends to misplaced sympathy for children who approached them begging for food. Many soldiers, who killed women and children to survive, suffered from severe depression and were suicidal.

The American platoon had taken Ayeza to the Kabul hospital where she was placed in the intensive care unit until she stabilized.

When Ayeza first arrived in Germany, there were men in physical therapy at the German hospital who had shared the recovery ward with her in Afghanistan.

Ayeza continued to train with the men and teach the women. Ayeza's skill surpassed that of the men in her weight class and she wanted the challenge, but in martial arts, size does matter. Although she became a legend on the base, she often showed up at the hospital unable to hide the bruises she endured when she took on the best of the best in the Special Forces who had learned to treat her as their equal.

Ayeza volunteered to work with the men learning to walk on artificial limbs and feed themselves with mechanical hands. Her own story of recovery and her accomplishments in the gym, and in the air, were passed on to new arrivals in Germany. A past product of the brutal Islamic society, the presence of the renewed, green-eyed beauty at their bedside was an antidote.

Ayeza's Pakistan roots and the lifestyle in her village were a normal topic with General Hudson and his wife. Five years after Ayeza arrived she was invited to a party at the American Embassy along with the couple. It was a chance to dress and Cathy Hudson never passed up the opportunity. She also enjoyed shopping for Ayeza. After a day at the spa, Ayeza dressed in an emerald evening gown matching her eyes.

They would stone her in her native Muslim country if she were to wear the dress in public. However, her black hair in contrast to her fair skin glistening from the scented lotion above the strapless gown made her the center of attention in a room full of unattached men.

The subject about a group of soldiers recovering at the hospital from wounds received in Iraq and Afghanistan came up at the dinner party. Heavy doses of antibiotics were administered, but infection was rampant among those left untreated that were allergic to the drugs. The subject turned to the squalor of village life in the mountain regions along the Afghan / Pakistan border.

Ayeza told them that not all Pakistani people lived as the villagers in the refugee camps and in the border towns run by the Taliban. Wahid, her uncle provided well for her village. He had been educated in the U.S. and worked in the Pakistan nuclear weapons laboratory near Rawalpindi where they assembled the warheads.

Ron Edwards was one of the guests. As a member of the CIA assigned to track radical Muslim cell activity in France and Germany, he took notice.

The subject of Pakistan came up at a CIA meeting in Paris. The beautiful young woman had impressed Ron Edwards. She not only addressed the French, German and English guests at the embassy in their native languages, she spoke two dialects of Arabic.

Eric had been invited to the party at the embassy in Germany, but was delayed in Israel. Eric was in transit from Tel Aviv to Washington and stayed over in Paris to dine with his associate who was also his friend, and to be briefed on the meeting in Germany.

Ron was younger, but both men had experienced failed marriages due to their prolonged absences from home that were a byproduct of their careers. Ron was still recovering from his divorce from a ten year marriage and had sworn off women, but the discussion turned to the subject of Ayeza and her uncle's connection to the Pakistan weapons laboratory. Ron grazed over the lab. His eyes sparkled and his voice was animated as he described Ayeza.

"What, Ron, were you that smitten by her?"

"It would be hard not to be, Eric, what with those emerald green eyes, black hair and ... well, let's just say she's drop dead gorgeous, smart and impassioned with ideals about helping her homeland."

"I thought you gave up women?"

"Not women, just marriage, at least until I retire from this job. She is a doll so I did some checking. She was a child bride in Pakistan, married to a brutal member of the Taliban. It's a long story, but her experience with him has left her asexual. She doesn't want anything personal to do with men."

"If that's the case, why the interest? I would think she would first need to get her head on straight."

"The CIA is always in the market for good recruits. Besides being a straight-A student she is fifth-degree black belt and trains with the men in the Special Forces. She also teaches martial arts to the women on the base and holds the women's parachute altitude record. She wants to go back and would be a remarkable asset if we could convince her to join."

Ayeza had received U.S. citizenship by the time General Hudson retired from the military. He and Cathy returned to Washington, D.C., where their daughter had settled. She had recently married and was pregnant with their first grandchild. Cathy was anxious to return to the States. General Hudson and Cathy wanted Ayeza to join them, but they knew her past would eventually lead her back to Afghanistan.

Ayeza had numerous choices, but she was a product of her past. At first she was undecided. She was offered an officer's commission and considered joining the American military as an instructor. She could have remained in Germany, or she could have migrated to the U.S. However, her life experiences and secular education had transformed the former female slave of Islamic ideology.

When the CIA approached her, Ayeza revisited the political and military scene in her homeland. With General Musharraf dethroned, what was left of Pakistan's secular society was spiraling into oblivion. Pictures of mutilated bodies of the innocents filled the European airwaves daily.

Although settled in her life in Germany, Ayeza's nightmares of the past turned to dreams of freedom for the Afghan and Pakistani women and children. They were once again being subjugated by the Islamic rule of the Taliban who were growing stronger in the tribal regions where she was born.

Ayeza accepted the CIA's offer and entered their training program in Washington. She was at the top of her class and as her confidence grew her mind healed. She was given a choice of locations when she graduated.

When she left Germany to return to Kabul she spoke six languages. She was also a confident, educated woman, free of the Islamic influence that separated her as a child into the classless society of Muslim women with no rights and no future.

Ayeza did not have proof she had been born in Pakistan. She left the country in a U.S. C-17 cargo jet as General Hudson's protégé and arrived at the U.S. Air Base in Germany as a refugee from the war. General Hudson and his wife filed U.S. adoption papers for the 14-year-old refugee shortly after she arrived.

Eight years of dedication paid off in an early degree in languages and Middle East history. The CIA upgraded her passport to diplomatic status when she asked for an assignment in Pakistan.

U.S. / Pakistan relations were decaying, and the Afghan / American war with Al-Queda and the Taliban was ongoing. The CIA traced her roots before giving her the assignment. Faisal had left Kabul, but he still had contacts in the city. Her emerald green eyes could be a problem. They were rare in the Caucasian race and almost non-existent in a people blended from a dozen Middle and Near East ethnic groups. Both Ron and Eric thought it a shame to hide her eyes, but she would need tinted contacts to go with her Afghan passport.

The camps along the Afghanistan / Pakistan border near the city of Peshawar are rife with political corruption. Corrupt officials were confiscating UN and U.S. aid supplies that were destined for the refugees and trading them for heroin. Most of the supplies ended up in the tribal regions of Pakistan where the American military could not go.

Ayeza's fluency in French, German and English and two dialects of Arabic gave Eric reason to provide her with British, French and German passports, as well as those she would need in Afghanistan and Pakistan. If the time came, Ayeza would be welcome in places where most Americans could not go.

CHAPTER 4

D ark lenses shaded Ayeza's eyes. She had not been to
her village since she was thirteen. The memories of
the backbreaking work she toiled at as a child and the
callousness her family had shown by selling her to Faisal faded long
ago, but now they flooded her memory.

They would not recognize her, but she had mixed feelings. As
a child, she had come to realize her labor in the poppy fields was
necessary to her family's way of life, but up until that day when her
father gave her to Faisal, she felt loved and cared for.

At times she could still feel the softness of her mother's body
and the gentle touch of her father's calloused hands when he lifted
her to his shoulders to watch the games the boys played. The
memories had haunted her, and although content in her new life,
she had missed her family.

A few months after the party in Germany Eric sent operatives
to visit her village to contact her uncle. Although the relationship

between the American military and the new Pakistan administration was deteroritating, Americans involved in the aid programs were still tolerated in the region.

They crossed into Pakistan posing as members of a U.S. / UN assistance program making an effort to steer the villagers from growing heroin poppies to farm produce.

The CIA sent a courier ahead with a message offering a reward and that they wanted to talk with Wahid. Isma'il, the leader of the tribe notified his brother at the nuclear laboratory that their opportunity to leave the regions may have arrived. Wahid came for the meeting.

The villagers had bitter memories of the Taliban who came once a year to collect the poppies. Isma'il and Wahid relayed a story of how, six years earlier the Taliban had come and killed a brother and his entire family.

Faisal had spies on the American base in Kabul. He had planned to kill Ayeza when she recovered and returned to her village. After he was told Ayeza left Kabul for Germany, Faisal arrived at her village with a dozen Taliban. He told her family she had sinned and how the Americans rescued Ayeza, but she was still alive and she had not asked his forgiveness. He wanted her dowry returned.

Her father refused, and when he said his daughter was innocent of any wrongdoing a fight broke out. Faisal killed her father. The Taliban then dragged his wives and children into the village square and executed them for Ayeza's crimes and her father's *apostasy* when he condemned the Islamic law specifying the punishment of stoning.

Since then the Taliban had cut the annual payment to the village for the poppies to half. Isma'il explained to the Americans that if they did not raise poppies for the Taliban, the Taliban would kill everyone in the village and give the land to others who would.

It was apparent to the CIA that Wahid's salary with the Pakistan government was insufficient to make up the difference between the income from the poppies and the cost of supplies for the entire village. Many of the villagers were malnourished and for those women who could still bear children, the infant mortality rate had grown to fifty percent. The village was dying.

Wahid was a nuclear physicist with a PhD, from the University of Michigan. His grant was cancelled and American Immigration denied his permanent visa after 9-11 when his roommate was connected to a militant Muslim student association.

Wahid's job in the Pakistan laboratory was to assemble the nuclear warheads. After hearing the story, the CIA recruited an eager Wahid. When the CIA approached him, he thought, *perhaps if he helped them, they might change their minds.*

The CIA men sent to the village were also to trace Ayeza's family. When they heard the story about the Taliban slaughtering a family over a child in Kabul, they mentioned a green eyed girl that had been rescued by the Americans, and that they thought she had been born near Wahid's village.

It had been almost eight years but Faisal still roamed the region where her village was. Eric did not intend to give her an assignment in the region. He decided not to tell her until after she returned to Afghanistan and had time to readjust to her new life.

The situation had changed with the nuclear threat to America. Admiral Michaels pegged it when he said, *everyone was expendable.* Ayeza was the only one available with the skills. She would have to return to her village where she would need to maintain an attitude of indifference if she had any chance to succeed. The only way Eric felt that possible, was to tell her the truth and give her the option.

She was to report to the administrator's office after the children finished breakfast and settled for the day. Eric placed the call at the appointed time. "We need you to go, but there is something you must know."

Ayeza felt that Eric patronized her, thinking she was still recovering from her childhood. Ayeza was not interested in men, but she knew the affect she had on most of them. Being a woman in a man's game did not help. A beautiful, smart woman capable of defending herself intimidated most men.

Cathy Hudson prepped her well for the role; one she was beginning to enjoy.

"Yes, Eric, I will remember to hide my eyes and not give myself away to my uncles or the other men in the village. It will be more difficult with my family, but I have accepted that they must not know who I am."

"You won't see your family, Ayeza."

"I have not seen them since my father handed me to Faisal. I have come to terms with that, but I have missed them. They do not need to know who I am, but I would like to see them."

"I'm sorry, Ayeza, your father and mother are dead, and so are your brothers and sisters. The only relatives you have left in the village are your uncles Wahid and Isma'il and their families. Now they too are at risk, but we have agreed to bring them out and relocate them in exchange for their help."

Ayeza sat, thinking she should be feeling more. The life in the fields take a toll, her parents' bodies were old when she left, and it had been years since her family had sold her to Faisal. Besides, there was no medical care and life in the village was difficult. Knowing she could never go back, she had dealt with the loss years ago; now there was just an empty feeling. "Do you know how they died, Eric?"

She could stumble on the truth herself. Eric would not lie to her and risk turning her against him. "Faisal and the Taliban went to the village after you left Afghanistan. He accused you of adultery and demanded they return your dowry. Your father defended you and refused. Faisal killed him and the Taliban executed your family."

Memories of the day Faisal dragged her down the streets, and watching him pick through the centuries old pile, encrusted with other women's blood, for the first stone to hurl at her flooded her mind.

Ayeza was expert in small arms and explosives, a field she selected on her own before she decided to return to Afghanistan. She would find him and kill him herself once the mission was over. She sat silently for a moment.

"Do you know where Faisal is now?"

Ayeza's psychological profile and her aggression in martial arts tournaments indicated she had an instinct to kill in order to survive. It was a trait difficult to teach, especially in a woman, but mandatory if she was to survive in her new profession.

The CIA psychiatrist assigned to her case believed Ayeza had a subconscious, but strong desire for revenge. It was an issue the CIA would have re-evaluated before sending her into the field. Now there was no choice. Either she went, or the Special Forces would have to do the mission. With the current standing orders against American forces crossing into Pakistan by both the Pakistan and U.S. governments, the chance of them succeeding without an incident with the Taliban or the Pakistan military was slim. Either situation could cause the mission to fail.

There was little option, but the calmness in Ayeza's voice sent a chill down Eric's spine. She was detached from the emotion of losing her family and concentrating elsewhere.

"He moves around the region collecting poppies for the Taliban and deals in heroin. The Afghan and American governments put a price on his head, so he does not stay in one place long. Ayeza, we need you focused. Can you put this aside?"

"Yes, Eric, for now, but someday I will find him."

Her tone and her response encouraged him. He would authorize the mission, but he was thinking, *he would not want to be Faisal when she did find him.*

A woman could not travel alone. Namir would escort Ayeza through the pass. He was born in the mountains of Afghanistan. He fought the Russians and then joined with the Americans as a guide to fight the Taliban. The Taliban put a price on his head when he led the Americans to some of the Al-Queda leaders on the Afghan side of the border. The remaining Taliban fled into the tribal regions of Pakistan where the Americans could not follow. Since then Namir had suffered burns masking his identify; his enemies would not recognize him.

Namir was waiting in the jeep as Ayeza left the office. The jeep would take them to the border near Parachinar, Pakistan, where they would set off on foot for the village near the city of Thal where Ayeza was born.

They would cross the Pakistan tribal region which had become a refuge for the Taliban. The Taliban would kill a stranger rather than chance an unwelcome visitor who would betray them to the Americans. The couple needed a reason to be there.

Eric had the American military deliver reward posters with pictures of Namir and Ayeza to Afghan moles living in the villages along the border that were sympathetic to the American forces. The Taliban would believe they were escaping Afghanistan and seeking refuge in the region.

Ayeza changed into traditional clothes she had not worn since she left Afghanistan. With her features covered and a little padding on her lithe body, Ayeza would blend with the women of the villages. They would pass themselves off as Afghan refugees seeking shelter and protection from the Americans who had posted a price on their heads. For the next week their lives would depend on her ability to act subservient to Namir.

Pakistan has very little industrial base. According to South Asia's Analysis Group, Pakistan's illegal heroin economy has kept its legitimate State economy sustained since 1990. Heroin and U.S. aid is the only thing preventing its collapse. The passes in the region, which are the conduit for the heroin trade, had not changed since she crossed them with Faisal as his child bride.

Heroin enables Pakistan to maintain a high level of arms purchases from abroad, and to finance its proxy war against India through the jihadist organizations. The use of heroin dollars for such purposes started after the Soviet troops withdrew from Afghanistan in 1988.

In the 1980s, at the insistence of the American Central Intelligence Agency, Pakistan's Internal Political Division started a special cell for the use of heroin for covert actions.

This cell promoted the cultivation of opium poppies and the extraction of heroin in Pakistan territory as well as in the Afghan territory under Mujahedeen control. The excuse at the time was that the heroin was being smuggled into the Soviet controlled areas in order to make the Soviet troops heroin addicts.

After the withdrawal of the Soviet troops, Pakistan's military heroin cell started using its network of refineries and smugglers for delivering heroin to the Western countries, using the money to supplement its legitimate economy.

America looks the other way, even today, because without heroin dollars Pakistan's economy would have collapsed years ago.

Namir and Ayeza left the jeep at the base of the pass. Namir bought a horse and a herd of goats at the first village they came to. A few hours later they joined a passing caravan crossing from Afghanistan into Pakistan.

In Muslim style, it was Ayeza's place to walk, pushing the herd of goats ahead of them while Namir sat comfortably on the back of the horse. The wanted posters had gone before them. Enemies of the Americans were friends of the Taliban. A copy of the poster, a bribe and cooperation with the Taliban were their only valid passports.

The narrow path separated one tribe's poppy fields from the other. Raw heroin drying in the shade of tent canopies covering the makeshift tables filled the village squares. Men and boys as young as eight or nine watched from the canyon walls through the scopes on their sniper rifles purchased from rogue American soldiers in a heroin trade.

Money was a useless commodity for the common people in the villages. The money generated from the heroin crop belonged to the Pakistan government and the religious tribal leaders. Members of the tribe would go to Peshawar a few times a year to buy provisions, but one had to buy permission in a land where heroin was the only cash crop.

There was insufficient feed to raise goats in the mountains. The goats were barter to use one side of the path or the other along the borders carved in the cliffs between the tribal territories.

The caravans they joined carried little besides guns and other munitions foreign soldiers traded for heroin. In Afghanistan or Pakistan, a kilogram of heroin will buy one shoulder fired missile, or 1,000 rounds of small arms ammunition, or three automatic weapons.

That same kilogram had a New York street value of $1,000 per gram before cutting. Profits of up to $80,000 per kilo the drug lords shared with the government and the tribal leaders were sufficient reason to treat strangers with suspicion.

Like Ayeza, Namir had been born in a village near Thal, Pakistan and was familiar with the local customs and fees. Twenty goats had been sufficient to bribe their way over the mountain and into the village where Ayeza had been born.

Eric sent word to Isma'il by satellite phone that Ayeza and Namir would be arriving, and that a new sample was needed. They arrived later in the day than expected and Isma'il was nervous. The women of the village were preparing the evening meal. The men were sipping tea and uncomfortable with Ayeza who was the only woman at the campfire.

"The Taliban are angry and come often to the village to check on us because of the Americans who were here before. When your people said a woman would come, I told them women are for raising children, not doing man's work. You put us all at risk."

"There was no one else, Isma'il. We are here, that is what matters. We need the proof. We understand you gave it to those who came before us, but they were killed. Do you know where it is?"

"It is lost. The mountains are vast and there are many caves. I think the men hid it before they died. If the soldiers or Taliban had found it, I would know and none of our people found it when the soldiers left. It was hard to get and it will cost much to move Wahid's family. It will be more difficult now and more expensive. You are strangers, the Taliban will find out you were here; now I too will have to leave with my family and I have no money."

"We have brought double the fee. It is enough for you to take your family to the safe house in Kashmir with your brother, Wahid. If your information is correct and Wahid brings proof, the Americans will relocate you to a safe place with others from the mountains. It will be a good life; they will provide money for you to live well with your wives and children."

"The money now, I will need to send my family ahead. Wahid will deliver the proof when we arrive in Kashmir."

"We need the proof now, Isma'il."

"I gave what we had to your friends; they lost it and I don't have more here. The message you need more came only three days ago. Wahid brings it, but there is no more plutonium; he will have to bring a weapons core. Soon they will discover it is gone. Wahid and his family must leave."

"There is enough money in the satchel. There will be more in Kashmir if Wahid gets the proof. Tell me what you know."

"We will have the proof. It is a good time for us because there is much trouble in the government. India is making threats over the recent bombings. The men they killed and captured are from the tribal regions in Pakistan and have ties to some of the new leaders in the government. There is talk of war and there are many convoys of weapons going to the border. Wahid says the new director ordered eight weapons and is sending a convoy to take them to the storage facility at Mardan, but there is much confusion and Wahid believes some will be diverted."

"How does he know that?"

"There are some he knows from our past who fought with the Lion Sheik working at the laboratory. He says the crates they sent are marked replacement parts for the oil refineries in Saudi Arabia. He questioned the man who delivered the truck and was told they were in a hurry and it was all that was available."

"Why to Saudi Arabia?"

"The Lion Sheik's money comes from Saudi Arabia. The Americans think the Saudis are their friends, but the Lion Sheik knows many in his homeland who are loyal to him and who hate the Americans. Our sources say they purchased the weapons for crusaders on an island off the coast of America."

"The Lion Sheik, you mean, Bin Laden? You have much information; how do you know so much?"

"I know Osama from the early days. Wahid knew him too, when we fought the Russians together. The Lion Sheik trusts Wahid, but not all of us like the old ways. His followers brag about their success against the Americans and talk of many plans that the Lion Sheik has designed. His crusaders come to our village to meet the caravan for supplies and to collect our poppies. They pay us little. It was better before. There are many who hate the Taliban, but it takes much money to leave so they sell information."

"What else do you know, Isma'il?"

"The Lion Sheik is ill and wants America subdued before he joins the Prophet. They speak of a February delivery. Now too much talk, you are not safe here, you must go now ... leave the money, we will meet in Kashmir ... *God willing.*"

Ayeza remained seated at the campfire. Isma'il was nervous and uncomfortable, but she needed to pry, "Who are *they*, Isma'il?"

"The loyal ones who share his campfire, now... you must go! I will send word when we have the package."

"No, we will go with you to meet Wahid. You will need our help with the Americans who will take you to Kashmir."

"We cannot cross into Afghanistan to meet the Americans. Wahid and I are known to the tribes. They know we have no business in Afghanistan. We will have to travel east and cross into Kashmir from Pakistan."

"I will ask the Americans to meet us at the border near Shandur Pass. Can you contact Wahid and tell him to meet us there?"

"No, Wahid's family will not leave the village without him so he must come here first, and I have four wives and many children. We will need a truck and provisions for the journey."

The package is too important. The longer it is in Pakistan the greater the risk. You must contact Wahid and tell him to go straight to Shandur Pass from Mardan. Someone will meet him there. We will go to Thal and get a truck and then bring his family."

"I will send the message tonight, but Wahid is stubborn and will do what he wants."

Ayeza climbed to the top of the canyon to send a coded text message by satellite to the American military in Kabul. She told them she had tried to convince Wahid to go to Shandur Pass, but they would be delayed if he returned first to the village for his family.

General Sampson forwarded the message to Eric's office in Washington, but by the time the message had been decoded and arrived on Eric's desk, the *try to convince* part had been deleted.

CHAPTER 5

———⬦———

The Hindu / Muslim conflict has a thousand years of brutal history. The 18th and 19th century British colonization process on the sub-continent of India resulted in segregating the warring Hindu and Muslim populations in order to bring stability to the region.

In 1956, bowing to Islamic fundamentalism, Britain carved the State of Pakistan out of Indian Territory.

In 1971, the Hindu ruler of the Kashmir region, which is predominantly Muslim, acceded to India. Pakistan has never accepted the transition in Kashmir, and military flare-ups have been an ongoing way of life since. To conform to the current treaty, Dr. Hakeem was required to notify India when there was to be a shipment of nuclear material.

After the recent bombings in India, the government of India was rattling its sabers. Wahid was told the Pakistan military did not want to put them on notice until the shipment arrived at

Mardan. Although a Pakistani inspector from Dr. Hakeem's staff would be at the laboratory to check the shipment when it left, the shipment was to be kept low key, and was not to be announced to the laboratory staff.

Wahid's first opportunity to steal the raw plutonium came as a result of the transition in the government and the replacement of personnel at the lab after Musharraf abdicated. There was much conflict in the ranks of the Muslim religious leaders and the new secular leaders in the government.

The inspectors discovered the earlier plutonium shortage, but the laboratory staff blamed the prior head of the agency, and explained it as a miscount of inventory. A second shortage could not be covered up and would expose Wahid.

When the CIA lost the first sample it would have been impossible for Wahid to smuggle more out of the lab until he was given orders to assemble more warheads. That could be months, possibly years. But others in the tribal regions were controlling the circumstance. The theft was planned by Al-Queda, and was being financed with Saudi Arabia oil profits and Pakistan heroin.

The world was focused on the recent bombings in Mumbai, and India was accusing the leaders in Pakistan of encouraging the militants. The flare-up in India justified Dr. Hakeem's orders to assemble nuclear warheads and ship them to the Mardan Weapons Storage Facility.

The shipment was timely for Wahid, but he was not aware the bombings in India were staged to justify it. Al-Queda intended to further destabilize Pakistan's government and they were succeeding. The angry rhetoric between India and Pakistan's new government was accelerating. Pakistan and India were both reinforcing their borders and preparing their missiles. The shortage would be discovered the next time they assembled warheads. If tensions or tempers continued to flair, Dr. Hakeem would order more. Wahid would have to disappear with the core.

The enriched plutonium cores were in the processing area. Wahid was the only one at the laboratory with access. His assembly team never entered the room unless he was there.

In its final form, a few seconds of exposure to the plutonium core without protective clothing would be a death sentence. It was a difficult process working with the thick gloves and robotic controls behind the glass barrier where all the weapons cores were stored. Although one could do it, past security required a two-person team assemble the units.

More bureaucrat than scientist, Dr. Hakeem was new to the agency and was not aware of the process of assembly. Wahid's opportunity came when Dr. Hakeem sent the two other physicists at the lab on an inspection trip to the Mardan weapons storage facility to prepare for receiving the shipment.

Wahid waited until the rest of the staff left and then dressed to enter the secure storage area by himself. After inserting the cores, he placed eight titanium assemblies and one plutonium core in lead lined containers. He put four of the containers with the assemblies in crates marked as replacement parts for the Jeddah and Yemen oil refineries and then loaded all of them in the transport truck.

There were only three trucks in the convoy. Wahid's orders were to personally take the assemblies to the nuclear storage facility at Mardan, Pakistan. The facility is seventy miles short of the Afghanistan border, near Peshawar, which is the hub of the militant uprisings in Pakistan.

Pakistan's conflict with India was not the only front. Al-Queda was at war with all but the Whahabi Sunni side of Islam. In the past, President Musharraf sent heavily armed convoys to escort weapon shipments, but there were some in the new government, as well as new military leaders who sided with the Taliban.

Others would betray their own for the money. After a conference with his benefactor assuring him the convoy would be allowed to pass safely, Dr. Hakeem decided he could justify an unscheduled shipment if it was discovered, and an unmarked convoy would not draw attention from the military.

After placing the box with the core in a satchel and storing it in the cab of the truck, Wahid prepared the shipping documents listing the contents of the truck as replacement parts for oil refineries in Yemen and Saudi Arabia. However, Dr. Hakeem's instructions were to delete eight units from the laboratory inventory and show them in transit to the Mardan Storage Facility. The only back up to the inventory was in Dr. Hakeem's office in Karachi. A physical count later would reveal that one additional core was missing.

Pakistan's relationship with the Americans was deteriorating under the new government. Accusations of mismanagement of nuclear inventories were made on the floor of the U.N. Security Council. As a result, the UN Nuclear Regulatory Commission, which was chaired by the American Ambassador to India, had been recently barred from the Rawalpindi laboratory.

Dr. Hakeem was an arrogant, corrupt bureaucrat. Even if the rumors were false and the warheads all arrived safely in Mardan, Wahid doubted there were hard copies of the inventories. However, Wahid knew if Dr. Hakeem discovered the missing core after he disappeared, he would shift the blame charging his predecessor with incompetence. Wahid and his family would be safe in their new life.

The transport convoy left at dawn. One of the physicists from the lab always accompanied the shipments. This time Wahid's driver was conveniently sick. Rather than delay the shipment, he told the inspector he would be driving the truck himself. With Wahid driving, the inspector did not check the cab of the truck.

Dr. Hakeem's business interests had suffered during the Musharraf regime and he had been forced to live a less lavish lifestyle than he had grown accustomed to as a youth.

As the convoy started north toward Mardan, Dr. Hakeem accessed the laboratory's inventory records. He deleted four titanium assemblies from the shipment and readjusted the inventory figures that Wahid had entered earlier.

Wahid and Dr. Hakeem had grown up in the same village, but Dr. Hakeem's family had strong ties to the Taliban. Heroin profits funded their fleet of fishing boats that were also used to transport slaves to sweat shops in India, and to smuggle arms, heroin and Islamic crusaders to the various camps in Yemen, Sudan and Somalia.

Wahid had been a dedicated student enrolled in a U.S. student aid program. He and Dr. Hakeem attended the same university and they had belonged to the same American Muslim societies. Dr. Hakeem believed Wahid was loyal to the Prophet and the cause of Islam and that he would not betray him; the shipment would arrive safely in Mardan.

Dr. Hakeem had purged the Mardan nuclear storage facility of employees loyal to the Musharraf regime and had replaced them with militants loyal to Al-Queda. Dr. Hakeem also barred the UN Nuclear Regulatory Commission inspectors from the facility until new security clearances could be issued. The clearances had been stalled in the corrupt bureaucratic system. When Wahid arrived at the storage facility, four assemblies would be isolated from the inventory and diverted.

Dr. Hakeem was at his desk when the e-mail came in notifying him the convoy had left the laboratory at Rawalpindi. He clicked on the send button forwarding the e-mail.

The fifty million would be in his Swiss account before he boarded the plane. Dr. Hakeem opened his safe to remove the plane tickets and his new French passport. He then returned to his desk to wait for the call.

His surgery was scheduled at a clinic in Amsterdam. Dr. Hakeem's facial makeover would be healed and he would be living in his new flat on the Island of Notre Dame sharing a bottle of wine with his French mistress in two weeks. The four missing warheads would go unnoticed until long after the scars healed.

Baraka's plane sat on the runway while he logged on to Dr. Hakeem's desktop. After forwarding Wahid's e-mail to a mountaintop near the Pakistan border of Afghanistan he placed a call to Dr. Hakeem's direct line in his office. Recognizing the number, Dr. Hakeem took the call he was waiting for.

"The shipment is in transit."
"The money is on its way."

It was three hours until his flight departed. Islamic laws forbid the consumption of alcohol, but Dr. Hakeem removed the bottle of cognac from his desk and was pouring himself a drink celebrating his new life. Baraka waited until Wahid's GPS registered on his screen before he moved the mouse to click on the icon that would send the signal to set off the charge beneath Dr. Hakeem's desk.

There were sufficient explosives to demolish the building. There were many unhappy with the new government. They would write it off as another suicide bomber unhappy with the secular bureaucrats who ignore Islamic laws.

Before putting the laptop away, Baraka activated the GPS tracking device in Wahid's truck, then signaled to the pilot to take him to the village near Thal.

Chaman, Pakistan

Yaq'ab rose from his prayer rug to greet the Lion Sheik. His mentor was picking his way through the dimly lit corridor. He was exhausted from the exertion of the past three days' travel between towering peaks. It had meant a steep climb and then a descent by rope ladders to reach the entrance to the new cave.

The crusaders stationed on the peaks of the canyon's walls guarded his new home. It was inaccessible to anyone except on foot. The shipment of shoulder-fired missiles arrived a week earlier; it would be suicide for the American helicopters to fly the valley, and the slow un-manned drones were easy targets. Buried far beneath the surface of the ground with three escape tunnels, the cave was impervious to America's conventional weapons.

Al-Queda's new headquarters were recently completed by hand tunneling with scarce tools and little light. They left an uneven cavern with jutting ledges of granite that had been impossible to be removed by hand. In frail health, his eyesight failing, the Lion Sheik moved his staff slowly ahead, feeling for residue left from the continuous calving of the stone walls.

Yaq'ab greeted Allah's frail messenger with a flask of stale water and his arm, to assist him to a stone ledge. A bed made of rags over a thin layer of straw stretched across the back of the shallow cavern. The ceiling of the cave above the bench was just high enough for him to sit. He turned to rest before crawling to his bed. "Is the shipment in transit?"

"Yes, they left Rawalpindi this morning."

"What of the greedy Doctor?"

"Baraka has completed his mission. The authorities are blaming India for the bomb. They say it is a response to the recent hotel bombings in India. They will search no farther. Have you picked the target?"

"Yes, but it could change. We will wait until the shipment arrives at its destination. If they are late we will pick something farther north."

"What of the crusaders, have they been chosen for the mission? Many will die; we must be sure we send only those who will choose martyrdom and a place at Allah's side."

"The Americans are fools Yaq'ab; we have many new recruits to choose from. America's famous *apostate* will guarantee many more. I have word from our friends in Somalia and Sudan; the camps are swelling with new recruits. Those from Sudan will join Ghalib to make the pilgrimage to Mecca before leaving for Nassau. Have the British agreed?"

"The crusaders from Somalia are accepted as refugees by the British and will be given visas for the island. The island berth is ready and the yacht waits off the shores of Saudi Arabia for the shipment."

"Dr. Hakeem promised four, Yaq'ab; will they be missed?"

"No, the inventory has been adjusted and Dr. Hakeem and Wahid had the only access codes."

"Codes can be broken."

"Only two outside our circle know of the shipment. One is dead and no one will look farther once Baraka deals with Wahid and his village. Now that Hakeem is dead and his office destroyed, they will reprogram and take new inventories."

The Lion Sheik was tired, the meeting was over but Yaq'ab paused before turning. "The *Apostate* is ignorant. He knows nothing of Islam's law. Muhammad left instructions to kill the *apostates*, and he travels freely to our sacred places. Are the others willing to leave him be?"

"Only for now, our Shiite enemies in Iran play the game well. The *Apostate* has offered to sit with them while they reinstate laws condemning *apostates* to the sword. He is a fool to think the Muslim world welcomes his leadership role in America, or anywhere else. Someday we will kill him and the others, for now we will use him. It has been difficult, but the leaders in the mosques will ignore him until the time comes. I must rest. Send food and then wake me when we control the shipment."

CIA Headquarters

Pakistan was off limits to the American military, but Kashmir is under the rule of India. When Eric received the message from Ayeza, he assumed Wahid would be traveling northeast toward Kashmir with the package.

Eric put General Sampson in Kabul on notice to ready a C-17 transport, three helicopters, and a team of Special Forces for a trip to Gligit, Kashmir as a staging area. One of the helicopters would fly to Shandur Pass and pick up Wahid to bring the package to Kabul. The other helicopters would wait for Ayeza and Namir to arrive with Isma'il and the others. Eric then patched into the satellite camera positioned over Pakistan's nuclear storage facility in Mardan.

When the convoy approached the weapons facility, the plan was on schedule. Eric assumed Wahid would head for Shandur Pass when he left Mardan. He sent an e-mail to General Sampson, sending the C-17 to Kashmir.

The truck backed under the canopy to the loading dock. Wahid passed four assemblies to the men on the dock. Wahid supervised while the men placed the assemblies in their racks in the secure area of the facility. The other crates marked, *Parts for Saudi Arabia* remained in the truck.

After leaving the storage facility, the convoy turned south toward Peshawar before moving on toward Thal. New drivers had been assigned for the trip to Karachi. Wahid moved the core before switching trucks to ride as a passenger to Thal. He believed the four remaining warheads were loaded in the truck behind him and that the convoy was in view of the American satellite that was tracking them.

Wahid was not aware that the crates had been switched while he was with the men securing the other warheads in the weapons facility. The four remaining warheads were now stored in a private produce delivery truck parked inside the maintenance building.

The helicopters had been off-loaded from the C-17 that was sitting on the runway at the airport in Gligit. Colonel Rogers and his team of Special Forces were ready to fly to the border for the rescue when Wahid left the weapons storage facility and turned south toward Thal, instead of north toward Shandur Pass.

Isma'il was unable to contact Wahid until after Wahid completed the delivery; when he did, Wahid refused to leave Pakistan without his family.

The orders from the State Department had been reinforced the day before. Jim Symington had met with the Congressional Military Oversight Committee complaining about Admiral Michaels and the CIA's involvement in the terrorist activities in the U.S. that they said were being directed out of Pakistan.

The Speaker of the House, who chaired the committee, contacted General Sampson in Kabul. She restated the Committee's position and told him to respect Pakistan's airspace. A follow-up e-mail came from the White House Chief of Staff stipulating America's military was to clear any incursions into Pakistan's air space with the Secretary of State's office.

The word nuclear changed the options. Both Eric and General Sampson overreached their authority and put their careers on the line when the truck turned south. Eric notified General Sampson. General Sampson then ordered Colonel Rogers to load the Special Forces in the helicopters and move to the border near Thal.

Colonel Rogers would fly north from Kashmir, crossing into Afghanistan, and then hug the border until they were opposite the village of Thal where a tanker would meet them to refuel. They would wait in Afghanistan until Ayeza confirmed Wahid was carrying nuclear material before they would cross into Pakistan to attempt the rescue.

Ayeza and Namir were to be dropped in Kabul, but Afghanistan would not be safe for Isma'il or Wahid and their families. They were to be taken to Kashmir to the waiting C-17, then flown to India for debriefing before being relocated to new lives.

It was a 300-mile trip from Mardan to Thal skirting tribal borders on congested dirt roads. It would be the next day before Wahid would be approaching his village. Eric hoped Admiral Michaels would be in his office.

"I have word from Afghanistan, Admiral, and our worst fears have materialized. Our source says we have as many as four nuclear warheads on the way to an island off the Atlantic coast. The arrival date is sometime in February. It may be coming by way of Yemen, or Saudi Arabia. We think it is going to Andros Island."

"Do you have proof, Eric?"

"Not yet, but we made contact with the courier. The package is en route. It also seems we have a large party to deal with. The two men supplying the package need new lives. However, between them they have half dozen wives. We do not have an accurate count, but there are also a couple dozen kids. General Sampson has a C-17 transport waiting on the runway in Gligit, Kashmir."

"The material will have to go to New Mexico for verification, why a C-17, the Lear would be faster."

"The C-17 is for the families, the Lear is in Kabul waiting for the woman. General Sampson and I figured to take the heat. We don't want a glitch and end up losing the package."

There would not be another opportunity. They needed transport helicopters and cover. It meant crossing into Pakistan with a substantial force.

"I have asked General Sampson to send in Colonel Rogers and his Special Forces team to bring them out. He agreed, if the girl makes contact and has the nuclear material they are going in."

"That won't go over big upstairs, Eric. Can they make the trip without engagement?"

"I doubt it, but if we get the proof it's worth the risk, Admiral."

"If the colonel makes the trip, I will be the one to tell the committee that I blessed the mission. Either way, no matter who made the decision, if we don't get the proof, you and I will be out of a job. What about the families? Assuming they make it out, you can't bring them here. The Social Services in this country would split them up."

"We haven't told them yet. It was short notice and we didn't want a leak, but arrangements are being made. If the government of Egypt agrees, they will be given new identities in a fishing village on the Red Sea. There is a group of Afghans and Pakistani refugees in a community called Hurghada. The other options are the desert in Botswana where there are communities of Pakistan refugees, or another country where they can maintain their lifestyle of multiple wives."

"It seems that's settled, but the real issue is the warheads in transport. We need proof in our hands. Symington scuttled the meeting with the State Department. I can't go back upstairs on hearsay; get me something concrete. If something is missing, our friends in Pakistan will know."

"We have few friends left. I checked, they say nothing is missing, but the country is in transition and loyalties are difficult to ascertain. The new President is insecure so security is lax, and shipments are not always tracked. Besides, if we ask too many questions before we get our hands on the package, we risk losing it."

"You are telling me Pakistan has lost a couple of nuclear bombs that are heading our way and we can't question them about it?"

"We don't think the shipment is lost, Admiral. We believe it is on a convoy heading for Karachi; our satellites are tracking the trucks. It is 800 miles of bad road; it will take them a week. If we get our people out with the proof, we can confront the Pakistan government. They will help if we threaten to pull the plug on their aid package."

"That's not likely with this administration. What have you heard from Ron?"

"The London moles are pointing to Saudi. Word is that they took advantage of the real estate crash, buying up land in the Bahamas and the U.S.; no one is aware of a package."

Thal, Pakistan

Al-Queda's leaders believed that Wahid was loyal and the theft had gone unnoticed. Dr. Hakeem was dead and the assemblies were safely on board the produce truck in a sealed compartment and buried under the load of tomatoes.

The truck would not stop until it arrived in Karachi where it would deliver to the vendors in the market place. The shipment would be split up and shipped by sea to Saudi Arabia.

The convoy was on the road to Karachi. If anyone questioned them and opened the crates, all they would find would be valves and gaskets for the oil refinery. The last loose end and the only risk to the Lion Sheik's plan was Wahid.

The Lion Sheik was growing frail. In the eyes of some, he had grown soft and more concerned with living than joining the Prophet. Nevertheless, loyal to the Prophet or not, and although he was a friend, he would not risk leaving the only outside link to the warheads alive.

Baraka's plane touched down by a remote village near Thal. Wahid's village was an hour drive. He was early; Wahid would be arriving later that evening and Faisal would not arrive with the Taliban until four pm.

Baraka had not been with a woman for weeks. He preferred them young. He had married Malika a few months earlier in the Islamic tradition of Muhammad, when she was nine years old. Her wedding night scars would have healed. He had time to visit his new wife before dealing with Wahid and the villagers who might betray the Lion Sheik.

Wahid was raised in Karachi, but his mother had been born in the village and made frequent trips visiting her family. Yalda was thirteen when selected by Wahid's mother. Her dowry was distributed among the tribe and Wahid was welcomed into the society. Years passed and Wahid married twice more. Although he worked in Rawalpindi, he preferred village life and commuted when he could to be with his family.

Wahid was a brilliant student and was privileged to have been educated in the U.S. After he returned to Pakistan, his appointment as lead scientist at the weapons laboratory assured his ability to support a family and help support the tribe.

Times change; his new tribe was poor and the Taliban had returned. They were forced to grow poppies. Each year the Taliban would collect the poppies, but as he had done in the years since Faisal killed Ayeza's family, he admonished Isma'il and the others for what they termed a meager crop.

Ayeza and Namir were strangers in the land of Isma'il's tribe. Believing they would pose a risk to Wahid, he left Ayeza and Namir in the village when he and three men left before dawn leading a horse and a pack mule to meet his brother at the road from Peshawar to Thal.

Namir and Ayeza woke to find Isma'il gone, but he had left word that he would be returning with Wahid later in the day. Ayeza climbed to the top of the canyon to call Kabul.

The Kabul flight tower locked in on her GPS and then conveyed the message from General Sampson. They were tracking the convoy and knew Wahid had met his brother and was on his way. Assuming the sample was on the pack horse, Ayeza was to wait for Wahid and bring the families to the top of the canyon where Colonel Rogers would pick them up.

Ayeza and Namir watched as Isma'il and Wahid approached the village. "We thought we lost you, Isma'il."

"I will not leave without my family. They must all come with us. I have a truck waiting near Thal. We must leave now for Kashmir."

"No, Wahid, it is not safe to travel that far with so many. The Americans will come here for us. What do you have for proof?"

Wahid took a container out of a linen bag. It was heavy and difficult for him to lift. "This, but it is enough."

Ayeza wore a simple bracelet that when turned inside out changed colors as it absorbed radiation. She removed it from her wrist and laid it on the case. The silver turned to bronze, a low level, but definitely proof that the container was contaminated."

"What is it?"

"It is the core of a nuclear device containing weapons grade plutonium. The case is lined with lead. It is too dangerous to open here. You will have to verify it where it can be opened safely."

"Do you know what is on the convoy?"

"The truck carries four 2-megaton nuclear bombs. I assembled them at the factory."

"Do you know where the shipment is going?"

"It's on the way to Karachi."

Ayeza remembered the conversation from that morning. The American satellites were tracking the convoy, but they would need the proof to intervene. "We must gather your wives and children and climb the canyon walls. The helicopters will pick us up there."

"We must collect our property and some of the children are very young. The climb will be difficult, why can't they land in the village?"

"They must stay above the valley floor. If the Taliban or the Pakistan army spots them coming in, they could get above them. The Taliban have many shoulder-fired missiles; we must climb out. There are many; leave everything behind but the clothes you wear, and hurry. It will be dark soon."

Ayeza stripped out of the traditional clothes to her army fatigues and climbed to the top of the canyon walls. After sending the message to the Kabul tower, she returned to the village. It was a steep climb. She would follow with Namir, helping the stragglers.

"Isma'il, do you have you any guns?"

"Ours are very old; the Taliban have taken the rest."

"Bring what you have. There will be many on the climb and we will be visible from the next valley and the skies."

Wahid led the column climbing the steep path leading to the plateau on the canyon ridge. Two boys took turns carrying the core while the others prodded the children ahead of them.

Namir was following Isma'il and his family to assist the stragglers. It was a slow climb for the women and children. Ayeza stayed back with the archaic weapons to defend their flank if they were seen from the valley floor.

Baraka arrived with Faisal and twenty armed men. All the men in the village, except for the very old and the young boys were away working in the cities or serving in the military. Ayeza and Isma'il believed the Taliban would leave the women and children alone since they were not related to Wahid. However, Faisal's men searched the village, dragging old men, women and children from their huts looking for Wahid.

Faisal hated all the people in Ayeza's village. When a woman, shielding her child from the angry and violent men, pointed to the canyon walls, Faisal remembered Ayeza and the shame she had brought to him, thinking, *I should have killed them all then.*

Although they were a half-mile away and a thousand feet above the canyon floor, the refugees stood out against the barren sandstone cliffs. If Wahid was running, Baraka knew he had already betrayed them.

He pressed the button on his satellite phone to send a message to the Lion Sheik, but the canyon walls blocked the signal.

Baraka thought Wahid a fool. He had taken his women and children; it was thirty miles to the border. There were many mountains to climb on the way, and the new government had denied the Americans permission to cross into Pakistan.

Baraka was not aware that Ayeza and Namir were with the refugees, or that the helicopters were on the way. He believed he would have no problem catching up before they reached the safety of Afghanistan and the American military camps on the border. He ordered the men to scour the village and bring everyone to the square.

Not knowing whom Wahid may have told, Baraka turned to Faisal and his men standing over a group of women and children huddled on the ground, "Kill them all."

In a prolific society where every woman able to conceive bears a child a year, four generations of the dead and dying littered the ground. Faisal and his men moved among them and in execution style put a bullet in each of their brains. They then moved to the truck to give chase to those climbing the side of the canyon.

Faisal and his men fanned out across trails leading to the top after leaving the truck at the base of the path. Baraka stayed back at the truck scanning the hillside through his binoculars.

Ayeza watched the carnage in the village and knew the Taliban would give chase. She settled behind a rock outcropping waiting as the men approached. Three old guns against twenty armed men, all she could hope for was to slow them down long enough for the helicopters to arrive in time to collect the package and rescue her uncles and their families. She committed herself to dying in the place where she was born, but then Colonel Rogers cleared the canyon walls.

Still out of range of Ayeza's ancient weapon, Faisal and the Taliban were moving within rifle range of the stragglers who had not reached the plateau where the helicopters would land. She waited while they moved closer and then took the first man out who raised his rifle. She missed Faisal when he ducked behind a boulder and started to make the climb to get above her.

One of them got off a shot sending shards of stone into Namir's calf causing him to drop the child he was carrying. One of Ismail's wives took a bullet in her shoulder as she turned to help, but still managed to take the child's hand.

Colonel Rogers turned the helicopter toward the approaching men when he realized they were pursuing the families on the cliffs. As he passed over, Namir stumbled again and then fell after a bullet passed through his spine and pierced his heart.

Colonel Rogers' first pass took him over the woman with flowing hair defending the others, and past the pursuing Taliban to within sight of the village. Colonel Rogers and his men were veterans of two wars and used to the brutality of men like the Taliban warlords. This was not the first village they had seen annihilated.

As Colonel Rogers hovered over the village one of the other pilots turned from the rescue to join him.

"Need help, Colonel?"

"We will deal with this, Captain. Pick up your passengers. Drop the sample and the woman off in Kabul and take the rest to Kashmir."

Baraka was a mercenary concerned with his own skin, but the Taliban were committed crusaders who would die before they quit. When the helicopters appeared over the canyon, Baraka boarded the truck and turned it toward the road leading to Thal.

Colonel Rogers moved down the hill to drop his men to cut off the Taliban from the valley floor. They would be trapped in the canyon between the Special Forces and the helicopter when Colonel Rogers moved back up the canyon to cover the retreating refugees.

Before returning to the hillside, he made a pass over the village sending rockets toward Baraka and the retreating truck. Baraka died in a fiery crash while attempting to send a message on a satellite phone with no reception.

Colonel Rogers turned to the hillside and the Taliban who were gaining on the straggling women and children. When Colonel Rogers approached the men pursuing the refugees, they hid behind the rocks waiting for the helicopter to pass.

As Colonel Rogers passed by, one of the men stepped out into the open and was raising a shoulder fired missile. Ayeza fired before he could take aim. Hit, the man stumbled and the missile passed below the helicopter burying itself in the side of the canyon below where Ayeza was standing. Colonel Rogers waved to her as she resumed her climb.

"Sergeant, we want them all. I'll kick them out and you take them down."

"Roger that, Colonel, do we take prisoners?"

Colonel Rogers' actions answered the question. As the helicopter moved in, lighting the walls of the canyon with rocket fire, the chain guns raked the debris sending a thousand fifty caliber rounds into the nooks and crannies.

"They won't surrender, Sergeant. You saw the village; find them all. I will make two more passes then move up hill in case someone survives and tries to climb out.

It was a slow process. Wahid and Isma'il were helping frightened, weeping women and children who had never been beyond the tribe's boundaries settle into a fearsome machine that would take them from a way of life that had remained unchanged for a thousand years.

The first helicopter was loaded and on the way to Kabul with the plutonium core. Two more followed with Wahid and women and children; they would veer off to Kashmir once safely in Afghan airspace. Captain Pitt's helicopter was loaded with Isma'il and the last of the refugees; he would also be going to Kashmir.

Captain Pitt hesitated for a few moments before lifting off. He had seen the carnage in the village when he had turned to join Colonel Rogers. He had also seen Namir take the bullet and plunge off the cliff and he thought Ayeza was on her own.

The voice from the Kabul tower settled the issue. The first three helicopters passed into Afghan airspace. F-15s from Kabul were flying cover, escorting one to Kabul and the other two to Kashmir, but the Pakistan Air Force was on its way to the village.

"Colonel Rogers, Captain Pitt, the package has arrived, but you are running out of time."

Captain Pitt's helicopter lifted off, but as he turned toward the valley below, he saw Ayeza scaling the cliff. He settled back to the plateau and released a trailing ladder, and then waited to give Ayeza time to reach the helicopter. She was still five hundred yards out when one of the Taliban stepped into the open and took a snap shot with a missile.

The missile passed above the rotors of Captain Pitt's helicopter just as Colonel Rogers turned in the direction of the plateau. "Captain Pitt, you have your orders, get the package to Kabul."

The radio signal from Kabul was blocked by the canyon walls. Colonel Rogers had missed the part of the communication from Kabul about the package. "The package is in Kabul, Colonel, but the woman is on the hillside, and there is a man above her. I'll have a shot if he moves into the open."

"I know where she is, Captain. You have your orders and my men are on the way. We will get to her."

"Yes Sir." Captain Pitt banked toward the canyon rim and once clear, turned for the border of Afghanistan ten minutes away.

Faisal managed to get above Ayeza as she concentrated on the others, but as he prepared to take a shot Colonel Rogers sent a rocket into the cliffs above his head. The cascading rocks knocked the rifle from his hands. The rifle slid off the ledge leaving him unarmed.

Colonel Rogers moved off as his men mopped up, waving to Ayeza as he made the turn. She waved back and resumed her climb.

He had missed the man, but she now knew of the threat above her. Some of Colonel Rogers's men had trained with the woman in Germany and practiced with her in Kabul. She was on her own, but from what he had heard, she was up to the task.

Ayeza turned when the rocket exploded above her and saw the man scrambling in her direction. She checked the rifle in her hands; the breach was open. It was empty. Knowing the others at her feet were too, she reached for the Glock 9 mm nestled beneath her arm and then moved into the shadows of the cliffs waiting for him to emerge.

After Colonel Rogers interfered Faisal tried to sneak back down the canyon, but Ayeza had climbed to the trail above her. Faisal turned a corner on a narrow trail and came face to face with a dark eyed woman in men's clothing holding a pistol on him.

"Sit you pig," was her first thought as she recognized the man who had killed her family and almost killed her.

The face looked familiar, but the hate toward a woman who would dare challenge him overshadowed his memory. As he sat back under the ledge above them, Ayeza wiped at her eyes dislodging the contacts. Her eyes down, moving back toward the edge of the cliff, she holstered the Glock, then looked up.

Sergeant Anderson stood quietly in the shadows, his gun trained on Faisal as Ayeza holstered her pistol. When she brushed her forehead and her dark eyes turned shimmering green, Faisal let out a howl and his face twisted in rage.

Sergeant Anderson knew her history and thought to himself, *there is more to this than a chance meeting in a remote village.* He had sparred with the green-eyed beauty after she returned to Afghanistan. He was glad that it was an exercise. The man was unarmed. Sergeant Anderson lowered his weapon, knowing she would not want him to interfere, or for that matter, need him to, and then he backed away.

The unmistakable emerald-green eyes of the thirteen-year-old child stared directly into Faisal's soul. "I understand you have been looking for me. You do well killing old women and children, Faisal, but I'm not a child any longer and your friends are not here to help you."

Fifty years of crossing the mountain passes between Afghanistan and Pakistan had turned the body of an aging man to bone, sinew and muscle. Faisal believed women were for a man's pleasure to be used, or abused depending on the mood, not feared.

"I killed your father and your family when you disappeared. Today I killed the rest of the scum in your village. I would kill you now and my honor would be restored."

"You are a pig, Faisal, and a coward. You kill unarmed women and children. Now, when you die at the hand of one of Allah's enemies, and a woman at that, he will cast you in hell for failure."

"Allah will understand. You have the gun and I am unarmed, but if you kill me now, what difference, you and me?"

Ayeza looked up and then spit in his direction, the greatest insult a woman can hurl at a man. "My gun is put away, what keeps you cowering like a jackal in front of a woman?"

Faisal lunged with the speed of a striking snake, throwing hands full of gravel toward the green eyes of the child bride that shamed him in his village, and then escaped from his wrath and her just punishment.

Ayeza deflected his charge and calmly stepped aside. As he stumbled past she grabbed the ledge above, lifting herself to plant both feet in the small of his back, throwing him face first into the stonewall of the canyon.

Goading him on, "What's the matter, Faisal, I thought you liked rocks?"

Bloodied, dazed and reeling from the fracture in his skull he stood there, but his hatred for the woman kept him focused as he measured the distance between them.

Martial arts are psychology as well as physical force, "I remember you ran like the cowardly pig you are when the soldiers killed your brother to save me; are you going to run from a woman now?"

Faisal reached to pick a loose stone from the ledge floor and staggered forward. Ayeza had moved back toward the edge leading to the vertical thousand-foot drop to the canyon floor. When Faisal raised his arm to cast the stone, Ayeza reached to the back of her neck and in a sweeping motion threw the knife, burying it in Faisal's shoulder.

Dropping the stone, he stumbled forward and as he passed, she helped him along with a blow to the back of his neck, being careful not kill him.

Ayeza stepped to the edge watching as Faisal fell, face forward, staring into the stone floor a thousand feet below, knowing a woman had killed him.

Ayeza stood at the edge of the cliff reflecting on the past eight years. It was anti-climactic and time to move forward. She was feeling no remorse and no sorrow.

Sergeant Anderson stepped out of the shadows. "We must go, Ayeza, before the Pakistan Air Force arrives."

"What of the rest of the Taliban?"

"Colonel Rogers and the others have dealt with them."

"You saw what they did in my village, I must see for myself."

"All right, but hurry."

Ayeza walked to the edge of the canyon to scan the canyon walls before turning toward the village. The dead Taliban littered the trails and the truck was still burning at the edge of the village.

Colonel Rogers was hovering above her not wanting to be on the ground if the Pakistan Air Force arrived. The rest of the Special Forces had moved above them and were almost at the plateau.

Colonel Rogers landed to pick up the men. Sergeant Anderson and Ayeza were the last to reach the helicopter. "Everybody make it, Colonel?"

"We lost one, Ayeza's guide, and one of the men took one in the arm, but it's nothing serious. What's the body count?"

"I found twenty-one, plus the one in the truck. You did not leave much for us, Colonel."

"Were there any survivors, and were any of them military?"

"There are no survivors. I was trailing him, but Ayeza took their leader out. The Pakistan military was not involved. All but her guide wore traditional clothes. I also found a satellite phone by the truck, no reception; they could not have made a call."

Ayeza stood on the plateau gazing at the place of her birth for the last time while Sergeant Anderson boarded the helicopter. Colonel Rogers waited a moment and then signaled Ayeza it was time.

"Where is the package, Colonel?"

"In Kabul, there is a Lear on the runway waiting to take it, and you to the States."

Colonel Rogers was flying an experimental helicopter capable of carrying a crew of two and eight men at a speed of two hundred fifty miles per hour. It was ten minute flight to the border and a thirty-minute flight to Kabul.

The rescue helicopters had approached the village from Gardiz, a hundred miles south of Kabul. The Pakistan radar had spotted them when they crossed the border, but lost them when they turned northeast and dropped into the canyons.

The first helicopters passed back into Afghanistan without incident. Captain Pitt was in Afghan air space before they arrived, but Colonel Rogers was still on deck when the Pakistan Air Force turned south toward the village.

When Pakistan's radar picked up the rescue helicopters, Pakistan's military contacted the American ambassador to lodge a protest and a warning. The ambassador called the American Secretary of State. She called General Sampson to order him to withdraw the helicopters. The General's assistant took the call and told the Secretary of State the General was in the field, but he would relay the orders.

General Sampson had ordered the F-15 pilots to hold at the border unless the helicopters were threatened. General Sampson and his wingman were flying a pattern at the border waiting for Colonel Rogers.

The Pakistan pilots had orders to engage the helicopters. Without cover, the outcome was predetermined. The chain guns would be a deterrent, but experimental aircraft or not, once he left the cover of the canyons, Colonel Rogers would not survive against any number of F-16s

The package containing proof nuclear weapons were destined for the United States, and the man who assembled the weapons, crossed safely into Afghan airspace. That part of the mission was over and the American military had not engaged the Pakistan military. It was still General Sampson's call. He had the option of leaving Colonel Rogers to run the gauntlet to the border before he intervened and deal with the aftermath of a successful mission. His only other choice would put their careers at risk.

General Sampson was in the air with his wingman approaching The Pakistan border. Admiral Michaels was with Eric and Ron following the action by satellite camera, and in contact with General Sampson.

"Bring them home safely, General. We owe them that."

"That's what I was thinking, Admiral."

General Sampson, like the military brass in Washington, was disgruntled with the American Congress' lack of support for the American forces in Iraq and Afghanistan even before the change in administrations.

At that moment General Sampson joined with Admiral Michaels and a select circle of military leaders in Washington. With nuclear weapons en route to America, they would risk their careers and even imprisonment defying the Congressional Committees and members of the State Department who were caught up in the power struggle of a changing administration.

When the satellite picked up the squadron of six F-16s taking off from the air base in Saidu, Pakistan and then heading southwest toward the Afghan border, General Sampson ordered a second squadron of F-15s into the air.

The American F-15s were overtaking Pakistan's American made F-16s in a supersonic test of speed toward the crossing point. They would join with General Sampson to escort Colonel Rogers to Kabul.

Colonel Rogers lifted off, turning northeast toward the pass leading to Kabul when the Kabul tower came on the air. "The Pakistan Air Force is on to you, Colonel, and on the way. Stay out of the canyons, turn southwest and head straight for the border."

The direction change gave Colonel Rogers one last look. When the Pakistan army found the village, they would also find those responsible. The bodies of the men Sergeant Anderson had located were mostly young boys twelve to fourteen years of age, as well as

Faisal. Colonel Rogers hoped they would treat it as a Taliban raid on the village, but he knew they would blame it on the Americans.

Captain Pitt turned south, passing the northern tip of Pakistan and was crossing into Kashmir when Colonel Rogers lifted off the plateau. The Pakistan Air Force radar followed them until they disappeared off the screen and then ordered a squadron of F-16s to patrol the Pakistan border from Kabul to Kandahar.

The Pakistan radar in Parachinar, Pakistan picked up Colonel Rogers as he cleared the canyon rim above the village and turned toward the Afghan border.

The Afghan / Pakistan border is a jagged line along the mountains. The F-16s were approaching from Saidu Air Base, but would have to divert to avoid crossing Afghan air space where the two remaining F-15s were flying the border. The Pakistan pilots would come in from behind Colonel Rogers, but the diversion would prevent them from reaching the helicopter before it reached the border. The Pakistani pilot's orders were to follow the helicopter into Afghanistan and to destroy it.

Colonel Rogers approached the Afghanistan border as two of the Pakistan F-16s broke formation to engage the helicopter. The F-16s broke off when the two F-15s arrived and locked their missiles on them before they were in range of the helicopter.

General Sampson and his wingman let the Pakistan F-16s go, but after they rejoined their formation the six F-16s turned to re-engage the helicopter and the two F-15s.

The four F-15s caught up and entered the fray scattering the Pakistan planes, and then the six F-15s joined in formation above the helicopter.

General Sampson contacted the Pakistan airbase telling them the F-15s were flying cover on a rescue mission of UN personnel out of the tribal region, and they had orders to engage the Pakistani pilots if necessary to protect the helicopter.

The F-16s were no match for the F-15s. The Pakistan Air Force would lodge a protest, but they ordered their pilots to return to base.

CHAPTER 6

Yaq'ab climbed to the canyon rim to place the call and then waited at the entrance to the cave for the Lion Sheik to finish his morning prayers.

"The Army has arrived at the village. They found Baraka, Faisal and the crusaders; they are all dead."

"They were only women and children and we disarmed the village long ago. Faisal was to take twenty men to the village. Who killed them?"

"The general said the Americans crossed in with helicopter gunships from Kabul."

"What of Wahid, Yaq'ab; did Baraka get to him?"

"Wahid and Isma'il were not among the dead."

"Then they betrayed us. Their families must be punished as an example. When the army leaves send more men."

"The Americans took Wahid, Isma'il and their families under their protection; the rest in the village were killed."

"The Americans bombed the village?"

"No, the general said they were executed, it looks like Faisal's work."

"Send a message to the general, Yaq'ab; they must burn the village and blame the Americans, but Wahid has betrayed us, what of the shipment?"

"The shipment is safe. Wahid thinks it's with the convoy, but it left Mardan a few hours ago."

"They know we have them; we will change plans. Tell Daqa to split up the shipment when he reaches Bannu. Send three with the plane to Somalia. Tell Butrus and Fawzan to stay with the fleet. We will drop three of the packages into the sea. They can collect them and deliver them to the offshore courier."

"What of the other?"

"Send it to Gwadar as planned. One of them will get through to our enemies in America, Yaq'ab, God willing."

Gligit, Kashmir

Ismail and Wahid boarded the C-17 in Gligit and were told they would be going to Cairo, Egypt. Wahid was aware of the laws in the U.S. against bigamy, but he and Isma'il argued that the agreement was for a new home in America.

Assimilating the families into the society of the U.S. with their multiple wives and a dozen or more children each would be an insurmountable task. When told they could go to America as promised, but they would have to break up their families, they refused and were given a choice of countries where the Islamic laws were acceptable. Just as Eric figured, they chose the seaside community of Hurghada in Egypt.

The Egyptian consulate granted them asylum and new identities. Wahid's American education and fluent grasp of the English language would help them blend into the multitudes working in the tourist industry. The financial reward from the CIA would assure them a lifestyle of plenty in a society otherwise ravaged by poverty and indifference.

The C-17 transported the families to a remote airstrip on the shore of the Red Sea. The debriefing on the way provided little additional information. Wahid was convinced the packages were on the convoy headed south to the Port of Karachi, but he was unaware that Dr. Hakeem had been killed.

No one believed the story about militants from India. The bombing had been reported by the American news media as an attack by Muslim militants on members of the Pakistan government who were continuing to promote secular laws. There was no mention of Dr. Hakeem's connection to the Pakistan nuclear program.

It was too much of a coincidence. The CIA put the Taliban raid on Wahid's village and Dr. Hakeem's assassination together. If, in fact, there were nuclear warheads in transit, it appeared an obvious attempt to silence anyone connected with the theft. Since Wahid had escaped, Al-Queda's plan had gone astray. The American satellites were tracking the convoy, but Ron Edwards and Eric Ludlow both believed they would attempt to split the shipment before it reached Karachi.

The Pentagon

Ayeza carried the core on the Lear. The supersonic jet refueled as it passed the island of Crete, then turned north and flew over the North Pole to New Mexico. Ayeza arrived at Holloman Air Force Base twenty hours after leaving the village. A courier from the Los Alamos National Nuclear Laboratory met her at the plane.

Admiral Michaels's secretary relayed the message when the call came in from the lab in New Mexico. "The tests are in, Admiral."
"What's the verdict?"
"If all four of them have the same core, they are tactical warheads with an effective kill radius of between two and five miles. If detonated at ground level, everything within ground zero

will be obliterated and collateral damage causing radiation burns will extend out another three to five miles."

"Are Ron and Eric in Washington?"

"They will arrive this afternoon."

"Tell the New Mexico lab to fax a hard copy under signature, then contact Jim Symington's office and ask him to set some time aside for us this afternoon. In the meantime set up a meeting with the Joint Chiefs; it's time to confront the civilians."

Ron and Eric joined Admiral Michaels and the Pentagon Joint Chiefs after the written report came through. "The tape indicates four warheads, Eric. How reliable is the source."

"Wahid brought one of their plutonium cores, Admiral. The arrangement was that he and Isma'il will not receive their final payments until we confirmed the information about the warheads. Wahid was the scientist in charge of assembling the warheads at the lab in Rawalpindi. He claims he assembled eight and loaded them in the truck, but that only four were unloaded at the Mardan storage facility. It appears Dr. Hakeem was the only other one connected to the Pakistan nuclear program who was aware that there were eight warheads in the shipment. All other records show Wahid only assembled four. We think Dr. Hakeem's death and the attack on Wahid's village was an attempt to cover the theft."

"How is that playing in Pakistan?"

"It's not. The Pakistan authorities are sticking with the inventory figures. Dr. Hakeem's entries the night he died showed only four in transit. Pakistan's nuclear agency claims only four were transported to Mardan and four arrived. They also say the inventories at Rawalpindi and Mardan have been confirmed."

"The UN has oversight at the lab in Rawalpindi. I would think the Pakistan government has an accurate tally; where is the credibility?"

"The new government of Pakistan has no credibility. Musharraf's military controlled the laboratory and the weapons storage. They worked with the UN Nuclear Regulatory Commission, but after he resigned, all of his inspectors were replaced by the new government, and the UN has been barred from the facilities. We believe Dr. Hakeem, the head of Pakistan's nuclear program, made the inventory adjustment from his office in Karachi when the weapons left the factory."

"Has anyone told the Pakistan government we have the man who was in charge of the Rawalpindi lab, and that he claims he assembled and shipped eight warheads?"

"Yes, but it is well known that Wahid had petitioned the U.S. State Department for residence status when he was in school here. The Pakistan spokesman claims Wahid made up the story to gain asylum in the U.S., and that it was only a coincidence that a few minutes after the trucks cleared the gate a bomb went off under Dr. Hakeem's desk killing him. It's too neat, Admiral. Somebody was covering their tracks and with Wahid now in our custody we think they will try to split the shipment. We do not have time to go to the Hill with this. The CIA team is ready to go, but we need your approval."

Turning to the other military leaders in the room, Admiral Michaels searched their faces for dissent; there was none. "We are in agreement. General Sampson in Kabul and the Special Forces are at your disposal. We will also notify the fleets in the Persian Gulf and the Arabian sea to lend their support."

"That does not help stateside, Admiral. We need access to the Miami estates and Symington still has the authority."

"Bring the Florida governor on board, Ron. I will ask for a meeting with the Congressional Committee and brief them on the situation. If they balk, I will tell them we will leak the story to the press and I will resign in protest of their actions. That will give this credibility. When FOX News picks it up the rest of the stations will have to follow. Once the news leaks, the local politicians will demand action. The Florida governor can call up the National Guard and I doubt the members of the committee have the balls to take the responsibility to try to stop him."

With the mission approved by the Pentagon, they moved on to the meeting with Jim Symington. Ron handed the Los Alamos report to Symington after Eric played the translation of the taped conversation between Ayeza and Isma'il.

Symington was not convinced. "You have no proof the warheads are on their way here, Mr. Edwards."

"Drop the formal cynicism, Jim, or should I say, Mr. Symington."

"I'm sorry, Admiral, but this is not proof they are coming here. The militant Muslims have left the U.S. alone since 9-11 and have been targeting European countries. Besides, Israel, not the U.S., is their primary target. Whatever is in that package could be headed anywhere. If it were coming here, someone would be expecting it. We took you at your word and we checked every source after the plane left Kabul and before it touched down in New Mexico. It is business as usual and the imams are all making overtures to the new administration. They don't want their communities to have to deal with another aftermath of 9-11."

"Wake up, Jim; we aren't talking 9-11. We are talking Miami or possibly four different targets on the eastern seaboard."

"That's ludicrous, Admiral. The Saudis did not buy a billion dollars of Miami waterfront to destroy it. Your Pakistan contact could be trying to buy a new life. I understand his relocation budget exceeds five million dollars. That's a lot of money in a country where the average wage is a few hundred dollars a year."

"That decision wasn't made until yesterday when he delivered the core."

"Still, that's a lot of incentive for someone living in a mud hut on Pakistan wages. My authority supersedes yours in this, Admiral. The Pakistan government's inventory is in balance. I don't consider this proof Al-Queda has a weapon or that even if they do, it is on the way here."

"If we have to, we will do it without you, Jim. The Joint Chiefs and the Florida governor came on board. The Navy is moving toward the Bahamas and you need to start banging on doors in Miami. Get the warrants. If you refuse, the Florida governor intends to send in the National Guard. His jurisdiction in Florida overshadows yours."

When the meeting adjourned, Eric remained seated and checked his voice mail. Admiral Michaels and Ron were at the door waiting, but Eric signaled them to sit back down.

"We notified the Pakistan government this morning when the core results came in, Admiral. The army inspected the convoy. A UN inspector and one of ours were with them when they opened the crates. There was a slight trace of radiation, but the truck carried the weapons to Mardan so that is expected. The only cargo in any of the trucks was four crates full of valve parts for a refinery in Yemen. We have had the convoy on camera all this time. They must have pulled a switch at the Mardan storage facility."

"They left Mardan four days ago; they could be anywhere by now, Eric."

"The flights in and out of Pakistan have been monitored and their cargo checked at their destinations. There have been no flights direct to Yemen or Jeddah. They have to be in a truck on the way to Karachi, and at best that will take them a week, Admiral."

"Eric, is the Pakistan government going to cooperate?"

"No, it means inspecting every truck on a road leading to Karachi. They were indignant this morning. They claim the inventory at the storage facility has been verified and there is nothing missing. They refused to search the convoy this morning, but the Pakistan aid bill is pending in Congress. When they were reminded, they changed their minds and agreed to the search. The convoy was bogged down in the mud three hundred miles from Karachi. The military arrived by helicopter. It was a mess. After the search they called the Ambassador, cancelled our man's visa and told us to butt out of their business."

"What now, Ron?"

"It's Eric's territory, Admiral, but it's obvious we are going to have to do this without the Pakistan government."

Eric paced the room a moment. "Admiral, the convoy has been bogged down in a storm that has turned the roads to a quagmire of mud. If they cannot move, no one else can. The convoy is still four or five days from Karachi and another transport truck has to be behind them.

If we want to find the warheads before they leave Pakistan, we cannot trust the new government, and now they have an excuse to ignore us. Wahid can brief a team on what we are looking for, but we need authority to go in."

"The Committee is nervous and the Hill is spoiling for a fight with the military. I say we leave the civilians out for now. It is always easier to ask forgiveness than permission, Eric. Go in covert. I will deal with it upstairs if they are caught."

"That leaves the CIA on the hook alone. I am not going to send my people in without assurances I can bring them out if the Pakistan military gets involved. Failure is not an option, Admiral. You and the military Chiefs are going to have to make the full commitment, regardless of what the Hill decides.

We are talking nuclear warheads in the hands of the Islamic militants. We can't do a repeat of half measures like we did in Nam or Iraq if we want to succeed timely. That means that if they interfere, we engage the Pakistan military head on with whatever force is at our disposal."

"If we don't find the warheads, we lose your way, Eric. If we take responsibility for recovering the warheads and a bomb does go off anyway, the Congressional Committee will make it our responsibility."

"What's our choice, Admiral?"

"We are not at war with Pakistan and have been ordered to stay out, Ron. This is the administration's responsibility not the military's. If we sit back and let Congress and Symington deal with it and a bomb goes off, the Task Force, the administration and Congress will take the heat."

"The CIA and the military can't sit back and wait for them to arrive in Florida, Admiral. We have to focus our attention somewhere, and while the warheads are still in Pakistan that's our obvious choice."

"Right now the government of Pakistan is not the enemy, Ron."

"Al-Queda is the enemy and Pakistan is protecting them."

"Al-Queda represents a religion not a country. Congress and the administration will stall and make it Pakistan's problem, that way they will have someone to blame if a bomb does go off."

"What about the million or more Americans who will die if just one of the warheads gets through, Admiral?"

"There is a chance your people could find them and get out safely, Eric."

"Sorry, Admiral, but if the military does not commit we don't go in."

"What other option is there, Ron?"

"We try to trace them, but we wait until they leave Pakistan."

"We'll lose them, you know that."

"More than likely, Admiral, the team can go in by commercial carrier, but they won't stand a chance without a military pick up if they find the weapons. I'm not sending my people in on a suicide mission."

"All right, Ron, but mutiny is not the answer. I will go back to the Joint Chiefs. This has to be unanimous. If we agree, we will need to bring the White House on line."

"The White House will balk, you know that. They won't take the heat from Congress if we fail."

"They can sit back and watch. We will tell them we will go with or without them and take the responsibility if we need to sort it out later, but if they object our hands are tied. In the meantime, notify your team and I'll tell General Sampson to put his people on alert. But, Ron, if we do go in, we had better find something."

Admiral Michaels believed it was a lose, lose exercise for the military. By definition, without Congressional or Executive approval it would be insurrection. If the administration tacitly agree and they succeeded in finding the warheads the administration would get the credit, but a threat ten thousand miles from home would be downplayed in the press.

An unsuccessful operation and an American Air Force and Special Forces confrontation with Pakistan's military without pre approval would be grounds for court-martial proceedings against all of the officers involved. If they lost the warheads in Pakistan and they made it to the U.S. mainland there would be no proof as to where they originated; their convictions would be assured, and Congressional hearings condemning the military for ignoring Pakistan's sovereignty would drag on for years.

The military had orders from Congress and the Executive branch of the government to respect Pakistan's sovereignty, and they had made it clear they would not change their minds.

The only way to go through channels if the administration refused would mean playing the connection between the *Apostate* and the nuclear card, and letting the press run with the story.

If the administration balked, the core was in safekeeping, under the control of the military, and the documentation could not be disputed. The military Joint Chiefs would conduct a press conference and tell the country that they were convinced that there were nuclear warheads in transit to the U.S., but their hands were tied by Congress and the administration.

Eric had a different opinion. The public's mood in America's heartland was growing somber. America was spiraling into a society of elected government officials, government bureaucrats and their employees, the very rich and the very poor, with little middle class left in between.

The outgoing administration and the incoming President had promised trillions of dollars for the Wall Street barons and the major American corporations. The CEOs of those corporations were lavishing themselves and their executives with billions in bonuses and perks, but jobs were disappearing in the private sector and nothing was filtering down to the working class or to the small business owners.

Under the new administration, government employees had no fear of losing their jobs and with the unions they would become tenured positions. The rest of the country was reeling from the economic melt-down and millions were out of work. Millions more faced layoffs and losing their homes.

America was on the verge of a depression. Even if they stood down waiting for orders, if the military split from the administration, what little confidence in the economy that remained would dissolve and a depression would become reality.

The new American President is the Messiah to some, but to many others he is the anti-Christ. The country was split along party lines. Eric believed the administration would have to act. A nuclear threat by militant Muslims against an American city that could be blamed on the *Apostate* could be the match that lights the fire. The possibility of panic, riots and looting in the major cities across the country was a great risk.

After conferring with the military Joint Chiefs it was decided to move forward, but to brief the President and suggest he call a press conference to tell the public the truth. It was a ludicrous suggestion and Eric knew it. The administration would stall, but they would tacitly allow the military to proceed.

Eric was right. The President refused to meet with the military leaders, but his Chief of Staff gave them an audience. Admiral Michaels left the White House after the meeting with assurances that the administration would keep a lid on the story until it was proved true or false.

The request for presidential authorization for the covert mission was granted, but any decision to engage the Pakistan military would be a decision for, and the responsibility of, the military leaders themselves.

This was a case where the end would have to justify the means. The administration would hold the military leaders responsible if it proved to be a false alarm.

Admiral Michaels returned from the White House in a somber mood. There was no choice. To trace them they had to start in Pakistan, but the chance of finding the warheads in Pakistan was slim. If they failed, the President would be asking for resignations of all those who challenged him. It would be the end of the American military and the beginning of the civilian militia the *Apostate* had suggested forming while he was on the campaign trail.

Pakistan was Eric's territory; he was also the expert on militant Muslims and Islam. Ron Edwards and Admiral Michaels would lend support, but it would be Eric's mission.

"Where is Antonio, Ron?"

"He is still on leave in Spain, Eric, but of all people, why him?"

"He worked with Pakistan's military in the tribal regions when Musharraf cracked down on the Taliban, and he was in Rawalpindi when they secured the nuclear laboratory. He speaks fluent Arabic and knows his way around Pakistan."

"I know he is your friend, but he's hard to control and he's sulking. He still blames me for the Lisbon foul-up."

"This is not a James Bond flick, Ron, he can sulk later. He's the best we have. Get in touch with him and tell him to meet our plane in Madrid, he has a mission. Where is Wahid?"

"He's settling into Hurghada, Egypt."

"That's out of the way and we don't have much time. He is the only one who knows what we're looking for. Send a plane and get him to the base in Kabul… Where is Ayeza?"

"She's at the Hyatt. Her cover is blown so she can't go back to Afghanistan. She thinks she is going back to Germany."

"Is she willing to go back to Pakistan? She won't be any good if she's reluctant."

"They raped her, killed her unborn child and her entire family. Still, it was her first kill and she is dealing with it. It could take a while longer."

"We don't have a while longer."

"Why the girl, Eric? I would think she would be in the way."

"A couple has a better chance. She was born in the Pakistan. A lone man would raise suspicion."

"I can have a private charter ready in an hour, but Antonio is bitter and may take orders better from you. He and I clashed in Spain the last time I saw him, his woman died. He was in love with her. You were there, but he blames me."

"This is no time for personal feuds, Ron."

"I know, but you can't tell him that. If you want him to take the mission, it's best you deal with him yourself. Besides someone needs to concentrate on Andros Island and Miami if we miss the warheads in Pakistan."

"That makes sense. I will take Ayeza to Madrid. Send word to Antonio to meet me at the Madrid airport in the morning. While I'm gone, find the fisherman. I want to know what is up on the island."

"Admiral, you have been quiet."

"Sorry, Eric, just making notes. I am an, *if it can go wrong it will, so plan for it,* kind of person. That way if we get lucky and the couple find the warheads we stand down, but in the meantime, nothing is lost."

"I'm not proud, Admiral, jump right in."

"Let's work with what we have. The airports in Miami and at Nassau are too well guarded and an amphibian landing anywhere nearby will draw attention from the Coast Guard or the Navy.

If we lose the package in Pakistan and the destination is Miami or Andros Island, I think they will ship it by boat or ship. We have satellites covering the coast of Pakistan, the Mediterranean and the Arabian Sea. If we start now, we can track the traffic and connect the dots to Andros."

"There has to be hundreds of ships, Admiral. How do we narrow it down?"

"If we believe the sources, Eric, we track anything that leaves a Pakistan port or docks on the coast of Somalia, Yemen or Saudi Arabia. We also track anything that leaves the countries and sails toward the coast of the U.S. They have to come through the Suez Canal, or around the Cape of Good Hope. We should have narrowed it to just a few by the time they reach the Atlantic. By the time it approaches the Bahamas we should be dialed in on the right one."

"You are talking a lot of man power and equipment dedicated to the task. I don't trust Symington or his staff. We don't need our actions leaked. Can the Navy tap into the satellites without our going upstairs, Admiral?"

"We are always logged on, Eric. I'll make this top secret and notify the ships' captains to assign only personnel with clearance. I will also shift a missile carrier group to the coast of Somalia.

The pirates are getting bolder and the tankers and yachts have been asking for escorts. It will appear routine. We have two surveillance ships in the Persian Gulf and the Mediterranean. One can join with the carrier group to track the ships in the Persian Gulf and the Arabian Sea, the other can track ships leaving the Sudan, Saudi and Yemen ports traveling north to Suez."

"Ok, we send Antonio and Ayeza to pick up the trail in Pakistan and the Navy covers the oceans. Ron's people are relocating to the islands so that leaves Miami. Symington and his people will not be much help. Does anyone have a suggestion of what targets we concentrate on if they slip through?"

"Eric, we are running out of time if you want to make Madrid tomorrow."

The meeting was over, but Admiral Michaels turned to Ron as he was leaving. "The governor of Florida is a friend, Ron. It is his state so I called him to see if he could pull some strings and influence Symington. He is in Washington at a governor's conference. Bring him on board, maybe he can help."

CHAPTER 7

—————⊃●⊂—————

The plane taxied down Washington National runway a little
after five pm. They would land at Madrid International
Airport at seven am Madrid time.

Antonio was naked, sitting in the chair by the bed. The clock
said 5 am. He had been awake since three. The girl was asleep, he
was thinking, *passed out*. She was loaded in the bar when he arrived
and had another half dozen brandies after he joined her.

He thought back, *the taxi dropped them at her front door; he
helped her up the stairs*. He got up and moved to the bedroom door,
looking for his clothes. Tripping over his pants, one leg inside out,
he remembered the shower. It started there.

He gathered his wrinkled clothes. His shirt was damp from the
shower spray; there was not room for two with the door closed.

He knew he needed fresh clothes, but what he had with him
would have to do. He was to meet the plane at seven. He looked

toward the bed as he dressed quietly. She had turned face up, legs spread. The bed was in disarray, the covers on the floor.

The woman was cute but not his type. She was tall, gangly, thick ankles and that tattoo! It would be hidden by the thong now lying on the floor, but in her current position it was quite visible, starting below her tan line, passing through her crotch and ending a few inches above her hair line in the shape of a snake's head. *That would take some doing; and I am glad it was dark!*

He quit binge drinking months ago, but when he did the loneliness and sleepless nights returned. She had filled the gap, as the others had, but the call the night before brought reality back into focus.

It had been a year. Thinking, *it was fun but it is time to go back to work,* he dropped three hundred dollar bills on the nightstand, three times the going rate. It made little difference, there was much more in the satchel. He was not sure how much; he had not bothered to track the bonds he cashed. He knew he did not need the money, but he needed a change and would take the new mission, no matter what it was.

Eric mentioned a new partner, another woman. He would prefer to work alone. He was not a good teacher and had not wanted his last partner. Ron had forced the issue the first time, but after a while, she grew on him.

His watch said five-forty-five. It was an hour taxi ride. He settled back to take a nap but the thought of a new partner flooded his mind with memories. He reflected on that night in the Semiramis in Cairo. They were posing as a couple but in a suite with two bedrooms, just as it had been for the three months they had traveled as a team.

They were apart for days at a time when not on assignment. When they were together the arrangement crimped his sex life; posing as a couple left him little time to himself.

Like the girl still in her bed, Aletha was also not his type. Before Aletha, he had liked short, full figured women, soft of body with long hair. Aletha was tall, five eight, maybe nine, eye level with Antonio when wearing heels. Her body was muscled, hard, not soft, her neck long, hair cropped short.

After their first assignment, they shared a bottle of wine and he made a pass. At the time, he had many women in his life and was not ready for commitment. She knew him to be a shallow womanizer and blew him off. It was business; she wanted to keep it that way.

Although not his type, she was a beautiful woman. It was a difficult arrangement at best. They would be traveling together, sharing the same room. After the first month, Aletha was growing on him. They checked into a suite at the Paris Hilton. It was a sunny spring day. Aletha suggested an outdoor café by the Seine, and a glass of wine to celebrate a successful sting against a Muslim cell in Brussels. It was the first crack in her shell. One glass turned to a bottle and a snifter or two of Hennessey.

The walk back to the hotel became a stroll along the river. He was not sure when, but at some point before they reached the hotel she took his hand in hers, or did he take hers? The memory was foggy, but he knew she held his until they reached their suite. The crack had widened, he opened a bottle of wine the concierge had sent to their room. It was that time of year in Paris, Beaujolais as he remembered.

She turned and opened the doors to the balcony letting the cool air crossing the river flood the room. She stood for a moment then turned around. He offered her the glass. She held out her hand, but the fresh air had a sobering effect; she smiled, sheepishly, *no, I have had enough wine, besides, I have made another commitment and I do not lie well.*

She retreated to her room. He heard the lock turn in the door behind her. He walked to the balcony and sat for a while sipping his wine, and then stood and gulped hers before leaving the suite and heading for the bar.

The woman walked in and sat two stools away. She was short, full figured and soft of body with long hair. He ordered another glass of wine. An American fluent in French piqued her interest. "Are you here in Paris alone?"

Aletha had mentioned a significant other whom she shared a flat with in Frankfurt when not on assignment, but had not gone into detail. Distracted by the thought of a woman growing on him, "No, I'm here with a friend. She has had a long day and is resting in our room."

She was new. For a time, their missions were uneventful but scattered. They traveled together in close quarters, but he kept his distance and she kept hers. It had become a routine, a suite with two bedrooms, but relationships develop; little things we notice at first. He found himself opening her door, ordering her favorite wine instead of his, putting the seat down, shaving daily and looking forward to her company when she was gone.

She smiled more. There were times when her hand would brush his, or their bodies would touch when in crowded elevators and public transportation, and she would move closer and linger longer than necessary.

He had mentioned he liked a new perfume, now it was all she wore. She did not want to rush, dinner took longer and they often lingered with a nightcap in the living room of their suite before going to their rooms.

They checked into the Semiramis a few months later, following the leader of a Muslim cell in Paris. The imam had incited his followers. The riots earlier in the week had taken the lives of a dozen Paris police officers caught in a crossfire. A Paris magistrate issued an arrest warrant, but he had fled the country. The CIA traced him to Cairo. It was rumored to be an interim stop for a new identity, and then a connecting flight to New York through Amsterdam.

After entering the narrow passageways of the bazaar following the man, his actions became erratic and he doubled back to the square rushing to the entrance of the mosque. It was noon on a Friday; the mosque and the square in front were congested with men performing the Muslim mandatory Friday prayers.

The imam shouted angrily, pointing in their direction. A few dozen men rushed at them. Antonio turned toward Aletha; she was frozen in place and there was panic in her eyes. Taking her hand, *I know; there are too many and we left our guns at home, there will be another day.*

It was only a split second; his comment jarred her. They had a head start and cleared the bazaar losing the men in the crowds. Shit happens! Even to the best. The good people do not always win, but there are times they walk away, lick their wounds and wake another day.

It was her first narrow escape. Out of breath, Aletha laughed about the incident. "I froze, how dumb is that?"

"We all do at first. That's why you get a partner for a time. It is not like the classroom and it cannot be taught; you do not flunk or fail, you live or die. It happens to us all. The first time there is a real threat we come to terms with our mortality. In this business, that feeling stays with you and you learn to live for the moment because it could be your last. It takes getting used to."

Having their cover blown meant a trip home or a vacation. Someone else would take over. "If that's the case let's celebrate our survival."

"Sounds like a plan; I'll notify Eric to send someone else before the imam leaves Cairo."

A glass led to a bottle, one bottle led to another and as they entered their suite, Antonio had reflections of the night in Paris.

Aletha had other ideas. "Why don't you pour us a glass of wine?"

"We just checked in this morning. There is no wine in the room, I'll call room service."

"This is Cairo, Antonio, remember, room service takes hours. Be a dear. I saw a Chandon De Brailles in the gift shop, it's my favorite."

Antonio returned with two bottles. Aletha was on the balcony. She had showered and changed into a sheer silk nightgown. He opened a bottle and poured two glasses, then walked to the balcony to join her. She was standing at the rail with her back to him.

"I'm cold."

Antonio set the glasses on the table and then, accepting the invitation, he stood behind her drawing her close, warming her body with his. He could smell the freshness of her skin and the scent of the perfume on her neck.

"What's changed?"

"My friend in Germany is jealous of us; he doesn't believe me. We had a fight and he moved out. It's a good thing, it was not working and I am beginning to like you, besides you convinced me. We live for the moment and I am in the mood."

She turned to face him. His hands moved to caress her back and the flesh on her ass. Her body was muscled and as hard as his was, but her lips were soft and the skin on her neck silky.

She purred, "Humm... you're good, what else do you do?"

"Whatever you like."

Aletha moved to the bed. "Bring the wine, I like a lot and sex makes me thirsty."

Her demeanor had changed; he watched her saunter across the room, discarding the gown as she swept the covers aside. He smiled, "It is hard to drink lying down."

"I meant after, and it needs to breathe a little so there is no hurry, the wine that is. Take a shower and shave, then come to bed."

He paused, "Picky?"

Picking up her glass she smiled, "Of course, besides, it's hot and dusty in Cairo, and it's been a long day."

Before they left Cairo, Antonio and Aletha were reassigned to a case involving a radical Muslim by the name of Jamal al-Din after a tip by an unnamed source in the Mediterranean.

The American Ambassador to Morocco found the message folded in his napkin when he rejoined his table at a dinner party in Casablanca. A maze of e-mail correspondence followed from numerous locations in the Mediterranean. They pinpointed the location when the source moved his yacht to an isolated berth on a private island off the coast of Spain.

The mole was obviously financially secure, but he had something of value to sell. The CIA agreed to pay the twenty-five million when the source delivered a personal hand written note from the Speaker of the House to Jamal al-Din that was written when she was a student in college.

The source had sent enough information to cause a stir, but without more proof it was all speculation. The mole sent records showing Jamal al-Din, whose name at the time was Jim Karcher, was a professor at Trinity College in Washington, DC when the Speaker of the House attended the campus.

Homeland Security tied Karcher to an account financing Hezbollah, but he jumped bail and disappeared before they brought him to trial.

The source said he had proof the Congresswoman had begun the affair while attending college, and that they had met again in Syria.

Karcher first re-surfaced as an advisor to Syrian President Bashar al-Assad in 2007. The House Speaker's 2007 trip to Syria and her meeting with Assad coincided with Karcher's return. The source claimed to have tapes and films taken during their meeting in Karcher's private suite at the royal palace.

Karcher's recent death during an American raid on a meeting of Taliban leaders in a village in Pakistan tied the Syrian to Al-Queda. Her private cell phone number was listed in his, tying Karcher to the Speaker of the House.

Antonio and Aletha arrived at the Port of Lisbon to meet the yacht from the island. Eric had arrived earlier. The mole from Morocco left the island for Lisbon when Eric told him the CIA approved the payment and the money was available.

Antonio and Aletha were approaching the yacht when Eric arrived carrying the satchel of bearer bonds. Meanwhile, Ron Edwards and his men were to have set up a perimeter to quarantine the dock and cover the trio.

Ron Edwards and his men were delayed. A CIA rookie notified the Lisbon police. It was new policy for the CIA that had been handed down by a Congressional Committee with no field experience.

The Lisbon police arrived, followed by the intruders who drove on past the barricades in an armored car loaded with explosives. The police opened fire with automatic weapons as they passed. Aletha took a stray bullet as the car left the dock, landing on the back deck of the yacht before the explosion.

They were above the dock and out of range of some, but not all, of the blast that engulfed the yacht in flames killing everyone onboard. Eric was in front of Antonio and injured by flying debris; Antonio was thrown into a pile of rubble.

The fire spread to nearby buildings. The police formed a barricade and no one approached. Choking in a black fog of smoke, Antonio crawled to Aletha. She had a faint pulse. Antonio missed the blood pooling beside her and assumed she was just out cold from the blast. He then crawled to where Eric lay unconscious.

Before the smoke cleared, he took the key from Eric's pocket and removed the satchel attached to Eric's wrist containing the bearer bonds. Crawling through the debris, he hid the satchel from the police, knowing they would confiscate it.

Aletha had no pulse by the time Antonio returned to her. She had died minutes after the bullet passed through her femoral artery. Antonio picked her body up and carried it out of the haze of smoke toward the barricade of police.

The Spanish government protested the CIA's actions. In the ensuing congressional hearings, the CIA buried the story of the House Speaker's ties to the terrorist, substituting a story of an Iranian nuclear threat. However, the story had leaked. It became tabloid news ignored by the public and discredited by the House Speaker's staff as political fodder, but not before it created an irreparable break between the House Speaker and the CIA.

With the yacht and its contents destroyed, the money gone, and the Syrian connection killed, it was a dead end. The Speaker of the House was in the clear.

CHAPTER 8

Eric briefed her on the mission shortly after they boarded the plane. An hour before they landed in Madrid, he described his choice of partners for her, and then qualified it with a brief history of Antonio's life-style.

Ayeza smiled, and then excused herself to freshen up. When Ayeza boarded the plane in Washington, she was dressed in a stylish suit, four inch heels and her hair was up, showing off her long neck and the emerald earrings that matched the color of her eyes.

When she returned she had changed into padded attire giving herself the look of a subservient Middle-Eastern woman. Catching the meaning of Eric's surprised look when she returned, she smiled. "After your description of him, I thought it best I changed into my working clothes."

"You can't hide forever, Ayeza."

"Are you hitting on me, Eric?"

"Not that it hasn't entered my mind, but no, Ayeza, you are a beautiful woman and old men like me may be on a diet, but we still enjoy looking at the menu."

"You're sweet, but men have never been my long suit, Eric."

"Your village and the streets of Kabul are only a sliver of real life, Ayeza. There are some good men in this world. We are not all like Faisal."

"Your description of Antonio does not put him in that category."

"I knew him well and long before Lisbon, Ayeza. He was settled in the relationship and faithful to Aletha. He would have given his life to save hers."

"Then why not give her memory some respect, Eric. From what you said, he has lost the ability to care about anyone."

"They made a great team, but what happened is a product of this business. Antonio blames Ron and the rookie who notified the Madrid police, but he blames himself more. Aletha did not have to be there that night. We were going to trade the bonds for the tapes and film. Antonio was the inspector. I was the courier. However, they had become inseparable. It was his decision, but she would not stay at the hotel and he let her come along."

For a time the scotch clouded his memories, now the women he paid filled the void. He decided he would not love again; it brought too much pain, but it had been a year and it was time to move on.

The taxi left him at the end of the runway. The Lear faced into the chilled December wind. The sound of the turbines humming caught his attention as he climbed the stairs. He had been told it was a briefing; he was not aware he was going on a trip. The flight attendant closed the door and pointed to a seat as the ramp pulled back and the Lear started down the runway.

The last time he saw Eric, Eric was strapped in a gurney, barely alive. It was the night Aletha died. By then Antonio had fallen in love with her.

Eric woke from the coma the day before Aletha was buried. He would make an appearance at the funeral, but he could not climb the stairs. Eric remained in the car while Ron and the CIA rookie entered the chapel. Antonio met them in stride. He was smoldering with rage. It did not matter that it was a police bullet that killed Aletha. Antonio blamed them for Aletha's death because they brought the police.

A few days later Antonio disappeared. The bonds had also disappeared. Antonio surfaced in Madrid a few months later and contacted Eric. By that time the CIA Internal Affairs hearings ended with the assumption that one of the Lisbon police or medical attendants had cut the bracelet off Eric's wrist and had disappeared with them. Although Antonio was Eric's friend, Eric was not completely satisfied. However, with Antonio's connections in Europe and the Middle East it would be impossible to trace his activities. Eric let the matter drop when it became apparent pursuing the issue would compromise other CIA operations in Europe.

Antonio had been on leave since the Lisbon foul-up. He was not Eric's first choice, but he was the top CIA operative in the field. His fluency in Arabic, his experience in Pakistan and his ability to pass himself off as Arab put him on top of the list.

However, when Antonio boarded the plane looking like he slept in his clothes, his eyes bleary from a lack of sleep and needing a shave, Eric questioned his own judgment. "Hello, Antonio, glad you could make it."

The memory at the Lisbon dock returned. Eric, out cold, bruised and bloody was lying on a stretcher with the medics working on him. "You're getting old, Eric. I thought you would have retired after that mess in Lisbon."

"I was tempted, but I'm still trying to get even. The committee was not happy. Losing twenty-five million in bearer bonds cost me a pay grade and part of my retirement. How about you? You look like the leftovers of a rough night. Have you got it under control?"

Antonio ignored the obvious. "I came for a meeting. I didn't know it was a formal affair. Where am I going?"

"Kabul, then into Pakistan."

"I've heard Americans are no longer welcome in Pakistan."

"Do you have an issue with that?"

"No, you said I had a new partner?"

"You do, say hello to Ayeza"

Ayeza was sitting on the lounge facing the door dressed in traditional Pakistani women's clothes, with her hair covered and body padding in place. Faisal was gone; there was no need for the contacts. Her green eyes sparkled as she watched the disheveled man in front of her, and to no one in particular, she said, "My new partner, my, this should be fun."

Having heard her, and then looking down at his soiled and wrinkled shirt and pants he thought, *a beautiful woman and here I am without my toothbrush.*

"Nice to meet you too, do you always dress like a nun?"

Reaching for her handbag on the seat, she drew out a pack of gum, tossing it to Antonio, a smile on her face, "These are pretty close quarters, Antonio, give us all a break, and those clothes, do you drink scotch or bathe in it? Gum won't help them."

Ayeza turned to the steward who was offering Antonio a cup of coffee. "Doesn't someone have a razor and something he can wear?"

Antonio settled back watching the sparkling green eyes, and the matching emerald earring Ayeza had forgotten to remove that had slipped out of the head scarf. Something was amiss. There was more to this woman he would have to rely on in a day-to-day world, where a misstep could put you in the ground.

"Steward, you look to be my size, help me out."

Turning to Ayeza, "I'm easy, a few hours of sleep is all I need, and it only takes ten minutes to shower and shave, but you are young and an unknown. Are you up to this? Or, didn't they tell you? The last girl died; I'm not good luck."

"Yes, I know, maybe we'll do better, but I don't know what, *this*, is Antonio. You are not what I expected. I heard that at one time you were the best the CIA had to offer, but you disappeared for a time. I also heard that before your last partner died you were a gentleman. That appears to have changed. You're a mess and I am not impressed, but it appears there is little other choice. I'll take my chances with the rest, but if I'm to play this part, you do need to clean up."

The steward handed Antonio a change of clothes and a shaving kit, refusing the wad of bills Antonio offered. Antonio was free lance and well paid, but he had been off over a year. Eric noticed the hundred dollar bills and the satchel of missing bonds flashed through his mind, but he was still amused, *under the circumstances he probably feels he earned it, but he is sober, maybe it is going to be alright.*

Antonio had not been briefed and was not aware of Ayeza's background or her talents. She seemed quite young and much too relaxed for someone embarking on a mission that could put them both in the ground.

For all he knew she could be an overconfident rookie straight out of a CIA training class in Washington and an attempt by the CIA to fill the gender requirements put forth by the new administration. Inexperience on a mission was dangerous. Inexperience combined with overconfidence was a recipe for disaster. Antonio watched the beautiful woman with green eyes for a moment longer and then moved to the rear cabin to shower and change.

Although Antonio questioned Eric's choice for his partner, Ayeza handled her first mission like a seasoned pro. Her chance meeting with Faisal put that part of her life behind her. What was left of her extended family arrived safely on the shores of the Red Sea; she had little reason to return to Pakistan.

Ayeza wanted to go back, but knew a woman could not work alone in the Muslim world. However, nuclear warheads in the hands of Muslim extremists were enough reason for Ayeza to accept the mission. She would work with Antonio, but Ayeza's return to Pakistan and her chance, face-to-face meeting with Faisal convinced her she did not want, or need, a male partner if she were to return to Europe. However, when Antonio turned in the aisle and left for the rear of the plane, she questioned her own motives.

Ayeza's hormones shut down, and her emotions were buried under the rocks on the streets of Kabul the day Faisal dragged her into the street with the mob following them. She was a child at the time and had never felt physically attracted to a man, before or since, until Antonio entered the plane looking like he slept in his clothes, but with an air of confidence about him.

When he was out of sight she shook it off. Ayeza had never considered a personal relationship. When this mission was over, she wanted a position in Europe. A lone woman who understood the society could help deal with the violence against women that was becoming accepted in the European Muslim communities and the secular courts as a part of their way of life.

Eric was aware of Ayeza's feelings. He watched as Antonio closed the door behind him. Ayeza's gaze in the same direction lingered. Eric watched her smile and started to comment, but he let it pass; he knew Ayeza's background. As asexual as she appeared to be in the past, her banter with Antonio on his arrival indicated she was comfortable in the company of men and in fact Eric believed she found Antonio attractive, even in his unkempt state.

It was Eric's turn to smile. The earring had slipped further from her scarf. Eric dropped his gaze when Ayeza caught him staring.

When the door closed behind him Ayeza turned toward Eric, "Do you think he is over her?"

"No, but he is in denial. She was his first serious relationship."

"He is in his forties, Eric, how is that possible?"

"The job doesn't lend itself to a personal life, Ayeza. Antonio has been at it over twenty years. He does have a place near Madrid, but for the most part, he lives out of a suitcase. Before Aletha, any attractive woman would do. I always thought him incapable of personal attachment, but he proved me wrong."

"What happened?"

"He was devoted to Aletha, and when she died he blamed himself as well as the Lisbon police and the CIA. It was downhill from there. For six months he disappeared. He has a few dozen passports. He would surface now and then, but it was usually in a skirmish over one of the women attached to the rich and famous who circle the globe looking for entertainment."

"If he is still unstable, why did you bring him on board now? There has to be someone else."

"I did not say he is unstable. He buried himself in a bottle of scotch for a time, but he's been sober for the past few months. We need the best for this job. In the past, on his worst day, Antonio was better than most of the others on their best day, Ayeza. He's ex Special Forces with a PhD in Middle East civilizations. He speaks five languages and he knows the country and the people. He also likes to jump out of airplanes above the trade winds. It's a technique no one else has tried. He can drop fifty miles from a target and he'll land on the rooftop. It's a talent we may need."

"I heard the story in Germany at the jump school, but I did not believe it."

"Believe it, it's true. He's no ordinary man, and these are not ordinary times. We need him, but you are a beautiful woman and we don't want him distracted; find a way to deal with him and he will keep you both alive."

Antonio returned as the captain entered the salon. "Eric, there is a call for you, it's Admiral Michaels."
"Thank you, Captain, I'll take it at the desk."

The convoy had been a dead end and sending in Antonio and Ayeza was a long shot. Finding the package in time before it left Karachi seemed an impossible task, but the Admiral and the military Joint Chiefs at the Pentagon did not want to leave the proverbial stone unturned.

When the news came that the Pakistan military searched the convoy and came up empty, Admiral Michaels ordered the technician on the surveillance ship, Tucson, which was heading for the Gulf of Aden, to review the satellite tapes from the cameras monitoring the activity at Pakistan's weapons storage facility in Mardan. When nothing out of the ordinary turned up the day before and the day after, she expanded the search to the week prior to the delivery and the week after.

They missed the produce truck earlier because they were focused on the convoy. The convoy left the lab at Rawalpindi and had an uneventful trip to Mardan. Four of the warheads were off-loaded under Wahid's supervision. Everyone assumed the other four were on the convoy when it left Mardan.

The produce truck arrived at the storage facility three days before Wahid arrived. There were many routine deliveries to the employee cafeteria. No one took notice.

The produce truck remained parked in the parking lot until a few hours before the convoy arrived, but then it had backed into the warehouse near the loading dock where Wahid parked the truck under the canopy out of sight of the satellite cameras. It did not leave Mardan until three days after the convoy left.

We are still tracking the produce truck, Eric. They have made a few stops, but nothing has been loaded or unloaded since it left the weapons facility."

"Yes, Admiral, that may be good news. Are the films clear enough to identify the truck and driver?"

"The driver no, but we don't think it's a local truck. It is a converted military six-by-six. It is in too good shape by Pakistan standards to belong to one of the local vendors. It is ideal for getting around the rockslides and the rutted dirt roads common on the mountain passes. It is slow and is not designed for paved highways.

There are a dozen roads leading south from Peshawar to the Gulf with connecting roads to Karachi, but they left the paved highway this morning and are on the road to Thal. That may be a coincidence, but isn't that near your girl's village and close to the area where the Taliban are expanding their activities?"

"Yes, it is, and I don't believe in coincidence, Admiral. The army searched the convoy. Even if the Pakistan government does not cooperate, Wahid has disappeared and the men they sent after him are dead. American helicopters were involved in the rescue. These people may be deranged, but they are not stupid; they will connect the dots."

"Thal is out of the way if Karachi is the destination, Eric."

"Al-Queda's leaders are tucked in somewhere near Thal, and they know we are searching for the warheads. They will probably split them up. That will be safer to do in one of the villages. I believe Karachi is too obvious, Admiral.... just a minute, Admiral."

Antonio was familiar with the tribal regions and the connecting roads.

"Antonio, if you had to get to the Gulf from Peshawar this time of year, and you wanted to avoid the military checkpoints and inspections, what route would you take?"

"They can pay off the military but this time of year there can be mud in the valleys from the heavy rains. I'd take the road through Quetta along the mountains. It's a hundred miles out of the way, but it's a better road and less traveled."

"Does that road go through Thal?"

"Yes"

"Where does it go from there?"

"When you leave Quetta you have four choices: Karachi, Pasni, Gwadar or Iran."

"It's not Iran; this is an Al-Queda operation."

"Anything is possible, Eric. Iran wants a nuke."

"The Sunnis and Shiites are at each other's throats, Ayeza. Iran would use the nuke on Riyadh. If Al-Queda has the warheads they are going to the States, not to their Shiite enemies. Antonio, is there a deep water port at Pasni?"

"No, but there is one at Gwadar, a little further north."

"Just a minute, Admiral, there is a map in my briefcase."

"Admiral, we are only going to get one shot at it before the Pakistan military gets involved. Tell your surveillance to stay with the truck. I am going to leapfrog our search to Turbat, which is on the road between Quetta and Gwadar.

We'll make the commitment and send the couple in with Special Forces helicopters, and F-15 back-up at the border. If the weapons are not on the truck, we will have to assume we missed them in Pakistan and move on to Jeddah."

Admiral Michaels was taken off guard. "You picked a couple to go to Karachi to give the man credibility. Now you have a woman involved in a Special Forces mission. What's her role?"

"It's the same circumstance; they will drop the couple near a village. They will need to buy a truck to block the highway. A refugee couple won't be as conspicuous as a lone man in a strange land."

"We were going to give Karachi a shot and then bring them out if they found them. They could have flown in and out on a commercial carrier. If they found the material, it would have been a quick trip in and out for the military. A full blown mission means double the exposure."

"There is little other choice, Admiral. The longer we wait the more risk they split the shipment.

"A rescue mission if we found the warheads was easier to sell. Sending our military into Pakistan will cause a backlash in Washington if we come up empty. The State Department will be up in arms. If you miss them and have to go to Saudi, it will have to be a covert operation; the Saudis won't give permission and our State Department will back them up."

"We will go into Saudi covertly if we have to. The terrain is different than Pakistan. We have friends across the Red Sea in Egypt. We won't need the military. The couple can parachute in and an amphibian can pick them up if we come up empty."

"You can't fly over Saudi airspace."

"We are still in Pakistan, Admiral, but trust me; we won't encroach on Saudi's sovereignty with our military unless we find the warheads there. By the way, Admiral, I know it's only been a day, but have you heard from Ron Edwards or Symington?"

"Ron and the Florida governor are on their way over, but Symington is stalling."

"What about the fisherman?"

"It's quiet in the Bahamas, nothing out of the ordinary."

CHAPTER 9

The satellite cameras zoomed in as the truck turned off after passing the city of Thal. When they arrived at the village, they backed into the shade of one of the tents covering the tables piled high with heroin drying in the breeze.

The USS Tucson was entering the Arabian Sea from the Gulf of Oman. Lieutenant Connie Holman watched as the men packed two-kilo bags in the wooden crates alongside the truck. "It looks like a heroin pick-up, Captain."

The Pakistan government was involved in the drug trade. The inspectors were made aware of the shipments in advance, but were paid for their silence. Boats connecting with friendly ports in Yemen, Sudan and Somalia were the safest means of transportation out of the country; they would not be searched.

Heroin was the payment of choice to the smugglers moving slaves, drugs and military hardware through the interconnecting waterways of the Middle and Near East.

On the table in Pakistan the Taliban paid fifty dollars a kilo to the villagers who produced it. Depending on its purity the wholesalers paid upwards of fifty thousand dollars a kilo. They would resell it for eighty thousand a kilo to the distributers who would cut it down and repackage it in nickel *five dollar* bags. The street value to the end user could be as high as one hundred twenty thousand dollars a kilo, depending on the quality and the supply available at the time.

The factories in Mumbai shipped thousands of containers of electronic merchandise each year to the port of New York. Batteries split into two compartments were routinely half filled with heroin and packaged with the equipment. The acid in the batteries masked the smell of the heroin; the dogs at the customs yards would routinely pass it by. After clearing customs in the States, some of the heroin-filled batteries would be replaced at the warehouses in New York before they were shipped to the retail distributors.

The original heroin-filled batteries would remain with the equipment shipped directly to the on-line customers who placed orders with shell companies in India and Pakistan.

The villages and training camps in the tribal regions were under routine surveillance by the American's satellites since 9-11. Al-Queda was familiar with satellite video technology.

While the men loaded the heroin, the hatch below the truck slid back, exposing the tunnel. Two men reached up to remove the bolts from the access plate in the belly of the truck.

They would be too heavy to carry through the tunnel or on horseback. After removing three warheads from their lead containers, they replaced the access plate and slid the sand covered hatch back into place, closing the tunnel.

Admiral Michaels logged onto Lieutenant Holman's station as the truck entered the village. "Patch it through, Connie. Have they made any other stops?"

"Only to switch drivers, Admiral, it's been slow going, but they haven't unloaded anything since they left Mardan."

Connie and the Admiral watched as the men packed one hundred bags, twenty-five to the crate. After heroin worth twenty million dollars on the streets of New York was loaded, the truck pulled out of the village and continued south toward Quetta.

The sand covered the tunnel below the truck. By the time the truck reached the highway, three warheads were in a shallow cave on the other side of the canyon wall. The transfer went unnoticed.

"Leave one camera focused on the village in case we missed something, Connie, but don't lose the truck."

Admiral Michaels returned a few hours later. "Anything new, Connie?"

"No, Admiral, nothing has moved in the village for the last four hours. It looks like they loaded a heroin shipment, but nothing was off-loaded."

"OK, re-focus on Quetta, but keep the truck in view."

Antonio and Ayeza met Wahid's incoming flight at Kabul. He had packed eight assembled warheads into lead containers making them immune to detection by most radiation units. However, since they were no longer with the convoy, Wahid believed the nuclear assemblies may have been switched to assemblies without plutonium cores while in the warehouse in Mardan. Antonio thought the idea far-fetched, but it was possible Al-Queda was leaving a false trail and moving the warheads in a different direction.

Wahid explained that the warheads could be detonated three ways; one, by programming the computer on the outside of the assembly. The warheads could also be detonated by cutting the leads from the keypad to the detonator. It did not matter which lead was cut, the normally closed switch would open if either of the leads were cut or the keypad itself were removed from the unit.

There was also a plunger installed in the warhead that is in place when the assembly is bolted together. The weight mass ratio of the warhead was calculated to set off the warhead if it were dropped from a height of two hundred feet or higher and the plunger entered the core, but any contact between the core and the plunger would create an electrical current that would set off the device.

The only way to disarm the warhead was to insert a probe to prevent the plunger from slipping into the core when the case was removed and then to disassemble the case and unbolt the core from its frame before the leads were cut.

If they recovered the warheads without an available probe the warheads would have to be shipped to the nuclear lab in New Mexico where the assembly could be stored until the government of Pakistan gave them a probe. Shipping an armed nuclear device to an American installation was an unacceptable risk.

The assemblies required special handling and equipment. If they recovered the warheads, they could not verify that they were the ones Wahid had assembled without opening the unit. If the core was in place, opening it without protective equipment would mean a lethal dose of radiation. The probe was equipped with a sensing unit that would identify the core and keep the plunger from contacting the core when the assembly was opened.

Someone would have to insert a probe through the inspection port, if and when the assemblies were found. The only probes available were in the Pakistan lab at Rawalpindi, or the storage facility in Mardan. Those at the lab were in the secure area of the facility.

It was assumed the codes had been changed since Wahid left. It would be impossible to enter the restricted area without them. Any attempt to navigate around the codes would cause the bank-like doors to lock down until someone reset them in the computers.

The probes in Mardan were carried in the trucks that transported the warheads to the missile base. They would be easy to access if someone could get on the base without being discovered.

The Pakistan government verified their inventory a second time when the American Ambassador met with the Pakistan Prime Minister that morning. Asking the Pakistan government to furnish a probe would be a redundant exercise and serve only to put the Al-Queda men at the storage facility in Mardan on notice. Once warned, they would secure the probes, and there were no other timely options.

Someone would have to break into the weapons storage at Mardan before the truck was intercepted at Turbat. That meant another trip into Pakistan for the Special Forces. It would be difficult to convince the brass in Washington, let alone the administration.

A successful assault by an American armed military force on the Mardan weapons facility would be impossible without engaging the Pakistan Air Force. Two Apache helicopters would not be a match for a squadron of F-16s, and the F-15s would be susceptible to the new missile batteries designed to defend Mardan against India's bombers at an altitude above ten thousand feet.

An early warning system had been installed along the border of Afghanistan near Mardan by the Americans during the Russian occupation. It would pick up the helicopters as soon as they entered Pakistan air space.

They would have thirty minutes at most. There would be resistance at the storage facility. There would not be time to drop a team, search the truck shop and return to Afghanistan before the Pakistan Air Force would intercept them.

Mardan was less than eighty miles from the border. They would have to cut the time and still enter Pakistan, breach the facility, find the probe and then call for the helicopters when they were ready to be picked up.

Antonio thought he knew a way to do that if the trade winds were favorable. It was a seventy mile flight from the Afghan border to the weapons storage. He and Ayeza would go in on the trade winds and if timed right, the helicopters could be in and out while the F-16s were still scrambling on the runway.

Antonio asked Eric to have the Navy access the weather satellite and patch it through to Kabul. The trade winds were favorable for a free-flight into Pakistan and to the weapons facility in Mardan from the border of Afghanistan.

Antonio glanced over at his new partner. He would go alone, but two had double the chances of leaving the facility with a probe. There was no choice but to take her along. "Are you up to a new experience, Ayeza?"

"What do you have in mind, Antonio?"

"We fly the trade winds from the Afghan border to Mardan. We find the probe and the helicopters come in to pick us off the rooftop. It's a walk in the park."

"It's over seventy miles. I understand your record is less than sixty."

"If we fly the trade winds it's closer to eighty, but it's doable. The winds above the Pakistan border are at thirty-three thousand feet; five thousand feet higher than those above Sudan when I flew fifty-five miles. Trust me, Ayeza."

When Antonio suggested he and Ayeza could make the flight, Colonel Rogers volunteered for the mission. Admiral Michaels and General Sampson approved it, even knowing that another incursion into Pakistan could result in an early retirement for all of them if they failed.

Wahid had been searching Ayeza's features while he described the probe they would be searching for.

Wahid was a scientist. When Eric turned to Ayeza and asked if she was up to a high altitude jump and a ride on the trade winds, Wahid questioned her involvement.

"When you came to my village you had dark eyes, now they are green. They are very rare, but I once knew a child with green eyes. You are older, but you look like that child."

"Things are not always as they seem, Wahid."

"That is true. Here you are dressed like a woman from our village. The last time you dressed as a woman, but changed to soldier's clothes, and then you killed a man. He was her husband. Are you my brother's daughter?"

"Yes, Wahid, you and Isma'il are my uncles. Were you there when he came and killed my family?"

"He said you sinned with many men, our laws are clear."

"He lied. Our family did not practice the old ways. He married me, but afterward he did not want me because he said I was unclean. His other wives beat me and threw me out, and then Faisal's brother and the Taliban raped me."

"Why have you come back? You no longer belong with us."

"To save the innocent ones in the villages we must find the weapons. If the crusaders use them against the Americans, they will come with their bombers looking for the Lion Sheik. Many in the villages will die."

"Only the Taliban are left in the villages and the Taliban are my enemies. The Americans can kill them all. I will go with you and help you because you saved my family."

"No, you must return to Egypt and your family. This is a job for two. We just need you to give us a map of the buildings and the codes, and tell us how to use the probes."

"You are a woman. It is a man's business. It is better I go instead of you. I know many of the men working at the facility."

"All the men you knew are gone. Besides, Antonio and I trained for this."

"Why do you do this, you have no business here? If they catch you, they will rape and torture you. Then they will kill you. You saved me and my brother and our families, now I will do this for you."

"We must jump from the altitude above where the big jets pass over. It will be very dangerous. You have never jumped, even close to the ground."

"You do not know how to use the probes, you could trigger the arming mechanism; you will need me."

"No, Wahid. You must return to Egypt and your family.

Antonio overheard the conversation. "He's right, Ayeza."

"He can't make that jump, Antonio."

"He can wait in Kabul. When we return, we will take him with us to search the truck."

There were rumors at the jump school in Germany of someone in the CIA who had intentionally bailed from a plane into a two hundred mile per hour jet stream above Sudan. He was on a mission into one of the Muslim training camps. According to the source, he traveled over fifty miles before dropping out of the jet stream to the stratosphere where the air is warmer and the winds dissipate.

The instructors said it would be an impossible feat and that if someone were to try it, the impact of falling from the calm air above the jet stream into the stream itself, would be like bailing out of a plane into the cone of a tornado.

Hurricane Katrina's 150-mile per hour winds devastated the gulf coast, tearing buildings from their foundations and destroying the city of New Orleans. Jet streams circle the globe at speeds to 400 miles per hour.

Antonio briefed her as he helped her with the oxygen packs and the equipment they would need on the ground. Ayeza then watched Antonio as the plane climbed to forty thousand feet, five thousand feet above the jet stream that Antonio said would carry them from the border of Afghanistan to the city of Mardan.

He chose the floor instead of the seat, resting against the bulky pack strapped to his back. It was a short flight, thirty minutes or less. It appeared he was dozing, his eyes half closed.

Ayeza leaned back against the hard bench seat of the C-17 reflecting on the past 36 hours. Watching Antonio and reflecting on her feelings, she found it difficult to believe that she had met the man less than two days earlier.

It started on the Lear shortly after they left Madrid. Antonio took the clothes from the steward and left for the bathroom to shower and shave. True to his word, he returned to the main cabin ten minutes later, refreshed. He smelled of Old Spice he had found in the shaving kit the steward had given him. He carried a tray of coffee and croissants.

After the call from Admiral Michaels, Eric stretched out on a lounge, his head turned toward the outer hull. He fell asleep quickly, a pillow muffling his snores. The flight to Kabul would take six hours. When Eric pulled the blanket over his head the flight crew retired for the night and fell asleep in their seats. Antonio moved to the rear of the cabin and refilled their cups.

As the Lear passed over the lights of the yachts and ships crossing the Mediterranean below them, Ayeza took the coffee and one of the croissants Antonio offered. He turned to sit across from her, and then turned for a moment to gaze at the lights dotting the sea below them. Without looking up he surprised Ayeza with his statement. "You are a long way from home, Ayeza, and your clothes are out of place."

Caught off guard, Ayeza stammered. "Why..... is that, Antonio?"

"Your earring matches your eyes."

Ayeza reached sheepishly, felt the earring and began to remove it. Antonio looked up, grinning. "Leave it be for now. Go in back and remove that ridiculous scarf and some of that padding; it does not suit you."

Ayeza slipped the scarf off her head, shaking it loose, letting her silky hair fall around her shoulders. Antonio smiled as he watched the brilliant emerald earrings dance, reflecting off the cabin light.

"Am I that obvious?"

"I don't know what you are, but I would remove those earrings before we land in Kabul. We aren't going to Paris; there are some who would cut off your ears to take them from you."

A woman knows when a man is attracted, but the stirring in her own body surprised her. When Antonio settled back sipping his coffee, Ayeza, smiling, turned to watch the lights of the ships below, and to avoid the stare of the man across from her undressing her gently in his mind. She did not want him to know that she was enjoying the attention.

Reflecting on their first meeting, and drawn to a man she hardly knew, she fidgeted, readjusting her harness. It was bulky and cumbersome compared to the moon suit she had used in her high altitude jumps back in Germany. However, that was for fun and to prove she was as good as the men training with her.

In the daylight it would be dangerous. It could be a nightmare to attempt a blind jump in the dark. The GPS strapped to their wrists were their lifeline to their destination. He said they would travel almost forty miles while in freefall, and then another thirty when they deployed the sail.

He was awake. Antonio preferred a moon suit over an oxygen mask and thick layers of clothing for jumps from high altitudes, but time was the determining factor, there were none available.

"Leave it be, Ayeza. It's uncomfortable, but it needs to be loose so you can shed it after we deploy the sail."

The winds were from the north. The C-17 turned in a bank at a height of forty-five thousand feet. They would brush, but not enter Pakistan airspace. The C-17 slipped down just above the jet steam and the pilot throttled back until the plane was pacing the wind.

The plane depressurized. Antonio waited until the pilot slipped the plane into the jet stream before opening the hatch. It was a moonless night, but the sky was full of stars. The constellations were the same as those above her village.

Ayeza thought back to her childhood and the circumstances that changed her life. She let herself lean toward the weight of Antonio's body bracing them against the wind from the open hatch.

He took her hand, turning to reassure her and then attached the line from his wrist to hers. Their thermal clothing covered all but their face masks which doubled for a screen. He typed the message on the keypad on his wrist. *It is a piece of cake, Ayeza, drop with me and pretend you're a bird.*

The plane banked to the left just before they reached Pakistan air space; Antonio and Ayeza dropped from the hatch as the pilot accelerated the plane and began his descent. As the plane accelerated and then dropped below the stream, the couple disappeared toward the city of Mardan.

The GPS homed in on their target, signaling it was time to end the freefall, deploy the chute and catch a thermal. Strapped together at the wrist and controlling the angle of their descent, the jet stream had carried Antonio and Ayeza fifty miles before they exited into the stratosphere.

They dropped to a height of fourteen thousand feet before Antonio tugged at the nylon cord. More a sail than a parachute, it was designed to carry two, plus their equipment.

As they settled into the glide path, they hung the packs containing the equipment they would need on the ground from their ankles. It was time to discard the outer garments that had prevented them from freezing in the minus 70-degree temperatures of the high altitude.

Part of the debris would fall to uninhabited wastelands in the mountains before they reached the villages on the outskirts of the city. The rest would stay with the sail until it landed on the other side of Mardan.

After lightening the loads and resettling their packs, they rode the thermal, maintaining their altitude until they were ten miles from the waypoint.

Antonio cut the strap between their wrists. They would be on their own when they deployed their individual parachutes. With the oxygen tanks as ballast, the sail would fly on for another twenty or thirty miles past the city where it would drop into the desert. If it was spotted on radar, or found before daylight, the Pakistan military would waste their time searching a barren area.

"When we are five miles out, cut loose from the canopy and deploy your chute. Ladies choice, you want to lead or follow?"

Ayeza was cold, but exhilarated by their flight and smiled at the barb. "I think we should go in side by side. If we are spotted, I don't want to have to shoot through you; or you through me."

Antonio and Ayeza dropped onto the roof of the warehouse before dawn. There was not room for a helicopter to land on the roof, and it would be suicide for the pilots to try to pick them up on the ground. The helicopters would have to pluck them from the rooftop in flight. They finished setting the arches with the hooks attached to the bungee cords between the air-handling units on the roof. From a distance, it looked like part of the assembly.

As the sun began to rise, Antonio crawled below the overhang of the parapet where the air-handling units butted against the wall. There was room for two, but barely. He motioned to Ayeza to settle in beside him "Take a nap, Ayeza; we have six hours before the noon call to prayer."

Antonio was snoring softly in minutes. Back to back, but pressed tightly together, Ayeza lay awake for hours, her body stirring. It was a first for her. The last time she had been this close to a man was on her wedding night with Faisal. She had been humiliated and when he was through, he had beaten her because he said she was unclean.

Because of her experience, Ayeza's asexual nature developed and she had shied from physical contact with men. As a defense, she had developed her skills and she knew she could take care of herself. However, her instinct told her this stranger, like the soldiers in the village who saved her life, would protect her with his life.

Ayeza was not sure what she was feeling, but she fell asleep thinking, *the rumors were true, but who was this man she seemed drawn to, sleeping next to her. They had just done what the experts thought impossible and would soon face a life threatening challenge. The mission was incredibly dangerous, but he slept peacefully, acting as if it was a Sunday stroll in Central Park.*

He stirred first, feeling the body of the woman next to him through his thin cotton shirt. Ayeza had turned in her sleep.

Ayeza woke when he moved, startled when she realized her arm was around Antonio and her cheek was resting on his back. She started to turn away, but he held her arm, looking at her watch. "Don't move; we have fifteen minutes until the call to prayer."

"I'm sorry, I turned in my sleep."

"That's OK, I don't feel a thing."

She laughed quietly and started to withdraw. "Nice try, Antonio, but the armor is in your pack."

She tried to move her arm but he held her firmly in place. "Stay where you are until it's time. There are offices in the taller buildings with windows facing this roof."

Antonio relaxed his hold, letting her settle back. She started to pull away, but then surprised him when she spooned in closer letting her arm rest against his chest.

Kabul

Pakistan radar would pick up the helicopters in Afghan airspace, but would lose them when they dropped below the radar and entered the canyons. Flights along the border were routine and they would be ignored.

However, Pakistan radar would pick up the helicopters the moment they crossed the canyon rim. The Pakistan F-16s would be in the air a few minutes later but could not follow the helicopters through the canyons.

The Pakistan Air Force would come in from the north and have to cross into Afghan air space to reach the mouth of the canyon where the helicopters would exit Pakistan.

General Sampson had readied a squadron of F-15s to fly cover for the helicopters. He intended to turn the Pakistan Air Force back before they engaged. "Your bird is on the runway, General. Colonel Rogers and Captain Pitt are in the briefing room with the other pilots. The couple will be leaving the roof in thirty minutes, ten minutes to take off."

"Thank you, Lieutenant."

General Sampson walked to the podium; the map of Pakistan and the plan of the Mardan facility were on the screen.

"Colonel Rogers, Captain Pitt will fly cover; you will pick up the couple. They will set a bungee connection on the roof of the warehouse."

General Sampson moved to the map. "The Pakistan helicopters are no match for the Apaches. They won't send them up against you, but in turn, you are no match for the F-16s."

"What about the missile batteries?"

"They are designed for high altitude bombers, Captain. If you stay on the deck you will be by them before they can leave their launch bunks."

"Where will the F-15s be, General?"

"On the border, Colonel. We will come in if we have to, but we do not want a confrontation with the Pakistan Air Force in Pakistan air space. Fly the canyons. It's longer, but you can go in below their radar. However, you will have to cross the canyon rim twenty miles from Mardan. When you do, their radar will pick you up and they will scramble the F-16s. You should have twenty minutes before they are on you. By that time you need to have the couple on board and be back in the canyons where the F-16s can't follow."

"General, it's only a one hundred mile flight to the weapons facility from the F-16 base. That's less than ten minutes for an F-16. If they are in the air, they will cut us off between Mardan and the storage facility before we can reach the canyons, and I doubt they will buy it's a UN rescue this time."

"It's Friday, Colonel. The couple will wait on the roof of the warehouse until they hear the noon call to prayer. It is a Muslim religious requirement for all the men to go to the mosque at noon on Fridays to pray. The guards at the storage facility will be either in the mosque or on the square in front of it, facing east for thirty minutes. So will the pilots at the air base and those watching cameras and radar screens.

When the sirens go off it will take the pilots fifteen minutes to gear up and get in the air. It is why the Jews keep kicking their ass; they take time out in the middle of a fight to pray."

"If they are late, The F-16 pilots could decide to come around and meet us when we exit the canyon. Once we clear the border, we will be in open country and sitting ducks. What's the back-up?"

"When you exit the canyon you will be back in Afghan airspace. If the F-16s are out of range, the F-15 squadron will be loafing along the border. However, if at any time it looks like they will intercept you we'll come in.

If you make it out of the canyon and they don't follow you, we turn back with you; otherwise, we will intercept them."

"Based on the recent rhetoric from Islamabad, that is a declaration of war, General. What does the White House say?"

"The State Department says you have to make it to Afghan airspace before we can intervene. Then it's the Pakistan pilots violating Afghan's borders. However, although the President's standing orders are to respect Pakistan's sovereignty, both he and the Congressional Committee are waffling now that we have the warhead core for proof.

The American Ambassador has asked the Pakistan Prime Minister to assist us. Admiral Michaels says the Pakistan government refuses, so the Joint Chiefs at the Pentagon are taking a stand; better a mess here than losing a city or two back home. My new orders are to get the probe and then find the warheads. It is not my place to question them."

"It sounds like the military loses either way, General. If we find the warheads, the President and Congress are heroes for sending us in. If there are no warheads and we engage the Pakistan Air Force, it will give them the excuse to bring us all home to face court-martial proceedings."

"It's worse than that, Colonel. If we do not find the warheads and one gets through to American soil, we are the scapegoats for losing them. If we don't find them, this could be the end of the American military as we know it."

The men were leaving the buildings carrying their prayer rugs a few minutes after the call to prayer resonated from the mosque. The outer perimeter of the weapon's facility was secure. There was no reason for the guards to expect intruders. The buildings would all be vacant for thirty minutes.

Antonio knew what failure meant. At best, he would be tortured then killed. They had talked about it. Ayeza had been through it once, and the rape and stones were fresh in her mind. She would take the easy way. He cracked the seal, blending the mixture, and then placed the cyanide capsule between his teeth and lower lip. He then offered one to her. They would disintegrate in thirty minutes. "We have twenty-nine minutes, it's time. Keep it between your lower lip and your teeth; you aren't apt to bite down on it that way."

On her first mission, Ayeza was up against men climbing a canyon wall from a distance of five hundred yards away, and then a sudden confrontation with a man she hated. She did not have time to anticipate the confrontation. Her adrenalin kicked in and she dealt with Faisal methodically, but it was routine.

"This is not like the classes, Antonio, and nothing like the villages. I almost froze last night and it's still difficult to breathe."

Their lives depended on the actions of the other. Reassuring her, Antonio checked Ayeza's harness; it fit tight, and it was difficult to fasten the clasp on her vest over the form fitting body armor. He lingered longer than necessary, but she did not resist.

"That nun's habit on the plane, what was that all about?"

Soothed by his tone and confidence, her green eyes sparkled and her heart rate slowed. "I gave up men, but I'm beginning to think I was wrong."

He felt himself drawn to her, but this was not the time. "We must go. Put your glasses on; if they turn them on, the laser fences will glow. Remember, we can cross the green; the yellow will set off the alarms telling them where we are. Don't try to cross the red; the laser will cut through bone."

They left the roof, skirting the square in front of the mosque. Ayeza had memorized the map and the access codes. It was just a tool so there would be probes in the truck used to transport the weapons to the air base. Wahid said it would be in the truck shop, the least secure building at the facility.

Two men, too lazy to walk to the mosque had spread their prayer rugs at the entrance to the shop. The overhead door was open. The transport truck was facing out, backed to the loading ramp with the door open. "They are moving materials, they will be back soon. Take the one on the left."

Ayeza hesitated; then fired her silenced weapon as one man slumped to the ground after Antonio's bullet entered the back of his skull. Ayeza's bullet caught the second man in the throat as he turned, preventing the cry of alarm from escaping. It was almost too easy. She had expected to have to search the grounds. "Nice recovery, move them to the wall out of sight. I will get the probe from the truck."

Antonio strapped the probe to his leg and then pressed the button sending a signal to the satellite receiver. Colonel Rogers and Captain Pitt lifted off the canyon floor and turned south crossing into Pakistan airspace.

General Sampson had quit flying missions when he received his first star and left the Persian Gulf to take the position in Kabul. He missed the action. If it was going to be the end of his career, he would fly the missions during the search. He had enjoyed the flight to Quetta and the adrenalin rush when the F-16s arrived. He was flying the F-15 leading the squadron pacing the helicopters.

General Sampson and the squadron settled in a triangle pattern on the Afghan side of the border at three hundred knots. Colonel Rogers and Captain Pitt dropped into the canyon and crossed into Pakistan airspace as Antonio and Ayeza approached the warehouse after retrieving the probe.

The couple turned the corner toward the stairwell when the laser security fences came on line, cutting off the passageway to the stairway. Antonio moved to the corner of the building below the parapet. "Someone must have found the men at the truck shop, Ayeza."

"No one is coming, we would hear them."

"They don't know where we are. They will be waiting until we cross a fence and sound an alarm. Colonel Rogers will be here in a few minutes. We can't use the stairs; we will have to scale the building."

Armed men were scurrying from the mosque to the truck shop. Others were milling, waiting for the alarm to tell them where to direct their search. Antonio lifted his arm toward the building roof three stories above his head and released the CO_2 cartridge sending the grappling hook over the parapet.

Handing her his weapon, "Hold this and climb on, we're going for a ride."

They were halfway up when the imam in the minaret of the mosque spotted them ascending the wall. Ayeza, hanging off his neck, turned toward the shouts of men rushing toward them. The winch would lift two hundred pounds three stories in five seconds. Their combined weight of three-twenty doubled the time.

At ten rounds per second Ayeza emptied the thirty round clip of the M-16 as Antonio lifted her over the parapet. "Here is another clip, spray the courtyard, I'll ready the sling."

Ayeza emptied the clip and then moved toward Antonio as Colonel Rogers cleared the facility wall and spotted the couple on the roof.

"They need some backup, Captain, divert their attention, but avoid contact with the buildings; there are nuclear warheads inside. I'm going after the couple."

Captain Pitt made a pass spraying the walls of the mosque with chain gun fire, sending the men on the ground to cover. Antonio looked toward the approaching helicopter as he slipped the loop between their harness rings before attaching it to the bungee sling. "Face me and hang on."

When the hook from the winch on Colonel Roger's helicopter caught the sling, the bungees cushioned the hundred knots per hour lift off. The helicopter accelerated to two hundred knots by the time the couple settled in the sling. The winch man would wait to bring them aboard until they were clear of the ground fire and Colonel Rogers slowed the helicopter.

They were face to face, her arms around his neck as the winch drew them to the helicopter. Antonio looked at his watch. There was fifty seconds on the timer.

As the helicopter slowed, Antonio turned his head to the side while taking her face in his hands to get her attention. He opened his mouth and dislodged the capsule.

"Spit it out, Ayeza!"

She had forgotten it was there. Lodged between her lip and teeth it was beginning to dissolve, "Spit it out Ayeza!"

She opened her mouth running her tongue between her teeth and her lip dislodging the capsule. As it left her lips, the gel dissolved in the air leaving a trail of foam behind them.

Still holding her face in his hands, "You need to pay attention to the time young lady."

Her arms tightened around him as the memories of her life in the village and Faisal faded. "I know, but I was distracted."

Accepting the invitation, Antonio kissed her as the winch-man turned the switch. Lost in sensations she had never felt before, she clung to Antonio as the winch man brought them aboard.

Antonio cut the straps binding them together. It was an awkward moment as the winch man turned to close the door.

Ayeza fastened her harness as Antonio joined her, and then huddled on the bench dealing with her feelings as Colonel Rogers and Captain Pitt turned the helicopters toward Afghanistan.

Lieutenant Holman on the Tucson was monitoring the satellite above the Pakistan air base; the tower in Kabul was patched in. "General Sampson, the F-16s lifted off the runway and are turning toward Afghanistan. It looks like they will try to intercept the helicopters at the mouth of the canyon."

"Where are the helicopters?"

"I've lost them, General. They dropped below the radar and are off the satellite screen. They should emerge from the canyon in ten to twelve minutes."

"That's too long, Lieutenant. The Pakistan Air Force is only ten minutes out. We are going in. Contact the Pakistan air base and tell them we are on a rescue mission and to instruct their pilots to stand down or we will engage them."

Three F-16s broke off when the F-15s lit up their early warning screens, but the pilot of the lead F-16 ignored the Americans and banked toward the mouth of the canyon. General Sampson dropped out of formation to intercept him and watched as the F-16 pilot locked on and fired a missile as Colonel Rogers and Captain Pitt cleared the canyon entering Afghan air space.

Captain Pitt crossed the border when Colonel Rogers ducked back into the canyon where the F-16 could not follow and the missile buried itself above him in the canyon wall. The pilot made a turn pursuing Captain Pitt into Afghan airspace after firing the missile. Seconds later General Sampson's wing man locked on the F-16. When the lock showed on his screen, the Pakistani pilot turned for home.

General Sampson believed the pilot had enough. "Let him go, Captain."

General Sampson's wingman released the lock and turned toward Kabul, but the lone F-16 turned toward the canyon where Colonel Rogers was emerging. General Sampson banked to intercept him and before the F-16 could lock on the helicopter, General Sampson fired a missile.

CHAPTER 10

G eneral Sampson escorted the helicopters along the border and then turned for Kabul. Colonel Rogers and Captain Pitt continued with the couple and the Special Forces on toward the Pakistan border near Quetta.

"Lieutenant, see to it the squadron is refueled. No one is going anywhere until the couple returns."

"Will you be going back up, General?"

"Yes, send an e-mail to Admiral Michaels that the couple has the probe and is on the way to Quetta. Attach the pictures with a report that a Pakistani pilot crossed into Afghan air space with hostile intentions. Tell him we acted in self-defense. Once we are refueled we will be covering the mission into Quetta."

Washington

Ron and Eric arrived at Admiral Michaels's office as Colonel Rogers was approaching Pakistan airspace. The Florida governor arrived a few minutes later.

The governor came on board, joining with the military in the search before Symington requested the subpoenas. His threat of assigning the Florida National Guard to the search and his intervention with the Florida judicial system expedited an otherwise lengthy process with liberal judges who would have stalled the requests.

"Have they found the warheads, Admiral?"

"No, we have an operation in process now, but there are no guarantees. We can't wait for the results to come in. Until we find them we have to assume they are coming here and plan for it. We have information the target date is February and the destination is Florida. What happens in Florida in February, Governor?"

"February is the height of the season, Admiral. Everything: hotels, beaches, restaurants and roads are packed. The inter-coastal waterways and the Atlantic are both jammed with yachts of all sizes. There is less boat traffic on the gulf side, but there is just as much high season activity."

"We don't think the Gulf side is a target. Our sources have them arriving in Miami by way of the Bahamas. We can monitor the activity on the Gulf, but we should concentrate along the Atlantic seaboard."

"Admiral, I'm inclined to agree with Symington. I can't see the Saudi Sheiks building mansions and buying mega yachts just to destroy them."

"Ok, let's make that assumption and narrow it down. Our source says the delivery is scheduled for February. We have the scientist from Rawalpindi so Al-Queda knows we are aware they are en route. If we don't find them, they won't delay long once they get here. If they are bringing the warheads to Florida the target has to be close. What special events take place during February and March?"

"Two big ones in February; either would be a tempting target. The Super Bowl will be in Miami on the seventh of February. The stadium seats eighty thousand and there will be as many more in town just for the party."

"If the source is right, the first week of February would be too early."

"You said two events. What's the other, Governor?"

"It's the brass ring in Florida, Eric. The Daytona 500 on the fourteenth of February is the event of the season, and the sporting event of the year. On race day there will be over two hundred thousand at the track and another hundred thousand in town.

Daytona Beach is just five miles away. Every marina, RV Park and hotel within fifty miles of the track will be full. The VIP list would fill a phone book. Many of the rich and famous come by yacht and anchor off the beaches. It is a weeklong party and it would be almost impossible to isolate the right yacht if that is how they choose to transport it."

"Admiral, let's not discount the Super Bowl. Either would make a tempting target. Our source says there are four on the way. How about you, Ron, any thoughts on what the others are meant for?"

"Miami may just be the landing point, Eric. If they come by boat to the east coast, they have a choice of targets. Spring in DC will find Congress in session and spring break for millions of students.

If the weather is decent every airport will be packed, so will the hotels and resorts. It is one of the busiest tourist weeks in Washington. Disney World in Orlando will also be mobbed. If they arrive in February and I was Al-Queda setting the timeframe, the bomb would go off in the spring when the crowds are thickest."

"I think we can discount Washington, DC, gentlemen. If a nuclear weapon goes off in this country, even the liberal press will assume it is Muslim related. The Muslim leaders know that if we don't have leadership in Washington, the general populations will turn on the Muslim communities and slaughter them."

"What is the point, Eric? Congress and the new administration have already proven they will make an effort to bend the rules for the Muslim communities at the expense of the constitution, and the general public. If the Al-Queda leaders believe the country will turn on the American Muslim community after an attack, why set back the progress they have already made?"

"Al-Queda is at war with the other Muslim sects; they don't care what happens to those who don't embrace their views. Besides, the President has made it clear he wants to bring the military home, Governor.

Under this administration the Muslim communities in America are not at risk. If a terrorist attack is successful, he will blame America's past policies, not the Muslims. He has the votes in Congress to back him up. Their response to an attack on American soil will be to cut a deal with Al-Queda to leave America alone in exchange for us leaving the Middle East for good."

"Ok, for the time being let's take Washington off the table, Eric. Andros Island makes sense for a Muslim base and Miami could be the landing point. However, I don't see them planning four fronts. It would be easier for them, and it makes it more complicated for us, if they come at one target from numerous directions.

If they do make it to the estate on Andros with more than one weapon, they can transport them to the mainland on four yachts, four private planes or a combination. With a dozen secure properties in Miami they have many options, and if they do manage to land them within our borders, their friends in Washington will see to it our laws protect them from search. Now that they have the weapons, if they are patient and careful, it's going to be almost impossible to stop them."

"That may be right, Admiral, but patience is not Al-Queda's long suit. We believe Bin Laden is very sick. Before he dies he wants to free the Middle East from American imperialism and drive the Royal Family out of Saudi Arabia.

I think they will rush training the crusaders and the transportation process. If they do they will make a mistake, we just have to be observant enough to be there and take advantage of it."

"They have waited a long time for a nuclear device. Iran is still in the process of developing them, but they are being hindered by the European community. I can't see Al-Queda wasting this opportunity, Eric."

"This is just one front in the Muslim war of conversion, Admiral. It will not be their last chance, and with the *Apostate*, as they refer to him, in office for another three to seven years, the volunteers will continue to flock to the training camps. They have plenty of time."

"Eric, are you saying that the leaders don't care if we find them?"

"What I am saying, Governor, is that the *Apostate* is filling their ranks with new crusaders. They have the money, time, and the incentive. Whether or not we win or lose this round, we are in for a series of attempts."

"That doesn't make sense, Eric. He has included the Muslim community in his inauguration and has made overtures to Iran, Hamas and Hezbollah."

"Governor, this country must face reality. The American press has downplayed his roots and he has demonstrated his sympathies toward the Muslims. Nobody knows what the President really believes, but it doesn't matter. He's been elected and he can't be impeached because of his religious beliefs.

The point is that no matter what he believes, both the President and Congress have an attitude of appeasement toward the Muslims. The world is also addicted to Muslim oil. The *Apostate* and his cronies in Congress have made it clear that they will continue to refuse to allow us to develop our own energy resources.

Oil prices will go back up and the transfer of wealth will continue to flow to the oil producing countries in the Middle East. With that kind of money, even if we find these warheads and shut this operation down, the Muslim militants can buy more from Pakistan or North Korea."

"Maybe, but if we do crack this and trace it to Bin Laden we will have the excuse we need to ignore Pakistan's sovereignty and invade the tribal region in Pakistan to find him."

"Finding Bin Laden won't help, Governor. He is only a symbol to the movement and there are dozens waiting to take his place. It's been accelerating since the *Apostate* came on the scene. Volunteers to be martyrs have been flooding the camps in Somalia, Sudan and along the borders of Pakistan and Afghanistan.

The imams seem to know something we don't and are keeping quiet, or they might simply want to believe a Manchurian Candidate was successful in his bid for the Oval Office. Either way, now that he is the President, they are playing the *apostate* card. There are thousands willing to die and more arriving each day. They can choose a target and then wait for the opportunity. If they fail, North Korea and Pakistan will cooperate and they will send more. Very soon, Iran will be building bombs and joining in."

"You paint a pretty grim picture, Eric, but if we put the pressure on these people someone will crack. If we can just find one of the warheads, we can warn the public. The administration and Congress will have to take a new approach.

"Perhaps, Admiral, but it is not likely the crusaders will panic even if we come close, so they will be difficult to stop. If we do not find them before they arrive in the States, and if they send all four to the same target but choose different routes and different means of transportation, the odds are, one of them will get through."

"Congress and the press do not believe there is a real threat, neither do the general populations. Do you really believe they will start a nuclear war, Eric? We have thousands of warheads pointed in their direction from locations all over the globe. With the naval fleets in the Persian Gulf and the Arabian Sea, our missiles are only minutes from the major cities. It would mean the end of their civilization."

"Whose civilization, Governor? We need to open our eyes; we are not at war with a government. We are at war with a religion. Bin Laden's sole purpose for existence is to spread his brand of Islam.

If he succeeds with a nuclear strike in the U.S., after the *weapons of mass destruction* debacle of the Bush administration, this Congress won't act."

"He's right, Governor. Even the hawks would know that if we take out all of Pakistan just to get to Bin Laden, it will not put an end to it. There are a few hundred million more like him scattered to every country on earth.

Orders originate in Saudi Arabia and a riot flares in London. Ahmadinejad spews his hatred and the streets in Paris erupt into flames. It's like that throughout the Middle and Near East, and it is flaring up again in the caucuses of Russia and on the outskirts of China.

Who does the administration look too? No, Governor, this administration may point fingers, but the Muslims do not believe the *Apostate* and this Congress will declare war. Neither do I, they will stand in the halls of Congress and do what they do best, condemn America for the misery in the world."

"Governor, there is another side of this nightmare. The military and the administration are split and the balance of power could fracture. General Sampson's report came in this morning. Pakistan is beginning to make threats against American intrusions."

"What happened, Admiral?"

"We sent a Special Forces unit into Pakistan last week and another yesterday. There was an engagement with General Sampson in the air. He led the squadron of F-15s and shot down a Pakistani F-16 when they crossed into Afghanistan and tried to intercept our returning helicopters. There is a third mission in process as we speak."

"What is Sampson doing in the air, Admiral? He is supposed to be running the show over there. Who is giving the orders?"

"The Pentagon is bucking the administration on this, Governor. We know the warheads are in the hands of Al-Queda and on the way here. The oral orders from the Hill are to stay out of Pakistan, but the military and the CIA has voted; we're going in."

"It sounds like mutiny, Admiral. What about the officers in the field, are they playing along?"

"The military and the CIA are committed to finding the warheads, Governor. The CIA is ignoring oral orders from the State Department until someone puts them in writing. No one on the Hill is prepared to take the heat if they are wrong, so it's a stalemate.

The CIA has a team familiar with the country, and the military is providing transportation and cover. I dispatched an additional F-15 squadron from the Fifth Fleet Carrier Group in the Persian Gulf to the Kandahar airbase last night as back-up for General Sampson.

Right now they think they are a training mission, but I will order them into Pakistan if we find the warheads and we need additional cover for the helicopters to bring them out."

"Admiral, we will be the invaders if our planes engage the Pakistan Air Force; the President will instruct the Joint Chiefs to bring the Air Force home. Congress will make an example and instruct the military to court-martial both you and General Sampson."

"We have confirmed Al-Queda has at least one, and possibly four warheads, Ron. They are coming this way. We know the President, the Speaker of the House, and her senator friends hate the military and want it disbanded.

The consensus in the military is that if the terrorists succeed and set off a nuke, the President would blame our military involvement in the Middle East to convince Congress to cut a deal with the terrorists and bring the military home anyway.

There are even some who believe they would cheer a successful attack on American soil for the excuse to do that."

"Admiral, Congress is split along party lines, but there are still some on both sides who believe if we stand down after a nuclear attack on American soil, it will also be the end of NATO and our alliances in the Middle East."

"Governor, there are bills pending in the House to withdraw from NATO and close most of the military bases in this country. The President and the House Speaker's goals are to disband the troops and give the UN another fifty billion a year to become the peacekeepers in the world.

Their excuse is that we are spending over fifty billion a year on the Fifth Fleet in the Persian Gulf and that it would be a cost saving measure to let Europe take care of its own. If the house and senate vote the party line, they have enough votes."

"Admiral, you are talking about giving up without a fight and the end of our way of life."

"If they set off a nuke in this country, that's exactly what I'm predicting, Ron. That's why we in the military believe there are some on the Hill willing to sit back and let it happen."

"Who are *we*, Admiral?"

"The Joint Chiefs are in agreement, Eric."

"Are we talking a military rebellion, Admiral?"

"We are all hoping we make our point. We have the core. It's proof the nuclear facilities in Pakistan have been compromised, which is the only reason the administration and the State Department is not condemning the military publicly."

"That's not an answer, Admiral."

"I know, Eric, but our military leaders are not going to stand by and allow our enemies access to this country with a nuclear warhead in their hands. Our enemies can call him what they will and use him as an excuse if they so choose, but *apostate,* Muslim, or Christian, it makes no difference, we have told the administration we are prepared to act independently until we find all four warheads.

It did not sit well, but short of firing all the military brass and then explaining it to the American people, they had no other option."

"The military cannot act alone; that by itself would go against everything this country stands for, Admiral."

"The President's advisors have taken a unique approach, Governor. The theory is that it is a win for the President and Congress, no matter which way it plays. If we engage the Pakistan military without clearing it first with the Secretary of Defense and we come up empty, they can bring us home. If there are warheads and we find just one of them, they take the credit because we cannot go public that we acted on our own."

"What about the other three? How do they explain calling off the search?"

"They become the hero if we find just one, and since the militants still have three, they will try to convince the public that it is time to make a deal. Worst case, if we lose them and can't cut a deal with Al-Queda and one goes off, the President and Congress will blame past policies and the military for allowing them to get through. Then they will cut a deal."

"How do I fit in? I'm not military and I have very little influence left in Congress."

"You have influence in Florida, Governor, which is where the threat is supposed to land. Symington will not use the Task Force to help; at best, he will stall. We want you to use the power your constituents gave you and bring the Florida National Guard and the local police departments onboard."

CHAPTER 11

The day after the truck left the village the men carried the weapons through the tunnel connected to a cave leading to a trail over the mountain. After loading the warheads on packhorses, they set out for the village and the waiting plane, fifty miles away.

"You're late."

"The Lion Sheik said to bring two hundred kilos. We had one hundred in the village. We stopped at the village in the pass to load more."

"We must hurry; the plane is ready and the fishermen are waiting."

The men packed the heroin around the warheads in waterproof containers. The beacons attached to the outer shell had a range of five miles.

Miles away on the border near Quetta Colonel Rogers took the long way in, flying the canyons below the radar before dawn. He dropped Ayeza, Antonio and Wahid on the outskirts of Quetta where they would buy a truck to intercept the produce truck thought to be carrying the warheads. He then returned to the staging area on the Afghan side of the border where Captain Pitt was waiting for a message from Lieutenant Holman. She would send it when the truck left Quetta, which was five miles from the fork in the road leading into the canyon where Wahid and Ayeza were waiting.

The jet carrying the three warheads left the runway three hundred miles away a few minutes before Lieutenant Holman sent the message to Captain Pitt confirming the truck left Quetta. Colonel Rogers and Captain Pitt lifted off on a direct course to where Antonio was waiting to intercept the truck.

General Sampson and his squadron were flying cover. When Colonel Rogers crossed into Pakistan air space, they dropped to twelve thousand feet, coasting in a triangular pattern along the Pakistan border.

Antonio was blocking the narrow road into the village with a truck he purchased in the village. Hijackings were common events in the lawless tribal regions and although the driver and his passenger were armed, they preferred to avoid a skirmish. The driver turned into the canyon straddling the trail bypassing the village to avoid the obvious trap in the road.

Wahid and Ayeza waited in the side canyon as Colonel Rogers moved in, dropping Sergeant Anderson and his men to plant explosives and block the trail from the north. Captain Pitt would close it from the south.

As the truck passed the village, Sergeant Anderson set off the charges just as Captain Pitt fired the rockets into the hillside starting the avalanche.

Ayeza and Wahid moved to the cover of rocks as Colonel Rogers made a pass strafing the ground in front of the truck.

Colonel Nichols and his squadron were from the carrier group in the Persian Gulf and believed they were on a Naval Air Force training mission. General Sampson called Colonel Nichols that morning and instructed him to meet him in the no fly zone along the Pakistan border. A confused Colonel Nichols and his squadron of F-15's were cruising along the border when Colonel Nichols picked up General Sampson and his squadron on his radar five thousand feet below him.

"General, we have lift-off from the Pakistan air base."

"How many, Lieutenant?"

"Six F-16s and four helicopters, but another six F-16s are approaching the runway. That's better than two to one, General."

"Contact Colonel Rogers, tell him he has fifteen minutes. Colonel Nichols and his squadron are above me. They will even up the odds, but contact the Pakistan Air Force. Tell them we don't want a fight, but we do want the contents in that truck, and that none of us will be leaving without it. I'll move to the other channel to contact Colonel Nichols and tell him to join us."

Ayeza was to keep Wahid and the probe out of the fray, but Wahid took it as a personal affront that a woman would need to protect him.

Antonio approached the truck as Wahid stepped out from behind the rocks with a rifle in his hands. Ayeza was off to his side trying to convince him to return to the cover of the rocks when the passenger in the truck sprayed the area with machine gun fire. Ayeza's body armor took four hits and saved them both when she tackled Wahid as the men in the truck opened fire, but a fifth bullet hit her helmet with enough force to knock her down and out.

Sergeant Anderson caught up with Antonio and took the driver out. He had left the truck and was approaching Wahid who was dragging Ayeza behind the rocks. Antonio fired through the cab, taking out the passenger.

Wahid joined Sergeant Anderson at the truck. When Ayeza did not get up, Antonio rushed to her and turned her on her back. Her eyes were closed, but she was breathing.

When available, armor piercing ammunition had become common issue for the Muslim militants. Remembering the night Aletha died, he stripped her body armor and then her clothes off of her, checking for a wound. There was no blood. He pulled off her helmet; her eyes opened, but they were glazed.

Dazed and confused she tried to sit. The course sand and sharp rocks scratching her body made her realize most of her clothes had been removed.

Stripped to her bra, Ayeza was attempting to cover herself. "What happened?"

"I told you I was bad luck. You took some hits, you have some nasty bruises, but the armor held."

"That's an excuse for taking off my clothes? Where are Wahid and the others? I can't be seen like this."

"He and Sergeant Anderson are inspecting the package. Here, I'll help."

"You've done enough. I can dress myself, now turn around."

Ayeza was covering herself, "You said package, just one?"

"There are four crates but only one assembly. Wahid is checking to see if there is a core in the warhead."

Colonel Nicholas took up a position off of General Sampson's wing man as the Pakistan Air Force lit up his early warning screen.

"Colonel Rogers, you are running out of time!"

"General, there is only one warhead. They searched the truck; there is a false bottom with a hinged access door. They must have moved the other three."

"The Pakistan Air Force is on the way, Colonel. Have you confirmed the package you have is hot?"

"Wahid says it is one of the warheads he assembled and the core is intact."

"Take it to Kabul, Colonel."

"There is lots of chatter on the air, General. Ayeza says the Pakistan Air Force has orders to engage us and recover the package even if they have to follow us into Afghanistan."

"Come straight across the border, Colonel. We will neutralize the threat."

When Colonel Nichols joined with General Sampson's squadron twelve F-15s fanned out across the sky on a heading to intercept the Pakistan Air Force.

General Sampson was familiar with the American equipment installed during the Afghan / Russian war to keep the Russian planes and helicopters from dragging Pakistan into the war. Pakistan's surface to air missiles along the border area with Afghanistan were outdated and posed no threat to the F-15s, but the helicopters would be at risk.

The Kabul tower relayed the waypoints as General Sampson turned east to meet the Pakistan Air Force. "Colonel Nichols, take your wing man to the deck and take the missile batteries out. We'll deal with the Pakistan Air Force."

Colonel Nichols had arrived from the Persian Gulf, but he was the ranking officer in Kandahar. General Sampson and Admiral Michaels had hoped to contain the threat and deal with it from Kabul without dragging him in.

"General, my orders have been to stay out of Pakistan air space, and those orders came from Washington."

"Times have changed, Colonel. Colonel Rogers has a Pakistan nuclear warhead onboard. We have proof it was destined for the U.S. mainland. There are three others in transit. We do not know how high it goes in the Pakistan government, but we know the head of their Nuclear Regulatory agency was involved."

"General, if it is not the Secretary of Defense, who is running this show?"

They were sixty seconds from engaging the Pakistan Air Force when a battery of surface to air missiles left the deck, lighting up their early warning systems.

"Under the circumstances, I'll take the responsibility, Colonel. Hit the deck and take the missiles out; that's an order."

A ground attack by a squadron of F-15s is awesome to watch if you are the one attacking. It is mind numbing if you are on the receiving end. Colonel Nichols made two passes and then General Sampson turned toward Pakistan air space to meet the F-16s head on. In the face of overwhelming odds, the Pakistan pilots returned to base.

General Sampson pressed the button contacting the tower in Kandahar. "This is General Sampson; find me someone who speaks Arabic."

"This is Lieutenant Myers, sir. I speak Arabic." "Contact the Pakistan air base and tell them we will escort their planes back to their border as far as Kabul and then patch me through to Admiral Michaels at the Pentagon."

The search for the other three continued as preparations were made in Kabul to ship the Warhead to Holloman Air Force Base in New Mexico.

With the redistribution of wealth from the west to the oil producing countries in the Middle East, the skies leading into and out of the area have become cluttered with private jet traffic.

After two mid-air collisions and more than a dozen close calls, a tracking network of the private traffic had been established to determine the safest altitudes and flight paths for the commercial traffic.

Legitimate private companies had been encouraged to participate and to use the international airports. Only some logged into the system. Those involved in the lucrative business of smuggling arms, child slaves and heroin avoid the international airports, choosing remote runways and less travelled flight paths.

Lieutenant Connie Holman had been tracking the flights crossing out of Pakistan over the Gulf of Arabia based on flight plans logged into the worldwide network.

"Captain, I have an unscheduled contact. It's a private jet at eighteen thousand feet coming off the southern tip of Iran."

"Track it, Lieutenant, and then find out what is on the water below it. I'll let the Admiral know."

Connie activated the GPS tracking that would plot the plane's flight, and then pinpointed the boats in the water along its flight path.

Two hours after the plane crossed the southern tip of Iran the copilot activated the beacon and dropped the first package.

The captain turned the trawler south toward the Gulf of Aden and set the net to skim just below the surface. The plane turned toward India where two other trawlers were near the Blue Coral following the school of tuna.

The third package settled more quickly into the waves than the other two had done. Wahid assembled the warheads by himself without the oversight of an assistant. He neglected to torque the screws on the third assembly and those connecting the outer case were loose. The men in the village had rushed packaging the heroin around the warhead and the container had been loosely packed.

The impact was not sufficient to set the warhead off, but it split the crate and cracked the seal of the assembly when the crate hit the water.

The warheads all seeped low levels of radiation, but with the crack in the seal, the radiation from the third warhead would leave a trail on anything it came in contact with.

After collecting their cargo, the three trawlers merged behind the Blue Coral to reset their nets. The diving chamber resembling a miniature submarine left from the access port on the bottom of the mother ship as the fishing boats approached. As they fanned out encircling the school, the captains released the tag lines and the three packages settled to the bottom of the Gulf.

Following the beacon signal to the targets, the submarine collected the packages and then turned to catch up with the Blue Coral.

If the American satellites were watching, it would appear a routine flight for the smugglers dealing in military hardware and heroin. It was a common exercise. It would not garner attention from the American naval force when they approach the Gulf of Aden.

"Admiral, General Sampson is on line three."
"Patch it through to my office, Lieutenant."

"Good morning, Admiral. We recovered one warhead. There were three additional crates containing the lead boxes the others were packed in, but if they actually had all four, we lost three."
"What were the readings, General?"
"There is a low level of radiation on the crates. Wahid says the readings confirm the warheads were in the truck. He also says that now that they are out of the lead cases, the warheads will leave traces of radiation on everything they touch. It will take a sensitive meter, but it could be a break for us. He thinks the New Mexico lab will have meters that will read it."

"The plane coming to pick up the warhead will have the equipment. They left New Mexico when you recovered the probe, but they will need the plans to dismantle it."

"Wahid can dismantle this one when the plane arrives, but he may not be around if we find the others and they are scattered. I contacted the Pakistan government and have asked for plans, but they are denying the warhead is theirs. No one wants to assume responsibility for losing the weapons and if they give us plans that match them, there will be no way they can deny they came from Rawalpindi.

Wahid has volunteered to remain on the team until we find all four. He says it's too dangerous to transport the warheads now that they have been tampered with. He assembled them. He's the only one who knows the sequence to dismantle them without activating the detonators, but he needs protective shields."

"The plane will arrive in Kabul tonight. We will notify them that Wahid will join them on the plane."

It was a rhetorical question. "Where could we have lost the other three, General?"

"They pulled a switch after they left Mardan, Admiral. The truck has a false bed, and Wahid says the crates confirm they had them on the truck. They dropped them somewhere on the way. We need to close the ports at Karachi and Gwadar until we find the others."

"That would involve the Fifth Fleet in the Persian Gulf and would be an act of war against Pakistan. It's a State Department move, General. I can't authorize it from here."

"There isn't time to go upstairs. We blockade the ports or we lose the warheads."

"Then we need to leapfrog to Jeddah, General. When the couple returns, send them to Saudi Arabia."

Admiral Michaels returned to his office and patched through to Connie Holman. "Connie, what did we miss?"

"I don't know, Admiral, the truck has been on the move and in the open. If they didn't pull the switch at Mardan, the only place they had the opportunity was at the village near Thal. If there is a false bottom and a hatch on the truck they could have been parked over a hole and hid them there, but that's farfetched and besides, that was three days ago."

"That unscheduled flight coming out of Iran, where did it go?"

"It flew an odd pattern, Admiral, but they landed in Marka, Somalia. It looks like a drug drop over the water."

"Did you map the boats on their flight path?"

"Yes, the boats were a fleet of trawlers working with the Blue Coral, a French research ship following a school of tuna. Pardon the pun, Admiral, but I think something is fishy so I am still tracking them. The trawlers and the Blue Coral are now spread out. The trawlers are in the Red Sea. The Blue Coral is approaching the coast of Somalia."

Admiral Michaels had learned to take the instincts of dedicated personnel seriously. Connie was a career officer who served under his command before he left the Persian Gulf. They were friends. "What's fishy, Connie?"

"I told you my father was ex-Navy. After he left the service he bought a drag boat and fished off the coast of Oregon. I used to fish with him when I was a kid and nothing the trawlers did makes sense to me.

They moved off course and they each set their nets and made a pass after the plane flew over. Twenty minutes later they moved in on the Blue Coral and reset their nets. Five minutes later the Blue Coral dropped out of the pattern and turned south."

"Maybe the school sounded."

"No, Admiral, I could still make out the shadow of the school on the surface fifteen minutes later. I checked on the last port of call for the Blue Coral. Its last port was Gwadar, Pakistan. I ran it by my captain. He thinks it was a drug drop. Maybe the French dropped the merchandise and the trawlers collected it in their nets, but we have no jurisdiction, we can only deal with direct threats."

"Assuming it is drugs, Connie, how does that tie to the plane?"

"It doesn't, but the plane flew out of its way to pass over the trawlers and shortly afterwards the three trawlers turned south toward the Red Sea. My captain also thinks the plane may have made a drop."

"If the fish holds are full they would head for the processors or go back to their ports."

"Yes, Admiral, I thought of that, but there are no processing ships in the Red Sea. I checked, they are catching a few fish there, but the big schools are in the Arabian Sea, south to the Indian Ocean following the sardine migration. The processors and the rest of the fleet are all off the coast of India. I also took a look at the trawlers' water lines, Admiral. I think the trawlers were empty."

"What else have you got that's unusual, Connie?"

"There is a mega-yacht lying off the coast of Yemen with the name, Crescent Tide. Since the Crescent is the Muslim insignia, I've been keeping tabs on it. The film shows it arriving yesterday at a speed of thirty knots, but now it's moving at an idle. It seems to me the captain is waiting for someone, or something to arrive."

"Connie, continue to track the trawlers and the Crescent Tide, I'll follow up on the Blue Coral."

"Admiral, wait, this is going to really sound off the wall, but this fisherman's daughter is having a real problem."

"We are all in the dark, Connie. If you have a hunch, put it on the table."

"Like I said, Admiral, this is bizarre, but I went back to the tapes. The three trawlers put their nets out as the plane approached and then hauled them back aboard shortly after the plane passed over. Then all three turned to join the French ship and made it look like they were fishing. We are looking for three packages, what if the plane dropped the packages and the trawlers scooped them up in their nets?"

"Connie, you said the plane came off the southern tip of Iran, not Pakistan."

"Admiral, the smugglers are pros; actually the plane came out of nowhere. I backed down on the trajectory of the vapor trail and plotted it back over Pakistan. I checked the other satellite tapes and it shows up at five thousand feet and climbing over Quetta. I think it left from a runway in the mountains of Pakistan near the city of Thal.

They know we have eyes in the sky. They could have detoured through Iranian air space to throw us off. They flew an odd pattern over the trawlers. They could have dropped the warheads, the trawlers could have picked them up and the trawlers rejoining the Blue Coral may have been a ploy to make it all look legit."

"You may have put it together. Keep tracking and keep this connection open. If the trawlers dock in Yemen or Saudi Arabia, it will tie the plane, the boats and the destination together."

CHAPTER 12

The American surveillance ships in the Persian Gulf routinely monitored the Middle and Near East countries, the skies above them and the connecting waterways, but spying on Saudi Arabia and Pakistan had become a sensitive public relations issue.

The Anti Terrorist Task Force monitored the Pentagon's satellite links, and each time someone at the CIA or the Pentagon tuned in to the Navy link over the Persian Gulf or Pakistan, Jim Symington would notify the Congressional Foreign Relations Committee. Within hours, Admiral Michaels or Eric Ludlow would receive a call demanding an explanation.

Admiral Michaels was in contact with the surveillance ship by satellite phone from Eric's office. The phone was equipped with a scrambler that was reprogrammed daily.

"Hello, Connie, where are the trawlers?"

"The trawlers are all at anchor south of Jeddah, Admiral, but no one has left the boats and no one has boarded them. I think they are waiting for someone to come to them."

"Connie, I'm in Eric Ludlow's office. Eric runs the operations for the CIA in the Middle East. We are also in contact with Ron Edwards who follows the Muslim activity and drug trade out of Afghanistan and Pakistan in Europe.

We have been mulling your theory. However, the trawlers are traveling together so it does not make sense for them to split the shipment; if we found one we would find them all. Your captain is probably right. They are most likely carrying drugs that they will be delivering to India when they leave for their next tuna trip."

"Admiral, they are not together. They were traveling together, but they split up and are in different ports on the coast of Saudi Arabia. One dropped out in Dawdah, the second at Hamdenak and the third is at Al Lith. Hamdenak is three hundred miles south of Jeddah. The ports are isolated and twenty-five miles apart from each other."

"We can't join you on the link, Connie. How active are the ports?"

"There is a lot of oil drill casing stockpiled, but there are no people in sight except the guards at the gates and the men on the boats. They have the appearance of construction staging areas for the offshore wells, but they look more like forts than ports, Admiral. All three are walled on the land side and the rock jetties protecting the harbors are fenced and have anti-personnel nets strung across the entrances."

"Do we know who owns the ports?"

"We don't have access to those records, Admiral, and the only sign I can find on any of the properties is an old one in the scrap pile in the Port of Hamdenak. It's faded, but get this, it looks like it says Bin Laden Construction Group."

"Good work, Connie. That's enough to tie it to this operation. How many men are on the trawlers?"

"I think just two on each boat, Admiral,"

"How many are on the grounds in the ports?"

"Just the guards at the gate, Admiral."

"Keep someone at your desk, Connie. If anyone shows up or the crew leaves, contact me immediately."

Antonio and Ayeza boarded the C-17 in Kandahar. The flight was the weekly scheduled military flight to Cairo and it would be passing over the Red Sea.

Captain Stevens was a seasoned paratrooper in the Air Force before applying for pilot training. Antonio had flown with him a number of times before the Lisbon affair. The captain was used to sudden changes in flight plans when Antonio was on board.

When the captain was briefed on Antonio's mission, he was given the option of following the orders of Colonel Sampson, orders that might conflict with the standing orders from the Pentagon.

Captain Stevens joined the ranks of the military searching for the warheads. The crew took a vote. They would abort the trip to Cairo and return to Kabul after Antonio and Ayeza dropped from the plane. He would make himself and the C-17 available until the warheads were found.

Captain Steven's extended family was scattered along the eastern seaboard of the U.S. He had a personal interest as well as a military duty to find the warheads. If the warheads were on the trawlers he believed it was imperative he deliver the couple to Saudi Arabia safely.

Captain Stevens was aware of Antonio's specialty of free flight, but as an ex-paratrooper he was skeptical as to Antonio's ability to control a free flight in the path of three hundred knot trade winds.

Lieutenant Holman had been monitoring the weather satellite and relaying the updates. The winds had shifted and changed velocity.

The earth rotates on its axis at a speed of over one thousand miles per hour and travels through space on its course around the sun at sixty-seven thousand miles per hour.

The captain believed the winds too dangerous to predict, and that it was too great a risk under the circumstances. When the forecast came in as they approached the narrow entrance to the Gulf of Aden, he reset the autopilot and then woke the couple.

"We are an hour out, Antonio. We can't fly Saudi air space without clearance. Their missile batteries are programmed based on prerecorded flight plans. If I crowd the centerline and stay below thirty-five thousand, I can get you to within thirty miles of the beach.

There are some thermals at the lower elevations coming across from Sudan lifting off the Red Sea. If you open at twelve thousand you should make it. However, if you land short, turn on the beacon when you open the raft; the amphibian will pick you up."

"The amphibian is to pick us up after the mission, not to rescue us before we start, Captain. What is the jet stream forecast?"

"It's not good, Antonio, it's at thirty-eight thousand and out of the south above Yemen and Saudi Arabia. It was at three hundred twenty knots ten minutes ago but it's changing continuously and has been as high as four hundred ten in the last few hours. As I told you, we will be west of the target and well below it, so it's not a concern."

Antonio pulled out a map. "That won't work, Captain. Turn north across the southern tip of Yemen above the stream. Climb to sixty thousand; when you approach the Saudi border, drop into the stream. When you are ten miles from the Saudi border open the hatch, and then turn south before you enter Saudi Arabia's airspace."

"I told you the winds are at thirty eight thousand. That's too high, and at three hundred twenty knots, it is too dangerous to bail into. Besides, the Yemen / Saudi border is two hundred miles from your target."

"At three twenty, two hundred miles is less than forty minutes, Captain."

"I've heard the stories, Antonio. The winds were two hundred sixty and you flew less than sixty miles into Khartoum. These winds are over three hundred and we'll be two hundred miles out, and you weren't tied to a woman, nothing personal Ayeza, or to a man for that matter."

"There is no other choice, Captain. Do as I ask. You have a ceiling of sixty-five thousand feet which is out of range of the Yemen missiles. Climb to sixty thousand and then drop into the top side of the stream.

Keep it at ten to twenty knots faster than the wind. One knot slower than the wind will kill us. Avoid Saudi air space after the drop, but remember they have a treaty with Yemen. As soon as we drop out of the plane climb back to sixty thousand and turn south."

The captain depressurized the cabin after Antonio and Ayeza put on the moon suits, which had been delivered to Afghanistan after their first flight into Pakistan.

They stood by the hatch as the C-17 dropped toward the stream. They could communicate but needed to activate the mike.

"I know this is not the time, but I haven't been afraid for a long time, Antonio."

"There is nothing to fear. It will be just like the last time, only a little faster. You won't notice the difference. We will be traveling the same speed as the stream. It will be like setting a stick in a river and letting it float with the current."

As the hatch began to open, Antonio turned to check the strap tying their wrists together. Ayeza took a deep breath wishing she had said something earlier. In her mind, the relationship had progressed as rapidly as the jet stream was moving, but there had been little time for talk since they returned from Mardan.

European society was a world away from the mountain village where she was raised. Men had been hitting on her since she arrived in Germany, but Ayeza had fended off the advances by the men at the base and at the CIA school with the confidence of someone simply not interested.

Men don't like rejection and after a while they left her alone. Ayeza's attraction to Antonio confused her, but the feelings he stirred in her drew her closer to him.

When she woke on the trail in Pakistan with her clothes half removed and his hands searching her body she had mixed feelings. For an instant she felt violated and angry, but when she saw the concern in his eyes she realized he was trying to help her. When he realized she was alright he seemed embarrassed, not at all like the worldly man she thought she knew.

He turned away, but she realized there was dampness between her legs she had never felt before. His back was to her as she dressed. He did not see her blush when she realized that she wanted his hands caressing her body.

Later, when they had returned to Kabul, Antonio had been busy planning the operation, but he had gone out of his way to spend time with her. The kiss while escaping Mardan burned into her memory, but he had not pressed it afterward and she thought that it had simply been a reaction to the moment of their bodies pressed tightly together and the euphoria of a successful mission.

Bailing into the jet stream was dangerous even if he would not admit it. He was the first man she had felt attracted too and the only one she had ever had feelings for. She wanted him to know. As the hatch opened she turned to him.

"I need to tell you, I am not sure what it is because I have never felt it before, but I think I am falling in love with you. The captain is right, three twenty and two hundred is….."

Ayeza neglected to press the call button in her hand. Antonio did not hear her or see her lips move through dark glass of the helmet. He confused her by ignoring her, and then he casually pointed toward the hatch.

"Trust me, Ayeza. Now step back out of the hatch. The wind is pushing us, but the plane is only traveling twenty knots faster than the wind. Fall forward and enjoy the ride."

Taken aback by what she took as a rebuke, Ayeza stumbled and fell back instead of forward. Had she not been tied to Antonio's wrist, the erratic entry into the stream would have caused her to be tossed about like a leaf in a hurricane. As it was, she spun like a top until the strap connecting her to Antonio would turn no more.

It came close to breaking their wrists, but Antonio rolled to his back when the strap tightened on his wrist, stopping her spin. Ayeza had blacked out. He locked his arms around her and then rolled over, placing her below him.

Ayeza's body grew rigid as she woke. After pressing the send button in his palm, "Take a deep breath, relax, and then open your eyes. We need to cut the strap; it has shut the circulation off to both our wrists. I am going to release one arm and attach a tag line to your suit. We will still be attached, but you will have to fly alone until we can unravel and reconnect. Ayeza did not respond.

"Can you hear me? .... Ayeza, can you hear me?"

Realizing her mistake, she pressed the send in her palm. "Yes, Antonio, I can hear you. I'm sorry, I slipped coming out of the plane, and then I blacked out when I started spinning."

"No harm done, when I let go, turn over, put your legs together, keep your arms at your side, palms up and arch your back, just like a free fall in the lower elevations. We need to stabilize and reconnect before we start our descent."

"Where are we?"

"GPS says one-twenty out, but five miles off course. We have ten minutes to correct or we will overshoot the target."

Antonio attached the tag line then cut the strap. After he unraveled the line he pulled Ayeza closer. "Ok, it's time. I will reattach the tag line, but it's the safety net, hold my hand and keep your head down we're going in."

Calm settled over Ayeza as she realized Antonio was right. She remembered a seasonal winter stream by her village that cascaded in torrents down the canyon. The wind would blow the chaff from the poppy harvest into the water and it would float delicately on the water.

Turning on his side, Antonio had pulled her to him with the tag line. "We are twenty miles out, but we will be ten miles west of the target when we leave the stream. At twenty-five thousand feet shed the moon-suit and use the re-breather. It will still be cold as hell, but your wet suit will keep you from freezing. As soon as you are out of the moon-suit, I will cut the tag line. We'll drop slowly; I will deploy the sail at eighteen thousand.

Five miles from the waypoint, Antonio cut the sail loose. At ten thousand feet, they deployed their chutes. When they settled in their glide path, Antonio's altimeter read six thousand. He smiled when he realized Captain Stevens had been right. The warm air cooling as it skimmed the surface of the Red Sea was rising in thermals and would have carried them to their target, but then he and Ayeza would have missed the ride.

Killing was not an option. An intrusion into Saudi Arabia sovereignty by American military or the CIA would be hard enough to explain if they were caught and the trawlers were clean. Antonio and Ayeza carried weapons loaded with tranquilizer capsules that penetrated the skin and lodged in the muscle tissue. They would not kill, but they would paralyze a two hundred fifty pound man in seconds and then induce a coma lasting two to three days.

It was after two am. Lieutenant Holman had said that by one am, the guards would be asleep in the shack and the crew would be asleep on the deck of the trawler. They had four hours until dawn.

Ayeza was to take the guards at the gate and then drive their truck to the dock. Antonio had the radiation meter. He would immobilize the crew and locate the warhead if it was on the trawler. They would then drive the twenty-five miles along the deserted shoreline to the next port and repeat the drill.

Captain Gamal nosed the yacht from her berth at Jeddah. While in port, men mingling with the crowds, dressed in peasant garb and fresh from the Al-Queda training camp in Somalia had climbed the gangway and settled in their bunks.

As the port of Dawdah showed on Antonio's GPS, the Crescent Tide left Jeddah, turning south to avoid the prying Egyptian military inspectors at the Suez Canal and America's Mediterranean Fleet stationed off the coast of Israel. The yacht would take a leisurely voyage around South Africa's Cape of Good Hope before turning north toward the Canary Islands.

When the yacht reached the coast of South Yemen, Captain Gamal contacted the U.S. naval fleet patrolling the Gulf of Aden and requested an escort through the pirate infested waters off the coast of Somalia. It was a public relations move. The Crescent Tide was well armed and Al-Queda and McMood Fajal, the owner of the yacht, had sufficient resources and contacts in Somalia to assure the yacht's safe passage.

The Crescent Tide's final destination at Andros Island meant dealing with the British and American Coast Guards, and possibly their Navies when they arrived. The Lion Sheik believed a friendly history with the U.S. Navy and a few calls to friends in Washington would assure the yacht would pass without notice when it arrived.

Lieutenant Holman had been monitoring the mission from the surveillance ship in the Gulf of Arabia. The dye in their wet suits glowed for the camera. When Antonio and Ayeza left the first port without setting the flare to signal success, she contacted Admiral Michaels.

"It looks like you were right, Admiral. They came up empty. The couple is on their way to the second port."

"Keep the line open, Lieutenant."

Satellite calls are routinely monitored into and out of the Middle East. Lieutenant Holman would monitor the mission, but Antonio and Ayeza could only make one call when they were ready to be picked up.

Admiral Michaels had not cleared the mission into Saudi Arabia with the Congressional Committee. Oil money had infiltrated all the agencies including the CIA, and leaks were common. Their call would be picked up and scramblers could be decoded, but the mission would be over in a few hours. By then the couple would be out of harm's way.

Antonio signaled the amphibian waiting off the coast of Egypt before he boarded the third boat. Ayeza joined him a few minutes later. After a search, they launched the net boat from the deck of the trawler.

When they deployed the sail and discarded their moon suits the air temperature was twenty below zero. The full body wet suits had kept them from freezing until they reached the lower elevations. They became a burden in the ninety-five degree temperatures on the surface of Saudi Arabia, and a hindrance to Antonio as he dug through the fishing nets, ripe with decaying carcasses of trash fish, looking for the warheads.

Antonio stripped to the waist and discarded the top half of his suit after passing the jetty. He started to unzip the shoes and leg zippers.

Ayeza smiled, "Keep your pants on; I'll move up wind to the bow."

The amphibian came across the Red Sea skimming the waves, under the radar. Antonio and Ayeza were forty miles off the beach when they arrived.

There was little time for introductions. Antonio settled in the seat behind the copilot and reached for the satellite phone on the console.

"You two smell like you have been rolling in rotting fish. There is a shower down the hall; there are fresh clothes in the closet and food in the pantry overhead."

Ayeza moved toward the back of the plane but Antonio sat in the seat behind the pilot. "Thank you, Captain, but the call comes first."

Antonio hit the send button on the satellite phone that would connect him with Eric in Washington.

"We were concerned. The pilot said the winds were over three hundred. That was a lot of risk for a goose chase. How is Ayeza holding up?"

They had been together just five days. Two high altitude jumps and the mission to Quetta had left little time for socializing. They had slept on whatever surface was available and had changed into the wetsuits and moon suits just before the jump.

Antonio's reflex turn caught Ayeza stripping out of her wet suit. There was a shower on the plane, but little room to dress. Both the cabin and the shower door were open. She was a beautiful, slim, but full figured woman. She caught his glance, paused and held it for a moment before she smiled and turned to close the door.

He was aware of her history in the village and on the streets of Kabul. She was unlike anyone he had ever met. He was drawn to her, as she seemed to be to him, but she was living for the moment and facing her mortality at every turn. The kiss in the air and her clinging to him boarding the helicopter over Mardan was fresh in his mind, but the circumstances at the time had been in play.

It had been her first free flight, a narrow escape, her first planned kill and her first bungee pickup. It was a lot to deal with on their first mission together. Fear seemed too strong of a word for her, but he believed there were still some unresolved adolescent feelings.

Antonio had read her profile the night they arrived in Kabul. He had protested to Eric that he felt she lacked the experience for the first jump and the mission that would require her to kill without hesitation.

There was no other option. One might make it, but two doubled the chance of success. Ayeza was the only one available with a combination of martial arts training and high altitude jump experience besides Antonio.

When he reflected on the missions, Ayeza seemed more robot than human, yet she also appeared fragile at times.

Antonio had watched her through half closed eyes before the first jump, wondering if he should leave her behind. A mistake or panic in the jet stream would kill them both, and a hesitation in the field could mean the mission would fail.

She seemed nervous and was fidgeting with her harness, not a good sign. However, as the C-17 settled into its approach to the Pakistan border above the jet stream and it came time to check each other's packs and adjust their helmets, he sensed a calm settling on her.

She bailed from the plane without hesitation and when they settled into their free flight, she turned in the air like a bird on its back and he could see a smile on her face. The fear was gone and it had not resurfaced, but for an instant the night before.

Her comment before the last jump about her fear was out of place. She killed without remorse and was as physically capable as any man he had worked with, but there was another side of her struggling with her past.

He would give her the benefit of the doubt, but he was not sure if she had really slipped, or had actually hesitated when bailing from the plane. Whichever, it had almost cost them their lives. Had it been a man of equal weight he would have dragged Antonio into the spin, causing them both to black out.

There was a twenty-year age difference and he was her mentor. The partnership was one of teacher and student. Antonio was trying to hold her at arm's length. It was becoming difficult at times; she seemed to be inviting him.

He was startled some, but smiling at the reflection of Ayeza in the back of the plane, and the events of the past few days. It had taken his mind off Aletha for the first time since Lisbon. "Yes, Eric, I'm a little rusty, but she is the best I've worked with. It has been routine, but tell Captain Stevens he was right, we could have ridden the thermals."

"We know the warheads weren't onboard the trawlers; was there any sign of them?"

"The second one had higher readings, too high for an enclosed case, but there are traces of radiation on the nets and the back decks of all three boats. They did split the warheads up. There was one on each of the trawlers, but they are gone now."

"Antonio, this is Admiral Michaels. Lieutenant Holman is on the line with us. We have been monitoring the trawlers ever since the plane flew past. No one has come aboard and there hasn't been another boat within miles."

"Admiral, the nets are full of rotting carcasses and there is no sign of fresh fish on the boats. We found taglines with radiation on the purse end of the nets and the purses were open. We also found enough heroin in the cabins to keep all the junkies in New York high for a year. Somebody paid a big fee for the trip, but not to go fishing. I think Lieutenant Holman is right, but we have been chasing the wrong boats."

"The Blue Coral?"

"Yes, Admiral, the Blue Coral is a research ship; they might have transferred them to it."

"That's a straw in the haystack, Antonio. The Red Sea is crawling with divers from all over the world. If the trawlers scooped the warheads from the ocean, it's also possible they dropped them at a prearranged location near a remote reef when they entered the shallows at the entrance to the Red Sea."

"Admiral, this is Lieutenant Holman. I tracked the trawlers. They steered a centerline up the channel. They never came within five miles of another boat. The water is too deep for free divers and the area is infested with sharks."

"Connie, you have a theory, what is it?"

"Admiral, I'm with Antonio. Don't research ships carry submersibles? If no other boats approached the trawlers, and the crews never left the boats, that has to be the way they recovered the warheads and where they are now."

"Then why three trawlers? They could have done it with one."

"Antonio, this is Eric. They left us a false trail, but I think they expected us to come through channels. We were lucky it was Lieutenant Holman on duty. Someone with less experience would have missed it. If she had not traced the plane to Quetta, and then not come up with the trawler theory, it would have been days before we put it together.

By then there would have been a dozen trucks in and out of each port. We might eventually have traced the boats, but I think the only reason the crews were still on board was that they were waiting for the heroin pick up. Based on the amount of heroin you say was on board, the value of the boats is insignificant."

"I still don't see the purpose of three boats."

"I have a theory but we haven't time, Antonio. Admiral, where do we go from here?"

Admiral Michaels paused to reflect. Eric thought back to the recent events. He had learned to put himself in their shoes and to think like his enemies. The trawlers were in two thousand feet of water when the plane passed over. Dropping all three in one container was too great a risk; they could have lost them all, and scattered they might have missed one.

Three crates, three nets, three boats; it made sense if cost was not a factor. Besides, if the military satellites were tracking the plane, by the time the trawlers were traced to Saudi Arabia and arrangements to search them were made, the crews and the warheads would be gone.

Al-Queda breached security at the weapons lab. They knew the warheads would leave traces of radiation once they removed them from the lead containers. They would have found the trawlers, but by then they would have assumed the warheads landed in three different locations. The CIA and the military would be chasing their tails all over Saudi Arabia.

"Antonio, if the warheads are still on the water the Blue Coral has to be part of the plan.... Lieutenant Holman, where is the Blue Coral now?"

"Seven hundred miles off the coast of India, Admiral"

"Zoom in on it and see if there is a submersible on deck or if there is a hatch large enough to place one below deck."

"Admiral, I've looked, there is nothing there."

"Look again, Connie, zoom in on the deck and look for an un-welded seam."

"I've been there, it's clean, Admiral. They are doing research on the tuna schools; they don't have need for a submersible."

"Admiral, we are looking for the obvious, but it's not going to be on the deck."

"What are we missing, Eric."

"I'm not a Navy man, Admiral, but .... Connie, this is Eric Ludlow, what about under the ship."

"It never entered my mind, Mr. Ludlow. I have been concentrating on the tuna. However, you may be right. Yes, it's possible; there could be an underwater hatch, or a saddle with a transfer tube."

"Antonio, tell the pilot to fly you and Ayeza to Mumbai. Lieutenant Holman will continue tracking the French ship. We have friends in India. I'll contact the authorities in Mumbai and ask them to detain the ship when it enters their jurisdiction."

"Admiral, Indian customs are as corrupt as the Pakistan authorities. Heroin is their mainstay and if the Blue Coral is involved they will warn the captain and he will lose the submersible with the push of a button."

"Lieutenant Holman, what is the speed of the Blue Coral."

"She has slowed to six knots, Antonio; she does not seem to be in a hurry."

The airwaves grew quiet. It had not been said but it was coming down to boarding the Blue Coral in international waters. If they refused to allow a search, it meant an assault on a research ship flying a French flag. If they were wrong, it would draw another country into the mess and give the administration more ammunition to use against the CIA and military.

Lieutenant Holman continued to scan the ship during the silence. When focused properly, the satellite cameras can read the signature on a check.

"Admiral?"

"What is it, Connie?"

"I'm still zoomed in on the deck of the Blue Coral. Five people just came on deck. They are climbing the ladder to the bridge. What are two men wearing traditional Arab clothes and carrying rifles doing on a French research ship?"

"Lieutenant, you may make Captain if I'm still here when this is over. ...... Eric?"

"Where is the closest C-17, Admiral?"

"If we want to keep it in our circle of friends, Captain Stevens is back at Kabul."

"Get General Sampson on the other line, Admiral."

It was Eric's call, but General Sampson and Admiral Michaels concurred with the decision to mount an assault on the Blue Coral.

"Antonio, if there are Arabs on that boat, it is part of their plan. We board it with or without a submersible before it can dock in Mumbai."

"How do we get on board, General?"

"The amphibian is a Special Forces plane. It has a double bungee harness on board. You can transfer to a C-17. Make a list; we'll load an inflatable and whatever else you need. The C-17 will leave Kabul within the hour. The amphibian and the C-17 will intersect in the Arabian Sea. You and Ayeza can make the in-flight transfer there. By that time, we will have a head count on board the Blue Coral."

"How do we get off?"

"The USS Miami is off the coast of India. Admiral Michaels will contact the captain and have him move the sub into position for the pickup."

"I think we are overreaching. There are just two of us, Eric, and from what the Lieutenant says it's a big ship with a big crew. I am growing fond of the lady and I do not want to deal with another Lisbon."

"Admiral, how about some help from the Navy. The Los Angeles class subs carry a compliment of Seals."

"I served with the captain of the Miami, Eric, but I have not kept up. I don't know his politics. I can send the sub on a rescue mission, but I would need to go to the Secretary of Defense to send in a Seal team to board a foreign ship. I am out of favor upstairs and the water off of India is outside our military jurisdiction. The Captain would want confirmation."

"Admiral, ask General Sampson for volunteers."

"That's off the wall, Eric. The general is on thin ice in Afghanistan, and the Indian Ocean is a long way from his jurisdiction."

"Ask him anyway, the couple is going to need some help."

CHAPTER 13

The Los Angeles class submarine, USS Miami was in international waters off the coast of India. Captain Jenkins set the message down and went up on deck to take Admiral Michaels' call.

"Hello, Admiral, it's been a while, but why the satellite call? I have a direct line to the Pentagon."

"There are too many new faces and I don't want this leaked, Captain. The Pentagon Joint Chiefs believe the Islamic militants have gotten their hands on some nuclear warheads and they are on their way to Miami. We are hoping we can enlist your help."

"We're named after the city, but we are in the Indian Ocean; that's a long way from Miami. How can I be of service?"

"I'm sending in a team to board a ship in India's territorial waters. They will need to be picked up after the mission."

"I have a Seal team on board, Admiral. What is it on the ship that you want?"

"I don't have time to clear a Seal mission, Captain."

"I would think warheads in the hands of the Muslims would give you some latitude, Admiral. Don't fence with me, what is going on?"

Captain Jenkins and Admiral Michaels had served together when Jenkins first graduated from the Naval Academy. They had become friends, but had drifted apart after Admiral Michaels left sea duty and joined the Pentagon staff. Jenkins was a man of integrity with a fierce dedication to duty. If he wanted his help, he would need to bring him on board.

"There is some sparring in the new administration, Captain. The President and his friends in Congress want to retire the military and leave these issues to the UN. They have loaded the civilian staffs at the Pentagon with people sympathetic to their ideals. We both know the kind, typical power seekers more interested in their careers than the welfare of the country. The military is in this alone, and if we stub our toes it could mean the end of our careers."

"The direction the President and Congress are heading is no secret, Admiral. From the rhetoric coming out of Washington, our careers will be short lived anyway. We were scheduled for another five months but I received orders to make this sweep through the Indian Ocean, and then return to my homeport. I've been waiting for confirmation from the Navy."

"None of this has come across my desk, Captain."

"It came direct from the State Department, Admiral, I assumed it was settled."

'I don't understand, Captain. What did you assume was settled?"

"I was told they will decommission the Miami after this tour."

"The Pentagon has been kept out of the loop, Captain, but it seems it's started. The civilians are making military decisions without our involvement."

"It's not official until I get orders from the Navy, Admiral, and if you don't know about it, those orders won't be coming soon. In the mean time we are at your disposal, Sir. Back to the question, how can I be of service?"

Captain Jenkins returned to the helm and called his communication officer. "Lieutenant, I understand you speak French; do you do English with a French accent?"

"I was on the stage in college, Captain. It's a talent I have, why?"

"Contact Lieutenant Connie Holman; she is on the surveillance ship, Tucson, in the Arabian Sea. Scramble the call and go through the back door by way of the satellite over India. Code it to look like you are the French looking for a lost chick. Get the waypoint and the plotted course of a French research ship called the Blue Coral. Tell her to update us hourly and to use the same communication route."

"What's up, Captain?"

"A rescue mission of sorts, Lieutenant, it appears a couple from the CIA may need help from our Navy Seals."

"That should be interesting, Captain."

"Yes, it definitely will be. Get the waypoint, and then tell the Seals to meet me in the galley."

Meanwhile onboard the amphibian Antonio had set the phone back in its cradle and prepared the list of equipment he and Ayeza would need.

"Captain, please, get this to the Kabul base."

Antonio stood to leave then hesitated. "What's our flight time to intercept, Captain?"

"Give or take eight hours, Antonio"

"Please, wake us in seven."

Antonio closed the cockpit door and moved toward the aft cabin. Ayeza had showered, but had draped her fresh jumpsuit and body armor across a chair. Rather than dress, she had wrapped one of the light cotton blankets, sarong style around herself, and was sitting in the dining booth sipping a glass of wine.

Antonio moved toward the table to join her. She smiled, but lifted her hand, pointing him the other way. "You have a short memory, Antonio."

"How's that, Ayeza?"

"I told you when you boarded the plane in Madrid, I'll take my chances with the rest, but if I'm to play the part, you do need to clean up. It has been over four days and you have been messing in fishnets. There is soap and a razor in the shower, and another blanket in the overhead."

"Are you sure?"

"This living by the moment changes timeframes, Antonio; one slip and we die. I have made three mistakes in less than five days, but because of you, I am still here. This is not the part I had in mind at the time; but yes, I was sure before we made the jump this morning. I tried to tell you, but I forgot to turn on the mike. I thought you didn't care, which is what caused me to slip. I thought I killed us both, and then I passed out. When I came to with your arms around me, I knew it would be all right."

"You said you were afraid before the jump."

"I'm not afraid of dying, Antonio, but I am afraid I will die before I live."

"You said ten minutes, it's been almost twelve and the cabin is cold." Ayeza had moved to the sofa where she was sitting with her feet tucked under her blanket.

The open bottle of Merlot and two glasses were on the table. Taking one, she offered the other to Antonio who had returned from the shower with a blanket draped across his shoulders, and a towel wrapped loosely around his waist.

Ayeza winced as Antonio lifted her feet to sit down and then placed them in his lap. "What hurts?"

"It seems like months, but it's only been three days since we left the canyon in Pakistan. The bruises haven't healed yet."

"I thought you took the hits on your side and back."

Ayeza smiled through the pain. "I woke before you had all my clothes off. I also took one on my thigh and another on my calf. The armor is thinner there so the bruising is worse."

Antonio lifted the blanket to reveal the black and yellowish stain running from Ayeza's ankle to her knee. Moving out from under her legs he gently placed them back on the sofa before turning to kneel beside her.

"You should have said something. You were in no shape to make that jump."

"If I had said something you would have left me in Kabul. We started this together, we'll finish it together."

Antonio moved the blanket and gently brushed her bruised skin with his lips. Avoiding the bruise, his tongue slid gently on the skin above her knee. Ayeza moaned softly and shuddered as she caressed the back of Antonio's neck.

Antonio mistook her reaction when he moved her blanket and the yellowish stain on her thigh glimmered in the cabin light. He backed off and looked up, but it was his turn to smile; Ayeza was shivering, but not from the cold. Ayeza opened her eyes and smiled, and then she patted the couch and offered him a glass of wine. "It's alright, come closer, there's room."

Later they were sitting on the couch. Antonio set the glasses back on the table next to the empty bottle. His blanket was lying on the floor and Ayeza's was tangled around her.

Antonio started to stand but paused and turned to take the hand she offered.

"Now it's my turn, what would you like?"

"What are my options?"

"Let's go to bed, Antonio; I'm new at this, but I'm a fast learner."

Reaching down he caressed her thigh. "Are you sure, those bruises look like they hurt."

"What bruises?"

The C-17 was at sixteen thousand feet, sixty miles out. It was approaching at three hundred sixty knots. The pilot of the amphibian set his autopilot to match the C-17's course and then set the speed of his aircraft at three hundred to let the C-17 catch up. "Wake the couple, they drop in one hour."

Ayeza was awake before the copilot knocked on the door. Antonio was sleeping soundly, but he stirred when Ayeza told the man she was awake.

"You promised to wake me, now it's too late."

Ayeza moved closer feeling Antonio's body stirring. Taking him in her hand she moved down to caress his chest with her lips.

"You keep that up and we'll be late."

"The shower is big enough for two and I left my makeup at home. I can dress in ten minutes. We have time."

Dressed and ready for the jump, Ayeza stared out the cabin window as they sipped coffee waiting for the C-17 to come within range. "What happens if we miss, Antonio?"

"Best case, we get wet and the sub picks us up."

"Do I want to hear the worst case?"

"I don't think so, Ayeza, the objective is not to miss."

The pilot slowed the plane as the C-17 approached. "Five minutes to zero, Antonio."

Ayeza had seen the Special Forces in Germany practice the in-flight transfer, but she had never done it herself. The transfer she watched was successful and the men made it look easy, but there were many other times she was not on board that there were mishaps resulting in major injuries and even a few deaths.

Antonio checked her harness and cleared the strap from her safety chute.

"Remember, Ayeza, the bungee is eighty feet long, we need to fly apart and extend it to its full length, but not stretch it. The line has to be relaxed for a soft pickup and the hook must catch it between the stops.

Keep the knife in your hand. If we miss, you will only have an instant to cut loose. If it is a clean pick-up drop the knife and turn to face me. When the bounce settles we should be side by side, but we could be pulled apart when the bungee retracts; you will need to hold on."

The C-17 was directly behind them and a mile back. The amphibian would pull up and to the left as the C-17 dropped toward the couple with the grappling hook trailing from the plane.

The bungee between them was coiled on their arms. "Now, Ayeza." He squeezed her hand then turned her loose. When the line came tight between them, Ayeza was above him. He was stretched spread eagle to slow his descent; she had been watching him. She tucked her arms at her side overcorrecting, but as she started to pass him, the roar of the C-17 above her head caused her to look up.

The hook caught between the stops and Antonio caught her as the plane lifted them out of their freefall. They settled from the bounce with their arms wrapped around each other, and then the winch closed the distance to the plane.

"It can't get much better than that, Ayeza."

"Yes, Antonio it can, but the next time we need to leave time for breakfast. I'm hungry."

Al-Queda's plan was making sense. Admiral Michaels was convinced the warheads were on the Blue Coral. Lieutenant Holman dug into the archives and viewed some old tapes and then checked with India's customs office. The ship was due in Mumbai where it would be docking at the container terminal. If they had the warheads, there were a million containers on the docks heading for U.S. ports. If they got them off the ship in India they would never find them.

The Pentagon Joint Chiefs blessed the mission and General Sampson asked for volunteers.

The Special Forces boarded the C-17 a few minutes before it left Kabul. Colonel Rogers and Captain Pitt were at the door and Sergeant Anderson was pulling gear from the overhead compartment when Antonio and Ayeza boarded the plane.

"Welcome aboard, Antonio, Ayeza."

Surprised, "You are a long way from Afghanistan, Colonel. I thought you were assigned there for the duration."

"If the warheads are not on the Blue Coral, we won't be going back to Afghanistan, Antonio."

Ayeza and Antonio stripped out of their flight gear and settled in the cabin. "How is the General?"

"He said to say hello, Antonio, but he is still bucking the system. Pakistan wants fifty million for the F-16 and another ten for the pilot's family. The administration questioned his actions and then threw him to the wolves.

Some congressional committee wants to conduct a hearing, but the Pentagon brass intervened. He was reassigned to the Eglin Air Force Base in Florida. He will be there until we find the warheads, or the Pakistan government proves their inventory is accurate."

"I would think the warhead we recovered would have convinced them."

"The Pakistan government has blamed it on Wahid. They say he set it up for the reward from the CIA. They also claim he adjusted the inventory entries before he left the lab. They say they did a thorough inventory and nothing more is missing."

"What about the core? The Pakistan government doesn't know we recovered that."

"We also have the films and tapes of the rescue. If it does come down to a hearing they will use it as a defense, but for now the Pentagon is holding it back. That way the Pakistan government will not have time to discredit it. The point is, the administration is buying Pakistan's story for now, and they will until we have proof the other three warheads exist and are heading for the States."

"What if the warheads aren't on the Blue Coral?"

"We'll be in limbo. This C-17 is our home until we find them. When we lost them in Pakistan, the Pakistan government got belligerent and sent an emissary to Washington. It's getting messy. We are all being transferred out of Afghanistan. Our orders from the Pentagon are to join General Sampson at Eglin and conduct the search from there."

"What convinced them to send you here?"

"They didn't, but when you came up empty in Saudi, the Admiral gave us the option to make this detour. We took a vote; it was all or none. The other six are in the back."

"Hopefully we will end it here, Colonel. Has anyone talked to the French?"

"Your boss did some digging, Ayeza. They are flying a French flag, but the French claim the government has no connection to the Blue Coral. What records they have say it is funded by some organization based in Oman, called Sovereignty of the Seas, with offices in Paris and Mumbai."

"If it's a cover for the terrorists, what's the point?"

"Oman is claiming jurisdiction over the tuna in the Arabian Sea out to two hundred miles, but the other countries that front the tuna migrations want free access to within fifty miles of all the coastlines. The Blue Coral is supposed to be tracking the schools taking an inventory."

"Did they get a crew count on the ship?"

"No accurate count, but some Navy lieutenant on the surveillance ship, Tucson, is tracking them. The crew has gotten careless since they moved out of range of our Middle East satellites and our ships in the Arabian Sea.

They probably aren't aware we can tap the weather satellites. They are moving freely about the ship holding armed, military style drills on the deck. The woman tracking them said it looked like a Boy Scout camp. There are a bunch of teenagers playing soldier. She took one head count and there were thirty-five on deck at the time."

Four of the Taliban involved in raping Ayeza were under sixteen. "Colonel, the boys in the villages of Afghanistan and Pakistan are carrying guns by the time they are seven years old. They are seasoned killers by the time they are ten. If you or any of your men treat them as children, they will have the edge, and they will kill you."

"I lost a man in Afghanistan who hesitated when a young boy approached his truck, Ayeza. The kid shot him in the face when he offered him a candy bar. We were all there for the lesson; none of us will make that same mistake."

"If we plan on landing on the deck, it would be nice to know what we are up against, Colonel, and what mounted weapons they have on board."

"The lieutenant on the Tucson is very thorough, Antonio. The ship was commissioned last year. She traced it to the yard that built it. Some of your people went in and got the plans. Lieutenant Holman e-mailed them to us before you came aboard. It's all a front. The fish hold is actually quarters for the trainees."

"What weapons is she carrying?"

"The lieutenant did a sweep of the ship searching for mounted weapons. There is nothing visible on the decks. It's pretty obvious the Blue Coral is a small arms and martial arts training camp for the Somalia pirates and Al-Queda, posing as a research ship.

Connie's research of port and satellite records showed the Blue Coral made a routine loop along the coast of Oman, Yemen and Somalia, picking up men from the fishing trawlers. They returned to Mumbai for provisions every three months.

When they left Mumbai they spent two months training along the southern India coast. They were now due in Mumbai where some of the men would be seeking refugee status to the US and to Canada."

"If it is a training camp, they just left the coast of Somalia, so the recruits will be green. Not all of them will have the stomach for killing, and it will take time to train them. They probably have modern weapons on board, but I doubt they are carrying them yet. The camps usually start them with junk and save the good stuff for those who show promise."

"I was raised with kids like these, Colonel. They are full of hate and they are dangerous. When we left Saudi Arabia we were dealing with a crew on a research boat; now it's an armed camp, and even with you and your men, it's over three to one. Those are stiff odds. Do you have a plan?"

"The Pentagon wants an answer, Ayeza. If the warheads are not on the Blue Coral, it's time to head for Florida."

"That's not a plan, Colonel, that's a travel schedule. With you and your men, we have eleven. You said they counted thirty-five and there could be more. By my watch we have two hours to jump time, we need a plan."

"We did not have the head count until a few hours ago and no one liked the odds before then. That's why we're here. The submarine, USS Miami, will be in range in four hours."

"The Miami is our pickup, that doesn't change the odds, Colonel. Dying is a by-product of this game, but suicide is not part of my plan."

"I'm glad you feel that way, Ayeza. So do we, that's why Admiral Michaels enlisted some help from the Captain on the Miami. When they realized it was a terrorist camp, the Captain gave them the option. The Seal team aboard the Miami volunteered. We will drop in and secure the deck, then wait for the Seals to board. If the Blue Coral has a submersible and drops it, the sonar on the Miami will pick it up and they have the gear to recover it."

"It's going to be a difficult jump, Colonel. The odds of all of us hitting the deck without a watch spotting us are insurmountable. We will be ducks with our wings spread for landing, and that is an easy target, even for a green hunter. Most of them will be asleep. I think Antonio and I should go in first and secure the deck."

"I appreciate your concern, but I don't jump out of perfectly good airplanes, Ayeza, neither does Captain Pitt."

"I thought you were going with us?"

"We are. This is a C-17. I told you, it is home until we find the warheads."

"I'm missing something, Colonel; the ship is thirty five thousand feet below us."

"Sorry, Ayeza, I left something out. General Sampson and I thought you two would be tired of jumping out of airplanes. Our helicopters are in the cargo hold. We can launch and re-board from the main hatch while the C-17 is in flight.

It's tricky, but Captain Pitt and I have done it before. I'll take Antonio and the Special Forces. You go with Captain Pitt and pick up the Seals from the deck of the Miami. We can go in under their radar to the back deck. I will drop Antonio and my men and then move up and take out the bridge.

We will be five hundred miles from shore and there are no ships on their radar or in their path. They will not be expecting us, and they should not see us coming until seconds before we get there. Even if they do, we should be in control of the ship before you arrive with the Seals."

"Now that's a plan. Thank you, Colonel."

"On that note, Ayeza, it's not foolproof. The weather report is in. There is a tropical storm approaching. We will be at twenty thousand feet to make the drop and bucking seventy knot winds.

I can't engage the rotor until we are clear of the plane and in the storm there is a risk of collision with the tail section of the plane.

The rotors will spin in the wind and slow our descent, but it's a free drop until the rotors catch. Wear your chutes, if anything goes wrong the Miami will pick you out of the sea and you will have to go to plan B."

"I love an optimist, Colonel, what's plan B?"

"That's anybody's guess, you will have to play it by ear; we haven't had time to come up with one."

The C-17 banked into the turn that would keep them circling until the helicopters returned from the mission. "We are 50 miles off the starboard side of the Blue Coral, Colonel. The Miami is ten miles out, approaching from the west. Commander Thompson and his Seal unit will be on deck and waiting."

"Thank you, Captain. Drop the hatch and lift the nose, we are ready to drop out."

Colonel Rogers was the first to go. Captain Stevens put the plane in a climb and when they started to slide the Colonel steered the helicopter to the center of the hatch and quietly dropped into the storm. The rotors on Colonel Rogers' helicopter caught as Captain Pitt waited for Colonel Rogers to clear the plane.

"It's pretty bumpy, Captain. No harm done, but I clipped the hatch on the way out. Tell Captain Stevens to put the nose up and increase the slope of the plane; it will help you clear the tail section. Then drop a few seconds longer than planned before engaging the rotors.

Captain Pitt dropped into the night and turned toward the waypoint where the Miami was waiting. "Drop to the surface, Captain, it's going to be bumpy on the deck, but it will mask us from the Blue Coral's radar."

CHAPTER 14

———————⟫●⟨———————

Lieutenant Holman watched the military style drills on the deck of the Blue Coral as the storm approached. When she zoomed in on the boat, she saw there were posters and mannequins painted to represent the President of the United States. They were fastened to the bulwarks and being used for target practice.

Lieutenant Holman patched it through to the C-17 and Ayeza translated the signs above the posters. *Death to the Americans* and *Kill the Apostate* were the primary themes with subheadings referencing Jihad and killing all infidels.

Since the subject matter confirmed *The Apostate Theory*, Admiral Michaels thought it should be patched to the Pentagon computers. It was also time to bring the administration and the State Department into the loop about the Blue Coral.

The State Department ignored the Admiral's call, but thirty minutes after the pictures were relayed to the White House, Captain Jenkins received his orders and then told the Seals it was a kill on sight mission. Some of the men objected, they were soldiers not assassins. "What if the boat's clean and they offer to surrender, Captain?"

"It's doubtful they will, but if they do, warheads or not, it's a terrorist training camp. Set the survivors adrift and scuttle the ship. We will notify the Indian authorities to pick them up."

Antonio and Ayeza split up; their fluency in Arabic would help if there were prisoners. Antonio would go with the Special Forces to secure the decks and passageways cutting the crew's quarters off from the front half of the ship. Once contained in their quarters, Ayeza and the Seals would do a room by room search for the crew and the crusaders while Antonio searched the ship for the warheads.

The C-17 moved out into a widening circle and a few minutes later, Captain Pitt hovered above the Miami. Commander Thompson came on board first. As he moved out of the doorway to make room for the others, the lone figure in the cabin shifted on the bench.

A startled Commander Thompson tripped when he realized the dome light was reflecting off the brilliant green eyes of a woman. He regained his composure and then moved onto the bench next to her, brooding silently as the other six men came aboard.

Commander Thompson was sullen. When the door slid closed, he turned to Ayeza. "Captain Jenkins told us there was a woman involved. We thought that since we joined the party you might remain on the plane. We have a count on the terrorists and it could get messy. My men and I work as a team and we don't have time to cover for a chick."

Ayeza smiled at the arrogance of a man whose life was a constant competition with his peers. Seldom did the Seals and Special Forces team up together. Commander Thompson would swallow his pride and take orders from another man in the competing service, but a woman, and a civilian at that, on the team giving orders was something he had not counted on.

"And here I thought chivalry was alive, Commander. Do any of your men speak Arabic?"

"No."

"Do you or your men have any combat experience against children, Commander?"

"What, you came along as a nanny?"

"Ok, you are one of those macho men who think, *I should be in the kitchen or on my back with my feet in the air.* I'll deal with that, Commander, but don't get in the way if those kids on that boat want to play soldier."

"Alright, I'm out of line, you know something I don't. What is it?"

"Most of them will be asleep and I doubt if they sleep in their fatigues. If they are out of uniform, or in their skivvies, some of them will look like children. To you and your men they will be. Most of them are between twelve and sixteen."

One of the Seals overheard the conversation. Like Commander Thompson, he was wishing the woman had remained the plane. "We did not sign up to kill kids, lady."

To Ayeza and her women friends in Germany the term lady was a four letter word. "Then you are the ones who should stay on the helicopter, soldier."

"Look, lady……."

"My name is Ayeza, use it, or stay on this helicopter. Now, pay attention. You will be dealing with what you think are kids, they aren't."

Ayeza turned to Commander Thompson. "Commander, I was born in a village on the border of Pakistan. It is the *kids* doing the killing. The terrorists have their hands on three nuclear warheads; those warheads could be on the Blue Coral. Even if they are not, those *kids* are being trained to kill your wives and children; that is, if your families are still alive after the bomb goes off. Even if you and your men don't want to live through this, my friends and I do. Tell your men to pay attention or stay the hell out of our way."

Colonel Rogers hovered until the Seals settled in the helicopter and then turned to lead the way. The winds had subsided some, but they were still gusting to forty knots and the seas were running over twenty feet. It meant a rough landing on the pitching deck of the boat, but there was a plus side, the storm would cover their approach.

Staying just above the waves, the curve of the earth would keep them off the radar screen until they were within twenty miles of the ship. Flying at two hundred knots, they would be off the stern of the ship and back off the radar screen in less than six minutes.

They came in skimming the waves. The night watch was dozing and missed the blinks on the radar screen. Colonel Rogers dropped Antonio and the men, and then the radar alarm sounded when the helicopter rose to eye level with the man on the bridge.

The laser radiation detector showed the room to be clean. The startled seaman looked up an instant before the rocket left its tube.

"Antonio, the bridge is secure; there was only one man on watch."

"The deck's clean, Colonel, we caught them in their beds."

The Blue Coral had been running with the waves. With the controls on the bridge out, the boat was wallowing sideways to the swells; the decks were awash with waves breaking over the bulwarks.

Sergeant Anderson secured the passageway to the bow. He then stood cover, waiting as Captain Pitt landed on the deck.

"Commander, it's time. Make up your mind. Deal with them as the enemy, or stay on the helicopter."

"We'll play it your way, but our orders are to kill on sight. I'm not sure we can follow that order if they are kids."

"You'll feel different after one of them kills one of your men, Commander. In the meantime don't get in the way."

Antonio and the other six men spread through the ship, sealing off the hallways while Commander Thompson and his men unloaded the explosives.

When the rocket took out the bridge and the boat slipped into the trough some of the crusaders were thrown from their bunks onto the decks. Two of Colonel Rogers's men were in the galley engaged in a firefight with a group who had heard the explosion on the bridge and managed to gather their arms.

The storm had caused a rash of seasickness on board the Blue Coral, which accounted for the quiet decks and empty hallways when Antonio landed. Men were now in the hallways gathering their guns. Antonio and the other three were trading fire with a dozen crusaders who had managed to slip out the door before they sealed the hallway.

When the sound of the small arms stopped, Ayeza began a search for Antonio. "Antonio, we are on the back deck, where are you and the Forces?"

"We are on level three below you, Ayeza. The fish hold is the quarters for the recruits. We have them contained, but a few got out; some were in the galley. You were right, they are a bunch of kids, but they are determined."

"What about the crew?

"The captain and the crew are Chinese nationals the pirates kidnapped off the coast of Somalia. They speak English and would like a ticket home."

"Who's left?"

"According to the first mate, everyone is accounted for on this side of the bulkhead. They said the captain's quarters are next to the bridge and the instructors' staterooms are on level two below the bridge. We cannot get there from here. I've lost contact with Sergeant Anderson; where are he and the Seals?"

"Sergeant Anderson is with me; the Seals are unloading the explosives. How many instructors are we looking for?"

"It depends on who was on the bridge. It could be as many as twelve, but we need to deal with the Boy Scouts in the fish hold before they break out. There are drop chutes from the deck to the fish hold on either side of the net reel. Clear the top deck, and then drop satchel charges down each side. We will mop up and then go below to look for the warheads. When the smoke clears, take the Seals to find the captain and then clear the instructors' staterooms."

"Any sign of radiation?"

"No, so far the ship is clean."

Ayeza dropped the probe through the vent, testing the air for radiation. It was clean. "Antonio, clear your men out of the passageway leading to the Boy Scout's berth."

Commander Thompson had been standing at her side patched into the conversation. "The Forces have the aft hallways secure, but the natives are restless, Commander. There are kids aboard, but we have friends in harm's way."

"I'm not sure I can indiscriminately kill a bunch of kids, Ayeza."

"Since you are reluctant, Commander, Sergeant Anderson and I will deal with the Boy Scouts. When we finish, we will deal with the instructors. Your men can mop up and then mine the ship."

Turning from the Commander, Ayeza called to Sergeant Anderson, handing him two satchel charges.

"There are chutes on either side of the net reel. When Captain Pitt lifts off, set the timers for twenty seconds and then drop them. When the smoke clears, bring the crew topside. The crew is Chinese and they are friendly. The captain's quarters are next to the bridge. He is also friendly. Get them in lifeboats and off the ship, then contact Captain Jenkins on the Miami and tell him to pick up the crew when you set them adrift."

"Some of the others may surrender, what do we do with them?"

"The crusaders will not surrender. Mine all of the other lifeboats."

Sergeant Anderson dropped the charges. After the smoke cleared, one of the instructors had managed to make it to what was left of the bridge and an open porthole. He emptied the clip of his AK-47 at the helicopter as Colonel Rogers passed above the back deck. Captain Pitt saw the muzzle flash and sent a rocket toward the flash.

Debris blocked their door when Colonel Rogers fired rockets through the window of the bridge. The instructors were digging themselves out of their quarters, but the captain was collateral damage; he died in his bed. The hallway leading from the instructors' quarters also led to the ship's stores.

Commander Thompson led the Seals on a room-by-room search of the forward section of the ship. Ayeza checked for radiation in each room, and then the Seals would attach an explosive charge to a wall and move to the next door.

Sergeant Anderson had set the crew adrift and rejoined them. He was checking the rooms off the ship layout. One of Thompson's men set a charge on a watertight steel door that closed the passageway off from the lower level. It was latched from the other side.

"Commander, this is the only way in or out of that passageway. It leads to staterooms in the bow. They are probably the quarters for the senior instructors. If it's secured from the other side, it's occupied."

"When the charge goes off, I'll launch a grenade, Sergeant."

"You can't do that, Commander. We are looking for nuclear warheads. Wait until Ayeza checks the hallway for radiation."

The charge blew the door off its hinges. Commander Thompson dropped back waiting for a response. The radiation meter showed negative, but Ayeza's night vision caught movement in the hall and the flash from a silenced weapon as the bullets bounced off the bulkhead next to her.

Ayeza signaled the hall was clean and Commander Thompson stepped forward and launched a grenade in the direction of the flash.

When the smoke cleared, Colonel Thompson and his men continued the search. In the laundry at the end of the hall, a boy who looked to be about twelve years old was huddled in a corner. He had torn a scrap of white cloth from a sheet and had tied it to the end of a rifle that was propped by a door with the barrel sticking out in the hall.

Colonel Thompson turned into the room waving his men off. The bullet caught him under the arm, where the body armor separated in the expansion joint, tearing through his arm and lodging in his armor. The force of the impact knocked him off balance. He spun and fell inside the room, dislodging his helmet.

Dazed and confused, the commander began to stand in the dimly lit room between the boy and the door. The boy was smiling as he stood and calmly pointed the rifle at Colonel Thompson's face.

The kick to his head sent the Colonel sprawling to the side, and caused the boy to hesitate long enough for Ayeza to aim and put a bullet through his brain.

Commander Thompson woke a few minutes later with Sergeant Anderson putting a tourniquet on his arm. "How bad is it, Commander?"

"I'll live, Sergeant, but my head hurts and my pride's bruised. My God, Sergeant, the kid was flying a white flag. He was actually smiling at me when he pulled the trigger."

"They aren't kids, Commander. Ayeza was raised with them. A bunch like this gang raped her and almost killed her when she was a child. They grow up fast in the mountains of Pakistan and Afghanistan. This is her turf and she knows what she's doing. If you intend to stick around, it will be best for us all if you and your men pay attention to her."

"She tried to warn me. I didn't listen. It was a woman thing. Thank you, Sergeant; help me up. When the men on the Miami find out I let a ten year old kid get the best of me and someone from the Special Forces saved my life, I am going to get a lot of ribbing."

"In that case I would not tell anyone it was the woman."

"Ayeza kicked me in the head?"

"She said you don't like women, but I doubt it was personal. I have worked with her before. You were in the line of fire and we did not have a shot. She would have gone for your shoulder, but you are a big man. Headache or not, you had to go down. You owe her your life."

Commander Thompson felt the bruise and the goose egg swelling on the side of his head. "I don't believe she kicked me in the head, Sergeant, she's a woman."

"Ayeza is a special case, Commander. I trained with her in Germany. She's expert in a half dozen of the martial arts. There is no woman, or for that matter, man, better than her in her weight class. I've been to the tournaments. She always steps up a weight class or two and spars with the men. Even the big boys respect her."

"I blew her off in the helicopter. I owe her an apology, where is she?"

"She's leading your men searching the ship. She told me about the *lady* crack in the helicopter, but their attitudes changed when you went down. We spotted other Boy Scouts. You were out cold. She told me to stop the bleeding, and then to take you topside, put you in a basket and have Captain Pitt take you to the Miami."

"I'm not going back to the sub in a basket, Sergeant. You have the bleeding stopped; tear up one of the sheets and make me a sling. I'm going to help send this Boy Scout bucket and whoever is left on it to the bottom."

The warheads had been in crates lined with packages of heroin when the trawlers plucked them from the sea. After the fishermen removed their share they dropped the crates back into the sea. The divers brought them on board the Blue Coral to unpack them.

The ship appeared clean until Antonio's radiation meter registered at the bulkhead door leading to the stern diving access port. He followed the direction finder to a pile of clothes next to the hatch where the divers had set the warheads before placing them in their cradles in the sub.

The hatch opened to a watertight room below the water line with access to the sea. The meter jumped when he opened the door, but the room and the submersible cradle were empty.

Ayeza and the Seals were searching room by room. "Ayeza, have you had any readings?"

"No, Antonio, the ship is clean, but there are still men buried in the nooks. One of them wounded the Seal Commander. We are cleaning them out, but it's going to take time. The Seals are still reluctant to kill the *kids*."

"We were led astray; the warheads were in the hold by the diving hatch. They would have left a trail if they moved them to store them elsewhere on the ship. They're gone. It's time to move on. Leave the Boy Scouts for the sharks and return to the deck. Seal the doors behind you, but be careful on your way out, there are many places for the young ones to play hide and seek, one of them could have doubled back."

Antonio and the Special Forces boarded Colonel Rogers' helicopter and then lifted off the deck to make room for Captain Pitt. Ayeza waited on deck with Commander Thompson while his men finished mining the ship.

"It's done, Commander."

"Thank you, Lieutenant."

"I'll take the transmitter if you like, Commander."

"I was wrong, Ayeza. There were no children on this boat, they are terrorists. My men and I will remember that. I was wrong about you too, sorry about the *chick* crack."

Ayeza smiled, her green eyes sparkling in the light of the helicopter. She took the hand he offered and then climbed on board. Commander Thompson boarded behind her after placing the transmitter in his vest pocket.

Colonel Rogers hovered five hundred yards off the ship while Colonel Pitt lifted off the deck and turned to join him. When they were alongside, Colonel Thompson looked toward the Blue Coral, and then pressed the button sending the Blue Coral to the bottom of the Indian Ocean.

CHAPTER 15

CDs showing the crusaders on the deck of the Blue Coral using targets resembling the President of the United States were delivered to the Congressional Committee on terrorism. A few hours later a call came from the White House authorizing a secure, isolated link between Connie Holman's terminal on the surveillance ship and Admiral Michaels's office.

After they came up empty on the Blue Coral, Lieutenant Holman and Admiral Michaels spent hours reviewing the film of the flight of the jet that left the Pakistan village for Somalia, as well as those of the Blue Coral and the trawlers. "How could we have lost them, Connie, and where can they be?"

"I don't know, Admiral. I have had four screens going and technicians watching them around the clock. Everything in the area has been under surveillance since the truck left Mardan.

They were a thousand miles from land when the plane flew over, but we managed to follow them to the trawlers and to the

Blue Coral's submersible. If they weren't on the ship, they have to still be on the submersible."

"We know from the way they reacted they were not ready, so they were not warned. Colonel Rogers took the bridge out before they knew he was there. The Blue Coral's communications were destroyed with the bridge and in that storm I doubt divers could have readied and launched a submersible after we boarded the boat."

"So, what happened to the submersible, Admiral?"

"I don't know, Connie, but with the Blue Coral sunk, they have no place they can go, and they cannot stay submerged forever. The submersible has to be somewhere along the trail. Hopefully it will be on camera when it resurfaces."

"It's a big ocean, Admiral; where do we look?"

"The Blue Coral was on the way to India, Connie. Activate the satellite link and have one camera concentrate on the Port of Mumbai."

"Admiral, submersibles are electric. There is no way they carry a sufficient charge in the batteries to get them anywhere near Mumbai. Besides, I've been in on the conversations. Eric Ludlow said that his Middle East connection was convinced it was coming by way of Saudi Arabia."

"We've been there, Connie. Saudi Arabia looks like a dead end. Keep the coast of Saudi Arabia, Oman, Yemen and Somalia in view as well, but we need to widen the search. We might get lucky."

When the C-17 reached the Gulf of Aden it climbed to sixty thousand feet and turned toward the coast of Africa. They were well above the commercial air traffic and would not need to clear their route with the air controllers along the way.

The helicopters were tied down. Antonio and the Special Forces were asleep in their bunks. Colonel Rogers was having coffee in the lounge when Ayeza walked in. "Where to now, Colonel?"

"Florida, we have been assigned to the Eglin Air Base until this hunt is over, Ayeza. With Saudi Arabia off limits, it is doubtful we will pick up the trail before the warheads arrive in the States, and everything points to the Bahamas."

"My understanding is we will be staying on the fisherman's boat while we search the islands. Two helicopters and a squad of Special Forces following us around will be conspicuous, Colonel. Antonio and I can deal with a few guards on a rich man's winter estate until we have a definite lead."

"We are going to the base to wait for you until you need us, but new information came in while we were on the mission. Admiral Michaels sent General Sampson a notice that British Immigration has cleared a batch of Somalia refugees, sight unseen. The brass believes they are from one of the training camps in Somalia."

"When are they scheduled to arrive?"

"The Brits say the end of January. Based on the information Wahid had, that ties them to the warheads."

"Do we know which estate?"

"No, but there has been a flurry of construction activity on one of the estates belonging to a Middle East oil baron who your boss thinks has ties to the Bin Laden family. It may be coincidence, but the Somalia terrorists are some of the best trained in the world. If the warheads are connected to Andros, you and Antonio will need some help and you won't get much from the Brits. That's why we came along. Get some rest, Ayeza. There won't be much time for it when we get to the States."

They were half a world away and would have to take the long way around. The American military was unwelcome in the airspace of the African and Middle East dictators who had been stockpiling weapons to fight the never-ending wars with their neighbors. European air space was also off limits to American military aircraft.

It would add thousands of miles to the trip to stay over international waterways and they would need refueling twice during the forty-hour flight to Eglin Air Force Base.

Get some rest, Ayeza. It's going to be a long flight."

Ayeza left the lounge and headed for her cot. The drone of the engines next to the bulkhead was enough to keep her awake in the private room the captain provided for her.

Ayeza was not bashful, and although it was a cargo plane and the quarters were close, there were enough bunks in the cargo area for everyone.

Antonio and the Special Forces were in a deep sleep resting from the ordeal of the past week. She climbed in a bunk where the men were sleeping, but people snore; it is an unpleasant fact of life.

Ayeza had earplugs, but they were uncomfortable. She was back pacing the floor of the lounge when Captain Stevens came through the cabin on his way back to the cockpit.

"You need to get some rest, Ayeza. It's a long flight and there's a lot to do when we get there."

"I'm a little restless, Captain. It's been a trying week."

"My cabin is empty, Ayeza. There is fresh linen and a private bath with a soaking tub. A hot bath might help you sleep. There is also a wine rack and glasses in the cupboard. My quarters are yours for the rest of the flight; make yourself at home."

"We have a long way to go, Captain; you will need sleep yourself."

There are twin beds in the copilot's berth and we take turns up front, it's decided."

"Thank you, Captain. Captain, I've lost track of time; where are we?"

"If my watch is right we are crossing over the Gulf of Aden, approaching the coast of Somalia."

Ayeza knew there was a reason, but Somalia seemed out of the way. "That's a long way around, Captain, why not cut across to the Mediterranean?"

"Everybody has an air force these days, Ayeza. It's quicker than getting the clearances we need over land. We will be flying over international waters along the coast of Africa, around the cape, and then up the middle of the Atlantic."

Ayeza changed the linen, and then took a hot bath. More relaxed, but still restless with an uneasy feeling, she couldn't sleep. She dressed and headed for the cockpit. Passing by his bunk, she changed her mind and paused, letting her hand trail along Antonio's neck and down his back. She was new at this, but when he stirred she leaned down, brushing his ear with her lips, "I know you are tired, but there is a hot shower and fresh linen in my cabin."

"I'm not that tired. Point me in the direction, and by the way, your cabin? How do you rate?"

"The captain is a fan, and he has to fly the plane. His cabin is empty, but if it's a burden…?"

Antonio smiled, and then followed Ayeza to the Captain's cabin. Antonio dimmed the lights, and then turned toward the bed. Ayeza moved to the wine rack and choose a Merlot. "We have a deal, Antonio, there is a razor in the shower."

"Have you always been this way?"

"Always is just you, Antonio. I could rough it, but if a shower is available, I'm willing to wait; ten minutes, that is."

Ten minutes and ten seconds later, he drew her to him. As she drifted off into her new world of sensations, the two-man submarine reached its maximum depth.

Antonio was asleep beside her. Ayeza was lying there content, but thinking, *men, we have almost forty hours to sleep, but he is finished and I want to make up for some of the lost years.*

She stood for a moment and as she looked out the window, the running lights of the Crescent Tide crossed from the Red Sea into the Gulf of Aden. They were flying well above the turbulence. The room was warm and quiet, except for Antonio's soft snores. Ayeza watched Antonio for a moment. He was lying on his back, his body outlined beneath the soft cotton sheet.

The Merlot was breathing on the counter. It was a shame to waste it. Ayeza poured two glasses and then returned to the bed, smiling. Antonio seemed to be dreaming, about her she hoped, because his body was reacting.

Thinking, *it's been an hour. He can catch up on his sleep later.* Ayeza set the wine on the night stand. She bent down to move the sheet aside and nuzzled his chest, waking him. "I thought you might like a glass of wine."

Smiling and reaching his arms around her to pull her to him, "I don't think that's all you have in mind."

Smiling back, "Well, like I said earlier, if it's a burden...."

Love at sixty thousand feet blocked out the reality of a nuclear threat that would forever change the free world, and the drama unfolding in the sea below them.

Shortly after the trawlers released the warheads from the taglines attached to their nets, the divers reattached to the Blue Coral's diving hatch. After removing the warheads from the crates and storing the heroin in the locker, they changed out of their diving gear and re-boarded the sub.

Connie watched as the plane landed in Somalia. She couldn't see beneath the waves when the crusaders turned the sub to follow the trawlers to the Red Sea and then attached to a trailing line to be towed.

The submarine detached from the trawler at Dawdah and turned toward the Central Median Trench. The captain of the Crescent Tide approached the way point and slowed the yacht to match the speed of the submerged sub. As the stern of the yacht passed over, the diver attached the sub and activated the hatch, opening the diving port below the room with no doors.

When they transferred the warheads from the submersible to their cradles in the yacht, the cradles settled under the weight of the warheads. The magnetic switch below the cradle opened the bypass valve to the oxygen tanks and activated the timer on the submarine's ballast tanks.

The crusaders filled their oxygen tanks from the Crescent Tide's compressor and then closed the hatch behind them. The gas would blend with the oxygen, it was odor and color free.

The sub dropped off the Crescent Tide and moved toward the waypoint to wait for the passing trawler to tow them back to the Gulf of Aden. The crusaders believed the Blue Coral would pass the coast of Yemen on their way to Somalia and pick them up.

However, the crusaders would sleep first, and then the timers would open the valves. They would settle toward the bottom of the Central Median Trench, seven thousand feet below them. The pressure would crush the hull when they passed four thousand feet and the seawater would free their spirits to join the martyrs who had gone before them.

The transfer from the submarine to the Crescent Tide went unnoticed by Lieutenant Holman and the military satellite cameras. The lead lined room would contain the radiation from the leaking warhead which would have seeped through a standard bulkhead and hull, giving them away. The sealed underwater access blended with the hull of the yacht, and the room with no doors would assure anyone searching the yacht would bypass the room.

The Crescent Tide became suspect when it slowed along the coast of Yemen and then accelerated after the plane landed in Somalia.

As they approached the southern tip of Somalia and the safe waters off the coast of Kenya, the wine steward on the Crescent Tide opened the bottle. Captain Avery from the USS Main sipped the Merlot and marveled at the luxury of the amenities of the magnificent yacht. "This is an excellent Merlot, Captain Gamal."

Captain Gamal invited Captain Avery and his officers for dinner and a tour of the yacht to thank them for the escort past the Somalia coast that was infested with pirates. "What are those tags you are all wearing, Captain?"

"The USS Main is nuclear powered, Captain; these tags record radiation levels. If there is a leak we want to know about it."

"Does everyone wear them, even off the ship? Is that standard, Captain Avery?"

"No, it is only mandatory for those who work in or around the reactor area, but my onboard policy is that all personnel wear the tags whenever moving about the ship. We will be returning to the ship tonight so we keep the tags on our clothing."

The tour of the yacht had taken four hours. Captain Gamal insisted on their seeing every spotless room.

Lieutenant Holman tracked the Crescent Tide from the time it entered the Gulf of Oman until it reached the coast of Somalia. The name on the stern and the passengers dressed in traditional Arab clothes met the profile.

Admiral Michaels looked over at Eric as the phone rang. Captain Avery's call was hours overdue.

"Hello, Captain, how was dinner?"

"Sorry I'm late, Admiral. The tour of the yacht took longer than expected, and then I had to field calls from a couple of our U.S. Senators' aides. They said the owner of the yacht called and wanted to thank the Navy. That said, Captain Gamal put on quite a show, Admiral. My crew was impressed as was I, but if the warheads are on board they are in sealed units. Our tags all came back negative."

"We understand he might have picked up a bunch of Somalia refugees when he docked in Jeddah, Captain. They could be stored in their quarters."

"I'm sorry, Admiral, we saw it all. They did pick up a group of refugees, around fifty I think. They also have instructors on the yacht giving English lessons, but everyone seemed over and above board and friendly."

"Captain, this is Eric Ludlow. Do they have any weapons on board? Most of the big yachts have a security force."

"Security was on duty, Sir; a dozen men, maybe more. They carried side arms tonight, but the real hardware was in a secure area. The yacht also has cannon and chain-gun mounts. The hardware was out of sight, but the Captain opened the storage cabinets. He was proud of the assortment.

He said they would be crossing the pirate area off the Canary Islands, but he was quite confident about it. It seems a little strange that he would request an escort here since he is willing to deal with the pirates in the Atlantic."

"The Somalia pirates have become very active. Piracy is Somalia's main source of income. You were available and the owner has friends in Washington. It makes sense to me."

"One other thing, Admiral. Besides a number of U.S. Senators, Captain Gamal dropped a lot of high profile Washington names. He said there will be a reception at the family estate on Andros Island sometime in February."

"Thank you, Captain."

"It looks like the Crescent Tide is another dead end, Eric."

"I don't know that that's true. It seems a staged show to me, Admiral. He had no reason to request an escort. I do not believe for a minute that the Somalians are refugees. I think they are from the training camps. With the number of men on board and the hardware they have, they had nothing to fear from the Somalia pirates."

"The trawlers and the Blue Coral showed signs of radiation, Eric. If the warheads are on board the Crescent Tide there would be signs."

"Lead is cheap, Admiral, and can be hidden behind panels. Besides, it looks like they were intentionally leaving a false trail. We followed the radiation leaks and still lost the warheads. It would not surprise me if it was part of the plan and the warheads were back in lead boxes."

"The boat is now off of Kenya, Eric, and heading south. The Suez Canal and a trip through the Med would have saved weeks. It doesn't compute."

"Do you have an open line to the Tucson?

"Yes, but it's 2 am their time."

"It's the Navy, Admiral; get Lieutenant Holman on the line."

"I was up, Admiral. I just got off the line with Captain Avery. I'm sorry. I seem to have us chasing our tail."

"Lieutenant Holman, this is Eric Ludlow. Keep chasing it, things are not always as they seem. In the meantime would you please check the speed of the Crescent Tide and then plot a course from their present location, around the Cape of Good Hope to Salvador, Brazil, and then to Nassau, and give me an ETA."

"If I was plotting the course this time of year, I'd come by way of the Canary Islands. It's longer but the weather is better."

"Captain Avery said the Captain on the yacht mentioned the Canaries, but I thought that was smoke. It's the long way around. Plot it both ways, Connie."

"Yes, Mr. Ludlow. I've been following her. The yacht picked up speed after Captain Avery returned to his ship. She is running at 20 knots. It is twelve to thirteen thousand miles by way of Salvador, and another thousand by way of the Canaries depending on what corners they cut.

If they maintain their current speed, it will take twenty-six days by way of Salvador and about thirty days if they come through the Canaries. I am betting the Canaries. Today is the second of January. They have come this far without fuel so they are well tanked, but if we assume they will refuel at Cape Town, and then again in either Salvador or the Canaries, they should arrive in Nassau the first week in February."

"Thank you, Lieutenant."

"Connie, this is Admiral Michaels."

"Yes, Admiral, but I will have to take your word for it; I can't recognize the voices through the scrambler."

"I wanted to be the one to tell you. You can add a bar to your shoulder, Lieutenant Commander Holman. When this is over, if I'm still here, and if you want the job, you will be on my staff in Washington."

"Thank you, Admiral. I love sea duty; but for you I will make the sacrifice."

"Keep the Crescent Tide on the screen, Commander, and let me know if it changes course or speed."

"I will soon have a problem with that, Admiral. I don't have access to the Atlantic satellites. I would need the codes, but if I patch in, I will alert the spies in the Pentagon."

"Pack your bag, Connie, I'll make arrangements for your transfer to a surveillance ship in the Atlantic."

"The dots are connecting, Admiral. February in Nassau, it does *compute*."

"Maybe, Eric, but they have the politicians in the bag; it will get messy if we are wrong. If that yacht and the fifty Somalia refugees are involved, the couple is going to need more help than Colonel Rogers and his men can provide."

"Who do you have in mind, Admiral? Our resources are limited."

Captain Jenkins picked up the decoded message from Admiral Michaels. Commander Thompson was at the helm. "Commander, turn us south toward South Africa and plot a course around the Cape for Miami."

"Are we going home early, Captain?"

"No, we are just going to take a detour. That green-eyed woman friend of yours may need your help. I just volunteered you and your team's services."

CHAPTER 16

C ommander Holman boarded the National Oceanographic and Atmospheric Administration (*NOAA*) ship when the Crescent Tide left Cape Town. The Atlantis was cruising a hundred miles east of the Bahamas tracking a storm.

Captain Paige served under Admiral Michaels in the Persian Gulf. Terrorists kidnapped two of his men after a helicopter crash. He had become disenchanted with the military after they charged the men with murdering an Iraqi family caught in a cross fire during a rescue mission. There was no basis for the trial other than an attempt by temporary reservists in the military to pacify a group in the American Congress soured on the military.

The military court acquitted the men; but after the trial, Captain Paige switched services. Admiral Michaels approached him when Commander Holman suggested that the Congressional Committee and Jim Symington's staff may not be focused on NOAA's weather satellites or the Pentagon's communication with the NOAA ships.

Admiral Scott was in charge of the NOAA fleet in the Atlantic. He was also ex-Navy and blessed the mission. He then suggested they use the Atlantis as the base for the search in the Atlantic.

Shortly after she arrived, Commander Holman watched from her new office as Colonel Rogers and Captain Pitt landed on the deck of the Atlantis.

The Atlantis carried a crew of thirty; leaks were possible. Admiral Michaels was still using the scrambler.

"Admiral, Colonel Rogers landed a few minutes ago and I checked with my replacement on the Tucson. The new surveillance officer transferred in from the Atlantic fleet before I left. She said the Navy may do a routine search every few hours, but the military satellites are not dialed in on the NOAA ships."

"Tell them to tarp the helicopters anyway, Commander. It is not just our Navy; the British have a satellite and might get nosey about Air Force helicopters on your deck. I want to keep this under wraps until we have some answers."

The C-17 arrived at Eglin Air Force Base three weeks earlier. Antonio and Ayeza had joined the fisherman in a search of every cove and inlet on Andros Island. There were numerous new villas and armed guards patrolling the shores, but nothing out of the ordinary.

It had been a year since the *Apostate's* inauguration. The first of February was approaching and the consensus was that Al-Queda would not wait another year. Admiral Michaels instructed Commander Holman to widen the search.

Antonio and Ayeza's connection grew with each passing day. Ayeza was in love and Antonio found it easy to return. They played tourist during the daylight, pulling into the coves of the island showing off their catch and sipping wine with the natives at the numerous waterfront cafés, while searching for information. No one had heard of the Crescent Tide. Although there were many new villas and docks where a mega-yacht could berth, it was beginning to look like another dead end.

January in the Bahamas is the real beginning of what the natives call, *The Season*. The weather, a balmy seventies and eighties during the days, would often grow chilly when the sun went down. The fisherman's yacht was almost seventy feet in length and comfortable, but privacy overshadowed the comfort of their stateroom. The fast skiff on the yacht took them to the isolated white sand beaches of the outer islands where clothing was optional and there were perfect places for lovers to camp.

When they did sleep, they slept soundly. Antonio had buried Aletha, and the nightmares of her time with Faisal had faded from Ayeza's mind.

It was a cool morning, but later the sun would warm the air. Antonio was asleep, Ayeza was watching the stars thinking, *he does sleep soundly, but he does not mind me waking him, and I like catching up.*

Antonio usually woke first, but on occasions when she woke before he did, she liked to play the game. Ayeza slid out from under the blanket and turned to kneel, head to head with Antonio. Placing her hands on the sides of his waist, she leaned down brushing the nipples of her breasts across his lips while nuzzling his chest.

He woke with a smile; placing his arms around her back, pulling her to him, he turned them on their side. She feigned a resist, "You're hogging the blanket and it is cold out here."

"You woke me, what do you have in mind?"

"What are my options?"

"Whatever you like."

"You know what I like; you forever." Ayeza slid down under the blanket for a time, and then turned to lie beside him. When the gift of sensations only a woman can offer a man and he could return passed, they slept a while longer.

The radiant sun, warming the air as the orange-red ball separated from the horizon in an hourglass figure, woke them. "I love you, Ayeza."

"Then why is it that I am the one who has to ask you to marry me? I've been waiting!"

"I was getting around to it. It has only been a month."

"Our job is chasing nuclear warheads, Antonio. February is upon us. The yacht will arrive next week and this could get messy. There is a lovely chapel in Nassau; the captain knows the minister. I don't want to wait too long."

Days passed without success. Eric Ludlow, frustrated by the dead ends in the Middle East, had joined Commander Holman on the Atlantis. Antonio and Ayeza concentrated on Andros and the islands surrounding Nassau.

Connie was career Navy, and had spent almost twenty years living on board a ship. Before that, she had lived with her childhood love for six years, working at whatever job she could find to put him through medical school. She enlisted in the Navy a month after he graduated, and then failed to show up for their wedding.

Eric had a small apartment in the old quarter of Georgetown, but he lived out of a suitcase hopping around the Middle East. He had a failed marriage and few relationships since, but they never panned out.

Eric and Connie connected as a team, and as a couple. It was a mutual attraction. They had moved past the formalities, and had talked about giving it a try. If they survived the current mission, Connie would join Admiral Michaels's staff in Washington and move into Eric's Georgetown apartment. Eric would give up the travel and settle as a Middle East consultant to the Pentagon staff.

"Where is the Miami, Eric?"

"They arrived two days ago, Admiral. They are shadowing the Atlantis, waiting for orders."

"Captain Jenkins arrived early."

Weather is not an issue for a sub, and with nuclear power, fuel was not an issue.

"They passed the Crescent Tide when the yacht fueled at Cape Town, and then they came straight up and across the Atlantic, Admiral."

"Where is the Crescent Tide now, Eric?"

"Admiral, we could save a lot of headache if we just sink that damn boat when it approaches the Bahamas. The Miami has gear on board to recover the warheads. They could then tow it to the Puerto Rico Trench and drop it in twenty-five thousand feet of water. No one would ever find it. Even if the warheads aren't onboard the yacht, we would get rid of the Somalians and be doing ourselves and the British a favor."

"That was discussed. If there had been traces of radiation on board, Captain Jenkins would have boarded the yacht to search for the warheads and then sunk the boat in the Indian Ocean. But as of this morning, that option is off the table."

"What's changed? The Somalians are still on board."

"Yes, but there will be other visitors on board for the Atlantic crossing."

"Who's on the list?"

Arriving at Nassau during the height of the season was one of the keys to Al-Queda successfully delivering the warheads. The island would be crowded with cruise boats and thousands of tourists would be milling in town. British Customs and Immigration authorities would be busy.

Even the weather was cooperating. The series of winter storms were predicted when the Crescent Tide passed South Africa's Cape of Good Hope. The Florida cruise ships would be going to alternate destinations and the harbor at Nassau would be deserted.

There was no mention of the pending storms by the local news networks; the Florida economy was dependent on the tourist season. The storm would be ignored until it actually approached the coast of Florida.

When NOAA first predicted the storm would hit Nassau, Gamal sent word to Al-Queda that they would have to delay their arrival. The Lion Sheik sent Gamal a message to continue on course and to keep to the schedule. Later that day a message arrived at the American State Department, inviting the American politicians to join the Crescent Tide on the crossing.

They would pick them up at the Canary Islands and drop them at the cruise ship docks in Miami. The message neglected to mention the required stop in Nassau to clear the refugees.

"The invitation was a surprise to everyone. The resistance to an *apostate* in the Oval office started to surface after the election, and the imams in the mosques started getting vocal after the inauguration. Since then, a number of Middle East rulers cooled toward the new administration."

"Who's on the guest list, Admiral, and who is doing the inviting. It would be nice to know who owns that yacht."

"The Senate press secretary sent a notice that the Senator from Nevada and his staff were invited by a nephew of the Crown Prince of Saudi Arabia; someone we have never heard of by the name of McMood Fajal. The invitation is for them to join him on the yacht for the Atlantic crossing."

When the invitation came in the Senator jumped at the chance. His office was billing it as a public relations achievement for the new administration. The Speaker of the House was also invited. They all left the night before from Washington National on a private jet owned by the Prince. The flight time was seven hours to the city of Santa Cruz on one of the Canary Islands, and then a short helicopter hop to the Crescent Tide.

"They should all be on board by now."

"Just a minute, Admiral. Connie, zoom in on the yacht."

"Shit... Sorry Mr. Ludlow."

"If you are going to swear at me, at least use my first name. What is it?"

"The Senator and the Congresswoman are on the back deck having cocktails with someone in Arab clothes and a checkered head scarf. I can't make him out."

"Admiral, the Senator and Congresswoman are onboard the yacht."

"I heard, Connie, Eric. *Shit* is my reaction, too. Where is the yacht, Connie?"

"It's two hundred miles northeast of Santa Cruz, Admiral."

"Brazil was closer; it did not make sense to add a thousand miles to the trip."

"It is summer south of the equator, Admiral. There are constant storm fronts. If I had the time, I would choose the route they took. This time of year the winds are coming from the northeast across the Atlantic. The hurricane season in this area is past."

"The Crescent Tide is fast enough to outrun a storm. There is more to this than a pleasure trip. Besides, a storm is building between the Canaries and us. It looks like they all made a lousy choice. Stay with it, Connie, and call me if anything changes."

The winter storm had built off the coast of Europe, moving southwest toward the coast of Florida. When he was certain the hurricane force winds were on a collision path for the Bahamas, Captain Gamal set course to intercept the headwinds. More ship than yacht, the Crescent Tide was maintaining a distance of three hundred miles from the storm front as it approached Nassau.

The Senator and Congresswoman entered the salon when the following waves reached a height of fifteen feet. "Can you outrun it, Captain?"

"Don't be concerned, Senator, we will make Nassau before the storm catches us."

"Eric?"

"What is it, Connie?"

"We may have a new player; either that or the skipper has a death wish."

The Sultan had moved out of the harbor of Agadir, Morocco as the Crescent Tide turned southwest after leaving Santa Cruz.

Commander Holman began tracking the Sultan when Captain Gamal slowed the Crescent Tide to pace the storm and the Sultan moved into the wake of the bigger yacht.

At over one hundred fifty feet, the Sultan was classified as a mega-yacht, but it was a common maneuver for a smaller yacht to follow in the wake of a larger boat in a heavy sea. None-the-less, the storm was building and it would have made more sense for the Sultan to outwait it.

The Sultan had moved out of the Port of Agadir at a speed of thirty knots on a direct course to intercept the Crescent Tide. It seemed an intentional maneuver. Eric traced the Sultan to a wealthy Saudi Arab. The owner was a sports car buff with an entry in the Daytona 500. The Sultan had left Jeddah and arrived in the Port of Agadir eight days after the warheads disappeared.

"Eric, is it possible?"

"Nuts.... I don't know, Connie. I was beginning to think we had this pegged, but that's too much coincidence. Contact the Tucson. Ask them to dig in the archives and e-mail us the films of the Jeddah harbor from the time the plane crossed out of Iran until Captain Avery had dinner on the Crescent Tide. Let's find out if the Sultan was in contact with the Crescent Tide. Trace the Sultan from Jeddah to Agadir; see where it's been and where it's made port."

Eric continued to watch as the Sultan rode in the wake of the Crescent Tide on a course for Nassau.

"The tapes are in, Eric. The Sultan was berthed alongside the Crescent Tide in Jeddah. She left a day before the Crescent Tide, but returned with a steel net cable in one of her props. Divers cut it out and they left within hours of each other. The Crescent Tide came by way of the east coast of Africa, but the Sultan turned north toward the Suez Canal.

"Which one is carrying the merchandise, Connie?"

"Hell... I don't know, Eric. I thought we had it pegged to the Crescent Tide."

"We all did, but there are three warheads unaccounted for. Maybe they split them up again. We need to trace the Sultan to the builder and get the specs. Ask the ship's operator to patch me through to my office in Tel Aviv."

The Crescent Tide and the Sultan came across the Atlantic following the curve of the earth until they were below Bermuda. The storm was building as the Crescent Tide continued on a course for Nassau. The Sultan surprised Connie when it diverted from the wake of the larger yacht and turned southwest toward the lower end of the Bahamas. Connie watched the yachts grow farther apart until the Sultan was almost out of her camera range.

"The Sultan's turned toward the south end of the Bahamas, Eric."

"You take the Sultan, Connie; I'll stick with the Crescent Tide."

"It's been a rough forty-eight hours, Eric; they could just be tired of fighting the weather."

"The Crescent Tide is on course for Nassau; plot the new course of the Sultan."

"I did. If they maintain their present heading they will arrive south of Turk's island."

"You're navy, does that make sense?"

"It doesn't, not with the storm coming or if they want to make the Five Hundred on time. Turk's Island is three hundred miles south of Nassau; round trip that's six hundred miles out of the way. There are numerous closer passageways between the barrier islands. Besides, they are fast enough to outrun the storm and they were running with the swells. If they had continued to Nassau they would have beaten the storm by a day. Now they are quartering into the swells and heading right into it. It's going to be a rough ride and as big as that yacht is, they will take a beating until they reach the lee side of the islands."

"The storm is due in Nassau tomorrow evening. Maybe the Sultan is planning to come in behind it and then follow it up the coast."

"That doesn't make sense either, Eric. The storm has been downgraded from a hurricane to a tropical storm. They could berth in Nassau and ride it out. They will now cross through the full force of the storm before they reach the lee side of the islands. These people have a plan, Eric, and turning south is part of it."

"On their present course, what's their ETA to Turks Island?"

"Noon tomorrow."

The Crescent Tide arrived at the cruise ship docks in Nassau six hours before the storm would hit the east coast of the island. The head winds were approaching sixty knots, but the storm front itself had increased in recent hours and was predicted to reach ninety by evening.

The Crescent Tide would ride out the storm at the dock in Nassau. A private helicopter waited to transport McMood Fajal and his uncle to McMood's estate on Andros Island. McMood's sport fisher arrived earlier and would transport the Somalia refugees.

The pending storm hurried the process of clearing the refugees as the authorities evacuated the tourists and non-essential personnel from the harbor. Miami was now off the table for the Crescent Tide. The U.S. Navy helicopters were waiting on the dock to transport the Senator, Congresswoman, and their staffs to the Florida mainland.

Captain Gamal requested security from British Immigration the day before their arrival. He then leaked it to the news wire service that the American VIPs would be arriving and departing from the cruise ship dock instead of Miami as planned.

Eric closed the distance, zooming in on the British security officers escorting the VIPs through the crowds of reporters that had arrived by private yachts. British Immigration had set up tables at the gangplank of the Crescent Tide. With the head winds of the storm approaching, the British staff was hurrying the process. Eric shook his head while watching British Immigration personnel rubber stamp the passports of the refugees without ever looking up.

Eric was focused on the departing passengers when Captain Gamal turned the switch. As the helicopters lifted off the deck with the VIPs and the rest of America focused on the milling reporters and their camera crews leaning into the wind, the hatch below the room with no doors opened and the latch released the warhead from the saddle dropping it to the waiting diver.

The cameras continued to roll, and in drive-by-media fashion the reporters praised the politicians for their courage for crossing the Atlantic in the face of a typhoon, and their reporters for covering the story.

Jawdah Fattah was born in Iraq. His Sunni family was displaced when the United States toppled Saddam Hussein's regime. His affluent lifestyle changed when his family moved to the Muslim ghettos of Paris to escape the Sunni / Shiite bloodshed on the streets of Baghdad. Jawdah was vocal at the mosque about his hatred toward Americans and he participated willingly in the student riots against the French establishment.

Jawdah was a struggling English major in college, working his way through school as a waiter in a Paris café, catering to the rich tourists from America when Al-Queda recruited him. Shortly after 9-11, he changed his name, and with forged documents he migrated to America blending into the Iranian community in Dearborn, Michigan.

The Muslim student association was mostly Shiite. Jawdah hid his Sunni roots and his loyalties to Al-Queda while attending the University of Michigan. He praised the American invasion and rallied with his Shiite enemies when the Shiites took control of the Iraq government.

He played the role well. His moderate Muslim attitude and his masters in journalism earned him a spot with CNBC. He was a bright student and a quick study in his new job. He moved quickly through his apprentice days to a permanent position as a reporter, and writing an occasional syndicated guest editorial praising the Muslim American community's struggle to assimilate into the culture.

After the *Apostate* was inaugurated, Jawdah left to care for his mother in Paris. His request for leave stated that his mother would be undergoing a series of chemotherapy treatments. However, Jawdah's mother was cleaning a French woman's home when he passed over Paris on his way to his connecting flight in Frankfurt.

After his arrival in Cairo, Egypt, he took a bus to a fishing village on the Red Sea, where he boarded a trawler bound for the coast of Somalia. Others from Dearborn, Michigan had been arriving daily since the Democratic convention confirmed the *Apostate's* nomination. Targets and posters with the *Apostate's* picture lined the cabin walls and bulwarks.

Jawdah mingled with the Congresswoman's staff as he was leaving the yacht. His friends knew him as Jake Jacobs, the name on his forged American passport. Jake left the Crescent Tide a seasoned terrorist, but his light skin and clean-shaven face did not match the profile of the rest of the refugees. When he flashed his American passport, the men from British Immigration never looked up.

"Hello, Sally."

"Hello, Jake, I thought you were on leave."

"My mother passed away last week. She was the last of my family and Paris is dreary this time of year. I decided to take a week in Florida before going back to work. I was watching the news in Fort Lauderdale. Nassau and this story was only a boat ride away. I arrived this morning, but the owner of the boat I came on chickened out when the storm was upgraded. He returned to the mainland without me."

"I don't blame him; it's going to be a rough ride back. You are welcome to ride with us."

"Thank you. Do you have room for two? My cameraman is with me."

McMood Fajal's sport fisher arrived when the Crescent Tide was settling at the dock. Abdul Hasib, who had changed his name to Alan Kent, arrived from Dearborn, Michigan and boarded the sport fisher the night before to join the caravan of yachts leaving from Fort Lauderdale. Immigration glanced at his press pass when he flashed it on his way to join the milling crowds.

When the helicopters lifted off the dock, Alan followed Jake to where the members of the press had docked. Pausing at the edge of the dock he smiled when he saw that a diver was leaving the water after unraveling the bowlines caught in the prop from the two chartered CNBC yachts tied bow to bow.

News anchors across America salivated. The political fodder for the President's early foreign policy success would divert attention from the disguised but doomed socialistic maneuvers the new administration had begun implementing in a misguided effort to rescue the financial giants in the industry. Their efforts were failing. They had spent weeks justifying them even though the meltdown of the financial and manufacturing base in the U.S. had spilled across the globe. The press needed a diversion.

CHAPTER 17

Eric and Connie eliminated the islands one by one and continued to expand the circle of the search. Eric was searching Cat Island. Connie was moving to a flyspeck of an island further south.

The satellite passed over the harbor on Rum Cay as the crane was lifting the bulldozer from the deck of the barge to the end of what looked like an airplane runway.

"Eric……"
"What is it, Connie?"
"I don't know, but it's out of the ordinary."
Eric moved to join her at her station. "Zoom in, Connie."
They watched as the crane operator climbed on the dozer and drove it to an area littered with survey stakes. The crusher was spewing gravel into a dump truck. More equipment was grading the area, clearing rocks the blasting crews were generating for the crusher.

"What does NOAA have in the files on the island?"

"It doesn't look like much, Eric, and I doubt the Navy has any more. At the beginning of the 20th century it was covered with pineapple plantations that have been converted to playgrounds for the rich and famous. The American Coast Guard has protested to the British that drug smugglers moving cocaine from Bolivia use the coves on the south end of the island to wait out inclement weather. It is under British rule and outside U.S. Coast Guard jurisdiction when it comes to drug smugglers. Since the drugs are destined for the U.S., it's not a priority for the British."

"Dig deeper, Connie."

Connie opened the archives to review the old films. There was not much. The island was small, tucked behind larger barrier islands protecting it from the full force of most tropical storms. The last time Rum Cay took a direct hit from a major storm that came up the inside passage was in 1926.

The buildings on the island were leveled in the 1926 storm that brought a sixteen-foot tide surge and 175-mile per hour winds. However, the cliffs of Rum Cay rise to an elevation of one hundred seventy feet above sea level. A hurricane wave surge would not be a threat to the new buildings showing up on Connie's screen.

The new communities were above the tide surge and solid concrete buildings were built to withstand two hundred mile per hour winds. They would warn the residents of a pending storm, but Rum Cay was of no interest to NOAA's research. As the senior surveillance analyst in the Navy, Connie knew the U.S. Navy would also have little interest in the island.

Connie zoomed in on the water surrounding the island. Coral shoals laced the shores on either side of the entrance to the cove. Swimming birds moved quickly, indicating swift currents. Divers attempting to navigate the currents in the channels through the coral leading to treacherous tidal surges at the base of the vertical cliffs would be embarking on suicide missions.

British maps and accompanying notes confirmed what Connie was seeing on the screen. The tourist brochures warned anglers and divers to stay clear of the south end of the island.

The British charts were dated 1938. There would be new channels cut by the currents. Connie began systematically mapping the island. There was a narrow channel cut through the coral leading from the open ocean to the cove.

Folklore had it that the pirates of the nineteenth century blasted the channel open, and that they would lure passing ships to the coral shoals by placing lanterns along the cliffs.

Bolivian and Cuban refugees also exploited it during the latter half of the 20th century. During that time, Rum Cay became a safe haven for smugglers transporting drugs as well as refugees. The island had become the distribution point. Fishing trawlers would transfer the drugs and live cargo to the high-powered open ocean racing boats for the final leg to Miami.

"Continue mapping it. I'll get Admiral Michaels on the line." Connie zoomed in to map the buildings and other improvements. The straight-line, dark blue color change of the water signified a clear, deep-water passage between the shoals. It was apparent a dredge had recently widened and deepened the channel.

Connie mapped the deep water of the channel to the cove. The dock was nestled at the base of the cliffs protecting it on three sides. A rock jetty sheltered the fourth side from exposure to hurricane winds, or for that matter, the prying eyes of the occasional British Coast Guard cutter or buoy tender patrolling the area.

The strange, flat roof structures, their foundations cut into the stone cliffs, were set obscurely between the rock outcroppings a hundred feet above the water.

Connie marked what she assumed to be a cave at the end of the dock leading to an elevator entrance to the largest of the buildings.

The view would be stunning, but there were few windows in any of the buildings. It made no sense. Neither did the steep concrete pathways following the contours of the rock cliffs that were too narrow for the motorized carts parked at the dock. Connie thought it odd; it seemed the surface amenities were gingerbread. There had to be underground access and a network of tunnels connecting the buildings.

Connie dialed the secure line to the Pentagon. "Admiral, there is a flurry of activity on Rum Cay."

"I'm not familiar with Rum Cay, Commander."

"It's a remote island about two hundred miles southeast of Nassau. We did some research, Admiral. The island has a surface of about thirty square miles. The area on the south end known as Black Rock has a deep harbor. It caught my attention. It faces directly into hurricane alley and would not be anyone's first choice for an estate. However, there are a number of new buildings. There is also a large dock, and now they are building an airstrip. British records show it was a pineapple plantation, but a hurricane destroyed the settlement in 1926. There are no roads from the settlements to the north so it is completely isolated from the other communities on the island. The old tapes show it deserted and overgrown just three years ago, now it's a bustle of activity."

Connie scattered the satellite pictures on the table. The buildings and dock appeared to be finished and they were building a rock runway, but containers carrying steel construction materials continued to arrive daily. There was more going on they could not see from the surface.

"E-mail me the pictures, Commander. I'll contact the fisherman and send the couple in."

"Admiral, this is Eric Ludlow. Give me one day. Rum Cay will be a tough nut for the couple to crack, and we don't want to warn the occupants if there is a connection to the warheads. The CIA is working on an experimental dye called TR-3 that will raise their body temperatures. Antonio has used it before, it works. If they use the dye, we can trace them with the infrared camera in the satellite and guide them from here. That way we can keep them separate from the men on the island. I will call Ron Edwards and have him overnight a supply to the couple."

Alex Parker had been doing research around the islands as a front for his activities with the CIA. He petitioned British immigration for visas and permits to photograph and study the scorpion fish. The long spines trailing either side of the fish carried a lethal poison. Two divers died a few months apart after a spine pierced their hands while removing a fish from a spear.

Divers began encountering the subtropical species a few years after an aquarium overturned in a flooded house in the Florida Keys during a hurricane in the 1980s. The tide surge carried the fish to Andros Island where divers started to report frequent encounters with them by 1990. The fish was small, less than eighteen inches when mature, but the voracious fish spread outward throughout the Bahamas, decimating the juvenile populations of native reef dwelling fish. It was now threatening to overrun the reefs off the gulf coast of Florida.

The expedition also needed a reason to navigate the open water around Rum Cay as well as the shoals along the shoreline. Schools of immature six to eight foot hammerhead sharks were common sightings among fishermen and divers at the edge of the shoals, but adult sharks preferred the deeper water. Cruise ship passengers in the Mayaguana Passage south of Rum Cay had recently reported unusual sightings of massive hammerhead sharks sunning themselves next to floating debris that attracted baitfish, which lured the dolphin in.

Growing to a length of twenty-five feet and a weight of close to two tons, the adult sharks, known to spawn in the Puerto Rico Trench five hundred miles south, were lone hunters and seldom left the deep water. The British tourist industry financed the portion of the expedition that would radio tag hammerhead sharks to trace their migration.

Greg Lockhart, the captain of the Viking, retired from the CIA to a life of leisure, fishing and diving around the islands of the Bahamas. He supplemented his retirement chartering to the CIA on matters of national security when it came to high profile immigrants trying to reach the safe haven of land in the US, and the DEA surveillance teams tracking the drug transport through the Bahamas.

After securing the permits, Alex, the fisherman from the CIA and his crew boarded the Viking in Nassau to cruise the reefs in the area around Rum Cay. Ray Cable from the British Coast Guard base in Nassau was there to meet them.

Greg was on the back deck and the British officer was pacing the bridge when Alex arrived. Alex met Ray Cable a few days earlier when he picked up the permits for the expedition.

"Hello, Greg, why the British brass?"

"Hello, Alex, welcome aboard. The Brits threw us a curve. Cable brought maps of some newly restricted areas. Have your crew stow their gear in the forward cabin and put your luggage in the suite by the salon, then meet us on the bridge."

"Let the couple take the suite, Alex. This trip is doubling for their honeymoon. I'll take one of the forward cabins."

A courier made the delivery as Antonio and Ayeza paid the porters who carried the diving gear aboard. Antonio opened the package and removed the vials of TR-3. He remembered the first time and then looked over at Ayeza. He was sick for a week afterward. Not knowing how she would react to the drugs, he was tempted to lose them in the harbor.

The word, RESTRICTED, stamped in bold letters, and the highlighted area on the chart around the south side of Rum Cay were not there when he picked up the permits. Alex turned to the

British officer with a questioning look. "That's where one of the divers died, Lieutenant. I have clearances for the reef in that area."

"I'm sorry, Mr. Parker; the owners of the estate in Black Cove also own the spit of land on the south side of the reef. We sent them a notice that your expedition would be doing research on the reef. The reef falls within their property boundaries."

We only need a few samples. We will be in an out in a few hours."

"I'm sorry, the currents there are treacherous. The owners are high profile; they want privacy and they do not want the liability if something goes wrong. I have been instructed to tell you that they have posted armed guards and that you are to stay clear of the area."

"It is an area of high interest, Mr. Cable, but I don't like guns, or threats. We will stay clear of the spit and off their reef."

"I don't mean to imply it's a threat of any kind. It's not meant that way."

"Lieutenant, when you refer to armed guards and stay away in the same breath I get the message."

"Then I can tell them you won't be going to Rum Cay?"

"San Salvador is east of Rum Cay, and on our dive permits. We will dive for the scorpion fish there. However, the biggest hammerheads have been sighted in the deep water off the south shoals of Rum Cay. Tell the owners we will be fishing at night, but we will stay offshore and respect their privacy."

They approached Rum Cay that evening. The harbor lights shined in the distance as Greg slowed the yacht six miles offshore. Alex readied the lines while Antonio and Ayeza prepared their dive gear for the swim to the harbor. The un-baited lines trailed in the red die that looked like a chum-line from the air. The shark repellant would assure Antonio and Ayeza an uneventful swim to shore.

The helicopter passed over the Viking as it trolled five miles off the edge of the shoal, then turned toward the landing pad on the island. The water was murky from the recent storm, but the weather had improved and the silt was settling. "They are getting nervous, Antonio. This is the best it's going to get. Based on the forecast there may not be another opportunity for some time."

"Tell Greg to cross in front of the harbor entrance, Alex, but keep the lights on and the gear in the water. If they come back, we want them to think you are fishing for sharks."

Ayeza and Antonio followed the Apollo diver propulsion vehicle through the transom door as the Viking trolled the deep water past the entrance to the harbor. The couple dropped to the bottom with the antenna following on the surface. The GPS on their wrists pinpointed the waypoint at the end of the dock four miles away.

"They are in the water, Eric."

"We have been watching the harbor, Alex. They are getting nervous. There is a lot of activity near the helicopter pad. Connie spotted some adult hammerheads two miles northeast of your current position earlier today. Move offshore and make it look real until the couple is ready to return."

Commander Holman zoomed in on the harbor, picking up the heat radiating from the men on the ground. She then widened the circle, mapping the rest of the men in the buildings above the cove.

Connie was their eyes. She monitored the signal from the antenna that was floating on the waves behind them as they approached the harbor. Antonio checked the distance monitor on his GPS. "We are five hundred yards out, Connie; how many guards are posted?"

"There are two on each jetty. There are also guards on the dock, and two on the hill above the main house."

"Is there anyone home?"

"I'm not getting a reading through the roof of the main house, but there are no lights, and no one has entered the building through the front door today. However, there are more than a dozen men in what looks like a military barracks off the north end of the dock. They are in and out. They could be workers, or guards, or both."

"Connie, I am going to leave the antenna here with the dive tanks and the Apollo and mark the waypoint on my GPS. Do the same on yours as a backup. It is a clear line of sight to the dock, but we will lose audio and your text messages underwater and we will be splitting up when we enter the harbor."

"Antonio, this is Eric Ludlow. Commander Holman can't track you underwater without the antenna and your audio is routed through a scrambler. If you mix it up with the natives we won't know who is who. I know you hoped to avoid it, but we want the package to arrive if it's on the way. We do not want to put them on notice. With that many men on the island you will need to drink the dye."

"I've been down that road, Eric, but it is her first time. There is no guarantee how her system will react, but we do know she will be sick for at least three days. Connie can track our implants and the GPS signal after we reach the shore."

"That is too much risk. You will be in and out of the rock outcroppings. We can pick up the heat trails once you leave the water and your audio is a sonar signal that will bounce off the walls in free air, but we may not be able to read your implants or GPS signals below the cliffs. You must raise your body temperature so we know who is who; otherwise, we will not be able to separate you from the others. Drink the die now; it takes a few minutes to kick in."

As the bitterness of the liquid dissipated and the warm glow filtered through their bloodstream, they closed the valves on their dive tanks and then removed them. The tanks settled to the floor of the channel strapped to the Apollo.

The re-breathing devices would prevent the air bubbles from giving them away to the guards posted on the jetties. Antonio and Ayeza set the waypoint on the GPS, but they would have to rely on their compasses while submerged.

The floodlights from the dock lit the surrounding water, but there was an added glow of light hidden from the satellite cameras by the canopy of the dock. Divers were welding the last sections of the tunnel to the dock as the couple approached in the murky water.

Visibility was less than ten feet. Antonio and Ayeza swam cautiously along the bottom following their compass. They paused as other divers working their way alongside the tunnel pulled themselves along a rope tied to the dock. The shift was changing. As one man turned to leave, another took his place.

The gauge on Antonio's re-breathing device showed one third of the oxygen was used up. It would take as much for the swim back. Antonio typed a message on the transmitter on his wrist telling Ayeza to slow her breathing and hold her position until the shift change was completed.

A few minutes after the message appeared on her mask the last of the divers passed by. Antonio turned to Ayeza who he knew would be feeling nauseous from the dye. *It's time to split up, are you okay?*

Her attention diverted, Ayeza gagged, but held it back. If she got sick, she would have to surface. Tapping on the note pad on her wrist, *I'm alright; I'll deal with it on shore.*

She swam off when the nauseous feeling passed, but he knew it would return. Ayeza faded into the murky water. He watched from the shadows of a cluster of piling as the shift changed, and then moved alongside the dock taking pictures.

Antonio passed the workers and then paused beneath the pavilion above the completed end of the tunnel. The access hatch was open, but the room was dark. Lifting himself through the hatch, he removed his glove and felt the floor. It was still wet where the divers had shed their gear.

His body glowing, Connie spotted him the moment he left the water. "Are you there, Antonio?"

"Yes, the router is working. Where are the guards?"

"The guards in the harbor are at the far end of the dock and on the jetties. There are men milling around one building we think is their quarters. The rest of the grounds are clear."

"Where is Ayeza, Alex?"

Connie picked her up when Ayeza crawled ashore and found a secluded spot to vomit. She had a fever, but then the nauseous feeling was gone. She rinsed her mouth with salt water and then scaled the wall to the path connecting the buildings. Connie continued to check the path in front of her as she roamed the grounds filming the unusual buildings and transmitting the images to Connie's computer.

Whoever the owners were, they built a fortress, not a villa. The concrete poured walls and seamless concrete roofs would be indestructible in a hurricane, and the inch-thick panes would withstand two hundred fifty mile per hour winds.

"She landed on the beach and scaled the wall. The dye is working, but her temperature has not settled and is climbing. Connie is tracking her and coaching her on directions. Do your job and let her do hers; the sooner the better. She will meet you back at the Apollo and the dive tanks when she's done."

"What's her temperature?"

"104."

"I know the drill, Eric, we are supposed to be on our own, but the rules changed with the dye."

"You have the plans of the facility and a clear passage back to the Viking, Antonio. This was your choice and hers; she has a capsule. If one of you is caught the other must abandon the mission and bring what you have. Either way, you have what we need, your mission is finished. Get back to the Viking; Ayeza will be along when she's done."

"The dye was not part of that deal, Eric. We don't know how it will affect her. If her fever climbs too high she risks swallowing the capsule, even if she is not caught. The plans show a tunnel to a manhole on the runway. When I exit the tunnel, Connie can lead me to Ayeza. The plans are a bonus. We have enough information. Tell her to spit the capsule out and return to the beach. We will make the swim together."

"We have her on camera; it looks like she is alright. Connie will send her a message. If something changes I'll let you know."

The pavilion was the construction office and temporary access to the tunnel. The plans were in the rack next to the drafting table. Antonio took the pictures then re-entered the tunnel in search of the branch leading toward the runway.

Eric homed in on Ayeza's waypoint and transmitted it to Antonio's GPS receiver. Antonio then left the tunnel at the manhole and returned from the airstrip with Eric guiding his path to skirt the guards. Ayeza was to wait at the top of the cliff above the beach.

Ayeza remembered the rape and the stones in the village square. She refused to dislodge the capsule when she reached the edge of the cliff. Her fever was climbing and she was having difficulty focusing. Disoriented, she started the climb down before Antonio arrived.

The ten minute walk took twenty while Connie led Antonio, skirting the guards and taking the long way around.

Ayeza paused, straddling a rock ledge to get her bearing and disturbed a nesting gull. Startled, she slipped and fell the last twenty feet.

She felt a sharp pain as she fell back but the sand cushioned her fall. Antonio found her asleep by her mask and fins, hidden in the brush, clutching her knees.

Connie had been monitoring her body temperature. "I think she still has the capsule. Make her spit it out and then get her in the water, Antonio; her fever is over 104 and rising."

There was a tear in Ayeza's dry suit where she had grazed off a rock when she fell. The cut on her ribcage was deep and seeping blood. Antonio pried her mouth open and swept the capsule from between her teeth and tongue. "She's cut, Connie, we need to stop the bleeding."

Cutting strips from his dry suit, he bound her chest, but the blood oozed from the makeshift bandage. She woke as he was stripping her suit off of her. "It's time to go, Ayeza."

He reached to help her, but Ayeza waived him off. "You go, let me rest, I'll be okay."

"You're not okay. Your suit is torn and it's soaked with blood. Help me, let's get it off."

Antonio stripped the suit off her. The bandage came with it exposing the nasty cut along her ribcage.

The numbing pain caused Ayeza to focus as Antonio turned her on her side. "What now, Antonio? Alex is fishing for sharks; they are hammerheads and have the best sense of smell of any predator on earth. The blood will bring them to us from miles out. You must go without me."

Ignoring her, "I'll cut my suit up and bind the wound again, but your temperature is over 104. We have to get you in the water. The water will cool your fever some, but we need to get you in some ice. I'm going to attach a line to your wrist for the swim back. Stay with me, but yank on it if you get in trouble."

"I'm ok."

Antonio checked the re-breathing device. They had less than 20 minutes. They could clear the harbor but would have to surface before they reached the dive tanks.

Ayeza winced at the pain from the salt in the wound when they re-entered the water together. Even though Antonio was swimming slowly, the line connecting him to Ayeza was stretched tight. Half way to the dive tanks Ayeza turned toward the rock outcropping at the base of the jetty. Antonio caught her, signaling her to wait until he checked the surface. She shook her head, she could not wait. Stripping her mask from her face she vomited, then gagged as she started to inhale the seawater.

Connie picked them up on the heat sensors and a message flashed on his screen when they surfaced. Antonio was dragging her to the rocks.

"You are off course, Antonio; there is a guard approaching fifty meters south."

"We need a minute."

"You don't have a minute."

"I'll deal with him."

"Antonio, this is Eric; don't use a weapon; make it look like he slipped and fell."

Antonio began to remove his mask and flippers when Ayeza whispered, "I'm alright now, let's go."

Waves lapped the jetty masking the sound. The guard passed by as the couple slipped below the surface and turned toward the Apollo and the dive tanks.

Ayeza waited on the surface while Antonio retrieved the tanks. She shied away as he tightened the straps after settling the tanks on her back. Antonio's light shined through her mask. Her eyes were glazed, but she was attempting a smile. She signaled with thumbs up, but when Antonio turned toward the Viking in the murky water, a disoriented Ayeza swam toward shore. When the line between them came tight, the message flashed across his mask. *Antonio, contact me before you come in, Alex.*

Alex was monitoring the screen. *Alex, we will be at the waypoint in twenty minutes, but Ayeza is sick. We will have to come in on the surface.*

You can't approach the boat. The helicopter is flying a pattern over us with their floodlights searching the water. We had to make it look real. We have an adult shark on the line. There are a dozen more in the water. Turn when you leave the channel. Let the current carry you to the alternate waypoint. Nine miles should be enough and she will not have to swim. The current is running at six knots. Keep it together for an hour and a half. We will lose the shark and then make it look as if we are heading home.

Antonio and Ayeza surfaced when they moved out beyond the channel entrance. Blood was seeping past Ayeza's makeshift bandage into the current.

We are on the surface, Alex, switch to audio.

"We will meet you at the waypoint in ninety minutes, Antonio."

"We can't wait that long; we need to get her in some ice."

"We'll cut the shark loose in a minute. One of the others has taken a chunk out of him. The others are milling closer with each pass. Soon they will be in a frenzy and will follow the carcass; come in deep, and then straight up to the transom. You can wait below the boat and we'll bring you in when the helicopter is out of view of the stern."

"Ayeza is cut and bleeding, we can't come through the sharks; we are leaving a trail of blood, but we can't wait. Her fever is 104; we need to get her onboard and iced down before it climbs above 105."

"How much time left on the re-breathing devices? If she is up to being dragged, we can set a diver on a tow line. You can latch on when we pass over and we will tow you out of here."

"The re-breathers are almost polluted; there is very little time left, and you can't tow us with tanks."

"The helicopter has flood lights. If they tail us, they will spot you on the surface, and we cannot stop and pick you up without giving the mission away. What are the options?"

"Where is the helicopter?"

"Circling about a quarter mile off of our stern, but they will probably move in on us if we pull our gear and head your way."

"There is a phantom bungee line with our gear, Alex. It blends with the night and cannot be seen beyond fifteen feet. Use the spear instead of the tagging pole; put it through his gills, he'll bleed more. Then cut the shark loose. Dump your chum to draw the other sharks in, and then head our way."

The helicopter was approaching. When the spear sliced through the gill of the man-eater and exited through its stomach the sharks circling the boat moved in on the cloud of blood."

"We have the sharks' attention, Antonio; now what? I've never seen a line like this."

"Tie the bungee to a cleat then set it in an outrigger with the spreaders and the loop pacing the outside of the rooster tail. Track our GPS signal. Tell the skipper to make a turn on the waypoint. Pick us up at twenty knots, but when the line leaves the outrigger, put the throttles to the wall and keep them there until the helicopter turns back and is out of sight.

Ayeza was becoming delirious, drifting in and out of consciousness. Antonio would need to free himself of Ayeza while he made them ready for the pickup. "Focus, Ayeza, keep the re-breather clenched between your teeth and tread water."

Antonio dropped their tanks, and then he ran the straps he cut from the tanks across her chest and under her arms, tying her to him.

He was drifting on his back face up. Her re-breather was polluted. He was supporting Ayeza on his chest when the Viking passed the channel of the harbor. The bungee line had divers attached that would keep the noose separated.

When the Viking came in sight with the helicopter following, Antonio stripped her mask off and placed his re-breathing device in her mouth. He then pinched her nose shut before he took a deep breath and let them settle just below the waves.

A dozen sharks had moved in on the kill. The mix of chum and blood carried in the currents attracting others prowling the edge of the reef. The scent of Ayeza's blood had spread, creating a new trail to follow.

A hammerhead has ten times the sensory perception of any other shark. Blood was the draw, but when the electrical charge from the transmitting GPS on Antonio's wrist crossed on the sensors of the four foot wide head, he turned his 23 foot length and homed in on the scent and signal.

As the Viking approached the waypoint in a sweeping turn toward Nassau, the two foot fin surfaced, matching the speed of the yacht racing toward the couple.

Alex spotted the fin and the wake of the three thousand pound fish as it moved beyond the bow of the yacht in a race to its prey. The waypoint was three hundred yards ahead.

"Now, Greg!"

In an act of desperation Alex knocked the bungee from the outrigger, signaling the captain to accelerate the yacht.

The turbochargers kicked in and the rooster tail of the yacht passed the shark a few seconds before the noose came tight around Antonio's outstretched arm. The bungee stretched, absorbing the shock that would have pulled his arm from its socket and then it retracted, lifting them out of the path of the charging predator and in position behind the nine foot rooster tail of the accelerating sport fisher.

The force of the water tore Antonio's mask away when he and Ayeza surfaced in the rooster tail. He turned, resettling Ayeza against his chest and watched as the shark picked up the flash in the water and turned, inhaling the mask and the re-breathing device.

The captain settled the Viking's speed at forty knots as the helicopter made a final pass. The trailing spray from the nine-foot high rooster tail hid the couple from view on the moonless night.

Missing its prey, the shark veered off toward the chum line. The helicopter turned toward Rum Cay when the Viking cleared the north end of the island and made the turn toward Nassau.

When the radar confirmed the skies were clear, the Viking settled in the waves. Alex helped Antonio bring her on board and put her in the fish box, packing the ice around her.

"What about you, are you all right?"

"I still have my arm, but it was close. That was some lift off, Alex. Twenty knots is about maximum for a pickup."

"The shark was doing twenty-five."

"Yes, I know. I caught the flash when he took my mask, he was almost on us. Not that it matters, but it looked like an adult, how big was he?"

"Over twenty feet, three thousand pounds, give or take. Tied together like you were, he would have got you both."

The drug was designed to maintain a temperature between 102 and 103 degrees, 104 to 105 would cause delirium; 106 and above, brain damage. Antonio reached to feel her skin; it was cooling.

"I have been through it, but my reaction was not as severe. It is still experimental; my fever got to 104, hers was pushing 105, but it is like the measles; once you go through it, you are immune. We will take her out of the ice when it drops to 103, but it will fluctuate for the next twenty-four hours and she will dehydrate. I need to get her to an infirmary and on IVs."

"There are medical facilities on Cat Island and there are a number of cruise ships in the local ports. They all have infirmaries."

"That won't work; we don't want the civilians to know we've been here. Tell the skipper to contact Eric Ludlow, Alex. He is on the NOAA ship, Atlantis. The ship has medical facilities and is northwest of Cat Island. Tell them to turn on a heading for the center of Crooked Island Passageway. We will take the skiff and meet them halfway."

"The Atlantic is still rough from the effects of the storm. Why not call for a helicopter? NOAA has them; so do the British Coast Guard on Cat Island. It's a short hop."

"The British will get nosey if NOAA makes a pickup, and we need to leave the Brits out of the loop. The owners of Rum Cay can buy a lot of information. It may just be a drug enclave, but if the warheads are headed for Rum Cay, we do not want to warn them off."

"What about us?"

"Go back to Andros Island. Spread a little money and some stories about the big one that got away near Rum Cay. See if you can draw some interest. If there is a connection, we need to tie Andros and Rum Cay together."

CHAPTER 18

The Atlantis intercepted the USS Miami northeast of Cat Island. After Commander Thompson and the Seals transferred to the Atlantis, the Miami turned south for the trip to the Miami's homeport in Bangor, Washington. The trip around Cape Horn, then back up the western seaboard of the Americas would take a while.

Commander Thompson joined Colonel Rogers in the galley as Captain Paige set course to intercept Antonio, fifty miles east of Mayaguana Island. "Welcome onboard, Commander, but I thought your orders were to go home."

"Admiral Michaels is bypassing normal channels. No one except the crews on the Miami and the Atlantis know we are here. The Miami's tour ends when they check in at their namesake. They can't use the Panama Canal. If they take their time around the Cape, it's a month trip to Bangor. We won't be missed."

"Did the Admiral brief you on the mission?"

"Yes, but it makes no difference. The Admiral said the green-eyed woman might need some help. He asked for volunteers. I hate to leave a job half done, and I have a debt to repay."

"Her name is Ayeza, Commander, and she has earned respect from all of us."

"No disrespect meant; I know her name, Colonel, she's the reason I'm alive. What is our part in the mission?"

"That depends, how is the arm?"

"It missed the bone. I can't swim for a while, but I can steer the boat. How is Ayeza? Rumors have it they used TR3 and that she's had a nasty reaction."

"I'm not familiar with it."

"It's still experimental. A couple of my men nearly died testing it. I know other Seal units who read our report and have refused to use it until they perfect it. Will she be well enough to go back in with us?"

"The report's not in, but she and Antonio are on their way. We know she is sick, but past critical. The indication is she will be alright, but if not, are you willing to go in without her?"

"We volunteered to help the woman, but there is more at stake. The crew on the Miami tried to entice the captain to stick around. We don't know the plan, but he felt it would risk the mission with a nuclear sub in their waters if the British got nosey. Either way, with or without Ayeza, if they connect Rum Cay to the Sultan or the Crescent Tide, or even to the militant Muslims, we are going in, so bring me up to speed, Colonel."

"The maps are on the wall, Commander; Admiral Michaels is waiting for our assault plan."

Ayeza's temperature was holding steady at 103, but she was dehydrated and weak. Her temperature would climb again until the dye dissipated from her body. She couldn't keep anything down. She would need intravenous liquids until her muscle tissue absorbed the balance of the dye.

After helping Antonio launch the skiff, Greg turned the Viking toward Andros Island. Antonio strapped Ayeza in and then settled back into the hydraulic seat next to her. "Stay focused, Ayeza."

Antonio started the three, three hundred horsepower high performance outboards and pointed the 28 foot skiff toward the waypoint at the entrance to the Crooked Island Passage south of Cat Island.

Ayeza's temperature began to rise as soon as Antonio removed her from the ice. The storm front had passed, but the open ocean was rough. Antonio stuck to the lee side of the islands and as exhilarating as it was at over one hundred crossing the slick water on the shallow shoals, Antonio slowed to fifty miles per hour when he entered the Atlantic. Ayeza was in the infirmary on board the Atlantis less than two hours after the shark missed their feet.

Rum Cay is the outermost island in the string. Captain Paige set a course to a waypoint fifty miles southeast of Crooked Island Passage in a straight line with Rum Cay.

When Ayeza was on board the crew on the Atlantis secured the skiff to the deck next to the helicopters.

Antonio helped plan the mission. The skiff would look like a high performance fishing boat crossing the shoals southeast of Rum Cay. The British patrol boats were used to the sportsmen who could afford the high performance boats outrunning them and wouldn't bother to give chase. Colonel Rogers and Captain Pitt would fly the center of the passage and approach the island under the British radar on San Salvador and Long Island.

Connie pinpointed the radar and communication center at the compound on Rum Cay, which would be the Special Forces' primary target. If Rum Cay was a drug distribution center, there was little risk they would be in a hurry to notify the British authorities.

Ayeza was recovering in the infirmary. Antonio turned the camera chips over to Eric, and then joined Colonel Rogers and

Commander Thompson in the galley. The brass in Washington would make the final decisions. For the time being, there was nothing more any of them could do.

The ship's emergency horn sounded at 4 am waking everyone on board. Eric entered the galley carrying a message Ron Edwards sent by e-mail after reviewing the pictures Antonio and Ayeza took on the island.

We traced ownership of the compound on Rum Cay to a company belonging to one of Bin Laden's cousins from Saudi Arabia who disappeared without a trace last year. Rumor has it that he is in the mountains of Pakistan advising Al-Queda.

Alta Al Rahman was high profile before 9-11, but the Bin Laden name was enough to condemn him in Washington. He moved to New York and dropped the Bin Laden from his legal name, and then added the Al, but he could not shed the association.

Rahman owns an offshore construction company based in Saudi Arabia. He also has ties to the Taliban in Pakistan dating back to the Afghan / Russian conflict. He was in bed with the CIA and the Pakistan government at the time. When the Russians pulled out, he crossed the CIA and instead of shutting it down, expanded the heroin network to the States. Rum Cay is also in line with Mona Passage, which is the route of choice for the Colombia drug cartels moving cocaine to the States.

Rahman's company has the permit for the project on the Island. Rum Cay could be nothing more than a receiving and distribution point for a drug enclave. We are still working on a connection between the Crescent Tide and the Sultan, but after Captain Avery's dinner with the captain of the Crescent Tide, and with the Crescent Tide docked at Nassau, we think that's a stretch.

Check with your people in Cairo, Eric; yards in Alexandria outfitted both yachts. From Captain Avery's description, the Crescent Tide is a five hundred million dollar toy and the Sultan looks to be at least half that. Somebody will know where the money came from.

Antonio reached for the coffee to refill his cup. "Drugs may be involved, Eric, but they could also be the cover. The plans show a four hundred foot berth on one side of the dock, and four smaller berths on the other side. The tunnel under the dock has diver access ports at each of the berths and also to a manhole on the runway. Once it is completed and they have underwater access to the yachts, there is no way our eye in the sky can follow the action."

Connie entered the room. "Eric, Admiral Michaels is on the line."

Ask the lieutenant to patch it through. We'll take it in here on the conference line."

"It's looking like the Crescent Tide is a dead end, Eric. Captain Avery said the captain of the Crescent Tide told him the party will be at the estate on Andros. We put feelers out. The party is the weekend before the Daytona Five Hundred. It's a Washington VIP affair. They will hold it on the yacht at the estate. After the party, they will be taking a smaller yacht to the race. CNBC will provide their yacht in exchange for exclusive rights to cover the party. We know of five senators and eight congressional representatives who have accepted the invitation."

"I'm not convinced and neither is Connie, Admiral. Jeddah and the cross Atlantic trip is too much coincidence. The yachts are the only leads we have. The race isn't until the fourteenth. Connie has been tracking the Sultan. It's still within range and the Crescent Tide has time to make the detour before the race."

"Is the dock ready at Rum Cay?"

"We think so, but we cannot verify it without another trip in, and now there is a string of buoys across the entrance to the harbor. From the air, it looks like a net of some sort. They have also doubled their guards and have armed them with automatic weapons. No matter how we go in, they will know we are there. We are going to have to wait until a boat arrives, then make an assault on the island and hope we picked the right target."

"The British won't like it if we're wrong, Eric."

"If we're wrong, they won't put up a fight, Admiral. But it does look like drugs or the warheads, or both. Either way the British win."

"The British may not see it that way, Eric. ... Where is the Sultan, Connie?"

"South of Turks Island, Admiral."

"That's off the path, Connie. Rum Cay is three hundred miles north."

"We clocked the Sultan at fifty knots; that's only six hours. There has to be a connection, Admiral.

"Keep me posted, Connie. We have no authority over the drug trade on a British island. I cannot authorize an assault on Rum Cay without some connection to the warheads."

"Yes, Admiral." Frustrated, Connie went back to her station and settled in. When the Sultan turned west toward Cuba, Connie was beginning to think the Admiral was right.

It was almost daylight and the shift at the screens was changing. Connie moved to the cot by her desk setting the alarm for 8 am. Ayeza was in the galley sipping coffee when she walked in. Connie had not met Ayeza, but her green eyes were her trademark. "I'm Connie. You must be Ayeza; may I join you?"

"Certainly, and thank you for the guidance on the island."

"You are resilient. I thought we lost you on the cliff, and then again on the jetty, and that shark, he missed you by inches. How are you? We all thought you would be in the infirmary for another day or two."

"My fever is almost gone and my stomach has settled, but I don't remember much after the fall. Antonio dragged me back to the boat."

"Where is this Antonio I've heard so much about? We are all on a first name basis, but I still haven't met all the players."

"He's asleep in the bed next to where I was in the infirmary. He's tired and he's a sound sleeper. I didn't have the heart to wake him."

Connie poured a cup of coffee and stood to leave. "I have to get back to the screen, would you care to join me? I could use another set of eyes."

Connie paged Eric shortly after 9 am. "Eric, the Crescent Tide is leaving Nassau on a course for Andros Island. She's not coming to Rum Cay."

"Where is the Sultan, Connie?"

"You don't want to hear it."

Connie had been tracking the Sultan as it approached the south end of Great Iguana Island. It was not making sense. She backtracked to review the films of the port of Jeddah when the Sultan and the Crescent Tide berthed side by side. Ayeza joined her at the desk. "There has to be something we're missing, Ayeza."

Jeddah was a mass of humanity making the pilgrimage to Mecca and Medina. The dock swarmed day and night with arriving passengers. Separating a few out of the crowd of millions was impossible for the human eye.

Ghalib boarded the Sultan unnoticed as Jawdah led the group recruited from the Islamic Center of North America in Dearborn, Michigan through the crowd. Jawdah turned into the passageway leading to the lower level entrance to the Crescent Tide to wait for the refugees from Somalia. The others continued on to join Ghalib on the Sultan.

Eric entered the room when the film was showing the refugees from Somalia mingled with the crowd waiting ten or more hours to clear immigration. "Eric, there are thousands of people on the dock. The men are all dressed alike and their heads are covered. The women are covered head to toe; some could be men posing as women. There are men coming and going from both yachts. I cannot tell one man from the other. How do we know who is on what boat?"

"Why do we care, Connie? We are searching for nuclear warheads, not illegals."

Frustrated, Eric and Connie left the search to Ayeza who was studying the split screen. Ayeza did not have a clue as to who was who, but one screen showed Jawdah and the volunteers from Moqtada al-Sadar's army in Iraq on the deck of the Crescent Tide performing their noon prayers at the dock in Jeddah. The mingling crowd on the dock at Nassau was on the other.

Eric and Connie returned to the room and were standing in the background when Ayeza zoomed in on the deck of the Crescent Tide to study the passengers. "It isn't about illegal immigrants, Ayeza. Forged documents are a foregone conclusion, and the British are only concerned with numbers. It's looking like the Crescent Tide is a dead end."

"Somebody has to deliver the warheads when they arrive, Eric. Do we have software to isolate the men on the boats and the docks in Jeddah and compare their features to the ones leaving the Crescent Tide at Nassau?"

"Not onboard the Atlantis, Ayeza, but my office in Washington does. What's the point?"

"We are all concentrating on finding the warheads before they make land. Maybe we should be looking for the people who will be delivering them as well. If we miss the weapons, at least we might have an idea who to look for."

"It's a long shot, but worth a try. I have the access codes. Connie can patch into the CIA photo imaging computers and start a scan."

"While she's at it, have the computer compare the features of those on the docks to known terrorists in our data banks and to Muslim students in America who have had a run in with our law enforcement. We might get lucky."

The computer works a million times faster than the human mind. The CIA photo imaging computers began comparing what features they could distinguish beneath the Arab garments of the multitudes on the docks at Jeddah to those in Nassau the day the Crescent Tide arrived.

Connie settled back after splitting her screen into quarters. The Sultan had turned toward the Windward Passage which separates Haiti from Cuba.

Rum Cay was quiet. The construction crews had left the island with the barge. They had also replaced the net across the harbor entrance after the barge passed. Men attached electrical cables leading from a new transformer to the net when the barge cleared the harbor entrance. Connie knew they were expecting someone, but whom?

Ayeza was concentrating on the features of a bearded Arab on the gangplank of the Crescent Tide in Jeddah and that of a clean-shaven passenger leaving the Crescent Tide in Nassau. The computer pegged him as a fifty-five percent match to a Muslim journalist on the CIA watch list by the name of Jake Jacobs, but the computer was still working on the images.

The CIA computer also identified a man on the dock who went to school with Jacobs in Michigan; the match was 100% but he was leaving the dock, not heading for one of the boats. His picture came on the screen identifying Abdul Hasib. Hasib had changed his name to Alan Kent after an altercation with airport security when he was profiled and then jailed as he was trying to board a plane from Paris to New York. Immigration records showed he had returned to Miami from making his pilgrimage to Mecca two weeks before the Crescent Tide arrived.

Alan Kent was on the same list with Jake and he was a person of interest on the FBI's watch list. Jake and Alan had been students at the University of Michigan and were associated with the radical side of the American Student Muslim Association until shortly after the 9-11 attack on the World Trade Center.

The computer picked up speed as it discarded the chafe. Other images began appearing on the screen. The computer was running random comparisons of men on the docks in Jeddah to those of a group of Saudi Arabian students whose visas had been cancelled after the 9-11 attack on the World Trade Center. The CIA lost track of them after they returned to Riyadh until two of them turned up on surveillance cameras in the mountains of Pakistan. It was assumed the others had migrated to Sudan or Somalia.

Connie had been monitoring the Sultan while Ayeza was downloading the films of the CNBC crew on the yacht as it left the harbor at Nassau. The Sultan slowed for a Cuban naval boat as they entered Cuban waters.

"Eric, it looks like the Sultan is planning on crossing into the Caribbean."

"That doesn't make sense. Our sources had them going to the race. Zoom in on the yacht, Connie."

Eric and Connie watched the Sultan's deck crane lift from its saddle as the Cuban patrol boat rafted alongside. The Sultan's crane moved the inflatable and then transferred twenty, what looked like bales of marijuana, into the hold below the hatch on the Sultan's bow.

After it was loaded, the patrol boat turned toward the coast of Cuba. Before the patrol boat was out of sight, a high-speed cigarette boat approached from the northern tip of Haiti. After lifting the four pallets of cargo, someone on the Sultan lowered a suitcase to a deckhand on the cigarette boat.

Connie assumed payment had been made and refocused on the deck of the Sultan as it turned and settled on a northerly course. Out of the corner of her eye, Ayeza saw the powerboat disappear off the screen on a course toward Jamaica.

Eric forwarded the film and then contacted Admiral Michaels. "The Sultan is approaching Rum Cay, Admiral. We sent the films to the DEA. They estimate marijuana worth fifty million was unloaded by the Cubans and cocaine worth over a hundred million was loaded from the Jamaican boat. We can assume the Sultan is also carrying a ton or more of heroin. At that rate it won't take many shipments to pay for the facilities at Rum Cay."

"We aren't chasing drugs, Eric, and Rum Cay is out of our jurisdiction."

Ayeza signaled to get Connie's attention.

"What is it, Ayeza?" "Connie, tell the Admiral the computer has a new match."

"Thank you, Ayeza, we'll patch in." The CIA photo imaging was updating. "Eric, Admiral, we have a positive match on one of the men that was at the dock in Nassau when the Crescent Tide arrived with a man on the dock at Jeddah when the Sultan and Crescent Tide were in port. He's a militant Muslim with ties to Somalia. He studied at the University of Michigan. The computer is catching up fast as it narrows the field, Admiral. We also have a sixty-five percent match of a journalist who was in Nassau and a man on the gangplank of the Crescent Tide in Jeddah. We also have fifty percent matches of men who approached the Crescent Tide's gangplank in Jeddah with this man, but then split off to board the Sultan. They all have records. Two of them were released from GITMO last year and the others were deported from the U.S. within a few months of one another."

"Is there any new activity on Rum Cay, Connie?"

"There are three big yachts approaching from the north and a Lear arrived on the runway a few hours ago, Admiral. The net across the harbor entrance has been removed; they are expecting company soon."

"Admiral, I can't see the Sultan arriving at a Florida dock with two hundred million worth of drugs on board. They will have to split it up and Rum Cay is the obvious place. We also have men on the Sultan tied to the Crescent Tide. Whatever is going down is gathering speed and the dots are connecting the two yachts and the militant Muslims. What more do we need?"

"Alright, Eric, if the Sultan docks at Rum Cay send Ayeza and the Special Forces in by air, and Antonio and the Seals in by water."

"We already put it to a vote. The Seals want to go with Ayeza."

"It makes no difference to me, who goes with whom, but this is not a school picnic, and we had better be right. The administration and the State Department are anxious to pull the plug on this."

CHAPTER 19

———————

Connie plotted the course when the Sultan turned northeast and settled at a cruising speed of fifty knots. It was on a heading for Rum Cay, and it was in a hurry.

Connie refocused on the harbor. There was a Lear jet on the runway and three seventy to eighty foot sport fishing yachts had settled at their berths.

"The yachts are at the dock, Eric. They are all off-loading what look like high performance cigarette boats. There is also a forty to fifty foot Fountain offshore racing boat approaching from Cat Island."

"What about the Sultan?"

"She is on course for the harbor, five hours out at her current speed."

Eric gathered the Seals and Special Forces in the conference room where Antonio and Ayeza were watching the satellite view of the harbor at Rum Cay. "The Sultan has picked up speed, Eric. She will be at the dock in less than two hours."

"We will wait to make the assault until all five boats are in the harbor, Antonio."

"Eric, do we have a count of the crews on the yachts?"
"We have counted six men on each of the yachts and four on the Fountain, Ayeza. We think the Sultan is carrying close to fifty men. Admiral Michaels is tuned in with General Sampson. We thought they intended to divide the drugs and the men among the yachts and the Lear. Now it looks like we have the cigarettes and the Fountain to deal with too. We need to contain all of them in the harbor until we finish the weapons search."

"That's a lot of expensive toys but there are close to seventy men on the boats plus the guards, Eric. Once again, the odds are a little steep."

"Colonel Rogers and Captain Pitt's assault helicopters will even up the odds, Ayeza. Captain Pitt will clear the guards off the jetties and then drop the Seals in the harbor. Colonel Rogers will drop Antonio and the Forces on the runway."

"They will take to the tunnels at the first shot, Eric."

"Antonio will take two men and enter the tunnel from the runway. One satchel charge will cut off anyone trying to get to the Lear. The rest of the Special Forces will secure the building and the cliffs above the harbor while Colonel Rogers disables the yachts so the Seals can do the search."

"You left me out. I'm going in with Antonio."

"No, Ayeza, you're not."

"I promised to honor, not to obey, Antonio. The marriage license does not put you in charge."

"It is not Antonio's call, so don't get testy, Ayeza. Commander Thompson can't swim yet, and you're still having side effects from the TR-3. Those cigarette boats can all do over a hundred knots; if they get out they will scatter. We mounted a chain gun on the skiff. You and Commander Thompson will take the skiff and close the entrance to the harbor. He will pilot the boat, you handle the chain gun. Nothing, not even a rubber raft is to leave that harbor."

"Colonel Rogers and Captain Pitt can deal with the boats, Eric. They can't outrun the helicopters."

"This is not about glory, Ayeza. We are looking for nuclear weapons. The men on the island have automatic weapons. We assume they also have shoulder-fired missiles. We could lose one or both of the helicopters. If we do, we need a backup. They are launching the skiff now. You and Commander Thompson will leave an hour before the helicopters."

Ayeza buckled her harness as Commander Thompson set the autopilot for Rum Cay. The Atlantic had calmed some, and they were running with the swells at over seventy knots. The helicopters passed above them when they cleared the shoals approaching the north end of Cat Island. Colonel Rogers and Captain Pitt settled five miles north of the compound waiting for the Sultan to dock in the harbor.

The Sultan was on the horizon approaching the entrance to the harbor on Rum Cay when Commander Thompson slowed the skiff to trolling speed five miles offshore. Commander Thompson watched the helicopter from the island approach when the Sultan entered the harbor. Ayeza, her back to Commander Thompson and wearing a topless bikini waved to the smiling pilot from the deck above the chain gun as she let the hookless jig drift back behind the skiff.

Connie watched as the Sultan settled at its berth. One deck hand left the bridge to toss the ropes to the man waiting on the dock. There was no other activity on the Sultan.

The three sport fishers and the Fountain were tied to their berths; the cigarette boats were rafted alongside. Two men were in the cockpit of the Fountain taking a nap and men were on the back decks of the sport fishers lazily making up fishing gear.

"Eric..."

"What is it, Connie?"

"They're playing tourist for the cameras. They must be using the tunnel."

"Send the Colonel in, Connie. Let's see if we wake them up."

The signal turned green. Colonel Rogers dropped Antonio and the Forces at the end of the runway near the Lear, and then turned toward the harbor.

After a firefight on the runway with the three men guarding the jet and the helicopter, Antonio and the Forces disabled the Lear parked above the manhole on the runway.

"Sergeant Anderson, I'm going in. Wait thirty seconds then drop a satchel charge down the manhole and seal it off from the dock."

"You won't have any way out if they come this way, Antonio."

"I won't be coming back this way. The men on the runway were in contact with the others. They will know we have the Lear and helicopter so they won't try to come this way. Take your men, secure the communications building first, and then do a building-by-building search. I doubt they will, but if they surrender, disarm them, move them to their barracks and immobilize them, but under no circumstances is anyone going to leave the island. Once you have the buildings secure, move to the cliffs and cover the Seals in the water."

"Where are you going?"

"To the main house, it's the logical place for them to make a stand. I'm going to seal the tunnel there."

Hearing the gunfire coming from the runway, the men on the boats quickly mobilized on the decks. Small arms fire coming from the Sultan bounced off the bulletproof windshield as the helicopter cleared the cliffs. "They are going to fight, turn your weapons to hot. Captain Pitt, drop the Seals and then concentrate on the Sultan."

"Colonel, the yachts are cutting loose from the dock and they are loading packages onto the cigarette boats."

"I see them, Captain. Clip the bow of the Sultan with a rocket at the water line; we want her immobile but intact. Then take the two yachts on the inside; same plan, aim for the bow at the water line. I'll take the one on the outside and the cigarette boats."

After Colonel Rogers made a pass through the harbor the yacht settled on the bottom next to the dock and the three cigarette boats bobbed in the bay. The men on board the boats swam to the dock to join their comrades. Colonel Rogers strafed the dock when it became apparent the crusaders would refuse to surrender.

Antonio was setting a charge to seal the tunnel leading to the main house, but he surfaced at the construction office when he heard men approaching from the dock. Thirty men passed in the tunnel on their way to the elevator. "Sergeant Anderson, I'll seal the tunnel here, you have company on the way. Their only out is through the front door."

"We have our hands full, Antonio. They are a determined bunch. I have two men down and there are still a half dozen in the barracks returning our fire."

Colonel Rogers and Captain Pitt were on the same channel. "Sergeant, this is Colonel Rogers, stay with the bunkhouse. Captain Pitt will take the main house. Captain Pitt...."

"I'm on my way, Colonel."

Connie had the cameras focused on the mission. Eric, like the colonel and the captain, was monitoring the open channel of communications. "Captain Pitt, this is Eric Ludlow. The house is like a bunker. Your rockets will not penetrate the roof and the floor is two stories below ground level. Their Achilles' heel is the windows. Fire your rockets through the windows, then keep the men pinned down until Sergeant Anderson can get there with a satchel charge."

"This is Sergeant Anderson. We are busy here. Sorry, Mr. Ludlow, they refuse to surrender. It will be a few minutes."

When the militants refused to surrender, the rules of the mission changed. Colonel Rogers rose above the harbor and turned toward the plateau. "Sergeant Anderson, back off from the barracks."

"But......"

"No buts, Sergeant..... Captain Pitt, put a rocket through a window in the barracks, then train your chain guns through the opening and settle that argument... Sergeant, leave one man behind with charges to finish the job and send two of your men to the main house with satchel charges. Seal the front door and then wait for me to open a window."

"Yes, Colonel."

Commander Thompson watched as smoke rose from the sinking boats and then moved the skiff toward the entrance to the harbor. "If any come through, aim for the water line at the bow. Avoid the back half of the boat where the fuel tanks are located, Ayeza. We want to sink them, not destroy them."

The dead and debris from the yachts and cigarette boats littered the water, but the Fountain remained tied to the dock. Captain Pitt approached the main house as the last of the yachts were settling to the bottom of the harbor.

Colonel Rogers headed for the harbor as Captain Pitt approached the main house where Sergeant Anderson was preparing the charges. The Navy Seals were in the water going boat to boat searching for the warheads.

"I'm going back to the harbor, Captain, but we need some information. Put a few hundred rounds through the windows before Sergeant Anderson drops the satchel charges. See if we can convince a few of them to surrender."

"If they don't?"

"Get it done either way, Captain."

Colonel Rogers assumed the Fountain had been abandoned. He passed by the Fountain when he returned to the harbor to patrol the dock and check the jetty for survivors. His back was to the yacht when the forward hatch on the Fountain opened.

Antonio had just left the tunnel when he saw the flash of the missile as it left the deck of the Fountain and separated the back section of the helicopter from the cab. The helicopter dropped like a stone next to one of the yachts, narrowly missing the two Navy Seals in the water.

The divers pulled Colonel Rogers and his copilot from the helicopter and then dragged them under as the Fountain passed over their heads. Antonio stood on the empty dock, watching as the Seals surfaced with the Colonel and his copilot. "Ayeza, the Fountain is on its way."

Commander Thompson had positioned the skiff over the shoals facing the dock a hundred yards from the end of the jetty. The Fountain drew too much water to cross the shoals. It would have to pass by in front of them. The chain guns fired fifteen fifty caliber rounds a second. Ayeza would send a hundred rounds at the water line to sink the yacht as it passed by, and then train the gun on the open cockpit, leaving the hull intact.

The two crusaders stood with missile tubes in their hands when the skiff came in sight. The Muslim training camps in the Somalia desert are flat. They had practiced firing the missiles from the back of a moving truck, but when the skipper kicked the turbo chargers in as the Fountain cleared the end of the jetty, the ground swells were running at eight feet. The Fountain lifted off the first wave at a speed of eighty knots exposing the full belly of the yacht. Ayeza's first burst from the chain gun opened the hull; as the yacht settled in the waves, the second sent the crusaders in the cockpit on the final leg of their journey of martyrdom.

Sergeant Anderson secured the buildings on the plateau. Colonel Rogers, wet but unhurt, gathered explosives off the dock and joined Antonio to seal the tunnel from its last open exit. Commander Thompson docked the skiff behind the Sultan. He and Ayeza joined Antonio and the colonel as they set off the charge after exiting the tunnel.

"Anyone left, Antonio?"

"Some of the crusaders may be hiding in the tunnel, and the captain of the Sultan is in the construction office under guard."

"Whose side is he on?"

"He would like us to believe he's on our side, Ayeza. He said he killed a couple of the crew members when he heard the gunfire on the runway and then locked himself in his quarters. The Seals found him in his cabin. He says he is Egyptian and claims the Somalians hijacked the yacht when they left Jeddah."

"They returned to the dock the day they left, Antonio, how is that possible?"

"He says they left the dock at Jeddah, but wrapped a line in one of their propellers. The pirates laid a steel cable between two submerged buoys. They were trying to clear it when the pirates boarded and killed his crew. They loaded a couple hundred kilos of heroin and then they returned to Jeddah to pick up the crusaders. He said they left the next day with the crusaders on board."

"Any sign of the warheads?"

"We got a slight radiation reading by the Sultan's diving port, but it's just a trace. The captain says they brought a package aboard at the dock in Jeddah and locked it in the yacht's gun locker, but he claims he does not know anything about the warheads. We checked the locker. It shows traces of radiation, but it's empty, and Sergeant Anderson says the buildings are clean. We are still searching the boats in the harbor."

Ayeza left with Commander Thompson in the skiff to pick up the Seals. "Antonio, the boats in the harbor are all loaded with drugs, but there is no sign of a warhead."

"Have the Seals checked the Fountain, Ayeza?"

"Not yet, the blood in the water drew the hammerheads in. There are a couple of big adults in the bunch that are pretty worked up. There is not much left, but we're giving it a few more minutes to let the currents dissipate the blood and the sharks to leave before the Seals go in."

Captain Pitt settled on the rooftop of the main house waiting for the Special Forces to mop up and bring their wounded out. Colonel Rogers and four of the Seals were doing a final search of the dock and the Sultan. Ayeza and Commander Thompson picked up the remaining Seals off the jetty and were approaching the Fountain.

Eric and Admiral Michaels had been following the action on satellite. After the crusaders opened fire on the helicopter and the Seals found the stash of drugs still on board the Sultan, Eric brought the British Intelligence Service on line.

"Colonel, this is Admiral Michaels. We have British MI5 on line. When you finish the search, mine the facility, but don't blow it. We'll send in a barge to collect the debris and then destroy the buildings. The British will write the mission off to a chapter in a drug war. Is there any sign of the warheads?"

"Admiral, Ayeza's on the line.... Admiral, they found a warhead on the Fountain, but we are still short two."

"Ayeza has the probe, have you confirmed it's hot?"

"Yes, Admiral, she says it's a twin to the one we found in Pakistan."

"That still leaves two in the pipeline somewhere, Antonio."

"The dots connect the Crescent Tide and the Sultan together with the men who boarded in Jeddah, Admiral. If the warheads were on the Crescent Tide, they could have passed this one to the Sultan when the divers were clearing the line. If it was the other way around and the Sultan had all three, they could have dropped two in Jeddah for the Crescent Tide's divers to pick up. Either way, both yachts are obviously involved."

"Ask the captain how the warhead was brought aboard. His story about a hijacking sounds too orchestrated. Killing a few of his own crew members would not be a concern to Al-Queda."

"Eric, the captain said the hijackers brought the warhead aboard in Jeddah. He opened the locker when they stowed it. They told him it was a case full of gold bars and diamonds the pirates in Somalia were delivering to a fence in the Bahamas. The captain swears there was only one and the locker is big enough for three the same size. There is no reason to think they hid anything elsewhere on the yacht."

"Who owns the yacht?"

"He says he doesn't know. He claims he's a contract employee from the yard in Alexandria that built the Sultan, and that the shipyard hired him to bring the yacht to Nassau. The hijackers took the opportunity to move the drugs and gold. He said that's all he knows."

"That's too convenient. Keep the captain under guard. We will need to talk with him. Then tell Ayeza to leave the skiff for the Seals. Captain Pitt will bring the two of you, the captain, and the warhead. The NOAA helicopter is on the way to pick up Colonel Rogers and his men."

"Colonel, this is Admiral Michaels. Are there any survivors on Rum Cay?"

"Only the captain, Admiral, those we did not kill had arsenic capsules. This was a suicide mission from the start. Sorry about that, I know we could have used a snitch or two."

"We are better off this way, Colonel; the new rules of interrogation imposed by the *Apostate* and his friends in Congress tie our hands. We wouldn't have gotten any information and they would have been free in a month. Put the dead in the tunnels and then help the Seals mine the facility. The cleanup crew will be arriving in six hours. MI5 will deal with the local authorities."

Colonel Rogers disliked the new President and was disenchanted with some members of Congress and the administration over their attitude toward the military, but he still had respect for the office. "I thought any direct reference to the President's ancestral role in this was forbidden by military protocol, Admiral."

"We recovered two, one less than four hundred miles from Florida, but definitely on its way. Finding one that close to home lends credibility to Wahid's story that there were four nuclear weapons in the hands of the Muslims, Colonel. The militants are using posters of the President under the heading *The Apostate* to recruit the crusaders to transport them to the US, kill our citizens and change our way of life. Maybe it's time we call a spade a spade and deal with the reality of his roots. Clean up Rum Cay, Colonel, and then return to the Atlantis. I'll make arrangements to replace your helicopter."

Ayeza joined Connie to watch the crane on the barge lift the last of the debris from the harbor entrance. The dock, helicopter, the destroyed yachts and boats still loaded with three hundred million dollars worth of drugs littered the deck.

Commander Thompson and the Seals mined the cliffs above the harbor and the channel entrance as well as the buildings. Commander Thompson and the Seals boarded the skiff and then waited at the harbor entrance. They would take a trip around the island searching for any stragglers that may have made it to the beach.

When the tug pulling the barge cleared the channel, and then turned south toward the Puerto Rico Trench to dispose of the debris, Connie sent the satellite signal setting off the charges.

When the smoke cleared, the buildings were gone. The tunnels collapsed under the weight of the debris and Black Bay was once again a barren rock-lined beach facing south.

Colonel Rogers and Captain Pitt flew Antonio and Ayeza to Eglin Air Force Base to deliver the warhead and pick up a replacement helicopter.

Jim Symington, the head of the Anti Terrorist Task force, Eric, and Admiral Michaels arrived earlier and were at the airbase when they arrived.

When the warhead was found in the Bahamas on a yacht headed for Daytona, the Florida governor requested that General Sampson be placed in charge of the Florida National Guard. A second plane carrying the Florida governor and General Sampson arrived as Colonel Rogers touched down.

The governor asked Symington to attend the meeting, but Symington was not aware of the mission at Rum Cay and he had not been brought current on the results of the search. The warhead was placed as a centerpiece on the conference table. A skeptical, but curious, Jim Symington found his seat as Eric, Antonio, and Ayeza entered the room.

The story of the beautiful, black haired Pakistani woman with emerald green eyes had circulated through the Pentagon, but Jim Symington was not impressed. "I'm sorry, Mr. Ludlow, but the CIA has been told to clear their operations in Florida through my office. I don't recall being asked, and I have not requested your help. You don't belong here."

"Perhaps this meeting may change your opinion, Mr. Symington."

"I doubt that."

Eric turned toward Ayeza and Antonio. "You can thank this couple for finding two of the warheads, Jim, but there are still two more out there… Ayeza, open the case and give Mr. Symington the radiation probe."

"The what?"

Admiral Michaels took the probe from Ayeza when Symington refused to take it. He then placed it in front of Symington. When Symington refused to pick it up, Antonio reached for it and then activated it and laid it next to the warhead. The radiation level hovered just short of the red zone.

"You said to bring you proof, Jim. This is the second of four nuclear warheads taken from the Mardan, Pakistan weapons storage facility. If the CIA had not located it, it would be in the hands of Muslim terrorists somewhere in Florida by now. The two still unaccounted for might already be here."

"Where did you find it?"

"What difference? But if you need to know, on a yacht in the Bahamas."

"Then it's a British problem, why bring it here?"

"A courier from the Los Alamos National Nuclear Laboratory and the man who assembled it in Pakistan are on the way to collect and disarm it."

Symington shied, backing away from the table. "What, you're making a point? It's armed and you brought it to the mainland, you and your people are more deranged than I thought, Mr. Ludlow."

"Not everyone agrees with you, Jim, including the British. With the recovery of the warhead and proof there may be two more, the British have given us free reign in the Bahamas. This warhead was on a high speed yacht headed for Miami. We do believe there are two more and that they may already have reached the mainland. Washington cannot ignore the threat any longer. The American military Joint Chiefs are meeting with the President and his cabinet as we speak."

"If there is a threat to the mainland, I would be at that meeting, Admiral."

"Your attitude toward the military is well known, and since we are now charged with finding the warheads, we asked that your office be left out."

"That's ridiculous; the Task Force can handle it."

"That won't happen. The NOAA ship, Atlantis, is off the coast of Florida. It will be the base of operations. There are Navy Seals and a Special Forces team on board, and Coast Guard and Navy ships are moving toward Andros Island. The military will run the operation in the Bahamas, but the CIA will be in charge of the search in Florida."

"I think the President and the Congressional Committee will see things differently after I call them, Mr. Ludlow. Congress has given me sole authority over terrorism on U.S. soil. If we are conducting an operation in Florida, it will go through my office in Miami."

"We don't have time for protocol, or hearings to replace you and your staff, Jim. You can follow orders and help us find them, or you can get the hell out of the way; your choice."

The military had hoped to garner cooperation from the Task Force research specialists. Jim Symington was a career bureaucrat; he would cooperate, but he would remain belligerent.

"I'll need this confirmed by Washington, but in the meantime, what is it you want me to do, Admiral?"

Admiral Michaels watched Symington in silence for a moment and then made the decision he had hoped would not be necessary. The *Apostate* Theory was beginning to have an effect, not only on the military, but also on the actions of the White House staff. If the *Apostate* was the target of extremists, those closest to him would also be at risk. Finding the warhead ten thousand miles away in Pakistan did not hit home; finding one in the Bahamas on a boat with a GPS dialed in on Miami less than three hundred miles away, was a convincing argument.

Admiral Michaels left the room to make a call. He confirmed a plan with the White House Chief of Staff that had been left on the table earlier that day.

The White House press secretary would release a statement that, as part of the closure of the prison in Guantanamo, the Task Force was being disbanded by executive order in favor of state by state control. Funding would be provided by the Federal government and members of the Task Force would be given opportunities to lend their expertise to the new organizations.

The Washington Post and the New York Times would run with the story, citing as the reason the prior administration's infringements on personal liberties of Americans who were still incarcerated and awaiting trial.

With a staff of over two hundred experienced researchers, Symington could have helped in the effort, but a disgruntled bureaucrat would subvert the efforts for his own political gain. Admiral Michaels returned to the room to cut the ties.

"Call the White House if you would like to confirm this, but afterwards contact your friends in the judicial system and get fifty blank search warrants. We will not have time to do it one by one. There is a Lear on the runway. After you make the call, Captain Pitt will take you to Washington. He will escort you home, and then to your office in the morning to pick up the warrants. When you have them, you will deliver them to Mr. Ludlow on the Atlantis, and be sure to bring a suitcase. You will be staying on board with a direct line to the Miami judicial chambers."

"That's impossible. I have other pending issues to deal with in Washington. I will send a member of my staff, Admiral."

"No, Mr. Symington, your office has more leaks than a thatched roof in a Florida hurricane. We want to keep this under wraps or we will start a panic. The President's Chief of Staff is waiting for your call. He will confirm what I'm telling you."

Admiral Michaels hit the send button on his cell phone before handing it to Symington. The conversation was brief, after which a belligerent Jim Symington handed back the phone.

"It appears that for now, you are in charge, Admiral. Where does the Task Force fit in, I will put them at your service."

"That's not how it's going to work, Jim. Put all of your staff on paid administrative leave. Tell them the new administration has reviewed the budget and will be turning your duties over to local authorities. Make the call from here, and then surrender your cell phone and laptop."

"That is absolutely ludicrous; you can't close the Task Force down. Congress established it and set aside the funds to run it. I want confirmation from the Speaker of the House. She is a personal friend of mine and I would have been put on notice."

"I doubt she will take your call. The congresswoman and the White House have been told that you and your staff are under investigation by the FBI and the CIA. It's not a bluff. You and some of your staff violated the terms of your secret status. We have dozens of e-mails and taped calls to the press leaking information on past issues, which is why we left you out of this search."

"The only information we passed on was the covert missions into Pakistan you and General Sampson had no authority to undertake. Somebody has to get you and the hawks at the Pentagon under control. I have a lot of friends in Washington, and before this is over, this is going to get messy."

"You forget, we did find two nuclear warheads that the Pakistan authorities denied losing. They were headed here. We also have solid proof there are two more in transit. Your politician friends have too much to lose if they subvert the hunt and one of the warheads goes off. They will distance themselves from you. I would jail you now, but you have friends in the judicial system we need. Captain Pitt and Sergeant Anderson of the Special Forces are on the runway. They will accompany you to your home tonight and then to the Atlantis tomorrow. And, Jim, your home phone is tapped. If you try to leak this meeting to your staff or anyone else, you will be taken into custody and isolated until this is over."

Symington was subdued. "What will I be doing on the Atlantis?"

"You will report to Commander Connie Holman and make the arrangements with the court clerks in Florida to fill in the blanks on the search warrants."

CHAPTER 20

The file on board the Atlantis began filling with pictures of growing bands of Muslim militants training in the deserts of Somalia and Sudan. Pictures of an assortment of posters and mannequins taken at a new camp in Somalia with the President's profile graced the cover under the heading, *Kill the Apostate / Death to America.*

The file was assigned the title, *The Apostate Theory,* by the research team on the Atlantis and forwarded to an elite group on the list of need to know personnel the military Joint Chiefs had provided.

It was printed without review, and the title raised a lot of eyebrows when it reached the Pentagon conference rooms. However, after an explanation by the research team, the title remained and it was allowed to be passed on.

Al-Queda's influence on some of Pakistan's new leaders had evolved exponentially after the election. Some literal translations of meetings showed they used the term *apostate* freely when referring to the American President.

It had become a sensitive issue on board the Atlantis and in the conference rooms where the military brass and the CIA were isolated from the mainstream politicians. However, the films of the Muslim camps in Somalia and Sudan showed the ranks of the crusaders swelling as the days passed. There were still two warheads in transit and there were many more in the Mardan weapon storage facility.

Korea's on again off again threats and Iran's pursuit of a nuclear weapon were no longer the current nuclear issues for the West to deal with. Al-Queda had two warheads and the possibility of a nuclear attack on an American city, or on the country of Israel, had become a reality.

Some of the people involved directly in the search began referring to the President as the *Apostate*, knowing that even if they found the two remaining warheads in time, the *Apostate* would listen to the doves in Congress and withdraw the military. Pakistan would then fall under the complete control of Al-Queda and the Taliban, and more warheads would follow.

When the Task Force was placed in limbo, the Congressional Committee became involved in the search. When an original copy of *The Apostate Theory* surfaced in the Congressional Committee's chambers it caused a cry of outrage that echoed off the walls of the White House.

It had become politically incorrect to use the *Apostate's* middle name or the word Muslim in any reference to the democratic candidate during the presidential campaign. The *Apostate* was canonized by American citizens relying on state and federal welfare for their support or employment. The American liberal press and the Hollywood celebrity crowd jumped on the band wagon.

After the election the subject came up as to how the *Apostate* would recite the oath of office. Knowing it would no longer affect the outcome of the election, he chose to use his full name, which is based in his Muslim roots. Even so, a directive by the White House Press Secretary caused the White House copy of *The Apostate Theory* to be edited and re-printed before being distributed. The name was changed and all reference to *apostasy* or the President was deleted in what was now just a chronological report dealing with the search for the warheads.

The real world could not be ignored forever and the thin veil of camouflage was transparent to the military leaders while the administration floundered in a sea of indecision.

After the 2008 presidential election, Muslim anti-American rhetoric had escalated in the tribal regions of Pakistan. However, to defuse it, the new administration simply ignored it and rather than face the deteriorating political situation in Pakistan and Afghanistan, they upped America's foreign aid to Pakistan to keep the lid on things, and then sent the new Secretary of State on a good will tour of Asia.

The lack of experience of the new leader of the free world began to raise some eyebrows, but the press followed the politically correct course and focused on North Korea's nuclear threat. To the press, it was an opportunity for another diversion from the lack of attention the administration was paying to the real threats in the Middle and Near East.

However, in repetition, *the real world cannot be ignored forever,* even by the liberal press. Time Magazine featured the story and the inner pages of the newspapers began carrying accounts of the Taliban's success in reinstating Islamic law in Pakistan and their steady gains taking back their ancient lands in Afghanistan.

The prophecies of biological and nuclear attacks on America made headlines in the conservative press for a few days, but they were subverted by the liberals. Reference to militant Islam was taken off the air when the conflict between Israel and Hamas flared up before the *Apostate* took the oath of office.

Once again, according to the Jew haters in America, it was America's military involvement in the Middle East and support for the State of Israel that was fueling the fire of Islamic hatred.

Like Colonel Rogers, there were many in the military disgruntled with the administration's lack of support for the military who still respected the Office. However, although the term *Apostate* to address the President of the United States may not be politically correct in the mind of some Americans, it is an accurate description of the President's relationship with the Islamic world.

The military personnel involved in the search for the warheads linked the two together. They felt the reference apropos and continued to use the term in the face of growing criticism from the White House and the *Apostate's* supporters who were making overtures to the militant Islamic world.

After assuming office, the *Apostate* continued to ignore his own roots and Congress followed the *Apostate's* lead. In many misguided minds, it was time to embrace the world of Islam, not shun it, or fear it any longer.

In a gesture of appeasement, the first order of business was for the *Apostate* to sign an executive order to close the Guantanamo military prison. When asked what they would do with the Muslim prisoners, some of whom are the most dangerous men in the world and who have publicly vented their hatred toward America, the response was, we *are working on a plan.*

At first it appeared that the new administration was waffling and that the Guantanamo prison would continue to operate for years. The press breezed over it, pointing out that during the presidential campaign the *Apostate* proposed that the prisoners in Guantanamo be transferred to the general prison system in the U.S. What they failed to point out was that he also suggested they be tried in the secular courts, where as an attorney he knows most of the evidence against them will be dismissed resulting in their being set free.

The, *We are working on a plan*, response undermined the real issue and no one in authority was paying attention to the predictions of the experts on Muslim terrorists. Their explanation was, there had not been a strike against American interests outside of Iraq and Afghanistan since 9-11, and the War on Terror, with its fronts in Afghanistan and Pakistan, had become too costly.

Cities, counties and states across the country were cutting their budgets in the face of record deficits. Millions of Americans lost their homes as the number of layoffs accelerated across the country.

The War on Terror was out of sight, therefore out of mind. Complacency toward the violent side of Islam resettled on the American public. No one seemed to care when it was pointed out that a number of Muslim militants who had been released from Guantanamo had returned to the fronts of their terrorist organizations and were once again killing Americans and anyone else who disagreed with them. The Congressional Committee's answer was to propose we bring the military home and leave the Islamic world to police itself.

The economy was in meltdown and the life-style of the middle class continued to deteriorate. Appeasement became the order of the day. Withdrawing our military and financial support for the new governments in the Middle East and using the money to expand the social programs at home became a rallying cry behind a decision popular with the *Apostate's* followers.

The civilian government offices managing welfare programs expanded exponentially, but the CIA and FBI suffered the same cutbacks as the military. It was another opportunity to reach out to Islam. Muslim profiling was suspended soon after the inauguration and it had been months since the data banks had been updated.

The captain of the Sultan was transported to the Atlantis on the helicopter with Ayeza and Antonio. During the flight Ayeza struck up a conversation with the man.

Ayeza was dressed in army fatigues; she sensed his Islamic stance on the subject of liberated women. He also preferred his native Arabic language over his broken English.

Ayeza did not believe the captain was from Egypt as he claimed. His attitude as well as his Arabic dialect was that of the Taliban in the tribal regions in Pakistan.

Ayeza voiced her concerns to Connie, who contacted the shipyard in Alexandria, Egypt. The information Connie received was vague. The personnel file of the man who had left the shipyard with the Sultan had disappeared. There were no pictures, but the captain of the Sultan did not match the physical description provided. Connie fed a picture of the captain into the CIA data banks and waited.

"I'm sorry, Ayeza, but the CIA records are clean."

"Let's send his picture to the FBI, Connie; he is not what he seems." Ayeza did not believe the captain was Egyptian. She also suggested Connie compare the pictures she took of the captain, to the mob mingling on the two yachts and on the docks in Jeddah the day before the Sultan left the dock the first time.

Connie zoomed in on the Crescent Tide and then the Sultan. The computer was capable of comparing over a million frames a minute. It picked out Ghalib ten minutes after his picture was scanned into the computer. Mecca was east of Jeddah. He had risen early and had left his headdress in his quarters. He was kneeling on his prayer rug on the deck of the Sultan facing into the rising sun. His beard covered his lower face, but the computer matched his eyes and the rest of his profile.

Eric and Admiral Michaels reviewed the films. A few minutes later Colonel Rogers and two of his men entered the cabin on the

Atlantis where the captain of the Sultan was isolated. "Let's go, Captain."

"Where are you taking me, Colonel?"

"To a base in Cuba. Make it easy on yourself, Captain. If you know where the other warheads are, tell us now. You can save us the trip and you may save yourself a lot of pain."

Ghalib's English suddenly improved. "I'll tell you nothing. You have new leaders, Colonel. Some of us who have been in your prisons are now free to train others. The *Apostate* has changed the mood in my world. Thousands more will volunteer. Even if you find the other two warheads, the Lion Sheik's followers will soon rule all of Pakistan. There are hundreds more available. Besides, Colonel, America has new leadership; I can handle psychological questioning by one of your new trainees."

"It's a wasted effort, Captain, and it will destroy Islam. If one of those bombs goes off, Muslims around the world will become pariahs. The rest of the world will join against you. None of you will be able to travel beyond your own borders, and your leaders in Pakistan and those in Saudi Arabia who pay the bills will be annihilated."

"We don't think so. America no longer has the stomach for war and the leaders in Pakistan will no longer side with you. Besides, Americans have proven in the past they will run from spilled American blood. When the crusaders succeed and destroy one of your cities, the *Apostate* will cower and your Congress will cave in. Your troops will leave the Holy Land for good. America will concede and I too will be free."

"Our Congress has tied our hands in the past, but the warhead you carried on the Sultan has changed the rules.

Ghalib made the assumption he would be interned in the prison at Guantanamo. "An American attorney will represent me, and your military prison in Cuba will be closed within a year. Your prisons in the States have comfortable beds, better than the caves in Pakistan that I grew up in. You will only keep me a few years; that is nothing. I have no more to say."

"You will not be put into the American system. Our cameras picked you and a number of your men out on the deck of the Sultan before you hijacked the yacht. From there we traced your Afghanistan and Pakistan connections in our data bank, Captain, or would you rather me use your real name, Ghalib. You have no American passport and you are not on American soil. We will assume you are from Afghanistan and return you to your country. Be assured, we still have friends among the Afghans. They have their own methods; they will convince you to talk."

"I am on board an American ship. You must first extradite me, and that will take years."

"We are in British waters and you won't set foot in the States, so that won't be necessary. There is a private jet sitting on the runway at Guantanamo that will take you to Kabul. The decision is made. Tell us where we find the other two or you will be turned over to our friends in Afghanistan for questioning. You have until we reach Cuba to make the decision where you would prefer to spend the rest of your life; a few weeks in a cold cave in an Afghan prison, or many years in a warm bed in a prison in the States."

He thought back to his pledge to Allah at the training grounds in Somalia, and his earlier promise to the Lion Sheik. Prison in America was one thing; interrogation by his Shiite enemies in Afghanistan was not an option. Ghalib slipped his tongue under the loose crown dislodging it and the capsule below it. He then crushed the capsule between his teeth as he climbed the stairs leading to the helicopter deck. The process was irreversible. Ghalib joined the martyrs buried on Rum Cay before he reached the deck of the Atlantis.

The captain's suicide cast a shadow on the mission at Rum Cay. No one wanted to be chasing their tail if the missing warheads were still hidden on board the Sultan, or if the Seals missed them on one of the boats sunk in the harbor.

Eric ordered the barge carrying the debris to lay off the Puerto Rico Trench to wait for a professional demolition team from the States. The search for the missing warheads would start with the Sultan, and then if they weren't there, they would cut the rest of the yachts apart, piece by piece.

The deck crew lifted the Viking's skiff aboard and tied it down between the two helicopters. When the tarps were in place, Captain Paige turned the Atlantis north toward Cape Canaveral.

Connie dialed in and took one last look at Rum Cay. The British patrol boat was leaving the island, and as a private helicopter flew past the corner of Rum Cay, Yaq'ab stood on the canyon rim above the cave near Chaman, Pakistan and closed the laptop.

Returning to the cave, Yaq'ab approached the ledge where the Lion Sheik was resting. "We lost Rum Cay, Osama; the Americans recovered the warhead and destroyed the harbor."

"What of the drugs?"

"That too, and all the boats."

"The crusaders?"

"They are all dead; those the Americans did not kill took their own lives."

"If they are all dead, no one will talk, and the others still have two warheads, Yaq'ab; one of them will get through, God willing."

"If they find the other warheads before they reach a target our benefactors will withdraw their support, Osama. Our loss at Rum Cay was over two billion dollars, and the price of oil is low. You must select the target soon."

"Have we had word from Jawdah and Abdul?"

"Allah is watching over them. Jawdah chose the Crescent Tide over the Sultan; he and Abdul are safe in Fort Lauderdale."

"Contact our friends in Florida, Yaq'ab. Tell them to protect God's soldiers and then get word to Jawdah. I have selected a target.

The congresswoman and the senators who worship the *Apostate* will be in range on the yacht, and the race track will be in the dead zone. Over a million will die. Our benefactors will praise Allah and refill our accounts."

Fort Lauderdale

Sally and the CNBC news team settled in the salon of the yacht for the trip to Fort Lauderdale. It was a rough ride back. They were taking water over the side in the heavy sea, which was washing across the back deck before spilling out the scuppers.

One of the crew members braved the wind to drag the camera cases into the salon. When they arrived at the dock, Alan shuffled through the camera equipment and picked up the case. Jake then turned to Sally as he stepped off the yacht. "Thank you, Sally, we owe you one. It would have been impossible to find another ride until this storm passes."

Sally was attractive, single and unattached. She preferred experienced Middle Eastern men who had traveled the world, to the dull Americans who hit on her routinely at the local pub. "You're welcome, Jake. When will you be returning to Washington, maybe we can get together?"

"I'd like that Sally. We have a flight booked Sunday morning. I'll be in the office on Monday; I'll call."

No one on the Atlantis was getting any sleep. Connie had patched her personal laptop into the ship's computers so she could monitor messages coming in from Washington.

Eric left Eglin Air Force Base and returned to the ship to rejoin in the search. It was two am, but Connie was at the computer in her quarters reviewing the tapes of the Crescent Tide's arrival at Nassau.

Eric, bleary eyed, was ready for a hot shower and some rest, but he couldn't sleep. Thinking a snack might help, he dressed and headed for the ship's galley. When he passed Connie's cabin he noticed the door ajar and the lights on. When he pushed the door aside Connie smiled and invited him in. Noticing his disheveled look, "You look like you could use some sleep."

"You do too. When was the last time you slept?"

"Not since you left. I can't sleep wondering how we lost the other two."

"Maybe we both need to get our minds off it for a while?"

"What are my options?"

"Well…. Most people sleep better in bed."

"Now, why didn't I think of that? Close the door."

The ship's bell sounded at 6:30. Eric sat up and started to dress. Connie set the alarm for eight. "Come back to bed, my shift doesn't start until nine. If something important happens they will call me.

"We'll miss breakfast."

"I have coffee here."

They fell back to sleep at seven; the alarm sounded at eight. "I'll meet you in the galley, let them make the coffee."

"I'll need to go to my cabin to change; I'll be there at eight thirty."

CHAPTER 21

A ntonio and Ayeza were seated in the galley with Eric when Connie entered the room. Connie turned to address the others while filling a cup with coffee.

"The watch patched through the results of the identity search a few minutes ago. It's not perfect, but we believe Jawdah Fattah was on the Crescent Tide in Jeddah. He is a sixty-five percent match to Jake Jacobs, a reporter at CNBC. Abdul Hasib was a one hundred percent match to Alan Kent going in. He works with Jacobs so it makes sense. The other men the computer identified in Jeddah boarded the Sultan. I'm assuming they are all buried on Rum Cay. I've told the watch to notify me if anything else turns up, but so far, we have no other matches of those who arrived on the Crescent Tide.

"How far along is the search?"

"Only sixty percent, but the computer is speeding up as the search narrows. I expect all of the results by noon today."

Antonio was reflecting on the statistics. *There were divers in the water at the dock in Nassau when the Crescent Tide arrived. Divers removed the cables from the Sultan's prop when they berthed next to the Crescent Tide in Jeddah. What was under that boat?*

Antonio did not believe it was a coincidence. He believed Ghalib had to have hijacked the Sultan the day the yacht first left Jeddah, and then faked the cable in the prop to return to pick up the warhead.

"Alex, Connie said we have a personnel match on the dock in Jeddah of Muslims with terrorist connections. The Crescent Tide has to be the transport ship.

"Connie, where did Jacobs and Kent end up when the VIPs left Nassau?"

"I don't know, Eric. I lost them in the crowd on the dock. The computer is still looking, but so far Jacobs did not re-board the Crescent Tide."

"Let's dig back into the tapes and find those two. They work for CNBC, they must have returned to the mainland aboard the press boat."

Eric and Connie returned to the surveillance room of the ship. Connie refocused the computer, concentrating on the films of yachts transporting the visiting press off the island. Narrowing the search sped up the process. "Eric, you're right, they boarded one of the CNBC yachts."

"Back up the film and see what they were carrying when they boarded the boat, and then download the satellite tape to the conference room, Connie. I'll get Antonio and Ayeza; maybe one of them will see something we might miss."

When the couple arrived, Connie zoomed in on the CNBC news crew. "We know Jacobs was on the Crescent Tide gangplank before the VIPs departed, Connie."

"He was, Ayeza, but all he was carrying when he left the Crescent Tide was his raincoat."

Eric watched Jake talking to Sally on the back deck of the yacht. Alan Kent was stepping on the swim step to board. "Kent is empty handed too, Connie."

Antonio was concentrating on the inanimate objects, whereas the other three were focused on the men. He tapped Ayeza's shoulder and then walked to the screen. "We have been concentrating on finding the men; we quit looking for the warheads. Connie, back up and rerun the last two minutes."

Antonio stood for a moment. The others were lost in the faces of Jake talking to Sally and Alan Kent who was moving past them empty handed.

"Connie, back up to before Kent enters the picture and zoom in on the aft cockpit of the CNBC yacht. There ... count the bags of gear next to Jake; I see four lying flat on the deck. Now forward to Kent coming on board and zoom back in on the bags."

Eric's face filled with surprise as Connie refocused. "Now I count five. You spotted it, any idea how it got there, Antonio?"

"I think the fifth one was dropped on top of the others when Kent boarded the yacht."

"By who?"

"I think the diver who was on the dock behind Kent put it on board."

"It's the right size, Antonio, but it looks like just another camera case."

"A lead box would be too heavy for a diver to lift out of the water. Find that yacht Connie. If one of the warheads was in that case, the swim step and back deck will show signs of radiation."

The search had a new front, but while Connie returned to the surveillance room to begin a sweep of the yacht clubs in Fort Lauderdale, the other path of the search had come to its end.

The demolition crew on board the barge started with the Sultan. When they came up empty they cut the smaller boats apart and fed them through a shredder. The Sultan's weapons storage area, the diver's access hatch and the back seat of the Fountain were the only areas to register on the radiation meter.

It was another sleepless night in the surveillance room. Eric joined Connie shortly after two am. The phone rang at three waking Antonio and Ayeza. "Sorry for the call at this hour, Antonio."

"We'll be there in ten minutes, Eric." Antonio and Ayeza joined Eric and Connie as the demolition crew fed the last of the debris onto the conveyor to be baled and then dropped into the deep waters above the Puerto Rico Trench.

"What now, Eric?"

"We have the warrants, Antonio. The CNBC yacht is tied to the dock in Fort Lauderdale. Colonel Rogers will take you and Ayeza to the harbor. We start our search on the mainland there."

"Have you located Jacobs and Kent?"

"Not yet. We can assume they have a dozen different passports so cold calling the hotels may not work. We sent a dozen agents with their pictures to canvas the check in desks of the hotels near the yacht club; maybe we'll get lucky."

"It's after three am; the day crews will be home in bed."

"We know. It's a long shot, but it's the only one we have."

"What about the Crescent Tide?"

"It's docked at its berth at McMood Fajal's estate on Andros Island."

"When is the party?"

"Wednesday, the Washington VIPs started arriving yesterday."

"Why are we ignoring the obvious, Eric. There were four warheads. Even if Jake and Alan are carrying the third and we get lucky and find it, someone needs to board and search the Crescent Tide."

"Commander Thompson and his men are with the fisherman, Ayeza. Security at the estate will be lax the night of the party. They will swim in to check the hull before the party, but we will have to wait to board until after the VIPs leave for Daytona."

"If Daytona is the target that will be too late. If they are on board they will find a way to move them by then."

"McMood Fajal has powerful friends in Washington and in London, Ayeza. We are going to need some proof. We know that if the CNBC yacht had a warhead on board, it had to come from the Crescent Tide. However, first things first; Captain Pitt and his men have sealed the harbor in Fort Lauderdale. Colonel Rogers is waiting for you two on the flight deck. Hopefully, by the time you get there we will know the whereabouts of Jacobs and Kent."

Colonel Rogers dropped Antonio and Ayeza at the harbor at 4:05 am. The back deck and salon of the CNBC yacht registered in red on Ayeza's radiation meter. The warhead case had been opened or had been damaged. Either way, prolonged exposure to the amount of radiation listed on the meter would be fatal to someone in close contact with the case.

Antonio passed on the information to Colonel Rogers who ordered his men to put on their protective suits. Ayeza and Antonio were changing when Eric's call came through. "We almost got lucky, Antonio. One of the porters recognized the pictures. Jacobs and Kent checked into the Fort Lauderdale Airport Hilton yesterday. They were feeling secure, but that appears to have changed. They checked out a few minutes ago, but they might have left a trail."

Ten minutes later Colonel Rogers touched down on the roof of the Hilton Hotel while Captain Pitt dropped his men on the grounds and sealed the exits.

The call came in at 3:45 am. The message was coded, but for the sake of anyone who might be listening they were told the midday flight out of Fort Lauderdale to Washington, DC was overbooked.

Jake and Alan were packed and had been waiting for the call. The taxi was on its way. They left the Hilton Hotel at 4:00 am after telling the desk clerk they had to catch an early flight to Washington.

Connie patched into the airline's data banks. The late morning Fort Lauderdale flight to Washington had open seating. Jacobs and Kent were not on the passenger list, but there was a J. Jacobs and an A. Kent confirmed first class on American Airlines flight 610, departing from Miami at 7:15 to Paris. Jacobs booked the reservation at 3:50 am that morning.

When questioned later, the hotel clerk said one of the men, the one named Jake, seemed a little pale and feverish. He also had what looked like a rash on his hands and wrists. They were nervous and over tipped the porter who had helped them with their luggage to the lobby, but then they carried their baggage to a waiting taxi themselves.

Traces of lethal radiation registered on the porter's cart and on the floor by the desk where Jake left his luggage while checking out. Antonio noted that the radiation leak was increasing the more the warhead was handled.

The elevator showed signs, but it was non-lethal, indicating the warhead had been placed in some luggage and then stacked on the cart.

"It's been here, Eric"

"Eric was waiting for the call. "Antonio, we have to keep the lid on this or we will cause a panic."

"What do we tell them?"

"I called the governor when you confirmed it arrived in Fort Lauderdale. It's his state, so it's his call. He has called a press conference for six am and will make an announcement that there has been a break-in at the Turkey Point nuclear power plant and one of the spent fuel rods has been stolen. In the meantime, General

Sampson is flying in with a troop of National Guard to seal the hotel, and then help with the search."

"What do we do with the guests and employees?"

"No one is to leave. For the time being, tell them the thieves were at the hotel and they are quarantined until they can be checked for radiation contamination. Tell Sergeant Anderson to get us an accurate head count. Admiral Michaels will send a fleet of helicopters from Eglin to transport the civilians to the base hospital."

It was two hours to flight 610's departure from Miami; they had time. Colonel Rogers and Captain Pitt's men locked down the hotel while waiting for General Sampson to arrive. It would have to be cleaned and the guests and employees who had been exposed would be treated for possible radiation poisoning.

Ayeza and Antonio let themselves into Jake and Alan's room with the passkey the desk clerk provided while the hotel staff began to evacuate the floor. The empty camera case the diver placed on the deck of the yacht was at the foot of one of the beds. The case and one of the beds glowed with high-level radiation readings. Both beds had been slept in.

"They took it out of the case and put it on the bed before they put it in their luggage, Ayeza. If they did it before they went to bed, the one who slept in this bed will show signs of radiation poisoning. That explains the burns on Jacobs' hands. I'll contact the taxi service. The driver and cab will need to be quarantined."

"There is no way the suitcase with the warhead will get through airport screening, Antonio; it has to be a ruse."

"It's the only lead we have. Besides, they could be handing it off if they are just the couriers and are trying to catch a flight out of the country. If they pull a switch we will be there ahead of them."

The taxi office had not heard from the driver since he called in with the drop location. Dispatch tried the cell phone and got the driver's voice mail. It was not unusual and he was not concerned.

The driver's ETA at the airport was between five thirty and a quarter to six. The round trip was an hour and a half drive from Fort Lauderdale and it would be the driver's last trip before his shift ended.

Colonel Rogers' helicopter crossed over the Florida turnpike as the ball of flame coming from the wreck below them lit the sky. He touched down by the American Airlines jet parked at the boarding gate fifteen minutes later.

Captain Pitt and his men met the chief of airport security at ten minutes after five. The concourse to the flight gates would not open until five thirty.

"Suspend all flights in and out until further notice. They will have to check their luggage. If they plan to make the flight they are booked on, they will need to be here by six. Let them come through and then seal the building and close the entrance and exits to the airport at six thirty."

Tom Adams had been chief of security at Miami International for twelve years and through a dozen false alarms since 9-11. "That's a hell of a way to start my day, Captain. We have planes at the gate ready to leave and incoming flights from all over the world in their landing patterns. Some are already approaching the runways and some of them are low on fuel."

"It's just a job, Mr. Adams. Let those on approach and low on fuel land, but park them on the runways. Divert the rest of the flights and shut it down, this may take a while."

Adams made the calls while Captain Pitt and his men changed into American Airlines uniforms and joined the staff at the baggage handling desks.

At 6:30, Tom Adams approached Antonio at the entrance to the concourse. "They might think it would pass through in a shipping crate, but they would never get it through in standard luggage or in a carry-on. No one is that stupid. They are not coming. If they were, they would be here. We have traffic backed up on the freeway and the turnpike for miles and it will take days to unravel this mess.

Someone from the mayor's staff is calling every ten minutes raising hell. He wants to know what's going on. What do I tell him?"

"Tell him to call the governor. You can reopen when the search of the public and private long term lots is completed."

"There are dozens of lots and thousands of cars; that will take days."

"I told you, it's just a job. You reopen when we finish, not before."

At 4:00 pm, the radiation search of the grounds and parked cars had progressed to the long-term parking lot. There was no sign the taxi had arrived or that they had handed off the warhead.

The driver had not checked in with his dispatcher. General Sampson sent a helicopter to the address listed in the driver's personnel records. It was a Pak-N-Ship store where he received his mail.

At 4:15 the police notified the taxi company that the taxi had been in an accident and the driver and his passengers were dead. When the ID number on the taxi was confirmed, the dispatcher called Antonio, and Tom Adams was left to deal with the aftermath of another false alarm.

"I know it's not them, but we need to check. A fire won't destroy the radiation, Ayeza."

Antonio arrived at the impound yard a few minutes past five. Ayeza was at the county morgue.

"They pulled a switch, Admiral. The trunk of the taxi showed signs, but the bodies were clean. We know one has made land, but we think it's damaged. Wahid says that if the case is cracked or has been opened and the core has shifted, it could still detonate and pollute a wide area with radiation, but it may not go nuclear. We can hope for the best but even so, there is a fourth one unaccounted for and enough evidence to tie it to the Crescent Tide. We need permission to search the yacht."

"*May not*, is not very optimistic, Eric. They could have dropped them both in Nassau. That might account for the higher than normal readings."

"That's not likely, Admiral. They couldn't carry two in a case the size of the one we saw on the CNBC yacht. They split up the shipment. We won't find two together. I believe Jake and Alan are somewhere near Daytona and the fourth one is on the Crescent Tide. I need you to clear it with MI5 and authorize a search.

"That won't happen without more proof."

"Then we need to break the story, Admiral."

"The White House and the governor say no. We would have to start an evacuation which would cause a panic. Jacobs and Kent will hole up and we would never find them in time. Besides, it's our best guess, but we have no proof Daytona is the target. They could be heading north to Washington for all we know."

"There is still one unaccounted for, Admiral. At least the senators and the congresswoman need to be told that the Crescent Tide is suspect and Daytona may be the target. That might get their attention."

"No one believes the truth, Eric."

"The Secret Service will be on board with the VIPs from Washington; maybe we can slip some of our people in with their security team."

"Whoever is planning the operation is ahead of us, Eric. McMood Fajal is on board the Crescent Tide. He has an estate in Miami as well as on Andros with his own security forces and has guaranteed their safety. No one will believe he is suicidal. The congresswoman and the senators believe it would be an affront to refuse his protection. They have canceled the secret services' invitation to the party."

"Who's covering the estate in Miami?"

"General Sampson sent a platoon of men to cover Miami Beach. He says some of the Somalia refugees arrived on Fajal's sport fishing yacht a few days ago carrying British passports. It was part of the bunch from the Crescent Tide. They needed clearance from U.S. immigration to travel freely back and forth to Andros. Twelve men left the estate yesterday, but only nine returned on the yacht. All twelve were supposed to be the security for the party on board McMood's sport fisher when it leaves for Daytona with the VIPs. Fajal's people are trying to sell a story that three of them were transported back to Andros by helicopter, but General Sampson is not buying it. He thinks we have three of them floating somewhere in Florida."

"Admiral, there were three men in the taxi that burned. That is too much of a coincidence to ignore and one more connection to the Crescent Tide. How much more proof do we need to go in?"

"There are U.S. Senators and members of Congress on board. They have told us Fajal is a personal friend and an asset to the *Apostate's* relationship with the Muslim world. The military brass wants to keep clear until they are gone. What did the Seals find?"

"Connie thinks the people on the estate know we're watching. They're bringing supplies on board, but they're making a point not to take anything off the yacht that is not out in the open. However, Commander Thompson found a concealed hatch on the bottom, mid-ship of the yacht. There is a diving port ten feet away so he almost missed it. There is a seam isolating a four foot section in the keel cooler. It looks like a dummy covering an access port."

"You think it's a hidden compartment?"

"We don't know what it is. The shipyard plans show a fuel tank above that area. With the hatch, it looks like a room with no doors, just a sealed compartment with an underwater access hatch, but it could be nothing more than fuel tank access. The Seals installed cameras on the pier; we are monitoring it. If the hatch is opened the Seals will move in. Otherwise, we will wait until the VIPs from Washington leave to find out what is above that hatch."

CHAPTER 22

Thursday: 6 am

The President and his staff were in the loop and notified that the military was certain one of the warheads had reached the mainland and that although Daytona appeared to be the target, it could be headed north to Washington. The Congressional Committee and a few select members of Congress were aware of the search for the nuclear warheads, but they were not aware of the details.

When the governor of Florida told the press that a spent fuel rod from the Turkey Point nuclear power plant had disappeared, the VIPs on Andros Island inquired as to the severity of the situation. When told that the search was concentrated in Florida north of Fort Lauderdale, the trip to Daytona was postponed.

The congresswoman from California and the senator from Nevada made separate calls. They were told in private that one of the warheads had reached Florida. They were also told that the

British Coast Guard would arrive with the U.S. Navy Seals that afternoon to make an inspection of the Crescent Tide.

Knowing a warhead had reached the mainland, the senator and congresswoman left from Miami a few hours later for their homes in Nevada and California, three thousand miles from the threat.

Commander Thompson would meet the British at the entrance to the harbor and had orders to board the Crescent Tide after the VIPs left the ship. Believing they had located the fourth warhead and that they were closing in on Jacobs and Kent, Admiral Michaels invited the Florida governor to join Eric and Connie on board the Atlantis to direct the search from there.

Shortly after 9-11, Homeland Security ordered twenty-five thousand radiation detectors equipped with GPS sending units. The original order was for one hundred thousand, but it was cut back by the congressional budget committee.

General Sampson wished he had more when they arrived from the armory in Washington, DC, but he ordered the National Guard to plant units in all the hospital emergency rooms and outpatient clinics in Florida north of Fort Lauderdale.

Connie repositioned the satellite over the Orlando, Daytona area and activated the sensors. "All we can do is wait for a signal, Admiral."

"The hotel clerk said one of them had a rash on his hands, Connie. By now they are blisters and he will have a fever."

"That's a needle in a haystack; he may not risk medical treatment."

Admiral Michaels had commanded a nuclear carrier; he was familiar with the effects of radiation poisoning.

"It's still three days until the race. If he has started to blister he won't be able to deal with the pain and still function by then; he'll try to get help."

Eric left with Admiral Michaels to wait for the governor in the conference room. "What if the fourth one is not on the Crescent Tide, Admiral?"

"Where else can it be, Eric?"

The file was open in front of a perplexed Admiral Michaels. A review of *The Apostate Theory* led them all to the same conclusions.

They would never have the whole story. Al-Queda planned the nuclear assault on the U.S. around men who volunteered to be martyrs in Islam's war of Jihad. Dr. Hakeem was the lone exception. He delivered the warheads into Al-Queda's hands for the money. Killing him was part of the plan, but they were all expendable and anyone directly connected to the warheads would die once their part in the plan was fulfilled.

The lead lined room with no doors and the equipment was installed by technicians on board the Crescent Tide who disappeared the same day Ghalib replaced the original captain on the Sultan. Any information as to how the warhead got aboard the Sultan and its actual destination died with the captain and the crew at Rum Cay.

The submarine left the Blue Coral to collect the packages dropped by the pilot who believed all he was carrying was heroin. The fishermen on the trawlers separated half the heroin from the crates as payment for collecting the package, and then dropped the crates back into the sea.

The fishermen believed the boxes packed with the heroin contained gold bars the Blue Coral would deliver to the arms dealers in India who were supplying the pirates in Somalia.

Dr. Hakeem had told Wahid that the physicists from the Rawalpindi laboratory were on an inspection trip to the weapons storage at Mardan. However, the physicists were onboard the Blue Coral preparing the submarine for the pickup and transfer. The same scientists had designed the racks which had been installed by the technicians on board the yacht that would carry the warheads to their destination.

Dr. Hakeem's instructions were to remove the warheads from the crates and to leave the heroin on board the Blue Coral. He had also given them a waypoint to meet an unnamed boat that would pass over them.

The men on the submarine delivered the warheads and fastened them into the storage racks above the access hatch that opened when they approached and transmitted the code to the boat's sonar. The only one beside the scientists who knew the warheads were on board the yacht was the captain.

The men had worked with Wahid and had assembled warheads themselves. They worked behind shielded enclosures in the laboratory and without constraints. However, when they separated the warheads from their crates on the Blue Coral in the dimly lit room they dropped the last one in the process. Dr. Hakeem had chosen them thinking whoever removed them from the crates would need to be qualified to handle them. However, fate stepped in and in their haste they dropped the one out of four that Wahid had failed to torque the screws down on. The men were not concerned; had the screws been tight, the fall would not have affected the titanium case. However, the screws were loose, and the physicists missed the tiny crack in the seal.

The leak would not be a factor with the warheads safely in their cradles in the lead lined room with no doors. They would go undetected so long as they remained in their racks.

The pressurized room would stay dry when Captain Gamal opened the hatch with a password on his computer. A second password would cause one of the racks to swing into place over the hatch and drop one of the warheads to a waiting diver. The racks themselves could be disposed of when the yacht was at sea. Once all the racks dropped into the sea, the hatch would seal and the valve would open, flooding the room with fuel from the adjoining tank.

When the submarine settled to the bottom of the Red Sea, the only crusaders left outside the tribal region of Pakistan who knew where all three warheads were, was Captain Gamal. The only ones outside of Pakistan aware of Jacobs and Kent's mission were Captain Gamal on the Crescent Tide, Jake Jacobs and Alan Kent.

The original taxi driver was murdered shortly after picking up the three crusaders at McMood Fajal's estate in Miami. His body was left at a friendly mortuary to be cremated that night. Jake and Alan switched cars with the three crusaders in the parking lot of the Marriot Hotel, a mile from the Hilton.

They waited twenty minutes. When they left they turned north on Highway 95 toward Orlando. The taxi on the southbound on-ramp to the Florida Turnpike fifteen miles away, exploded in a ball of flames when Jake dialed the number of the cell phone he left in the trunk.

The crusaders in the taxi believed they were just a decoy, but the accelerant guaranteed the fire would quickly spread through the cab, sending the Muslim crusaders on their final journey.

The explosion separated the license plate from its loose mount. It was swept up and thrown in with the debris by one of the spectators posing as a department of transportation employee. After the bodies were removed, the car was towed to the police impound yard. By the time the police made the effort to decipher the VIN number on the taxi, it was after 3:00 pm.

The police also found Jake and Alan's forged passports in Jake's fireproof briefcase, along with their plane flight schedules to Washington, DC. Their CNBC press cards were clipped to the passports.

The taxi driver was a Muslim refugee who had arrived from Somalia a few weeks earlier. His employer said he had no family in the U.S.

The police notified the CNBC office in Washington. When CNBC tried to contact the next of kin listed in Jake and Alan's personnel files, the phones were disconnected.

The taxi driver's Muslim connections prompted the local police to send a routine fax to the Anti Terrorist Task Force office in Washington, DC, and then follow it up with a phone call. A disgruntled employee cleaning out his desk ignored the fax, and when the call came in he told the police the Task Force was being dismantled and that the responsibility would fall back to the local authorities.

Florida police are used to dealing with illegals with no kin and no address. They wrote the three off as illegal immigrants and shipped what was left of the bodies off to the county morgue to be cremated.

"If the warhead is leaking radiation, Eric, it will kill them."

"How long with it take?"

"The readings you gave me are pretty high; it depends on how much worse the leak gets. It may take a few days to kill them, a week at most, but if they stick by it and are moving around, they will soon be contaminating others."

"They can't be that stupid, Admiral. If one of them has a rash it will soon blister. When it does he will know he's contaminated. Florida is God's waiting room. There are lots of seniors in frail health. If they keep moving they will leave a trail, probably to a hospital or the morgue. We are going to have to warn the authorities about what they are dealing with."

"Have our people moved north?"

"Antonio is in Orlando with Colonel Rogers; Ayeza is in Daytona with Captain Pitt. They will move to the hotel at Daytona Beach tonight. General Sampson is on his way with the National Guard to install detectors randomly around Daytona and at the track to monitor for signs of radiation. The governor has made some discreet calls. The hospitals will report cases of radiation poisoning, but he's waffling. He says if we don't find it within 24 hours he is going to cancel the race and evacuate Daytona."

"They could set it off in their hotel room, Eric."

"I know, but that's not Al-Queda's way. These are tactical weapons with a limited radius. They will want to make a statement, and if it is going to be in Daytona, the middle of the race track is the logical place to assure a high casualty count."

After living years in the U.S. they had adjusted to their American names. Jake and Alan moved off Interstate 95 to Highway 1 and reached the safe house in Daytona Beach before noon. By evening, the burns on Jakes hands and arms had blistered and his fever had passed one hundred. "That damn thing is leaking, Alan."

"I'm not sick, it must be something else; besides, we have the target and it won't matter soon."

"The Lion Sheik said the beach on Sunday. This is only Thursday. You have not handled it, I repackaged it. It's very painful, I need something."

"Our instructions are to use room service and not to leave this hotel until Sunday."

"There is too much pain. I won't make it until Sunday, he would understand."

"There is heroin in my luggage. I'll prepare a shot for you, but we cannot leave the hotel. That would put us at risk and we would break our vow."

"Allah will understand."

"Allah does not have to understand, He makes the law. Take the shot, Allah will remove the pain."

Andros Island: 12:30 pm

When the VIP helicopter cleared the island, two U.S. Air Force Apache helicopters moved in to train their rocket tubes on the Crescent Tide. McMood Fajal's security team converged above the dock to face the onslaught, watching as the fisherman brought the Viking alongside the British ship after dropping the Seals at the jetty.

Captain Gamal signaled to his security force to stand down as the British Coast Guard cutter approached the dock with the deck guns manned and ready. When the cutter pulled alongside he stepped to the rail and waved to the British officer. "What can I do for you, Lieutenant?"

"We are making a routine inspection, Captain. There has been a fuel spill and we are checking all the yachts for leaks."

With U.S. attack helicopters in the air and British deck guns locked on the Crescent Tide it was a frail excuse and the lieutenant knew it. He also knew that if they came up empty handed he would be pulling duty in the North Sea along with whoever authorized the mission. He turned to Alex and Commander Thompson with a perplexed look. "What now?"

Commander Thompson knew by the smile on Captain Gamal's face that the warheads were no longer on board. "Tell him to ask his security force and whoever else is on the estate to move to the dock. The divers will do a hull inspection and we are going to board the yacht, Lieutenant."

"Permission to come aboard, Captain."

Thinking they would find nothing he invited them to board. "Be my guest, Lieutenant, and bring the U.S. Navy commander with you. I'll have my chef prepare a snack."

"This is not a social call, Captain."

Knowing the yacht was clean, Captain Gamal was more cocky than angry. "What then might it be, Commander? My friends in Washington will be curious when I tell them you have invaded my privacy with your weapons loaded."

"The British are on a training mission, Captain, and we asked to come along. There is nothing more to it."

"Then come aboard, my chef makes excellent crab cakes."

The Seals moved through the water checking the hull while Commander Thompson looked for the room with no doors. Not finding it, he began shuffling through the closets and cabinets. There was a concealed inspection port below a loose carpet on the floor of a closet above the area where he had found the access hatch on the bottom of the yacht.

After removing the port cover he took the radiation probe from his satchel and lowered it into the tank full of diesel fuel. The fuel was contaminated. Taking a drill from the satchel he started to drill through the top of the fiberglass tank, pausing when lead shavings began to show on the bit.

Captain Gamal and the British officer watched from the bridge security monitor. As Commander Thompson turned to hold the drill bit to the light, the Captain moved toward his cabin door. "I need to excuse myself for a moment Lieutenant, you don't need me do you?"

The lieutenant was not expecting to find anything and was more concerned with his future than keeping the captain by his side. He watched as the captain entered his quarters and closed the door.

Captain Gamal walked to his prayer rug to kneel and bow towards Mecca. He then slipped his tongue under the edge of the crown to expose the capsule.

Commander Thompson moved to the deck to place a call to Eric and Admiral Michaels. "I found the room. It's lead lined and full of contaminated fuel. They were expecting us, Admiral. There isn't anything else on the yacht. The captain was convinced we would not find it and at first treated it as a joke. I wouldn't have found it if I had not spotted the hatch on the bottom."

"Has there been any resistance from the others?"

"No, he gave orders to his security force to stand down before we came on board. Everyone has been disarmed."

"Where is the captain?"

"Sorry, Admiral, we lost him. He took the same out as the captain of the Sultan."

"There is no way to prevent that method of suicide, Commander, but it's a plus. I'm sure an autopsy will confirm the poison matches with what killed the Sultan's captain. It will help tie the two yachts together."

"What do we do with the yacht and the crew?"

"I have the British Admiral on the other line. Tell the Seals to collect all the weapons and immobilize everyone on the estate. The British will send another cutter to pick up the crew. I'll send a helicopter to Turkey Point to pick up a cleanup crew to drain and clean the tanks."

"We won't find the missing warhead in the tank, Admiral, it's gone."

"I know, Commander. When you're finished, I'll send a helicopter to bring you here. We are going to have to regroup and do some backtracking."

Friday: 6 am

"Admiral, the governor's helicopter is approaching."

"Thank you, Lieutenant. Show him to the conference room."

The governor began preparations when he was notified that the warhead had arrived in Florida and Jacobs and Kent *may* have a defective unit. However, there was no guarantee and after coming up empty on the Crescent Tide, the fourth was unaccounted for. If they don't find them both, they would have to evacuate a section of Florida. The governor would want to direct the civilians and calm the local politicians, a safe place to do that from was the conference room on board the Atlantis.

Connie was at the computer on the conference table. Maps of Florida covered one wall. Admiral Michaels arrived the day before General Sampson. Florida's highway patrol chief and the Florida secretary of transportation arrived with the governor.

Eric had joined Connie and was at the computer moving the icon out of the view of the marina at Daytona Beach. The icon would flash if a GPS signal came in from one of the radiation monitors. "Is there any word from Daytona, Eric?"

"No, Governor, Antonio and Ayeza are at the Regency in Daytona Beach standing by, and there are CIA agents or volunteers from the National Guard at or near all the major medical facilities. So far, no signal and no one matching Jacobs or Kent's description have visited any of the clinics or emergency rooms."

"Are you sure there were four, Eric."

"I'm not sure about anything, Governor, but our source from Pakistan claims he put eight together. He put four in the racks at Mardan. We found one in Pakistan. There were three trawlers and three packages. Why three to transport two? I'm betting there is a fourth one out there somewhere?"

The governor was pacing the room. Stopping in front of the map of the Florida inter-coastal south of Daytona, he turned to Admiral Michaels. "Ok, we assume there is another on the way, but then why only two yachts? You suggested different fronts, Admiral. Is there another boat out there and if there is, which way is it coming?"

A frustrated Admiral Michaels threw up his hands. "Connie?"

"We have had everything on the east coast under surveillance, Governor. The Crescent Tide never came within reach of another boat except at the dock in Nassau and we pegged that transfer. From what Commander Thompson said, the captain of the Crescent Tide was too cocky to have been hiding another one. He purged his tanks on the way to McMood's estate after he dropped the warhead to Jacobs and Kent in Nassau. He never thought we would find the room and the rest of his yacht was clean."

"Then we missed something. Think, Connie."

CHAPTER 23

They had been sleeping in shifts since their arrival. Antonio was in bed. The sun was breaking on the horizon on what promised to be a beautiful day in Florida. The balcony of the penthouse twelve stories up gave Ayeza a sweeping view of the white sands on Daytona Beach.

It was still two days until race time, but every hotel room for fifty miles was booked. Joggers were on the boardwalk and fishermen were scattered along the shoreline braving the chilly fifty degree breeze that would warm into the mid seventies by noon.

Ayeza scrolled the icons on her laptop, quartering her screen, and then patched into Connie's computer. As the satellite view of Daytona Beach lit up the screen, Ayeza's instant messaging icon flashed a good morning from Connie. Connie wanted to say hello, but did not have time to chat. The meeting was to start at six. Ayeza noted the time and smiled, it was 5:45. As usual, Connie had been at her desk since two am.

Women have a way of dealing with crisis separate from that of men. Ayeza typed a, *have a nice day, we'll tune into the meeting, give Eric a hug,* and then zoomed in on the Regency Hotel and the balcony she was sitting on. When she came into her own view she noted the count-down clock, fifty nine hours to race time. It was time to wake Antonio.

General Electric over manufactured when the bill was before Congress to authorize the purchase of the radiation detectors. When the order was cut back, GE discounted the units to the health care industry and installed them in emergency rooms and ambulances across the country. Florida was at the top of the list and had been aggressively pursued because of the nuclear power plants that were built in hurricane alley, and the aging populations scattered across the landscape.

General Sampson silently thanked GE for the head start, and then sent a convoy of National Guard in civilian cars and clothing to meet the C-17 at Daytona Beach International Airport that was carrying the additional equipment.

By four am Friday morning, radiation detectors had been planted in every emergency medical facility as well as the hotel elevators and public rest rooms within fifty miles of the race track.

Nothing more could be done except to wait. The mood on board the Atlantis was growing somber. The deadline to begin evacuation was approaching, but what to evacuate, and in what direction should they send the crowds was the question. Resignation was setting in, and preparations to deal with the disaster were replacing the search for the warheads.

Admiral Michaels contacted the Pentagon and the White House. If the bomb did go off, the military would move in and quarantine whatever area was affected. No one had a clue as to what casualties to expect or how big of an area would need to be cordoned off.

The mood in Washington was also growing nervous. An original copy of *The Apostate Theory* was on his desk. The White House Chief of Staff pointed out that no one knew for sure that Daytona was the target, and by race time Jacobs and Kent could be sitting across from the White House steps.

The President's plane was standing by, and the congressional members and military personnel who were aware of the search for the warheads were cleaning out their desks.

"Admiral, the President is on the line."

"Good morning, Mr. President."

"No, we aren't any closer than yesterday."

"Yes, I understand, and the governor is in agreement. Noon today is the deadline."

The evacuation of Florida north of Fort Pierce and south of Jacksonville would begin at noon. The *Apostate* and his cabinet would be leaving Washington at two pm. He had called a press conference to make an announcement and to plead with the Muslim world to call off the attack.

Admiral Michaels surrendered to the inevitable. "We lost, he's going to close all our bases in the Middle East and bring the military home."

CHAPTER 24

Friday: 10 am

Admiral Michaels turned to leave the room. Eric and the governor were at the maps on the wall choosing evacuation routes out of the area. The Florida Transportation Secretary was placing a call to close the roads into the area and to order the marinas and hotels from Jacksonville south to Fort Pierce to evacuate and send their visitors home.

"Eric, Admiral!"
"What is it, Connie?"
"We have a signal from a hotel in Daytona."

After Rum Cay was destroyed the Lion Sheik sent a message that they would be watching the gates and parking lots at the racetrack. They had reservations at a hotel five miles from the track and a stone's throw to the edge of the surf that had been purchased by an anonymous buyer who was represented by a law firm in Miami.

The friends of the *Apostate* would be anchored in the harbor or near the beach later that day with a thousand other yachts, and by race time the beaches and the surrounding area would be packed with hotel guests.

It was lying on the floor between the beds when he woke, but now that was too close. Transporting the warhead in a suitcase without proper packing had caused the crack to widen.

Jake had removed it from his luggage when they arrived in order to set the timer. He then placed the warhead on his bed behind the pillow and covered it with the spread to hide it from room service. When they finished dinner, he set it on the floor, but then fell asleep in the other bed.

The tingling in his arms woke Alan from a restless sleep. His bed soaked with sweat and his blurred vision were a product of the radiation poisoning. The room was dark, he had lost track of time. Disorientated, Alan moved toward the other bed to wake Jacobs; then the nauseous feeling overtook him. He vomited on the floor, and then in the dark room he slipped in the slime trying to get to the bathroom.

Recovering slightly, Alan stepped into the shower. The spray of cold water refreshed him, but it quickly turned hot, rinsing the sweat from his body. As the blisters absorbed the spray they began to ooze, and then the pain started.

His judgment clouded, Alan again tried to wake Jake. They would go to a clinic together for medication to control the pain he was now feeling. However, it was too late for Jake, the pain left him when the heroin spread through his veins, but Alan had been too generous. Jake slipped into a coma shortly after he fell into bed.

Alan turned the lights on to dress. He panicked when he realized Jake would not be getting up and then realized that the festering sores spreading across Jake's face were a prophesy of his own fate.

The memories of the mountains of Pakistan and the pride he felt when he was told the Lion Sheik had chosen him for the mission flooded his mind; despair now replaced it. He looked at the clock; the race was still two days away. The timer could not be reset. Housekeeping would knock on the door; he would need medication to survive that long or they would find the warhead. Thinking back to the night before and Jake's plea for help, it was his turn to believe that Allah would understand.

Alan made it as far as the elevator; the sensor sticking through the roof had been one of the last to be installed.

His clothes were sticking to his body, tearing at the open sores; the pain amplified with every move. When he started to exit at the lobby he remembered the heroin in his luggage.

Colonel Rogers was on the pad on the roof of the hotel. By the time Alan reentered his room Antonio and Ayeza were in the helicopter putting on their protective gear and the helicopter was lifting off the roof. "How far is it, Colonel?"

"Not far, you pegged it pretty close, Ayeza. It's coming from an elevator in the lobby of one of the older hotels across from the harbor where the politicians had planned to dock."

Colonel Rogers and the Special Forces sealed the building and began evacuating the guests. As anticlimactic as it was, Ayeza and Antonio followed the trail of radiation from the elevator to the door of Alan's room. The door was ajar. One man was asleep on the bed, and the bathroom light reflected off the ceiling by the door.

Ayeza let herself in quietly and found Alan in the bathroom in a daze of pain, mixing the raw brown powder in a plastic cup. The radiation was settling in his brain accelerating the pain in his eyes and the burning of his skin. He looked up with his eyes pleading for help, and then remembered his oath just as Ayeza jammed a baton in his mouth to keep him from crushing the capsule she knew was lodged beneath one of his crowns.

Antonio checked Jake's pulse. Finding it faint and the man hardly breathing, he moved the warhead to the desk. Following the procedure Wahid had showed him, he dismantled the assembly and removed the core. Wahid said the screws would be tight and he would need the special wrench. One of the screws was missing, the others loose to the touch.

Ayeza secured Alan with plastic ties and then returned to join Antonio. "Wahid was wrong, Ayeza, the core had not shifted. It was leaking, but it was still intact. The timer was set for noon on race day. They both could have died in this room and it would have still gone off."

"If it's leaking, Antonio, why didn't the radiation register in the elevator when they installed the meter? It would have been contaminated when they checked in."

Antonio stood perplexed with the meter in his hand. They had followed the trail from the back of the CNBC yacht to the hotel and then to the trunk of the taxi. The hotel room they were in was saturated.

Looking around the room, Antonio spotted Jake's open luggage and the odd looking shoes by the bed. Thinking back, *the suitcase must have been in the taxi when they switched cars.* The trail ended when Jake removed the warhead from the camera case and placed it in the new luggage with the lead lining. Antonio moved to the bed and picked one up; it was heavy. The sole of the shoe was glued to the lead lining.

"They switched cases after they left the hotel in Fort Lauderdale, Ayeza. The shoes and their clothing have a thin layer of lead. It's heavy, but manageable. Whoever planned this knew there would be some leakage, but they did not plan on a defective case. We got lucky, there was a one in four chance for this one to end up here.

If they hadn't been poisoned by the radiation, well...................
All I can say is it's our turn to thank God."

"There is still one out there, Antonio."
"I know, and there is no reason to believe its case is cracked. If it's here and planted somewhere, it's going to be damned hard to find."

They had forty-eight hours until race time. The third warhead was set for Sunday, which was when the race was set to start. Committed, Antonio and Ayeza returned to the balcony of the hotel and patched back into the Atlantis computer, waiting for another signal. Captain Pitt with the Navy Seals and Colonel Rogers with the Special Forces sat in their helicopters side by side. Everyone was dialed into their GPS screens, which were tied into the satellite monitoring the radiation devices.

By three pm Friday, 48 hours before race-time, it became apparent the fourth nuclear warhead would not be found in time. Admiral Michaels asked Captain Paige to move the Atlantis fifty miles offshore to serve as the command post.

There were thousands visiting their families from out of town. Every hotel and marina within fifty miles of Daytona Beach was booked. They could close the hotels, but forced evacuation of the resident population would be impossible. When the deadline set by presidential executive order arrived, the Florida Governor established martial law and people were given the option of leaving or remaining sequestered in their homes. A twenty-four hour curfew would go into effect at 6 am on Sunday morning.

The National Guard moved in to assist the State Police closing the roads north of West Palm Beach, Florida to the Georgia border and from Highway 1 along the east coast of Florida to the center of the State. A one way traffic pattern was established; people could leave, but no one would be allowed to enter.

TV and radio programming was superseded. The governor made an announcement that martial law would be imposed. The population had to be told why. Pleading for them to remain calm, they were told the CIA and military had reason to believe an armed nuclear bomb was planted and set to go off somewhere in the Daytona area on race day, and that the terrorists were holed up someplace in the cordoned off area of the state looking for an opportunity to move the bomb.

In the rush to leave, panic on the highways set in. The first accident caused thousands more. When race time passed and the bomb did not go off, silence settled on the communities. Many people, unable to return to their homes, mobbed the churches and had passed the time in prayer while the CIA searched for the terrorists and the military patrolled the vacant streets enforcing the curfew.

CHAPTER 25

Monday: 4:30 pm

The military and the search team had remained in Daytona Beach hoping for a miracle. Twenty-four hours after the scheduled start of the race, when the skies remained clear, the crisis passed.

"Daytona is not the target of the last warhead, Admiral."
Then what is the target, Eric, and where is it?"

Everyone on the Atlantis sat in silent concentration, their laptops open, drafting the orders to the agencies to deal with the aftermath.

The room was silent until Eric turned from the screen. "Maybe it was never on the Crescent Tide."

"Then where is it, Eric?"

"Maybe it was on the Sultan, Admiral, The captain of the Sultan was the only one alive on Rum Cay who would have known if they had another on board and if they transferred it to someone else on their trip from Jeddah to Agadir. The Afghans would have made him talk. I think he killed himself to cut us off from the information."

"We all thought the Crescent Tide was the prime transport, Eric."

"We know they passed one to the Sultan in Jeddah, Admiral. They could have passed two. Why else would Ghalib kill himself unless he knew the location of the missing warhead?"

"Someone help us out. What did we miss, Connie, do we need to start from scratch?"

Ayeza had sectioned her screen and refocused on the empty boardwalk; she could see Admiral Michaels in the background shrugging his shoulders and gesturing in the air with his hands. Antonio had joined her at the table with coffee. Ayeza had patched his laptop into the conference room, separate from hers. Antonio's split screen showed Eric sitting at the conference table on the Atlantis and the open water in front of Daytona Beach.

Antonio looked up when Admiral Michaels passed the question to Connie. It was on everyone's mind. *Maybe there were only three. They found one in Quetta, if the trawlers hauled three warheads out of the sea and the fourth warhead was not on the Crescent Tide, what did they do with it?*

Antonio looked across at the empty harbor; the only movement on the horizon was a Coast Guard cutter that had been involved in the evacuation. The light came on as the cutter passed in front of the hotel. Antonio sent an instant message to Eric. *We all thought it was a payment for the drugs. Have Connie patch into the film of the deckhand on the Sultan passing the satchel to the cigarette boat after the Cuban Coast Guard cutter left.*

Eric passed the message to Connie and then turned to the room where Admiral Michaels was pacing the floor, still reflecting on the past search. Eric's body blocked the view of the screen when Admiral Michaels approached. "We shredded every boat in that harbor, Eric. It wasn't there. So if it was transferred to the Sultan in Jeddah, where is it?"

Eric turned to Admiral Michaels, and then looked over at the screen in front of Connie thinking, *how could we all have missed it?*

Admiral Michaels reached past Eric for the coffee. Connie zoomed in on the transfer. He was searching for answers as the Sultan and the cigarette boat filled Eric's screen. Connie fast forwarded the film until the deck hand on the Sultan passed the satchel the size of a commercial camera case to the man on the cigarette boat. Eric froze the film and printed the picture.

"Haiti, or maybe Cuba, Admiral. We all thought that was a drug pick up; it could have been a trade. The Sultan picked up two hundred million dollars worth of drugs. Take a look."

The Admiral and the governor moved in. "One of the drug cartels may have it, Eric, but that's a guess; we don't know for sure that it's not here. It could be in any hotel room or closet in Florida."

It was Eric's theory, but it was just a theory. America had embraced the Apostate; he would be the prime target. When they found the third warhead and there was no trace of the fourth, Eric believed the plan had been to hold one in reserve to deal with the real insult to Islam, the *Apostate* himself, and that the fourth warhead was still in transit. It would hold America hostage until it arrived. "It could be anywhere, Admiral, but I don't think it's in Florida."

The President cancelled the press conference after the immediate threat was neutralized. Admiral Michaels and the governor would deal with the aftermath in Florida.

Many residents had been unable to leave, or had returned to their homes when road rage took over the highways. Thousands of accidents caused traffic to gridlock; they had no other place to go.

Hundreds of thousands already out of work and in the process of losing their homes were sequestered and running out of supplies. When it appeared to be a false alarm the anger that had been building months before the threat replaced fear, and then the riots started. Looting began with the grocery stores, but it quickly spread.

Hours after the news teams began arriving by helicopter to cover the riots, street gangs moved in from the neighboring cities. They started with the homes in the wealthy communities, and then spilled into the high-end shopping districts, burning the buildings to cover their tracks, and killing anyone who challenged them.

The Florida National Guard had been depleted by assignments to the wars in Iraq and Afghanistan and there were few willing to re-enlist. When the term nuclear was attached to the mission, desertion became rampant in the ranks of the Guard and local law enforcement as the soldiers and police tried to move their families to safety. Fires burned for a week from Fort Pierce to Jacksonville while what was left of the Florida National Guard and police tried to deal with the looters.

When it became apparent that they could not contain the riots spreading across the Florida landscape, the governor enlisted the help of Admiral Michaels who had remained on board the Atlantis. A few hours later, Colonel Rogers and Captain Pitt led a squadron of Apache helicopters from Eglin Air Force Base into the area. They were followed by helicopter gunships, tanks and armored personnel carriers transporting volunteers from the regular army and Special Forces stationed in the surrounding states.

Hospitals had been evacuated by air; they were reopened. Local doctors and nurses who remained behind were joined by volunteers from neighboring states who were flown in by helicopter along with medical supplies. Those caring for the sick and wounded slept in the wards alongside the patients and ate the military rations provided.

The sick and wounded littered the hallways of the hospitals and clinics, waiting their turn. The dead were transported by military helicopter to Eglin Air Force Base, where temporary freezers had been set up to house the bodies until they could be identified.

After local police equipment was replaced with military hardware and combat troops with orders to kill the looters on sight, the rioting and looting diminished. Once the military quelled the riots, they rounded up the last gang members trying to escape the area with stolen trucks filled with loot.

There was no room to house the thousands of prisoners. Makeshift wire enclosures were set up in the streets. People who could prove they were residents within five miles of an area where they were picked up were ticketed and released.

The military tried to maintain the curfew, but many had joined in the looting because they were running out of food and supplies. Some had gone days without food or fresh water and could not be contained until military convoys moved in with food and water, distributing it neighborhood by neighborhood.

The fourth warhead was forgotten by the press or dealt with as a military mistake, and people were ready to get on with their lives. After a week passed without incident the barricades were lifted.

People were returning to their homes searching for loved ones they had been separated from; many would never be found. Others, who had been trapped in the traffic and had managed to return home before the military sealed off the streets, were beginning to venture out to the few stores that still had food on the shelves.

The CIA insisted there were four warheads. Unconvinced, but not willing to take responsibility, the President sent the Secretary of State to Pakistan to meet with Yaq'ab, the Lion Sheik's second in command. However, the meeting was to be kept private. Publically she gave her reason for going was to tour the American air base in Kabul. However, before she left, she publically apologized for America's interference and promised Pakistan's new Parliament that in the future, America would respect Pakistan's sovereignty and allow the people of Pakistan to guide their own destiny.

Yaq'ab returned from the canyon rim in Chaman, Pakistan. He passed the message from the American Secretary of State to the Lion King. "She will be in Karachi; she wants to negotiate for the last warhead."

"The warhead is in a safe place. She has nothing to negotiate with."

"We lost the other three; we could lose it when we transport it."

"There is no hurry; we will wait, they will believe we only had three and they will call off the search. The crusaders will take it to Washington and deliver it to the *Apostate* himself; in the meantime he will help recruit thousands more crusaders for God's army."

"What about the woman?"

"Meet with the woman, she is like her husband. She will give us something for nothing, just to appease us."

The Secretary of State extended her trip leaving Kabul for Karachi and a private meeting with Yaq'ab and then Pakistan's Prime Minister. At first he denied losing the warheads, but he changed his tune when pictures of the three recovered warheads were delivered to his office, and after the Secretary of State told him the American President would use his influence to accelerate a new multi-billion dollar aid package in exchange for assistance finding the fourth warhead.

The Prime Minister agreed in private to search for the warhead, but both the Americans and the Pakistani governments would publically deny the existence of a fourth threat. Pakistan's nuclear agency then acknowledged that seven nuclear warheads had been shipped from the assembly laboratory in Rawalpindi to the storage facility in Mardan. At the time, India was rattling sabers over the bombings in Mumbai; it was a justified response.

Their investigation showed that during the transport of the weapons the head of Pakistan's Nuclear Agency was murdered after the lead scientist from Rawalpindi disappeared with three warheads. They said they believed the man by the name of Wahid, who had fought alongside Osama Bin-Laden against the Russians, had been working with Al-Queda.

They thanked the Secretary of State for recovering one in Pakistan and told her that they understood the American military recovered the other two before they arrived in the United States. The President of Pakistan sent a request through channels asking that the weapons be returned.

Eric was called to Washington to attend what were supposed to be closed congressional hearings. The meetings were held in private, but an unabridged copy of The Apostate Theory was placed in evidence and copied for members of the committee. Shortly thereafter, copies made the rounds of the congressional offices, and then it found its way to the press.

The Apostate Theory contradicted the report from Pakistan's new head of their nuclear program, claiming four warheads were stolen and three recovered. Eric refused to rewrite the Theory and insisted there were four.

When questioned by the media about the fourth warhead the President discounted The Apostate Theory for what it was, a theory. He had received assurances from the Pakistan government, as well as the UN Nuclear Regulatory Commission, that Pakistan's new head of their nuclear program had researched the theft and only three warheads were missing from the inventory. They understood all three were in a proper storage facility somewhere in New Mexico.

The President of Pakistan also assured the Secretary of State that the Rawalpindi laboratory and the Mardan weapons storage facility had been locked down and the Al-Queda personnel had been replaced. The crisis passed and the American press re-focused on the looming depression.

The Lion Sheik sent an answer a few days after the Secretary of State returned from Pakistan. Admiral Michaels asked for a conference with the President and his inner circle. Antonio and Ayeza were in the reception hall. Admiral Michaels, Eric Ludlow and Ron Edwards joined them and were then shown into the conference room.

Eric removed copies of the new file from his briefcase and spread them around the table. The President picked up a copy titled, *The Olive Branch*, and then moved to the display table where Antonio was setting the cradle with the nuclear warhead he and Ayeza found in Daytona.

No longer a warhead, the assembly had been cleaned. The core had been removed and a mockup had been installed in its place. The assembly was now an empty shell, but it was a duplicate of the real thing in the picture Ayeza placed on the easel.

The only difference was the wording on an engraved plaque in the shape of an olive branch that matched the logo on the title of the report next to it. The wording on the plaque in the picture was in Arabic, Ayeza had translated it.

"We had the assembly flown in from New Mexico this morning. As you can see it's a duplicate of the one in the picture, Mr. President."

"When did the message arrive, Admiral?"

"We received advanced notice a week ago. The pictures were dropped off in Georgetown early yesterday. The courier paid a premium for same day service."

E-mail can be traced. There was a DVD in the snail-mail package with the picture and the plaque. The message was in Arabic and the letters on the plaque were in Arabic. Translated, the wording on the plaque referenced an olive branch which had been etched above it.

"An olive branch is an offering of peace, Mr. Ludlow. That seems a strange name for a nuclear bomb."

"It's not exactly a peace offering; it is meant to hold America hostage, Mr. President. The CD accompanying the pictures listed the demands."

Eric presented the President with a copy of the list of demands that would have to be met or the warhead would be set off in the heart of one of America's major cities. At the top of the page was the logo for the new file, an olive branch.

- America would respect Pakistan's sovereignty and withdraw from Iraq and Afghanistan by the end of the year.
- Israel would leave the Muslim Holy City of Jerusalem and close the settlements in the West Bank.
- America's Muslim communities would be allowed to govern themselves under Islamic Shariah law.
- America's schools and workplaces would allow Muslims to practice their religion freely.
- The Apostate would renounce Christianity and Judaism and embrace Islam.

The President glanced at the list then handed it back, ignoring the Apostate reference. "It appears they are giving us some time, Mr. Ludlow. Get word to them that we will evaluate their requests. Ask them to meet again with the Secretary of State."

"You can't be seriously considering meeting their demands, Mr. President!"

"How many died in the riots, Admiral?"

"Just shy of thirty thousand, Mr. President, but we haven't an accurate count yet."

"When our military lost track of the fourth warhead, you believed they sequestered it in a safe house somewhere, but you have no idea where. We may never find it."

"We did not exactly lose it, Mr. President. We never had it. What the military did was to find three out of four."

"Close doesn't count, Admiral. It could be sitting next to Times Square, in a locker in the Capitol Building, or in the trunk of a taxi in Washington, DC across from the White House. We cannot search every square inch. How many will die when the bomb goes off?"

Eric stood to field the question. "Granted, possibly millions, Mr. President, but if it's not here yet and we can get them to move it we might still find it. While we are looking, if you cut off their money and send in the military to shut Pakistan's weapons facilities down, and then let Israel deal with Iran's nuclear production facilities they won't get their hands on another, at least not in our lifetimes."

"We are no longer going to police the world, Mr. Ludlow. Our future military role outside our own borders has already been decided, even without this... *Olive Branch*... whatever it is. However, they reopened negotiations so the Secretary of State will take this opportunity and return to Pakistan to try to negotiate a settlement. In the mean time find the fourth warhead or I will use my executive authority to begin compliance with their requests."

"Mr. President, if we give in, as long as they have that warhead, or if we simply believe they still have it, the blackmail will escalate."

"I've worn many hats, Admiral. Perhaps now it's time for another. I have always believed we should live by the principals our founding fathers set forth and let the people practice their religions freely. I see nothing wrong with what they are seeking."

"What about the Constitution, Mr. President? Islamic and secular laws cannot co-exist."

"Perhaps not in the past, Mr. Ludlow, but this is a new era. The Muslim community is not our enemy. Find the warhead, or we are going to have to find a way to live side by side."

EPILOGUE

A dmiral Michaels joined Eric, Antonio and Ayeza on the Atlantis as it was approaching the Straits of Florida. They would pick up the search there. Captain Paige was with them in the conference room watching the presidential address to the nation.

The Secretary of State had returned. America would accelerate their withdrawal from Iraq and Afghanistan and look into an accord in the Middle East where Israel would withdraw from the occupied territories; America's continued financial aid to Israel would depend on it.

The questions remained unanswered. Who do we fight? Who do we defend against? Who will we take our revenge on when the bomb goes off?

The enemy is a religious ideal, not a country, not just one people. It lives in the minds and hearts of a brutal cult founded in the seventh century that has remained unchanged for fourteen hundred years.

Islam has no fixed base and is splintered within its own ranks, but its war of Jihad against its common enemies bridges the gaps.

Islam reaches from Mecca throughout the Middle East, from Pakistan to the peaks of the Himalayas and to the camps in Sudan and Somalia, the hills of the Philippines: the caucuses of Europe: the islands of Indonesia, most countries in Africa, the frontiers of China, and the mosques in America. Mecca is its heart, Medina its soul, Iran its voice, the crusaders its children, and although they change from time to time, the generals in the war of Jihad now call the mountain caves of Pakistan and Afghanistan their home.

Shiites and Sunnis will slaughter one another when all others are subdued, but in the meantime they have joined together and focused against their common enemies, the People of the Book, *Jews and Christians.* Our constitution and secular laws protect them; they will move to the others governed by the dictators in Russia and Asia when we are conquered.

In a mea culpa to the Islamic world, the President re-embraced his ancestral roots and acknowledged America had unjustly invaded Iraq and caused havoc with the way of life in the Taliban regions of Pakistan and Afghanistan. As a method of reparations he would raise the ceiling on the number immigrants to one hundred thousand per year for five years from each country.

In order to assimilate the refugees into mainstream America there would be religious concessions in America's schools and workplaces. Secular laws pertaining to multiple marriages, divorce and criminal punishment would be reviewed to accommodate the growing Muslim communities.

In his final statement he stated that the warhead that threatened Florida had been found before race day and that there was little proof that a fourth warhead existed.

When the news broke that the warhead had been found two days before race day, the general population's fear changed to anger, but by then Al-Queda had found another soft spot in America's armor. It was apparent that fear would impose panic. Hundreds of thousands were stranded in the traffic jams; others looted homes of the rich and the business sections of the cities. Threats alone could be enough to win the war of Jihad.

False alarms breed false hope and raise questions. Was the threat real, or was it just another attempt by those in charge to control the lives of the common people?

The general populations settled back into their lives, and as the argument raged, the real threat was forgotten. Some Americans were angry at Islam and the Muslims, but after a few weeks it evolved into politically correct politics as usual.

Later, as the President moved to embrace the Islamic world, the liberal press and politicians defended the moderate Muslims and placed the blame on past American policies in the Middle East. The majority in the halls of Congress silenced the opposition as they continued to shred the fabric of America's military strength along with its financial backbone.

As he promised pre election, the *Apostate's* administration moved on with their agenda of *change*. The economy was in shambles, diverting the public's attention. They would leave it that way and create more havoc by indenturing America's future generations to a multi-trillion dollar debt.

Change meant real change. People would become dependent on the government's handouts, and since in the mind of the Apostate, the government knew best and the general populations should be subdued, the wealth would be redistributed until everyone who did not hold a position of power in the government was equal.

Connie returned to her station after the President's address and dialed in on Haiti looking for the cigarette boat. Al-Queda stood by, secure in the mountain region of Afghanistan and Pakistan while Mash'al loaded the warhead into the false bottom and then finished fueling the boat.

The Lion Sheik was ill, but he would live another year. Yaq'ab helped him to his prayer rug as the boat left Port au Prince for the trip to Belize. Mash'al would lead the crusaders waiting to begin their journey to Washington and the Halls of Congress.

End

Printed in the United States
148093LV00001B/208/P

9 781438 961095